FALLEN AWAY

BOOKS BY MARGARET CULKIN BANNING

A Handmaid of the Lord
Pressure
The Women of the Family
Mixed Marriage
Money of Her Own
Prelude to Love
Path of True Love
The Third Son
The First Woman
The Iron Will
Letters to Susan
The Case for Chastity
You Haven't Changed
Too Young to Marry
Out in Society
Enough to Live On
A Week in New York
Salud! A South American Journal
Letters from England
Conduct Yourself Accordingly
The Clever Sister
Give Us Our Years
Fallen Away

FALLEN AWAY

by

Margaret Culkin Banning

HARPER & BROTHERS, PUBLISHERS
New York

This book is neither biography nor autobiography. I knew none of these characters until I began to write of them. But the theme, the struggle, and some of the settings, both here and abroad, may be as familiar to many others as they are to me. To them I inscribe the story.

TRYON, NORTH CAROLINA, 1949
DULUTH, MINNESOTA, 1950

Book I

. . . in the mist of tears
I hid from Him, and under running laughter.

—"The Hound of Heaven" by
Francis Thompson

Chapter One

Late in the afternoon Kenneth telephoned, as she had known he would when the directors' meeting was over and he was free to talk to her. For an hour Barbara had been expecting the call, but when it came she was not ready. It flung her into panic.

"Somebody wants to speak to Mrs. Field," said the other girl in the office, as if that were no surprise. She offered the telephone to Barbara meaningly.

Listening to him ask how soon he could see her, Barbara felt herself resist, fear her own love almost to dread, grow faint at the thought that in conscience she must argue for an ending, and yearn to have him near to share this anguish of decision, perhaps to lift its weight from her in spite of anything she might say. All that before it was even time to answer him.

"Not tonight, Ken—it's better not," she said, coming back in the swift circle to the resistance she had promised.

"But I must see you. You don't sound natural, darling, not like yourself. Tell me what happened."

"I can't, not on the telephone."

"You did see the Bishop today?"

"Yes. I saw him."

"I'm coming out," he stated briefly and certainly, "to your place. About six o'clock?"

"No—I won't be home that early."

"All right, I'll go to the club when I leave here and wait. I'll call again before I come. Barbara, listen—stop worrying. It doesn't matter what he said. We know what's right and what we should do."

She said good-by and tried to put the telephone down as if it were not an important conversation, then looked across the room at the wall clock. The small hand jerked suddenly forward to five. Sally

Frick, who worked with Barbara in this office of the Co-ordinated Social Agencies, was hurrying records back into the files.

"I guess everything else will keep," she said. "I'm through for the day. Aren't you, Barbara?"

"Not just yet. I took an hour off this afternoon, so I've some work to finish."

But when Sally was gone, in her usual quick rush toward her flat and her husband, Barbara Field did not finish anything. There were several case histories of people who presented special problems to the relief agencies waiting for attention on her own desk. She drew the folders toward her. Bright yellow memorandums were clipped to the manila binders which held information about each case, and every yellow slip bore some comment or question. Barbara was supposed to supply data for answers. She tried to do it now, but she could not clear her own mind and make room for thought of these others.

Was this indigent family to be placed on the public relief rolls or could some more personal group be induced to carry the load of maintaining them? Automatically Barbara searched the record to see if the family had any religious ties. Yes, it was Roman Catholic. I could ask the St. Francis Society to take over, she thought. They usually will help if I ask them. But would it be different now? The Bishop's words echoed in her mind. "You would separate yourself from all good Catholics. You would create a scandal—"

She closed that folder. Somebody else could handle that case better than she could, under the circumstances. Here was another problem. What institution would have a place for this boy who was becoming a sex menace? He must be put under control before something disastrous happened. I will get that settled definitely tomorrow, Barbara told herself.

Tomorrow would come only after she had seen Kenneth, after she had told him that Bishop Tarrant had said that there could be no dispensation for her, no exception made in her case, that she could not marry Kenneth without excommunication.

Confronting her now was the case of James and Pearl Riggs.

[4]

The calamities of the world had poured malignantly on the Riggs for years, but they and four of their children had survived. The folder with their unhappy life story bulged with reports of visits, interviews, physical and psychological examinations, and expert recommendations. The modern machinery of social service had been trained in full force on the Riggs family. Barbara thought, it's as if tanks and rockets and fighter planes had been sent out to save some obscure village from destruction. And maybe they do, but when the shooting is over the village looks very battered and pathetic and not much better off. Like the Riggs.

James Riggs was about to come back once more from the work farm, with the liquor sweated out of him. A memorandum from a public health nurse stated that Pearl Riggs should do lighter work than scrubbing in office buildings. The oldest boy who did not get on well in school had been given a detailed aptitude test. Copy attached. The Riggs twins had been placed temporarily in a foster home. The baby was left with a neighbor while Pearl scrubbed lavatories. There was a tangle over which agency properly should pay the bill for enriched milk, which a pediatrician had said was absolutely necessary. Yet on the yellow slip was written, in ink that seemed to have dried with a firm edge, "This family unit should be restored."

That was the theory, always the goal. Barbara knew that. But she doubted that the married life of James and Pearl Riggs could be put together again. There was no use in shutting them up in a few rooms and waiting for the brawl to begin once more. How could those two people be brought back to the point of hope and desire at which they had joined their lives? After so much cruelty and shame and disappointment and exposure, was there a chance? Did Pearl Riggs, mopping some floor today, still want that man or did her nerves shrink at the thought of him? Did Riggs want her? If they don't, nobody can restore a family unit for them, Barbara said to herself. I ought to know. I couldn't do it for myself and Leslie, and I tried for years. That was what I told the Bishop today, not that it made any difference.

No. He says that there must be no other family for me. Because I was a fool, an infatuated girl at twenty, I must live alone as long as Leslie is alive somewhere. Or pretend to live alone, though the Bishop didn't say that, of course. I must wait for Leslie's death. And, God help me, I must keep my thoughts and my hopes from doing murder, while I wait.

It doesn't matter that I love Kenneth, or that he loves me. It isn't important that two lives are being thwarted and wasted. Better to have your love in a corner than to let it have a decent, orderly place. I couldn't tell the Bishop everything. But he must know the kind of spot that Kenneth and I are in. Certainly he does. That was why he told me I must stop seeing Ken. "My dear child, you know what you must do. You must avoid the occasion of sin."

In other words, leave town. Run. I would have to go away. I know that I could not go on living here and not see Kenneth. I've tried before to cut it off. It was in March, just before Easter, when I really tried. But it didn't work. There would have to be distance, a long stretch of space between us. I would have to be the one to go, for Kenneth couldn't, without giving up his position and wrecking his whole future. I wouldn't let that happen. He's had setbacks enough, with the war and then that woman. I have nothing here to give up, of any importance. Except him. I could go to some big city, Chicago, San Francisco maybe, and get some little job in a social agency. Grow old in a boarding house. Wait for Leslie to die. I won't wish that. I never have wished him dead, even when it was worst. I never shall. Maybe he gets something out of life even now. The use of his ego, anyway.

She had given up pretending that she could consider the problem of the Riggs family, closed their folder and stacked it with the others, and then walked with her thoughts to the window, fearing to take them out of the office in such confusion on their way to that inevitable, cruel, desired meeting with Craig. From where she stood, trying to gather control and resolution, she could see a wide part of the city, for the office of the Social Agencies was

[6]

in an old building on one of the southerly hills from which commerce had drifted away.

Lights had begun to pick out the bony structure of the town. It had naturally handsome lines, bending into a deep, hollowed curve where the glacial river valley lay heavy with bridges and railroad yards and rising to slim heights on the ancient irregular banks. On one of these stood the Cathedral, assuming a kind of architectural authority over the city, and certainly commanding the farthest and longest view. Behind the Cathedral was the Bishop's Residence, hid from sight, but Barbara knew where it was, how it looked, how it felt to approach the ugly dignity of the house. She had gone there today, hoping that Bishop Tarrant would give her permission to remarry, in spite of the fact that her divorced husband was living.

The cross on the gilded dome was bright in the afterglow of sunset, and a clean white star showed in the sky between its upper arms. Good luck, thought Barbara. It was always good luck to see the first evening star and an especially fortunate accident to see it close to the cross. She remembered how, when she was a little girl, she often used to say her prayers before a window in her bedroom which had a view of the Cathedral's cross, and the symbol seemed to give praying a special potency. Sometimes in summer, when the dusk came late, she would see a star right where it was now. They told me it was superstition, she thought, but I used to slip in a wish on the star. And how I prayed. Quite often for the most worldly, unlikely things—but savagely. How wonderful it was when a prayer was granted—and maybe the boy in the filling station spoke to me, as prayed for.

She spent a moment in the past. I gave God no peace at all until I was made a Child of Mary at the convent and had a right to wear the blue ribbon at Priems. I remember all those Rosaries I said, and that I made myself kneel stiff and upright while I said them, when I was storming God for a Catholic burial for Uncle Stephen after he killed himself. I suppose Aunt Agatha must have prayed even harder, but we got nothing that time except the cold

[7]

blessing of his grave. On a rainy day. Young as I was, I felt the whole family was outcast.

That was another time when the Church made no concession to a member of the Braniff family. I suppose I really hoped—Barbara turned irony into her mind—that the Bishop would find a way out for me because I am a Braniff and the family did a lot for the Church here once upon a time. It seems to have worked just the other way. The Bishop said, "Your family have always been strong in the faith, Barbara." To have a Braniff excommunicated is scandal scandalized.

She thought, we've been identified as Catholics so long in this region. Many stories had been passed down in her family about priests, even about the old Archbishop who had pioneered this territory and had been her great-grandfather's friend. Familiar, affectionate, but not always too respectful stories. A certain kind of lemon pie was always known to the Braniffs as the Archbishop's pie, because once he had eaten four pieces of it. They would say, "Sin of gluttony—I'm as bad as the Archbishop and his pie that your mother—your grandmother—used to tell about."

There were stained glass windows in the Cathedral, mosaics of saints that memorialized Barbara's great-grandmother and other members of that generation. The Braniffs had given the first high altar, though now there was a better one. When they had money, the Braniffs had been generous to every Catholic project in the diocese, as a graven name here and there still testified. But that was a long time ago.

Barbara asked herself mercilessly, was I expecting special handling in return for what the family used to be and do? Was I really trying a sort of blackmail? Or was I counting on the fact that it is Kenneth who wants to marry me, and since he has been made vice-president of the railroad, he is becoming important in the city. In my heart I didn't think the Bishop would refuse. If I went to him myself. I hated to go because I knew the law. The Bishop rubbed that in. He said, "You know the law of the Church, Barbara. You've been brought up a Catholic girl and well instructed. The

[8]

fact that Mr. Craig may be a very worthy man has nothing to do with it."

It has everything to do with it as far as I'm concerned, she thought stubbornly. I was honest when I got the divorce. I had no intention of remarrying. The last thing in the world I wanted was another husband. All I wanted was to be sure to be free, so that Leslie couldn't come back, so that he couldn't claim it was a temporary separation. I had no thought of marriage when I first knew Kenneth.

He would have left his office now. He would be troubled and impatient. How I have disturbed your life, dear love, she thought, and more than anything else I would like to bring you happiness and peace and trust, and the firm, easy, day-to-day relations that a man should feel flowing along with his work. Instead there are all these stresses and entanglements. But there's been joy. He's never been happy before. And to him it looks so simple. He can't understand this tangle of complications. He believes that everything can be straightened out, just as Nina was able to get an annulment of her marriage to him.

I didn't mention Nina and her case to the Bishop. There were so many things I didn't say. It wasn't that I was afraid. I suppose it is the reverence I grew up with that makes obedience and docility second nature. It was impossible to sit there today and tell the Bishop that I would marry Kenneth no matter what the Church said, with or without permission. But I did try to make it clear that I do not believe that it would be turning against God or my religion.

Barbara trembled. She felt again the involuntary yielding, the compliance with authority that had come over her in the Bishop's house. There had been a sense of being unable to escape from mighty controls, a consciousness that the Church had a right to control her life. The compliance was not so strong now. But when she left the Residence, she had been ready to tell Kenneth that their marriage was impossible.

I must still tell him. I must explain that if I did marry him

[9]

we would be living in sin, adulterous in the sight of the Church and all Catholics. But I have already told him that. He laughed. He doesn't take it seriously.

Then I shall tell him that there would always be a spiritual gulf between us. I don't really believe that. But it will be better for him to give me up and find someone else to marry, someone who doesn't present so many problems. Barbara plowed that thought cruelly into her mind and heart. She would tell Kenneth that, after talking with Bishop Tarrant, she felt bound to accept the decision of the Church and to obey its laws of marriage. As she left Bishop Tarrant, she had intended to do that. Sick and faint with disappointment as she had been, she had felt that she must go through with telling him that. And there had been a kind of exaltation buoying up the sacrifice.

It was not an unfamiliar feeling, that lift of spirit which could come with resolution and the prospect of self-denial. Barbara had known it at intervals ever since she was a child, its frequency varying with the patterns and routines of her life. It came at the end of a good confession—and confession was unthinkable if not honest—when the act of contrition, perhaps begun automatically at the admonition of the priest, suddenly came alive with sorrow and regret, and the purpose of amendment changed from words into active intention. There was often a moment of pure strength, when one need never sin again, never disobey. Childish failures in duty, temptations of a girl's curiosity, forbidden married practices, anger, rebellion, despair in grief—in less than thirty years Barbara had known them all, and many times, rejected them as many times and felt the brief, ecstatic reward of spiritual confidence in herself. The feeling had repeated itself today at the end of the Bishop's inflexibly kind denial. She had thought, I must go without Kenneth.

But she knew that the exaltation faded and the resolution always loosened its hold. The lift was gone now. So she must remember what she had intended and force herself to say that they must give up all hope of marrying now. Now meant forever. For if there was to be no marriage, the Bishop was right again. She must go away, soon and far. Without marriage their love would deteriorate, shame him, embarrass him, become what he wanted least. Kenneth wanted a wife. And I wanted to be a wife, thought Barbara, not a woman left with aftertastes, waking up to doubt and humiliation and that creeping sense of resentment. That is the sin. That is the scandal.

I must go to tell him now. Quickly.

Chapter Two

Restlessness and impatience had pervaded Kenneth Craig all day, as well as a feeling that too many people were not minding their own business. Barbara's visit to Bishop Tarrant to obtain permission to marry was at the bottom of his mood, of course. It seemed to Craig a strange and medieval procedure, and the exposure of emotion which it involved was very annoying to him. But since Barbara had felt it so necessary to her peace of mind he had not tried to keep her from going. It was his knowledge of that interview, Craig told himself, which probably was making him imagine things which did not exist.

His old friend and previous employer, Theodore Kilmey, now president of the Central and Eastern Railway, had called him today on the long distance telephone to say that he would be arriving in St. Anthony on Friday, and hoped that Craig would dine with him and Mrs. Kilmey and a small party on his private car. Craig's mind had immediately leaped to the thought that Barbara might enjoy that kind of party, and he had asked if he might bring her.

"—Mrs. Field, a very good friend of mine and a charming woman. You may know her," he had said.

Was it hesitation, or was Ted Kilmey merely being deliberate? He seemed slow on the uptake, for a cordial, hearty Irishman.

"I don't think I do. Not personally. Was she a Braniff girl?"

"Yes. That's right."

There had been another pause—or had Craig merely thought so? —before Mr. Kilmey said, "Why, yes, by all means. I'm sure Mrs. Kilmey will be happy to have you bring the young lady."

What more could he have said? Craig asked himself that, frowning, thinking that probably there was talk, that some people had nothing else to do. But for Barbara's sake, it was time the situation was settled. People were bound to wonder what went on, for he and Barbara had been seen in each other's company for months. Almost a year now. But at first, he remembered, I didn't want to marry anybody. I didn't want to be hooked again. And Barbara said she wasn't free to marry. That seemed all right at the time to both of us, but something has to be done about it now.

He was again annoyed with himself for taking note of the fact that Miss Noyes, his secretary, seemed to be lingering in the outer office after he had told her that he wouldn't need her any more today. Was she listening to find out if he would call Barbara? Or was it only his eagerness to talk to his love that made him self-conscious even about Miss Noyes and her delay? Were all these clerks and stenographers in the railroad offices talking of his affairs among themselves? Of course any man who wasn't married was their meat, as far as gossip went. But he didn't like it about Barbara and himself. He felt vulnerable. He thought that it had to be stopped, if it was going on.

Craig did not have any idea that a stout, middle-aged woman, called Agatha Braniff, was at the moment on the eighth day of a nine-day series of prayers which had his frustration for their object. His name did not enter into the prayers Miss Braniff offered that her dear niece Barbara might never live in sin.

He did not know either that Ted Kilmey had had quite a time with his wife that noon when he told her on the telephone that Craig was bringing Mrs. Field.

"But I don't know what the situation is," said Agnes Kilmey. "I've always liked Kenneth Craig. But I don't know what I'm getting into."

"The boy's had a hard time," answered Kilmey tolerantly, "with

[12]

that wife of his walking out on him. Maybe it was a good thing for him that she got an annulment. But poor Ken's never had a normal life. You can't blame him for wanting a little fun."

"There are plenty of nice girls," said Agnes Kilmey, "if he just wants fun. And since his marriage was annulled, Ken's quite free to marry."

"The Braniffs were a fine family. Well known in that whole area at one time."

"They were all Catholics," answered his wife. "One of them was in the convent with my sister years ago. Marie Braniff. This girl must be her niece. Anyway, she's married and not living with her husband. Someone from up there told me that she and Ken go around together all the time. You know what kind of thing that leads to. I just don't know," repeated Mrs. Kilmey, "what we're getting into!"

Craig had never seen Sally Frick, although he had heard Barbara speak of a girl by that name who worked in the same office with her. But Sally, after she had put the chops and salad on the table in her tiny dinette and summoned her husband, began her dinner conversation with Craig's intimate affairs.

"I get so sorry for Barby Field," she said. "She looked so sort of desperate today when that Craig man called her up. He calls her all the time. He's crazy about her, and I think she is about him. She doesn't ever go out with anyone else. I can't see why she doesn't just break down and take him."

"Maybe he hasn't asked her."

"Oh, he must have. Anyway she wouldn't have much trouble getting anyone in that state to come to the point. No, it isn't that. It's religion. She's a Catholic. He's not."

"What if he isn't? Catholics marry Protestants. I know a lot of fellows who have."

"But she's divorced, and that makes a difference."

"Can't they fix that up? The priests, I mean?"

"I always thought they could. But Barbara's a very good Catholic.

I think a divorced Catholic isn't allowed to marry anyone else as long as the first husband is living."

"No second try?"

"No, and it seems such a shame with a girl like Barbara. She's not even thirty, and sometimes she is really a beautiful creature. And that Leslie Field was a washout."

"He was a bum. I remember him around town. He got to be the worst kind of drunk and deadbeat."

"I remember seeing him too. Do you know this other man, Craig?"

"I know who he is. He's with Northeastern and Mississippi. On his way to the top, I've heard. If your girl friend has a chance to get him on the hook, she's doing all right."

"Her religion won't let her."

"Aw," said Jack Frick disbelievingly, "there must be more to it than that. After all, it's their own business."

That thought led all others in Craig's mind when he was on his way to see Barbara. He must convince her that the decision was their own to make, and only theirs. But when he saw her, paler than usual tonight, but smiling and trying to offer him serenity to start with, love overtook all his thoughts. He did not begin with argument.

Against his heart he heard, "I'm so sorry. It's going to be so hard."

"My poor, darling girl," he soothed her, "you've had a bad time. I shouldn't have let you go there alone, that was my mistake. But it's going to be all right."

"No. It can't possibly be."

He lit a cigarette for each of them, asked her if she wanted a drink, refused one for himself.

"Not just now."

The room was too small for him. She often felt that. But they had been happy in it. It was a distinctive little sitting room, better than her income, for it was furnished with things left from the days of Braniff affluence and from the glittering beginning of her own

[14]

marriage. Long yellow curtains shut out the clutter of little shops and unsorted houses in the neighborhood of the apartment building. A very old gilt-framed mirror almost covered one narrow wall and repeated all they did, giving back the tenderness of his embrace, his height and firm, aggressive shoulders and the almost fluid beauty of Barbara's figure.

Craig moved about restlessly, not quite guest and not quite host, never quite at ease here.

Trying to make her smile, he said, "I'm not going to let you run around with Bishops if they upset you so much."

"It isn't funny. I wish it were."

"Well, tell me, what did he say?"

"He was very kind and very inflexible, that's all. He said that as long as Leslie is alive, I can't marry again."

"But he isn't alive as far as you're concerned. He's completely out of your life and has been for several years. The Bishop doesn't want you to go back to that fellow, does he!"

"Oh, no—he didn't suggest anything like that."

"He just wants you to live like a nun."

"Like a nun—"

"Well, that's what you would do if the Bishop had his way. I tell you, Barbara, it doesn't make a spark of sense. And you know in your heart that it doesn't."

"I know that it doesn't to you."

"Nor to anyone else who understands the situation. I'll bet that it doesn't make sense to the Bishop himself. Of course he's got to take a stand. I was thinking, on the way out here, that he has to put up a certain front."

"Front! Oh, Ken, you don't realize—"

"Let me finish, darling. Maybe I realize more than you think. What I mean is that in his position he has to be a stickler for the rules, lay down the law for his organization. That's his job. I'd be in the same spot as he is if someone who was working for the railroad came and asked me to make certain exceptions to company rules. I'd say it couldn't be done, that we had an established policy and had

[15]

to maintain it. But that doesn't mean that we don't make exceptions when there's reason enough for doing it. And the same thing must be true of your Church. Did you talk to the Bishop about an annulment?"

"There wasn't any use. I told you, all that ground has been gone over before. When I first got a legal separation from Leslie and later when I had to make it an absolute divorce, because Leslie wouldn't take the separation seriously, I talked to both Father Moore and the Bishop. They would have preferred an annulment, and went over all the possibilities. What we call impediments. In my case, there weren't any of the right ones. Leslie had been baptized, and he had signed the papers to have our children brought up Catholics, and—you know what the other impediments are, don't you? Things like impotency, abduction, consanguinity, that would make any marriage no good. There was nothing like that."

"Just the same, they do a whole lot of annulling in your Church," he persisted. "That's how they fixed Nina up, after she was divorced from me, and wanted to marry her well-fixed Catholic boy. They annulled her marriage to me, wiped me clean off the slate."

"Wasn't that because you had never been baptized?"

"I guess that was the excuse. Something like that. As if any amount of holy water would make much difference with Nina! What I mean is that if they can fix it up for a girl like her, who—"

Barbara interrupted. She didn't want to think of Nina, who had been Kenneth's wife. Nor to have him think of her. She said, "Every case is different. It seems inconsistent if you don't understand the laws of the Church. It seems unfair. But of course you don't always know what's back of an annulment. Actually, I never really wanted one for myself. Let me tell you why. I couldn't possibly have gone on living with Leslie. But in spite of what he became, we had had a child. And even though David died, I didn't want to wipe out his birth that way. It seemed to me that an annulment would have destroyed the little that belonged to David, his decent birth—there would have been nothing!"

Kenneth said, "Don't, dear," for he could hear the pain rising in

[16]

her voice. But she went on as if she must say all that was true about that.

"Annulments may be all right when people are tricked or frightened into a marriage, or cheated in one of those ways so there can't be an actual marriage. But even if I was a fool, I knew what I was doing. And for a while Leslie and I were happy. I thought so anyway. Happy enough."

Craig walked up and down the room as if waiting for that memory to pass. Then he came back to her side.

"An annulment is a technical matter," he said. "I understand how you might feel about it. I only spoke of it because I thought it might be the best way out for you and would clear the decks completely. It shouldn't be necessary at all. It isn't. What I can't understand is why any private institution, church or not, has any right to consider the law of the land and judgments of the court invalid. That's what your Bishop evidently is attempting to do. You have a full divorce, and with it the right to marry again. Bishop Tarrant refuses to acknowledge the law of the country he's living in. He seems to claim that he has a higher authority. That may have been all right in the Middle Ages, but this is America, in the twentieth century. He hasn't a leg to stand on. He can thunder at you, but we can go and get married and he can't do a think to prevent it."

"He doesn't thunder. All he says is that we can't get married in the Church, Ken."

"That's all right with me. Any justice of the peace can do the same job and make it stick."

Barbara's thin hands pushed back the curves of hair from her forehead. The shining, rose-colored nails were like ornaments against the dark, roughened hair. He loved her more because she often would be careless with her own beauty, indifferent to provocation, as she was now with her face pale and strained from this struggle caused by their love. Craig had never known that a woman would resist a man she loved for such a reason. She made love very important, all inclusive, and he was glad of that in spite of the drawn-out argument and the delay. He had no intention of giving Barbara up nor

[17]

of allowing her to give him up. She would not do that, he was sure, no matter what pressure these Church people put on her. But the reasons for the pressure were still obscure enough to Craig to excite his impatience.

Barbara was explaining as best she could. "To a Catholic, marriage isn't just a legal bond. It is a contract, but also it is a sacrament."

"That's a fine way to look at it. I think marriage should be sacred. Of course it very often isn't. But our marriage would be, Barbara. I promise that to me it would always be the most sacred thing in my life."

The words made her tremble, but she put his hands gently from her and went on.

"Darling, don't break me down. There again you don't quite understand. A sacrament isn't only a sacred thing or an attitude in your mind. It is a cause of grace. I mean that it is something that brings the supernatural into the natural life. All the sacraments do that. From baptism to the one you're given as you are dying."

He said, "I know about the way they do that. We made arrangements for that sometimes in the Navy. For the Catholic boys. They took it very seriously. I got to know quite a lot about your Church during the war."

"That's why marriage is so important for a Catholic," she repeated, "because it is a sacrament. And if you don't have the grace which goes with the sacrament, then it's just as if you were living together without being married. In the eyes of the Church."

"So nobody who doesn't do it the Catholic way is really married?" he asked skeptically.

"Of course that's not true. The laws of the Church only apply to Catholics. But if you belong to the Church, and want to stay in it, you have to accept the laws."

"It's amazing how they have worked it out," said Craig, consideringly. "Of course the people who run the Catholic Church have always been past masters of psychology. They know how to control great masses of people. They take over the big spots in life and make themselves indispensable. Tie religion into marriage and

[18]

death and even sex relations. I've always given your church a good deal of credit for the boost it can give certain kinds of people. It was good for morale in the Navy. I don't question that for a minute. As a matter of fact, it was the only control over some of those boys. But they'd go to Mass no matter what they'd been up to on their last leave or looked forward to on the next one."

"As do I," said Barbara.

"I don't mean anything like that! That's just what I'm getting at. You can't class yourself with the kind of person that these rules are set up for."

"They're set up for every Catholic."

"Theoretically. But you can think things out for yourself. You surely must realize that a lot of the discipline, or whatever you call it, was worked out in the first place because the priests wanted to hold very ignorant people in line. They had to throw a scare into them, to make them toe the mark, and keep them reporting back. But you're beyond all that mentally. You can see through it. What can they do to you?"

"They can refuse me the sacraments," answered Barbara, "or rather they wouldn't have to because I wouldn't approach them."

He looked blank, not sure of what she meant. "Approach them?" he repeated. "Would that matter so much to you?"

"Yes." The word was unhesitating, just audible above her breath.

"Darling, couldn't I make it up to you? Wouldn't our life together make up for it?"

"I don't know. I can't quite think what life would be like, or what I would be like."

"You'd be yourself. Lovelier than ever."

"I'd be what they call a fallen away Catholic."

"Well—aren't there a great many of them? People who can't take the dogma and the rules after a while? I've known a number of people who used to be Catholics and stopped working at it."

"Most of them lose their faith," she said, "but, you see, I haven't. I want to marry you. But I haven't lost my faith. I really believe in my religion. I'm angry because I can't have what I want. It seems

[19]

unjust and unfair because I did try to make a success out of that marriage to Leslie, as long as there was any chance. Any hope at all. But he and I have lived apart for years now. And I'm still fairly young—"

She was on his side now. He didn't interrupt. She was saying what he wanted to hear from her, to make herself believe.

"I want you so much," she said softly. "I want you to have all the honor and pride and help that a man should get along with the woman he loves. I want it more and more."

"So do I—"

"Please let me tell you. If my religion didn't mean anything to me, it would be easy. I could go off with you to a justice of the peace without a qualm. I've never talked much to you about being a Catholic, except about this one obstacle. But it's deep in me, just the same."

"You were brought up in it."

"Yes, we've always been Catholics on both sides of the family. But we weren't very parochial, at least not in the last couple of generations. The Braniffs were never priest-ridden, my grandfather used to say."

"I'm very glad they weren't."

"My family always laughed at a lot of pieties and bigotries. Plenty of Catholics do. But they accepted the basic discipline and the privileges. They had to, if they wanted to stay in the Church. Once an uncle of mine committed suicide, and everyone in the family was bitter because he couldn't have a Catholic burial. There was a terrific row. We haven't always been very docile Catholics. But I was brought up in it, as you say. I took it for granted until I married Leslie. Our priest tried to talk me out of that, but I wouldn't take anybody's advice."

"I guess Leslie Field fooled a great many people at that stage of his career."

She did not pause to think about that. There was more she must tell Kenneth, and her head was lifted now, her eyes concentrated.

"When things got really bad, I can't tell you what my religion

[20]

meant to me. It was all I had to turn to. My father failed and grew strange, and then he died. David was a baby, and Leslie was drunk all the time—wild drunk. If I hadn't had any religion—but it came alive more and more. It was bigger than anything that was happening to me, stronger. And then Davy died—"

"Barbara, you'd better not. Don't tear yourself to pieces."

"Let me tell you," she repeated. "I thought I was going quite crazy. If I hadn't been able to believe that there was something beyond that awful emptiness—that somewhere David still had some care, that he wasn't quite lost—you see, one reason I hung on to my faith desperately was because it kept David living—it was being able to trust in it—" she broke off helplessly— "I can't explain. I can only tell you that it was the only rest I had, the only source of courage or hope. Of course that's nearly six years ago now."

"And you're never going to suffer like that again."

"In those years I might have become so cheap, so vicious—"

"You? There was never a chance of it. You're too fine-grained, too delicate, too decent. Yes, you are. I know."

"You don't know what it's like to live alone as I did. It's not easy for a grass widow, or a separated wife, or a divorced one who can't remarry. I was all those things, one after another. People tried to be fair and kind. I wasn't dropped entirely by old friends of the family, and not even by all the young married people who had started out when Leslie and I did. I got asked here and there, when an extra girl was needed in the married section. There were chances to play around. Men get tired of their wives, and they fight. I was a natural to hear their troubles."

"I suppose you must have been. But none of those people meant anything to you? You said—"

"That was true. I didn't feel much except excitement occasionally. You get starved for feeling and excitement can fill in. Music and the extra drink. But I tell you, Ken, if I hadn't had any religion—if I hadn't kept going to church, and to confession too—if I hadn't known where to find decency and cleanness and goodness—I might have become anything. There were times when I felt like a lost

[21]

soul, and that's the reason why the Church means so much to me. It's not what you think, a bunch of dogmas forced into my mind by priests. It's routine and habit, and pieties and things that bother me sometimes. But it's been my friend and my refuge and my angel so often! I'm not sure I could exist without it."

He said, "I begin to understand. I can realize what's been on your mind."

"I don't blame you for being critical or even hostile. I know how the Catholic Church looks to outsiders sometimes. No one could do the kind of work I did in the war, and since then with the Social Agencies, without rebelling against the laws forbidding birth control and divorce. I'm not the only Catholic woman in a tough spot. And some priests are ignorant and almost intolerable. But beyond all those things is the religion, my religion. If we marry outside the Church, I'll be denied the sacraments. I couldn't go to confession. That is, I could go if I liked, but if I told the truth no priest would give me absolution. I never could receive Communion. I'd be excommunicated."

"I remember that you were worrying about that last spring."

"Yes," she said. "I was, last spring."

"You got away with it then."

He had not meant to say anything that affected her that way. Her face went whiter and her eyes were shocked.

"Yes," she answered slowly, "I'm afraid that's what I did. I've never been sure. At the time it didn't seem so. I thought I was honest."

His mind went back to that disturbing time last spring when first they had realized their love for each other. Vaguely he had known that her religion was bothering her, but she seemed to get over it after Easter had passed. He had never asked how she had worked it out with the priest, but he had guessed that she had gone to confession.

"I shouldn't have put it that way. You mean that you didn't tell the priest then that we were in love?"

"Yes, but I told him too that I was going to stop seeing you, and give you up. I meant to at the time."

"Then you fooled him," said Craig, gravely now. "Maybe you even fooled yourself. But not me. I knew better than that then, and I know better now. That's the one thing that isn't going to happen, Barbara. Not unless you can tell me that you don't want to see me, and don't love me. We couldn't take it. After only a few hours I begin to want you, to see you, hear you, be sure you're there."

"I'll have to go away. That was what I was trying to think out this afternoon. I hoped so terribly that the Bishop would make an exception. He wouldn't. So I have to do what he said, and not see you."

"You won't do that, no matter what he said."

"I could live somewhere else."

"I'd follow you."

"You couldn't leave your work. That's why I'd be the one to go. The Bishop wants me to go."

Craig frowned. This was getting past theory. This was direct interference, and he did not like it.

He said so. "The Bishop went pretty far, it seems to me. It's all right for him to state his opinion, but to suggest a thing like that is overdoing it. What was his idea?"

"He wants me to avoid the occasion of sin."

Craig laughed, not as if it was funny. "Sin? Well, if your seeing me is his definition of sin, it's not mine. It's good, and right. It's heaven. It's the first happiness I've ever had that I could trust or believe in. Barbara, you wouldn't let anyone or any institution take that from me, would you? From us? We've found each other, after a lot of mistakes and grief and personal misery. After trying to keep straight in hard years. We're good for each other. Sin! We've found what we need to make us stronger and finer people, and able to do a better job with our lives. That's what you should have told the Bishop!"

"I did. I tried. To him that doesn't matter. Not in comparison with breaking the law of the Church."

[23]

Craig's answer surged back impatiently. "If it doesn't matter to him, you know why. It's because there is something abnormal in the outlook of men like that. They've lived unnaturally, as best they could, always compensating for not having a normal man's life. They're bound to write it down and write it off as unimportant to be normal and happy. They're frustrated. Cold."

"The Bishop wasn't cold, Ken. He was almost sorry."

"Well, I think I'd better go and see him."

"It wouldn't do any good."

"I'm not so sure. It might be easier for him to talk to a rank outsider. Someone outside his organization."

She had a flash of hope.

"That's the next step," he decided. "I'd like to do it your way, darling. You've made me see how much this means to you. But no matter what, we're going to get married. I'm not going to let you go. You don't want me to let you go."

"But you should!" she whispered. "You'll have to!"

"You know I won't. I've been doing some pretty thorough thinking myself. At first when you told me you weren't free to remarry, I accepted the situation. But it's no good. Gradually we've come to care more for each other and to want marriage more than anything else. It proves the depth of the feeling we have for each other. What's more, there's no hiding it from our friends or the public any longer. Everybody who knows either of us is wondering what is going on. I don't care except for your sake, but I don't want you to be the subject of that kind of speculation up and down the street."

"Most people know there's a religious barrier as long as Leslie is alive."

"That doesn't stop anyone's tongue."

"I know."

"Do you believe that anyone, looking at this situation and knowing how we feel, wouldn't think that apart from anything else, the decent, orderly thing is to get married?"

"Anyone except a Catholic."

"Catholics too, I'll bet, if any of them were in a similar spot. It's

[24]

not any way for us to live. I can't take care of you. I'm thwarted, humiliated."

"It's beastly for you—I know."

"Worse for you. We've been fighting windmills long enough. Now here it is. If Leslie Field were dead, you could marry me next day. Is that right?"

"But he's not."

"He's a very dissipated fellow. He might die any time."

"I won't hope for that!"

"I wouldn't want you to. But I'll bet money that Bishop Tarrant hopes for it. In any case, when and if that happens, the Church will okay our marriage?"

"We'd have to be married again."

"That would be all right. In the interim, if the Bishop won't come across, you're blacklisted by the Church. Technically you'll be living in sin, which nobody will believe and the Church probably won't either. But Barbara, actually, morally, wouldn't that be better than tearing ourselves to pieces the way we do now? Wouldn't our heads be higher?"

"Oh, you know how I feel! How I want to be honest."

"Your Church puts us in a situation where we can't be honest."

"They don't want to."

"Well, they ought to realize that they are dealing with human beings and get down to earth and make their rules workable. I know what we've got to do. I didn't talk about it until now because, as a matter of fact, I was pretty sure that Bishop Tarrant would clear things up when you went to see him. He held out. So the next procedure is for me to have a talk with him myself. Possibly I may get farther than you did. The Bishop might say things to me that he wouldn't to a girl, one of his own congregation."

"I don't think he'll change his mind."

"It's worth a try, isn't it?"

The crack of hope widened. "Perhaps. If it isn't too difficult for you."

"Not difficult at all. I've talked to a lot of tough customers in my day. But, Barbara—if that doesn't work out—we are going to be married anyway. Quietly and quickly. By anyone and anywhere that is legal. No—don't stop me, and don't object. I'm going to take charge of this situation from here in. I think that we've been on the wrong track. Not handling the situation correctly. I'll tell you what I mean."

She listened. What she heard through all he said was that it was not over, not ended. Perhaps need not be.

"I have a certain sympathy for the Bishop," said Craig. "Anyone who is connected with an organization, even the way I am with the railroad, can understand his position. He has to keep his crowd, the people under him, close-knit and make them take direction. I have the same problem. Any executive has. But it often works out this way, and this is what you don't realize. If somebody doesn't always toe the line and yet is a valuable person in the organization or conscientiously does something in his own way, that person isn't tossed out on his ear."

"He would be tossed out of the Church."

"I doubt it very much. Maybe that might be the threat. Maybe I myself might give that impression so that everybody else wouldn't want to jump the fence for no good reason. But if the thing I didn't authorize were done and I was confronted with a fact and not asked to give a green light, it might be a different story. I'd judge the situation on its merits. My guess is that the Bishop might prefer to face an accomplished fact rather than to make an exception beforehand. For that leads to the necessity of allowing other exceptions. You see what I'm driving at?"

"There's some truth in it. The Bishop talked about my case being a bad example. Every little girl in the diocese who isn't satisfied with her husband, he said—"

"Exactly. So it might be a whole lot easier for him if he didn't have to commit himself in advance."

She moved her head in doubt. "What could he do afterward?"

"He's in complete authority, isn't he? He could do what he pleased. And there is another thing I want to look into. You've been

[26]

fighting this all alone. A little influence might be brought to bear on the Bishop. A word from the right quarter might do a lot of good. Smooth it all out."

"But whose word?"

"Well, I was thinking of Ted Kilmey, the president of C. and E. He's a good friend of mine. I had my first job with his line, in the Chicago office. I used to be asked to their house, and I dated one of the Kilmey girls for a while."

"What was she like?"

"She was all right."

"Why did you stop dating her?"

He laughed and said he'd forgotten. "Anyway I didn't stay with that outfit very long when I got a chance to go with Northeastern."

"Why didn't you?"

"Well, that ties right in with what we're talking about. There was never much real promotion under Ted Kilmey except for a good Catholic, and I didn't qualify. Maybe it just happens that way, but they call his road the Catholic Railroad, you know."

"I didn't know that."

"But Mr. Kilmey's a good friend of mine, just the same, and he's been quite a booster for me. So when I was talking to him today—before I knew all this about the Bishop—"

"You mean he's here in St. Anthony and might talk to Bishop Tarrant?"

"I haven't gone that far. That's premature. No, he's not here, but he and his wife are coming through this week on one of his inspection trips. He makes them periodically. He loves to ride in that car, and so does she. They do a lot of entertaining on it. Anyway, he asked me to have dinner with them on Friday, and I thought you might enjoy the evening so I asked if I could bring you. It all fits together, doesn't it?"

"I wonder. I don't know the Kilmeys. Do they want me?"

"Why, of course they do. These affairs are basically business parties, fairly free and easy. There will be people you know. I told Mr. Kilmey I'd bring you. That's all fixed. What I would like to do is to introduce you to him and his wife as the girl I am about to marry. Come right out with it."

"Oh, no, Ken! Not as things are. Please don't tell anyone that. Not until you've talked with the Bishop."

"All right. You just turn plenty of charm on the Kilmeys. The thing I want is to have them ready to put in a word at the right time. If it should be necessary. It probably won't be."

"Darling, it's all too bad. I don't want to have you connive and plot. I hate to make things hard for you. I wish I could say it doesn't matter. But it does. If we could do this in the right way, it would make me so happy. It would be everything. You do understand, don't you, that it isn't just for myself? I want you and our love to have every blessing, every grace—"

"My lovely mystic girl," he said. "And I love you for it. But you must belong to me soon. And I won't stand for any more talk about your running away from me, either from you or your Bishop."

"It seems the only way."

"And what do you think would happen to you in some other place? Don't you think it would be the same thing all over again?"

"Oh, my God, no! Don't say that."

"You're a very beautiful woman. And you're human too. And mine."

"You think we've a chance? I was quite hopeless when I left the Bishop's house. I gave you up on his threshold. I remember."

"You forget that. You were a little hysterical. I've always heard that priests have a queer power over women, a kind of hypnosis."

"That's nonsense."

"Maybe. Anyway you look a different girl now from the way you did when I came in tonight."

He took her cheeks between his hands, warming them at the flush that rose, watched the question rise in her eyes, and quieted it with answer.

"Don't worry. I promise you that you cannot get away. And I want to promise you something else. I shall not worry you with my love, not until we are married."

[28]

She did not speak, but her eyes thanked him.

"When you were talking just now," he said, "I realized as I never have how some things have worried you, been a weight on you. I know you've been happy, but you must be happier. We'll wait. We won't have to be separated too long."

Chapter Three

The company invited to dine on the private car of the president of the Central and Eastern Railroad was small and important. Theodore Kilmey, even when he was traveling, always preferred to have people come to him and to be himself the one who put others under social obligations. Some awkwardness or humiliation, long buried in success, had left its mark and made him want to control any party he attended. So he and his wife made a habit of entertaining on the car, which was almost their second home, and most of their guests found it a pleasant novelty to dine in luxury in the railroad yards.

The car had been shunted on to a side track close to the station, and a special gate left open on the platform, with a watchman in attendance to make sure that no one came through without a pass. The steel body of the long, specially constructed Pullman gleamed in the moonlight that was breaking through mist and drizzle. Shades had been drawn down tightly over the windows, and from without there was no sign of the bright activity within the car. A colored steward was laying crisply folded damask napkins at places for twelve on a table centered with the red roses which were the only flowers that Mr. Kilmey did not regard as trivial. In the lounge end of the car, a Filipino boy had opened a built-in bar as soon as Mr. Miller, the president of Northeastern and Mississippi, had arrived. Mrs. Kilmey was knitting and listening slightly to what the men were saying. She was a pretty woman, with a white skin that had loosened only a little after more than fifty years, and her curly hair still mixed brown with gray.

Mr. Miller had arrived so promptly that he was early. He explained that there was never any chance to talk after a crowd came.

"It's only a small party," said Kilmey.

"I think it's so much nicer not to have too many people," said Mrs. Kilmey. "Our space is so limited."

"We can only take care of twelve comfortably," remarked Ted Kilmey with no humility, "so we had to hold it down. Couldn't ask everyone I'd like to have on the car. Dudley Harrison and his wife are coming, and the David Ryes. Who else, Agnes?"

"Blair Wyatt. He's just back from Europe and should be very interesting."

"The women can't do without Wyatt. He's a great beau of Agnes's."

"Oh, he's everybody's beau. Blair is the perennial bachelor," said Agnes Kilmey with comfortable lack of originality. "But I'm very fond of him."

"Wyatt is a smart fellow. He's made a lot of money lately, I hear. Not in Europe."

Agnes Kilmey went on checking the names of her guests.

"Mr. and Mrs. Lyman—"

"I've never had Joe Lyman on the train. I though he'd get a bang out of it," commented her husband.

"And Kenneth Craig is coming. He's bringing Mrs. Field."

"She was a Braniff girl, I understand," said Ted Kilmey.

"Yes, I know," said Mr. Miller. "She's very charming."

"My sister knew her aunt," Mrs. Kilmey contributed. "She was Marie Braniff before she married. The aunt, I mean."

"Ken asked if he could bring her," said Kilmey, "and Mother here said yes."

"What else could I say?"

"Is Ken pretty serious about her?" inquired Kilmey of Mr. Miller. Mr. Miller did not commit himself too far. "I don't really know.

I've met him with the young lady several times. But I believe the situation is a little complicated for some reason."

"Ken was one of my boys, you know. He worked for me. I gave him his start."

"I know you did. And he's always been very much attached to you."

"He's a fine fellow," said Kilmey. "He's able too. Let's see. He was with us in 1938. Yes, it was about three years before the war. That's right. Before he was married to the Howe girl. Lord, it's more than ten years ago."

"Nina Howe," Mrs. Kilmey supplied the rest of the identification. "She's married to one of the Longman boys now."

"That was what she wanted, I guess," said Kilmey. "A whole lot of sure money, no matter what went with it."

His wife frowned lightly at him. "Ted, they're nice boys."

"I never liked her," Kilmey declared, not arguing about the Longman brothers. "I have an idea she gave Ken Craig a very bad time. Kept him under a continual strain. And I guess she walked out on him, didn't she, Agnes, when he was overseas?"

"I really don't know. And you don't know either, Ted. Of course the marriage was annulled."

"Lucky thing for Ken that it was, in my opinion. How's he coming on?"

"Fine," answered Mr. Miller. "He's junior vice-president."

"And Marcus Croy must be sixty-five? Not much between Ken and your shoes, John."

Mr. Miller smiled without denial.

"I'd like to see Kenneth Craig well fixed and settled down," Ted Kilmey went on. "He ought to have a family. It's too bad if he's getting himself mixed up with another unfortunate situation. Agnes says she's heard something about it."

Agnes Kilmey said, "Only that she's a Catholic, Ted—all the Braniffs were. And her husband is still alive, I understand."

Mr. Miller asked, "Pardon my ignorance. I don't want to say anything out of order. But isn't it possible to make some arrangement in a case like that?"

Kilmey chuckled and said, "Depends on your pull with the proper authorities."

His wife protested again in her quick, mild way, "Ted, dear, you shouldn't talk like that. I'm actually ashamed of you."

"I was just joking, dearie."

"It's a poor subject to joke about. You'd better make that remark a matter of confession. It has nothing to do with pull, Mr. Miller. It depends on circumstances, on whether the marriage was valid or not in the first place."

John Miller spoke reminiscently. "I used to see Leslie Field around the club. He was a bad actor. Drunk all the time. They had to put him in institutions several times. I suppose she really had to get rid of him. He owed money all over town."

Mrs. Kilmey went on diligently with explanation, as if it was a matter of duty and conscience to make up for the unfortunate impression about the Church that her husband might have given to Mr. Miller.

"The Church is very broad-minded about cases like that. It allows separation. It doesn't expect a woman to live with a man who isn't any good. And sometimes people who are quite good Catholics have civil divorces, especially when the marriages have been mixed and the non-Catholic wants to remarry. But of course a Catholic cannot marry a second time when her first husband is alive. You see, the Church doesn't recognize divorce."

"No, if you're hooked, you're hooked," said Kilmey. His wife shook her head at him, and he leaned down to kiss her fondly. "And sometimes it works out pretty well."

The Lymans came in, interrupting the conversation. Harold Lyman had an easy, burly manner. He looked like the immensely rich contractor that he was, as if he had stood in the cold and wind and superintended the jobs that made him wealthy. He was glad to have dinner on Ted Kilmey's private car, pleased to have come this far socially, loudly cordial to prove he was not impressed. His

[32]

wife was unsure of herself in spite of all that the beauty parlor had done for her today, in spite of the white mink cape that Mrs. Kilmey admired.

Carol Harrison brought genuine ease into the party. She always did that, with her gift for social affection and her roving imagination. She always brought gaiety enough for two with her, because her husband was so inhibited. Jennifer Rye and her banker husband came next, playing each other up. Blair Wyatt, handsome and tall enough to carry off his overweight, arrived and got a double welcome because he had been abroad. He kissed all the women except Mrs. Lyman. Wyatt was sophisticated, even a little erudite. His manner was that of the great world. But the men knew that it was based on a local fortune which he had not only inherited but shrewdly increased. Finally Barbara Field came in, with Craig behind her.

"How nice of you to come, Mrs. Field," said Mrs. Kilmey. "You know, your Aunt Marie used to be quite a friend of my sister's, I think. My older sister. They went to the Sacred Heart Convent together. Wasn't that where your Aunt Marie went?"

"Yes, and my mother too," said Barbara. Her voice was full of happiness tonight.

Theodore Kilmey took Barbara's hand and gave her a covering glance which ended in admiration. He thought, she's a beauty all right. No one could blame Ken Craig. Looks a nice girl too. Sweet expression around her mouth.

She seemed younger than he had expected she would be, with that story of divorce and a drunken husband clinging to her. In her black velvet suit, and hatless, as if that were her custom, she had no look of hard experience. A nosegay of hothouse violets, their stems loose and long, was pinned to her jacket and that sign of love and attention brought a feeling of romance into the company. They all were conscious of it, of beauty and desire, the rumored problem between the two, the possibilities of their present relationship, the questions of its tenacity and outcome.

[33]

"How are you, darling?" asked Blair Wyatt, kissing Barbara as if he always did so.

"I've never been better."

"And you look it. Must I fall in love with you again?"

Kenneth Craig watched her with Wyatt, heard the interchange of frosted words. He wondered if this had been one of the men who had made Barbara's life a problem, driven her to the confessional for refuge. The thought distracted his attention from what Theodore Kilmey was saying to him.

"I'm sorry, sir. I didn't quite get that."

Kilmey chuckled. "I don't blame you at all. Too many attractions around here for serious conversation. Tell me, how are you?"

"Well, I've got a good job, sir."

"Fine. Come on over here and let's have a drink where it's more quiet."

They had the drink and Craig felt confident as always of the older man's friendship as they talked of his own business progress.

"You can always come around to me if you get in trouble, Ken," joked Kilmey.

"There is one thing I'd like to talk over with you, Mr. Kilmey. I'd like your advice very much."

"Getting on all right, aren't you?"

"This is a personal affair."

The older man began to look wary. Something in his manner closed up as Craig went on talking.

"I know you're a very well-informed Catholic, Mr. Kilmey, and I thought you might tell me what the procedure is in regard to what they refer to as impediments. In a marriage situation."

"Ah-ah, that's very touchy business. You'd have to talk to a priest about that. Or better yet to a Bishop. A layman like myself can't speak with any authority."

"There's no fixed practice?"

"Very definitely there is. Let me see—it's Tarrant in this diocese, isn't it? Do you know Bishop Tarrant?"

"Not personally. I've met him a few times at civic affairs."

"Well, if you have something on your mind, he would be the one to approach. He's a good man. Broad-minded. Stands high in Rome."

"It's always possible for things to be arranged, isn't it?"

"I wouldn't say that." Mr. Kilmey's eyes strayed in the direction of his wife, as if he wished that she were close enough to hear him and edit his answer. Then they returned, with kindness as well as keenness, to Kenneth Craig's grave face. He went on, "It is true that Bishops have great experience in these matters. And discretionary powers to a certain extent. There is even a special court at Rome for the consideration of extraordinary cases." He did not pretend to be surprised that Craig was asking such questions. "You should have a frank talk with Bishop Tarrant, my boy. That's the thing to do."

"I'm going to do that, Mr. Kilmey. As soon as possible. But tell me, sir—surely they must discriminate in enforcing laws—church laws, I mean—between cases which deserve special consideration and those which do not?"

"Well, Ken, the Catholic Church is a very wise institution. If exceptions can be made, they know the when and how."

"That's what I've been wondering about."

"Don't misunderstand me—"

But Mrs. Kilmey put an end to their conversation. She thought that the guests had drunk enough for a prelude and led the company back to the dining salon. Outside a freight train with a hundred cars rattled by, and the guests did not hear it, locked in their own noisemaking. A string of tourist coaches on a nearby track filled up with people who were going to funerals and weddings and new jobs and back to their homes and away from them forever. The lights in the cars were too dim for reading but bright enough to show the weariness and sorrow and worries in the faces of passengers. A priest, pallid and unhandsome, but with full power to marry and bury and absolve from sin, hoisted his black bag to the rack and settled into one of the seats. He looked through the dingy window beside him at the shining private train on the siding and

[35]

began to mold the contrast into his first sermon for the mission to which he was traveling. In which car would Christ prefer to ride? In the shining one or in this coach where the woman was munching chocolate bars?

On the private car they ate wild ducks with melted currant jelly and drank red Burgundy, a vintage wine, for Mr. Kilmey traveled with a little stock for occasions like this. He liked entertaining these guests. He had made his own money and position. Once his job had been on top of freight cars like those trundling by, and now it was in this luxury. Like the traveling priest he enjoyed an obvious contrast and found his own moral. Kilmey had never forgotten the savor of a new importance. Tonight he enjoyed having Joe Lyman here, who was making a fortune building railroad bridges now but had started with nothing in his jeans. He liked to show David Rye that he could be host and epicure as well as direct a railroad's finances.

Harrison bored him with his stale Harvard manner, but Ted Kilmey liked to have Harrison's wife around. She could be counted on to keep things going, and she never forgot that men were male. Blair Wyatt wasn't up his own street, but Agnes got a kick out of that society patter, and Wyatt was nobody's fool. He was a very rich man. Tonight he was playing up Mrs. Field. Could there be anything to that? Of course if she couldn't marry the one she couldn't marry the other. She was a lovely woman to be living alone. No children, she had told him. Too bad. Mr. Kilmey looked at his own wife, her rosiness now a little purpled. He thought of the six children, of the ten grandchildren, of the way she had kept an eye on the whole lot of them, including him, and he was lovingly proud of her.

They had finished the sweet and were having coffee and liqueurs when the local train pulled out with a clatter. A girl on it burst into tears as it moved out of the station. She had just been given a divorce that day, and now she was going back to the little town where she had left the children with her mother. She couldn't have done anything else, and she had told herself that a hundred times

[36]

in the last week. But she was cut off now from the only man who had ever even said that he loved her, and, oddly, the break with the taverns and the debts hurt. A failure, a mess behind, and terribly hard going ahead, she thought as she sobbed.

Mrs. Kilmey had Blair Wyatt on her right, sharing his talk with Carol Harrison. Mrs. Kilmey was becoming personal with wine.

"I thought you'd come back from Europe this time with a bride, Blair."

"A little displaced maiden? Clinging to me for a passport?"

"No, a nice, young, impoverished countess."

"The nice ones aren't young," he said lightly.

"But aren't you ever going to get married?" asked Carol Harrison.

Most of the dinner guests heard the question as it crossed the table, and listened for an answer that would certainly be amusing.

"I doubt it. All the women I want are married. Or beyond my grasp like Barbara."

Barbara heard her name. She had been listening to Mr. Kilmey state his political preferences, but he would go on without attention. She leaned forward and asked, "What's that about me?"

"I was just saying, darling, that I'm thwarted because you are out of my eager reach. That I'm thwarted, because you are canonically unable to marry."

It could have meant nothing, as he had intended. But the words seemed to strike conversation into silence. There was no laugh except the brief one that Wyatt ended on. They all saw Barbara's look, strange and frightened. Then standing, with his own chair pushed quickly back, Kenneth Craig was behind her.

"How wrong you are, Blair," he said quietly. "Didn't you know that Barbara and I are going to be married?"

Down into their minds, cracking the conversation and the surface frivolity like the thin ice it was, went Craig's statement, sinking as deep as it could in each one of them. This was no joke. This was the kind of seriousness, an exposure of love and determination, which sent the thoughts of the people who heard him to the depths of their own minds.

I made a mistake, thought Kilmey. I shouldn't have talked to him before dinner or given him any encouragement. Now the fat's in the fire. He thought it with worry even as he said aloud, "Well, Ken, this certainly is a surprise. Well, young lady! Well—this calls for a little toast. I must go and see if we have some champagne in the locker."

"So very surprising—yes, Ted, do—shall we go back into the other car?" Agnes Kilmey rose as her husband did, breaking up this embarrassing and distressing scene. She did not like this announcement, coming intrusively and roughly as it did. Not at all. Could the husband conceivably have died? I should not have allowed it to happen here, she said to herself. I ought not to have let Kenneth Craig bring the girl. I should have put my foot down. Because if she is not permitted to marry and they do it anyway, it will almost look as if I connived at it. Gave opportunity. Of course I didn't know a thing about it, but our name will be dragged into it. Blair Wyatt is bound to dine out on this story, and he will tell everyone that it was announced at my table. In Ted's private car! The Archbishop won't like it at all. And just when they are suggesting that Ted may be made a Prince of the Church.

She felt the hand of authority laid firmly on her, even though she was the wife of Theodore Kilmey. As she had felt it before during that dreadful time when Kitty, her own daughter, had wanted to marry a divorced man. That trouble came back to her in a rush, the struggle of wills, the child's wild hysteria, the miserable trip to Europe with Kitty sulking all the way, the novenas and the prayers, the arguments and the bribes. Ted had never realized how difficult that winter had been. He didn't realize that, even now after Kitty was married and had the two children, she was still a worry. She was not back to normal yet. The things she said about what she would do if she had more children! Kitty had always been the beauty of the family, but she was losing her looks. Something close to jealousy as well as admitted moral anger swept through Mrs.

Kilmey's heart, as she saw her guests congratulating Barbara Field. Any girl who would throw over her religion—if that was what she really was doing—for a man deserved no luck. She tried to smile in a noncommittal way that would fulfill the letter of hospitality while she withheld the spirit.

Carol Harrison was exclaiming, "But this is wonderful! I'm so glad for you both!"

She was not very glad, though she had a charming way of convincing people of her enthusiasm. Carol thought cynically that Barbara had put it over. Barbara Field could make men jump through hoops for her, however she did it. Leslie Field had been the same way before he went to the dogs. Or maybe that was why. The story around town of course was that there was a heavy affair between Craig and Barbara, but those things usually took care of themselves in time. Ran into boredom. But apparently not, with Barbara. The tiresomeness of Carol's own life with her inexpressive, egotistical husband seemed at the minute unbearable in contrast to the way Barbara obviously was loved. Carol had a spark of delight in wondering what Nina Longman would say to this, how Nina would like having a successor. Nina thought that Ken Craig never had got over her.

The Lymans were a little out of it and slower with congratulations, not knowing the other guests too well. But it seemed to Mrs. Lyman that the Field woman was very lucky. For Joe had told her that Kenneth Craig would be president of the railroad one day. Barbara Field didn't have a thing to bless herself with now. Just some little charity job, and yet she had managed to land a man. Mrs. Lyman had worked in an office before her own marriage and knew the limitation of opportunities for girls who earned their livings.

Jennifer Rye thought, I suppose she'll go everywhere now. Of course everyone thinks that they've been living together. Maybe he has to marry her. She's not too old to have a baby. I wasn't so much older—she must be past thirty—when I got in that fix. And I had to—right in the middle of the private car, lifting her glass of champagne in congratulation, Mrs. Rye remembered the terror, the lies, the abortion room, and how she had felt when she found she could never have another child even when she got ready to have one. And these years of pretending to David that it was his fault! Well, it was, in one way.

Blair Wyatt raised Barbara's hand to his lips and found it cold. Some thoughts that he always kept well covered, for fear some fool would laugh at him, came out from under their wraps.

"Forgive me, Barbara, that was the most stupid thing I ever said. There is no one I would rather see happy than you. This is fine."

The words were true and affectionate, but there were other things in Wyatt's mind. Curiosity and speculation. He thought, I never believed she would be willing to do it, being a good Roman. Perhaps she's getting an annulment. But there is no ground for one in her case. Barbara herself told me that once. She and Leslie were quite properly married in the parish house. Unless he has finally drunk himself to death—which would be the best thing that could happen. But that would have been known around town.

Besides, there is something about the way Craig came out with the announcement, and the way she looked when he spoke, that showed they were beating the gun somehow. They seemed under terrific strain. She didn't expect him to say that tonight. I forced it out of Craig with that remark. Craig lost his head. He could hardly have picked a worse place to tell the world than to assemble it in the Kilmey's private car and let fly. Surely he must know that they are tremendous Catholics. Almost bigots. It was a divorce situation that ruined Kitty Kilmey's life. She is a pathological case, she's a drunk, but they were willing to let that happen rather than go against their religion.

Blair Wyatt himself took church affiliation seriously. It was one of his sophistications. Divorce was not countenanced in the High Church of his own faith—he was an Episcopalian by birth and social feeling. He liked the rule against divorce. It had been a protection to him, more than once. But for a second now he wondered whether, if he had known that Barbara Field would ever consider herself free to remarry, he might have made the test. He had known her in the first false brilliance of her marriage, lost sight of her in the bad years, known her well again in the midst of her flirtations and confusions. I've always loved her a little, thought Blair Wyatt, watching the beauty of her smile at Craig.

Chapter Four

His own interview with Bishop Tarrant, to which Craig forced himself as soon as possible, left a taste of humiliation in his mind. He approached the meeting only as a concession to his love, in the hope of making Barbara's happiness complete. But it was an appointment which he disliked and, as he kept it, he felt again that it represented unwarranted interference in his personal affairs.

On a November afternoon he waited, rather ill-at-ease, in the Bishop's reception room. It was a square, high-ceilinged room, furnished with expensive dignity, indifferent to charm. Liver-colored shades were drawn down to half the length of the windows even on this dreary day, and lace curtains and stiff draperies stole more of the daylight. Two electric lamps on standards had been lit in compensation, and sent a cold, thin glimmer over polished and waxed surfaces. Craig took an upholstered chair with arms that curved slightly. It felt a little like a witness chair. He had an uncomfortable sense of being out of his element, and the huge gilt-framed portrait of the Pope at the end of the room was his only company for ten minutes.

Like most educated Protestants, Craig's attitude toward Catholicism was inevitably a mosaic. It was made up of tolerance, prejudice, jokes, bits of history and impressions left by seeing Catholic practices without sharing them. He had a certain admiration for the Catholic Church as an organization, because it had for so long a time been able to keep its grasp on its great possessions and millions of people, but along with that went some cynical suspicion as to the methods the Church had used to maintain its power. Craig was not naturally arrogant but it had been bred and schooled into him to feel superior to the ordinary Catholic, who could not, as was well known, think completely for himself, and whose entire life was conditioned with prerequisites of belief and conduct.

He had attended Catholic weddings, always held at an inconvenient time in the morning, and felt that the personal vows of the bride and groom were obscured by all the chanting and bowing at the altar. He had gone to the Catholic funerals of men whom he liked, and they had seemed unpitying, ritualistic services which gave neither place nor time to the proper praise for a dead man's achievements.

It was natural too that Craig had an uncoded business attitude toward Catholics. He knew that the top men in many corporations thought twice before putting a devout Catholic in a place where he could hire and fire many people, for he would be apt to fill every possible job with those who shared his religious faith. What he had told Barbara was quite true. He had not wanted to stay with the Central and Eastern Railroad because the Catholics in the organization had more chance of preferment under Ted Kilmey, if other things were equal, and sometimes even if they were not.

Craig had often been a buffer between his present chief, Mr. Miller, and priests who came to the offices of the railroad with requests for money. As a rule, they wanted to build new churches or lift the mortgages from old ones. At times they asked for donations to seminaries or parish schools or Catholic hospitals run by nuns. The priests were often raw young men, earnest and awkward. Occasionally they were older, shrewd churchmen whose approach was as easy and skilled as that of any politician.

The requests were rarely refused, though the amounts asked for were usually cut down. No corporation with important political dealings could afford to ignore or offend such a large segment of the voting public. A man often was elected to the legislature largely on the recommendation, passed around busily, that he was a good

Catholic. The railroad did not want enemies in the legislature or on the Interstate Commerce Commission.

That was all common knowledge. Like most businessmen, Craig believed that the influence of the Church was useful at times, as a deterrent or a handle. It worked diligently and with authority against the spread of communism. It was the only agency which could get close to certain groups of foreign-born people. That was not discounted by business executives. What worried them now and then was that the priests might build up a too-dangerous control. In a Protestant country that had to be guarded against, and it was.

Craig sat on several boards of directors which included a Catholic, as well as a Jew, and some representatives of labor organizations. The majority of the directors were always Protestant. To Craig that was fair and good sense. He was sure that he had no prejudice against any religion. He contributed to movements fostering religious co-operation and human brotherhood. But that did not mean that the last good story going the rounds about what was said by or to some priest in the confessional wouldn't get a laugh out of him.

He did not like to think of Barbara in a confessional. He could not possibly imagine himself in one. The position and relation would be ridiculous. He felt rather absurd at the moment, waiting in this stiff room to ask this Bishop if he could marry the woman he wanted without objection or criticism. But for her sake—

The Bishop came in with no pompousness, but cordially. He was sorry to have kept Mr. Craig waiting. He was a vigorous, graying, balding man in his human sixties. Nothing about him was pretentious. He wore calm easily, as if it were part of his robes. His blue eyes seemed to prefer gentleness and even be ready to welcome humor as he offered a few comments on the weather and the nation's business.

Craig did not waste time. He soon stated his errand. He was going to marry Mrs. Field, and she was disturbed because she believed the marriage would displease the authorities in her Church. Craig said he greatly hoped that wouldn't be so.

[43]

"If it were possible," said the Bishop as directly, "it would please me very much to have Barbara marry. I am sure her life presents many difficulties and includes many deprivations. Unfortunately, her husband is still alive. Or so she told me recently. I have no knowledge that the impediment has since been removed."

Craig went over it all again, Barbara's justification and her courage. Then he listened, frowning and now smoking, at the Bishop's hospitable insistence, to an explanation of the law of unity and indissolubility of marriage. It didn't sink into his mind deeply. It was only words and he countered them reasonably.

"Ordinarily," said Craig, when the Bishop paused, "I am sure that is a very wise position for a church to take and urge on its members. But there are always exceptions."

"There are occasional reasons for dispensations, but I believe not in Barbara's case."

Both men saw her imaginatively before they spoke again and it made them both resolute. The Bishop remembered the young woman, sitting here in this room, struggling with her faith and training against her human desires. His trained perception had felt a true devotion.

And Craig thought, I certainly must get her out of this, poor darling. This Bishop has a pretty hard shell. No wonder he beat her down. But there must be some way to get to him.

"Bishop Tarrant, I'm not a Catholic, but of course one hears from time to time that special arrangements are made by your Church."

"If certain impediments exist, yes."

Craig said, a little awkwardly and yet with determination, for after all he had come here to get right down to cases and not discuss theology, "Bishop Tarrant, if there is a question of money involved, some customary payment, or any contribution that is usually made in return for effort of this kind, I'd be glad to take it on. I'm not a rich man, but this means a great deal to me."

That was what he wished afterward that he had not said. The Bishop showed no anger, nor even surprise at the suggestion. He

[44]

almost smiled as slowly he shook his head, but it was not a smile of connivance. He closed the door on that idea.

"No money is involved, Mr. Craig."

"I did not mean to suggest—"

"I quite understand. There are stories of course that divorces, annulments—marital adjustments of one sort or another—are for sale. Mr. Craig, believe me when I tell you that invariably they are unsubstantiated by the facts. The administration of canon law in regard to marriage is possibly not completely free from error, if false evidence is brought to bear on a case and, in spite of great scrupulousness in judgment, should go undetected. But the latitude in dealing with exceptional cases to which you refer comes from the fact which I have mentioned already, that the Church recognizes a number of impediments which defeat the real purpose of marriage. I personally have inquired into the facts of Barbara's case, both previously when she came to me seeking the separation which the Church allows under cruel circumstances, and recently. Hers was a good marriage."

Craig answered, "I can't agree with any description that calls that marriage good, Bishop Tarrant."

"I am not speaking of its happiness. I mean that it was a valid marriage and therefore a sacrament."

Craig remembered that Barbara had been worked up about that same thing.

He said stiffly, "There are a great many valid mariages, Bishop Tarrant, which are not performed by a Catholic priest."

"You misunderstand me, I am afraid. It is not the priest who makes a marriage valid. From the Catholic standpoint every proper marriage between two baptized persons is a sacrament, whether these are Catholics or non-Catholics. The marriage of two Protestants before their minister is just as truly a sacrament as the marriage of two Catholics before their priest. It is true, by the law of the Catholic Church a priest must be present at the marriage of a Catholic. But the priest is present, not to administer the sacrament, but to act as the Church's official witness and to impart a blessing."

"I don't get that. Somebody has to marry them. Who does the job?"

"The couple themselves administer the sacrament, each conferring it on the other in the act of giving and receiving consent."

"Then it certainly is in the power of the couple to decide if they want to dissolve the contract."

"On the contrary. The contract, elevated to the dignity of a sacrament, is indissoluble, once the marriage has been consummated."

They run around in circles, thought Craig. He tried to be courteous as he stated, "The courts of this country hardly uphold that fact, Bishop Tarrant."

"Nor have they affected the sacramental nature of Christian marriage."

He spoke with finality. His manner had hardened. He's going to hold that offer of money against me, thought Craig. I shouldn't have put that up to him. It's probably not done outright, in any straightforward way. But it's done. Everybody knows that.

"I am not well informed on the fine points of Catholic doctrine," he said, "but I am puzzled on one point if I may cite my own experience. As you may know, I have been married. My wife divorced me. Then she remarried and she married a man who is a Catholic. In fact, she got what is called an annulment to our marriage. And there was no trouble in her getting it because I had never been baptized."

"That would invalidate your marriage. I remember hearing about the case and I believe there was also the argument of the Pauline privilege."

"I'm afraid I don't understand."

"It is possible to break the bond of a natural marriage in favor of a sacramental marriage. Saint Paul—"

But Craig did not listen to the quotation of authority. He was thinking, it is all hokum. Nina, the little bitch, did what she pleased and the priests blessed her. But they won't turn a wheel for Barbara and me.

[46]

He spoke coldly when it was his turn. "It is very difficult for a person who is not a Catholic to understand that technicality. We are more apt to consider personal and moral values."

"The Church never forgets them, Mr. Craig."

"I don't want to take up your time uselessly, Bishop. However, if you can spare me a minute or two more—"

"All the time you want, Mr. Craig."

"I'd like to ask in what way Barbara would be penalized if she and I are married by a justice of the peace. What will she be let in for? Will that mean she can never go to any Catholic Church again?"

The Bishop smiled with patience. "Anyone can go to any Catholic Church, Mr. Craig. She can—you can—the Church door is always open."

"I'm glad to hear that. But would anyone make it hard for her if she did go?"

"Hard in what way?"

"That's what I don't know exactly. I mean she wouldn't be talked about—by some priest—or made conspicuous?"

"You're thinking of public excommunication?"

"That sort of thing, yes. I don't know the procedure."

The Bishop said, "That would not happen. We have never done that in this diocese nor is it done—except rarely—in America. No, Mr. Craig, the penalty is more serious. It would consist in Barbara's inability to receive the sacraments. She could not be absolved in confession unless she renounced any civil marriage to you. Therefore, she could not receive the Holy Eucharist, a Catholic's greatest privilege. She would, in the tragic misadventure that you suggest, put herself outside the fold of practicing Catholics. She would be one of those unfortunates who have fallen away from their faith. The penalty would be in her own serious deprivations."

Craig did not look impressed.

"I deeply hope and urge," the Bishop went on, "that you will never subject Barbara, nor aid her to subject herself, to that kind of life."

[47]

"Barbara is going to marry me, Bishop Tarrant. I myself naturally abide by the laws of the state and Barbara is legally quite free. I have her promise."

"Release her from that promise, Mr. Craig."

"That's impossible. I care for her too deeply. I want to make her happy."

"You cannot make her happy," the Bishop stated gravely. "Not under such circumstances."

Craig had regretted mentioning money and having put himself in the awkward position of having tried to offer what might seem like a bribe. But this last assumption of the Bishop stung him even more, angered him because he could not laugh at its absurdity here and now. It would have been a satisfaction to tell the Bishop to his face how preposterous his statement was. Happy—only he and Barbara had come to realize slowly and certainly what joy they could make for each other. They were only within reach and sight of happiness when they were together. Sex was only part of it, and, as he had found that out, Craig had been deeply reassured, for he had seen the shabby side of his own passions. But with Barbara he had found the new delight of meeting subtler moods and thoughts. This denatured prelate, thought Craig, sitting here in his robes, has no idea of what happiness is or can be for a man or woman in love. They must beat that all out of the priests while they're young.

No, there was nothing to worry about on that score. Craig knew that he could make Barbara happy, that she had been happy with him. Given a chance, he could keep her that way, do it all better. For the way things were now, with the two of them living under different roofs, torn by their feelings, gossiped about, worrying, was bound to be unsatisfactory for people who had decent self-respect.

He did not want to go into some things with the Bishop. But he had to make one point clear. He tried to do it respectfully.

"Perhaps, sir," said Craig, "living as you do in a world a little removed from the rest of us, you can hardly realize that Barbara is in a very difficult position. As things are, I'm not able to take care of her, to give her the protection she should have."

[48]

"I appreciate that. It's very unfortunate," answered the Bishop. "That is why I strongly advised Barbara to do the only thing that will bring her ultimate peace. And you, as well, Mr. Craig. Your best course is to stop seeing each other and sever—"

Craig interrupted, "I shall not agree to that under any conditions. I am going to marry Mrs. Field."

"I shall pray that she will not take such a terrible chance."

At that moment the words did not seem funny to Craig. He stood up and ended the interview with a few, stiff, courteous words. But when he was out of the house and getting away from it in his car, the words came back to him as almost comic. Her marriage to him was a terrible chance. He must tell Barbara that one! No, he had better not.

So he couldn't make her happy. The doubt was like an insult. The Bishop was a monk. He didn't know what it was all about. His idea was that Barbara ought to be happy on her knees in some church, bowing down before some priest. They deliberately try to keep people, especially women, in a bondage of fear and superstition, Craig said to himself. It's all part of their system.

And the penalty for marrying him would be that Barbara couldn't get a priest to absolve her from her sins. From what sins? It was nonsense. It was morbid. The breakdown of this whole situation showed that the Bishop had no real control. He had almost said as much just now. He couldn't stop Barbara from going to church when and where she wanted to. As for that confession business, thought Craig, I'd be just as well pleased if she didn't go in for that after we're married. Who knows what those priests ask a woman, what they try to find out, how far they go to satisfy their own curiosity?

That other threat that the Bishop made so much of, saying that she would not be able to have any Communion, was only more of the mystery and taboo. It was a survival of a medieval rite, from what Craig had heard. The Jews celebrated it one way. The Catholics had another. Some Protestant churches gave out Communion too. They even advertised that they did. All these religions were looking for customers to keep themselves going. Craig recalled seeing a sign on the grounds of an Episcopal Church only recently, telling the hours when people could get Communion. Perhaps Barbara could get it in one of them just as well, if she wanted it very much.

Craig did not mention to Barbara the two things that left the bad taste in his mind after that interview, his own rebuffed offer of money and the Bishop's preposterous doubt that he could make Barbara happy as his wife. He was in a disturbed state of mind when he left the Diocesan Residence and calmed himself down at his office among practical, well-understood, sensible duties. But he could not reach Barbara for several hours by telephone and the little separation nagged at him like a threat. He did things that he wanted to do for her and set others in motion. He bought her a pair of pale-rose camellias. He stopped on his way uptown to look at new models of cars. He drove out past Mr. Miller's house in the early evening and looked at the neighborhood. And finally he saw Barbara again, in the same room with the long yellow curtains and she was more precious than ever. She looked like a schoolgirl to-night, wearing a white blouse and swinging gray flannel skirt. She looked as if she would be wholesome for a man, that with all the rest. The sight of her did him good, her touch dissipated the Bishop's challenge.

"I haven't had time to make myself glamorous," she told him. "I didn't get here until seven and you are right on my heels."

"You'd better get used to that."

The camellias delighted her. She put one deep in the curve of her blouse and he knew that the stem rested between her breasts.

"Where were you? I couldn't find you."

"There was a long, late meeting. With representatives from agencies all over the city to plan what we would do when we get displaced persons over here. A man who's just come back from seeing the situation in Germany and Austria talked to us, sort of briefed us. It was grim listening. I wish I could have gone over there myself. You know I did apply—more than a year ago—as soon as the European war was over. But nothing came of it. They took one girl from our organization but I suppose they had hundreds of applications like mine. The girl who went had more experience than I have."

"I'm very glad you didn't get to go. Europe is still dangerous, with diseases and crazy people everywhere. It's not safe. And what would I have done if you had gone?"

"Done better, maybe. Avoided a lot of trouble."

He felt a little distance between them and deliberately brought her back to him with the statement, "I had a talk with the Bishop today. Your friend Bishop Tarrant."

"You didn't tell me—"

"I didn't want you to start worrying. But I saw him."

Barbara grew utterly still, waiting to hear the answer.

"And I'm glad I did," Craig went on with deliberate ease. "For it absolutely convinced me on one point. The thing for us to do is to get married. Then everything else will fall into line."

"The Bishop didn't say that, did he?"

"Not in so many words. But after talking to him, I realize that he has to hew to the line pretty closely. What he did make clear to me was that there wouldn't be any open row. He won't take any action, or get rough about it."

"No—I suppose not. Of course not. He wouldn't have to."

"He told me that there was no reason why you couldn't attend your church after we are married."

"Anybody can."

"That's what he said."

"Plenty of people go to church who aren't in good standing. So he said no—to you too. I thought he would, Ken. I'm sorry you had to go through that on my account. I shouldn't have let you do it. I knew there was no chance. It must have been difficult."

"No," protested Craig, "it was my job. I found him quite an interesting fellow. Not very realistic. But what can you expect, living the way those priests do, half in the world and half out of it?

[51]

What impressed me was a kind of unworldliness about him. He doesn't realize how normal people feel. How could he?"

"It doesn't matter to him how people feel. He's not thinking of that. Suffering doesn't matter."

"I don't get the idea," puzzled Craig. "That's a queer twist."

"The idea is that suffering is good for you. You offer it up. It is better for you to sacrifice what you love and want."

"God, it's downright morbid!" exclaimed Craig, breaking through his own calm. "I feel more strongly about that now than I did before I saw your Bishop."

"But what did you say, yourself?" she asked. "How did you leave it?"

"I told him that we are going to be married," answered Craig, "and as soon as possible. Without waiting for anyone to die. I said that we were in a perfectly sound legal position, that it was better for you, essential for me—that we are going to be married."

She lifted her eyes and for once he could not read them.

"That was right, wasn't it?" he asked her soberly. Almost sternly. It was agreement he wanted now, not any emotional submission. "I told him the truth, didn't I?"

"Yes. You did."

The words of love broke through the tensity. "Oh—my darling—" "I can't let you go—" "You'll never regret—"

But along with his triumph Craig had a sense of pity because she was so tightly and implacably claimed by forces he had failed to reconcile or subdue. He wished that he could give her whatever she might fear she was losing, whatever the Bishop might hold out on her. Not that she would need it for long. The care he would give her and the happiness they would have together now would fill her whole life.

Craig promised, to balance that odd, irrelevant sense of pity, "Everything's going to be all right. We're doing what we must do, what we should have done before now. We've been fighting windmills, running around in circles with theories, and it's time to go ahead and live our own lives."

"They can be such good lives," said Barbara. "I can't believe that God wants them to be spoiled."

"Spoiled," he repeated, "would be it. You couldn't do it, dear. You couldn't go along with these priests and their ideas of frustration."

"No. Because I don't believe that God wants me to be a tramp or to have you angry and miserable and full of hate, going on to some other woman."

"I couldn't do that."

"After a while."

"And how about you?"

"I hate to think—it's all so inconsistent. They say I have a husband. Where? I don't know where Leslie is or have the slightest feeling that he is married to me or I to him. Even the Bishop admits that I can't live with him. But a husband is someone you should live with. We were taught from the time we were in parochial school that a girl should follow her vocation. She can be a nun, or stay unmarried, or marry. I know my own vocation perfectly well. It's marriage. I couldn't be a nun. And I'm not good at being unmarried. I don't do it well as some women do. I don't like to walk alone."

"You never will again as long as I live. Barbara, I've tried to hold myself in and not say too much about this business because it's been tied in with your church and I respect anybody's religion. But these so-called laws that they've been trying to put over on us are really pretty devious. They're clever. Designed for a purpose, and from a certain political angle perhaps it's a good purpose. But they tie sensitive girls like you up in knots, and try to make you believe that it's a mystical business, when it's obvious that men set up these laws at various periods in history for their own reasons. They were trying to tighten up controls, make nations homogeneous, breed them to think alike. They hold people in fear and ignorance. For my money, the Catholic Church would be doing a better job if it brought its marriage rules up to date and made them conform to the laws of civilized states. I nearly said that to Bishop Tarrant today. For him to sit there and say that your marriage to Field was good—"

"I know what he meant."

"Well, I didn't, not even after he had talked all the way around the bush. It was an unfortunate affair and it's long past. You're free and those people should admit it."

"I have no living husband, no matter what they say."

"You're going to have one soon."

She said, "We've both tried. We've waited and done our best. We've shown respect—"

"I'll say so. Plenty. More than was warranted by the reception it got."

"Don't be bitter, Ken. Not ever."

"Oh, I'm not. I'm just angry at the attempt to crucify you."

"They won't. I don't think we can do any more. Unless we gave each other up. And I'm sure now that would be wrong."

"It would be wicked."

"Anyway, they can only punish me," she said softly. "They won't shut anyone out except me."

"They won't even do that. Don't you worry. It will all blow over. Once we're in command of this situation instead of running around to ask favors, it will be a different story. I know how these things work."

"Can you find someone to marry us?"

He laughed aloud. "Why, they'll be bidding for the chance. What I have in mind is to ask one of the older judges. You leave it to me. All you need do is to pick the day."

"I'll talk to Mrs. Cunningham, the boss of our office, and see when they can let me go."

"Tell her it has to be soon. We must fix the date before I go to see the judge. And now I've something else to tell you. The day after the dinner on the Kilmey train Mr. Miller called me in. He said first of all that he was very glad that I was going to be married. I suppose—"

"I suppose he's heard plenty of gossip."

"I don't know about that. But anyway he was all for us. Then he asked me if I'd be interested in buying his house."

"The one out on Prospect? Is he selling it?"

"He'd like to."

"But that's too big for . . . us."

"Don't say it so hesitantly. It is us, from here in. No, it's not so big as it seems."

"You've looked at it?"

"I've been through it. Then I drove around again this afternoon to take another look. I think I could swing it all right, especially since Mr. Miller wants to be rid of it and would give me a price. The place is a burden to him since his wife died. His family is scattered all over the country and none of them wants the house. But he has a certain sentiment about it—he built it—and would like to see it in the right hands."

"To belong to his successor? Is this part of grooming you for his job?"

"He didn't say anything like that," answered Craig, with a grin that didn't rule out the possibility. "And of course, if you don't like the idea of that house, it's no good."

"Why shouldn't I like it?"

Why not? Why did the suggestion make her feel as if she were being torn out of her setting? She had no setting. Why feel any pang about leaving this apartment with its makeshifts and basic loneliness? Kenneth had never fitted into this room—nor into her life so far. He had sought her out in this place almost against his own will.

It was the realization of how complete the change would be that jolted her imagination. The Miller house was on Prospect Road, a boulevard laid out among the western hills in the past twenty years, as the city changed its habits. That had never been her part of the city. Her grandfather, when he was rich, had owned one of the big turreted houses on Cathedral Avenue. After his death the house had been sold and now it was a dingy rooming house. But her mother and father had chosen to live in the same district. They had built a house within walking distance of the Cathedral, and Barbara's mother never would move, even when the district ran down. For Mrs. Braniff went to Mass every day and was a devout member of the League of the Sacred Heart which was pledged to take charge of the Adoration of the Blessed Sacrament when it was exposed on the First Friday of every month. I used to make the First Fridays, thought Barbara. But, about a year ago—

Kenneth said, "Of course we can look around a little before we decide. Only I don't want to live in one of those apartment buildings on the Ridge, if you don't mind."

Certainly not in one of those. That was where he had lived with Nina. He would feel about that as she did about the Green Park district, remember it with misery, remember it as little as possible. She and Leslie had once lived in a house in Green Park, at the beginning of the seven years which she had spent trying to make a marriage work. It was rather a pretentious house, and Leslie had paid a little money toward purchasing it but never any more. Finally the mortgages and interest payments drove them out. That house had a recreation room and a bar. For a second Barbara saw that bar clearly. She had not visualized it for years but there it was in her mind, like a picture against the wall, until a thought turned it over. There were the red leather stools, the shine of chromium, the pewter bowls of popcorn, the rows of bottles, and the endless chase of the horses around the foolish wallpaper. Once it must have seemed a good idea; at least she had gone along with it. Drink at home, that's the best thing to do—home, what a word for what a place and for what went on—

"The chief thing to consider about the Miller house—"

"Is whether it would be our house," she cut in, "with no dregs of other people in it."

"You bet not," he said, thinking the same thing, understanding perfectly.

It was like that now. Neither of them was holding anything back, or thinking separately. The invisible guards were down. Until tonight, even in happiness and love, the fears had been there—

[56]

I wonder if this is hurting her—if this is doing him harm—I should go away—I should send him—can I be sure he will care as much tomorrow—this is no way to live. None of that tonight, which in routine was like so many other evenings, with its brief city drive, its choice of food and lift of drink, and yet to each of them a new and exalted experience.

"Where shall we go on our wedding trip?"

"Where do you not want to go?" meaning Nina, of course.

"Florida."

"Nor to Bermuda," she added, trying not to remember anything about that.

"Would you like to spend your first Christmas in New York?"

"Christmas? As soon as that?"

"The sooner the better. For every reason."

"Yes—every reason."

"What are you thinking? Your eyes look so deep."

"That I never really believed until this afternoon that we could be married unless the Bishop gave us a dispensation. But when you asked me this afternoon if you had said the right thing to him, when you told him that we were going to be married, whether or not, I knew it was what I wanted you to say and should have said myself to Bishop Tarrant. And saying it—or being glad that you had, which is the same thing really—clarified me. I'm willing. The intention is there. If it is a sin, I've already committed it. Because in my mind I accepted marriage with you this afternoon and defied the Church. But only in that one respect, Ken. Don't think I've lost my faith. I believe everything else that the Church teaches and what it stands for."

"Of course you do."

"The strange thing is that I don't feel wicked. I feel good and more honest than I've been in a long while."

"You've been terrorized, poor girl. And suddenly you've waked up and found out that nobody can do a thing to you."

"It's not what anybody can do to me. It's what I can't do. But I

[57]

feel strong enough to face that too. As long as I must. For I'm sure this is right."

"Of course we're right, darling. There would be no life worth living for either of us without the other."

Chapter Five

It was no longer a matter of speculation. The news was like a current of electricity, making contacts wherever there was any connection and interest in Barbara Field or Kenneth Craig. In the offices of the Social Agencies everyone knew about Barbara's plans because the director was looking for a new girl to put in her place.

When she came back from lunch early one day, Barbara overheard Sally Frick delivering an opinion to someone. Pausing in the vestibule to shake the first wet snow of the season off her coat, it was impossible for Barbara not to hear what Sally was saying. She stood still for a minute and listened. It did not seem like eavesdropping but as if she were looking at a picture of herself which had suddenly been dropped in her way.

"But she hasn't seen that man Field in years!" exclaimed Sally on a note of protest. "He's absolutely nothing in her life. She doesn't get a cent from him, for it wasn't that kind of divorce. She just had to get rid of him. He was a horrid character, from what I've been told by people who knew him. Someone told me that once at the Town Club he was so crazy drunk that he hit her right in the face—"

That's right, he did, thought Barbara. I'd completely forgotten that dreadful night. How funny, to think that Sally heard about it before she knew me and has been carrying it in her mind ever since, probably wondering how I looked with a black eye. That was just before we put Leslie in the sanitarium. All that fuss to get him in there and it didn't do any good.

"—and Kenneth Craig is a wonderful man. He's really going

places. Barbara's just terribly lucky, that's what I think. And I'm glad of it."

"All I say is that I don't see how a person who pretends to be a Catholic can consider such a thing."

Barbara recognized that voice too. It was Anna Kelly, the field worker for the Catholic orphanage, who was talking her over with Sally.

"Barbara is an awfully good Catholic," declared Sally. "I know that for a fact. She even goes to church on those special days when they celebrate the Virgin Mary or something. And she carries a rosary right in her purse."

"That doesn't make any difference. She can't marry Mr. Craig or anyone else while her husband is alive. And he is, isn't he? I understand the Bishop himself found out about that. She can't marry again and stay in the Church."

"Then I know what I'd do in her place. Why, she'd be just a fool not to! A girl doesn't get too many chances at Barbara's age, even with her looks. My goodness, what do they expect her to do? Stay here and bury herself in case histories for a hundred and sixty a month for the rest of her life? Work with a lot of human wrecks when she can marry a man like Kenneth Craig and have a home of her own? And he's crazy about her and she is about him. I've seen him when he's called for her—"

Barbara called, "I'm back, Sally. You can go for your lunch any time. It's beastly stormy out."

There was a scurry of unintelligible words in lower voices. Barbara came into the office as cheerfully as if she had heard nothing. Anna Kelly was immensely busy making entries on a filing card. But when she looked up at Barbara, her eyes were sharp and curious. They were wondering if Barbara dared marry. The eyes knew what was involved, what it meant. Barbara had seen thousands of such faces listening to priests, as marriage laws were explained from the pulpit and those who broke them denounced as adulterers.

The cheap fur collar of Anna Kelly's coat looked bedraggled and so did the stray wisps of brownish hair that fell against it. But there was a pride that was almost defiant in her manner as she spoke to Barbara. It implied that not only was she as good as Barbara but might be better.

They went over a few routine matters and then opportunity came to Miss Kelly.

"I talked to Sister Cecilia about the Everett boy, Mrs. Field."

"About that nice couple who want to adopt him? Is it all right?"

"No, Sister doesn't approve of it at all."

"But why not? We've had several reports on the home and the people. The Child Placing Agency for the state looked them up thoroughly and okayed the family."

"It's a broken home. I suppose you didn't know that."

"There was nothing of that sort in the report I saw."

"The wife was divorced before she married this man. In Chicago. Sister Cecilia found that out when she talked to her. I think someone wrote to Sister and told her."

Barbara frowned. "It seemed such a break for that boy. Apparently they didn't mind his being delicate and were willing to do everything for him."

"Sister Cecilia says that his religion is more important than luxury."

The bright and curious eyes scanned Barbara for her reaction to that statement.

"Well," said Barbara with no change of tone, "she's in authority. She has the last word."

"She's almost a saint," commented Miss Kelly but Barbara did not answer.

"Has any organization offered to give the orphans a Christmas treat?" asked Miss Kelly. "Sister was wondering about that."

"Not so far. That should be looked into."

"Will you do that for us?"

"I'm sorry but I shan't be able to see it through. I'm leaving the Agency."

"You are? I heard a rumor to that effect but I could hardly believe it! Leaving for some other kind of work?"

[60]

Barbara knew that the surprise was false. Don't dodge, she told herself. Let her have it straight.

She met the other woman's searching eyes. "Yes," she said, "I'm going to be married."

Anna Kelly's face stiffened. Her mouth seemed to twist slightly as if it screwed up unspoken words. There was more than disapproval in her look, something different from moral shock. For a second Barbara saw actual anger, directed at herself, as if she had offered personal insult to Miss Kelly. She thought, it's frustration as well as religion that makes her angry. Maybe she gave up something once, when she had it to give. Some man. Or perhaps she has never had a chance to marry anyone and thinks I'm having more than my share. It's not piety in that face of hers. She really hopes that I'll go to hell. She doesn't want me to have Kenneth.

"How interesting," was all that Anna Kelly said. She committed no venial sin for the sake of being civil or conventional. She did not wish Barbara happiness.

Nor did Nina Longman. The news came to her from Carol Harrison, who was particularly anxious to see how the woman who had once been Craig's wife would react to his plans for a second marriage. It was great luck for Carol to meet Nina at the Town Club one noon, before anyone else had told her about it.

When she came to the city, where she no longer lived since she had married Bill Longman, Nina usually lunched at the Town Club where she was sure of seeing people she knew and of being talked about again. Chic and emaciated, she would appear once or twice a month in one of the cocktail rooms or the corner of the ladies' dining room. She might be on her way to New York or just coming back from Florida, for the Longman money made travel with the seasons very easy, and getting away from the Longman family made it very desirable. Nina said frankly that she could take just so many Longmans and then she broke out in a rash. She had a dentist in St. Anthony too. And a furrier. There were numerous reasons for coming and there were plenty of men who liked to lunch with her and buy her drinks.

She was a showpiece of a woman. There was always something about her that heightened her effect more than that of most women, a conversation, piece of jewelry, a mad hat, or no hat and a madder hairdo. She was not beautiful but almost the better off for that. Beauty might have interfered with her bold strokes of chic and made her less exciting.

She knew how to amuse and stimulate men. Blair Wyatt said she was one of the best human cocktails he knew anything about. She was wise and pornographic, always with a few little stories rotting in her mind. Yet there was something else. She could make her worldliness, her love of excitement and her doll-like looks pathetic. She had aroused so deep a sense of protection in the slow-thinking Bill Longman that he had waded heavily and uncomfortably through the gulf between them and carried her off. He was determined to give her what she wanted. And the story was that she still could make him believe that he was happy. Kenneth Craig, after the first few months of being married to her, had never been fooled about happiness.

That had been a hopeless marriage. There had never been enough money. Nina's restlessness at the lack of it, her avid need of spending, astonished Craig. It was hard for him to believe at first that she liked things better than people. But she did. She wanted clothes more than children and she made no bones about the choice. She had a passion for Craig himself, but she wanted passion to be carried out decoratively and amusingly. He often found that difficult, after a few months. He had to make his living, for the depression had disposed of any surplus capital in his father's family. Also before long he had to go to war and he chose the hard, undramatized way of the infantry. Nina did not even like his uniform. It was while he was overseas, thinking rather solemnly and often that he would do a better job on his marriage if he got back home, that Nina discovered the unattached Bill Longman and all that money could buy.

She was wearing some of the best of it when Carol Harrison met her with exclamations.

"You look too wonderful! It's black mink, isn't it? And soft as velvet. You would have that, before anyone else."

Nina said, "I think it's rather nasty stuff," and dropped the enveloping stole. There was a ruby bracelet on the edge of her black glove and it was the exact color of her mouth. Her face was pale and a little freckled and very vital.

"Will you lunch with us, Nina?"

"I wish I could. But I've got Peter Collins coming. We're re-decorating and he's helping me with colors. He did some marvelous things in Palm Beach."

"So I heard."

"Speak no evil," said Nina. "What's new around here? Pete never knows. Who's getting married or divorced or living a lie?"

"Ken is the big news, of course."

"Ken? My old Ken?"

"Didn't you know? He's going to be married again."

"You don't say. I thought he was just being talked about with the Field woman."

"It's past the talking point."

"I don't believe it," said Nina. "Why should they? Anyway they can't."

"Ken says they are. And he should know."

"What does she say about it?"

"She was right there when he told everybody on the Kilmey private car and she certainly didn't deny it. Just beamed. And I think everybody is delighted to see Ken get settled down. His life's been a bit gruesome. Not that I'm blaming you, Nina. If people don't get on, it's their own business."

Nina snapped open her cigarette lighter. In the tiny blaze she held to her face, the skin seemed stretched over her cheekbones.

"But I thought Leslie Field was still alive. In fact I heard that someone saw him not long ago in New York. Looking, I heard, like the wrath of God. Like an utter bum."

[63]

"Well, she's divorced. She's through with him."

"But she's a Catholic. The Braniffs were simply pillars."

"Maybe they fixed it up for her."

"It's not possible," said Nina Longman shortly. "If she couldn't get an annulment in the first place, she can't now."

"There must be some other way—"

"Not unless they are going to live as brother and sister. And my reminiscences of Ken make me believe—" she laughed, interrupting herself. "I suppose she would be ready to do anything to get him. My Ken is becoming something of a catch, I understand."

"He'll be president of the line, they all say."

"That's too wonderful! I guess I was all that stood in his way. It will be too bad if the poor guy makes a second mistake in his women because he's lonesome."

"He's utterly crazy about her. It's not lonesomeness."

"Why doesn't he pick a young girl while he's at it?"

"Oh, Barbara Field can't be more than thirty. No, not possibly," answered Carol. "I'm sure of that. Don't you remember that she was in that dancing class of parochial school children that Miss Powell used to have before our class? They were all at least a couple of years younger than our crowd."

It was the vulnerable point and Carol knew it. Nina did not care about being beautiful. But she wanted to be young.

She did not look young now. She looked as if she had been made to order after a strange, suggestive design, that wanted to show outline without body and expression without emotion.

"I wonder how she can get away with it," said Nina. "I mean with the Church. It's a tough proposition. I know, because I'm married to a Catholic."

"You managed it after your divorce."

"It was all right in my case. Ken had never been baptized so my first marriage wasn't really valid."

"You mean you were never married to Ken?" asked Carol, her tone mocking the words.

Nina smiled, not innocently nor prettily. The smile matched her thoughts which also were neither. Sometimes now she thought she had been a fool. Perhaps all Kenneth had needed was better handling. He was showing now what he could do if he wanted to. If she had it to do over again? Sometimes she thought she couldn't stand it any longer, the tough, leathery kindness of Bill Longman, no matter what she said, the holy acceptance of her by his stupid family because she was Bill's wife. Sometimes Nina even had thought that, if she and Ken could get together again—it was different now that he was making money, and she herself had all that jewelry—but here was that Irish girl walking off with him. And she herself wasn't in a position to do much about it or say anything. Carol Harrison would of course repeat anything she did say. That was certain.

"Not according to the law of the Church," she said over her thoughts. "Naturally that didn't matter to Ken. Not to either of us at the time. But I had been baptized a Catholic and of course the way we lived and his lack of belief was a hindrance to the practice of my faith."

She can say it with a straight face, thought Carol. Her faith didn't get in her way until Bill Longman came along.

"Dear Ken," said Nina. "Between you and me I never have been able to get over him. Or stop being terribly fond of him. But there were some things about a woman that he didn't understand."

Let Carol repeat that. It couldn't do any harm in some places and she could always deny that she said it.

"Well," said Carol cynically, "you won't have to worry about his lack of understanding women any more."

"I wonder," doubted Nina. "From what you say he still doesn't know when he's had enough."

The story about Kenneth and Barbara went back to Chicago along with the Kilmeys. The business and social pattern of the great cities of the Middle West interlocked and so it was an interesting piece of gossip. Mrs. Kilmey told it one afternoon in her own house. A number of friends including her married daughters had come in for what Mrs. Kilmey called tea and was almost invariably cocktails, and someone asked whom she had seen in St. Anthony. Mrs. Kilmey related what had happened at dinner on the car, with several declarations that she had never been in a more difficult situation. Later on, she wished that she had never mentioned the incident, not at least in Kitty's hearing. She had not thought of how it might affect Kitty.

Kitty, now Mrs. Aloysius Pond, had been silent but attentive. She stayed on after the others left and spoke of it again as she had another drink.

"That must have been something. I wish I'd been there when Ken Craig came out with that."

"It was dreadful! It was very embarrassing for me. I was very sorry I had let him bring the girl. But that was your father's doing. Of course it may come to nothing. But if they actually do get married under the circumstances—"

"I'll bet they will," said Kitty, "and I admire them for it."

"You don't mean that, Kitty," answered her mother. "You know better."

She said it gently, though she had to protest. But she did not want to stir up Kitty's mood. Mrs. Kilmey worried nowadays when Kitty looked as flushed as she did now. It meant, though Mrs. Kilmey didn't like to admit it, that Kitty had probably begun drinking at noon. By this time of day she did not look like herself and was apt to be argumentative. She was putting on weight too and nobody wanted to speak of that to her, for Kitty had always been happily vain. But her dainty, small-boned beauty could quickly disappear in this extra flesh.

"Kitty, dear, do you think you need any more?" asked her mother as Kitty went back to the tray that held the shakers.

"I can't make up my mind," said Kitty, pouring one out. "I've never been good at important decisions."

"You'll begin to lose your looks, if you drink too much," advised her mother, driven to frankness.

"My looks aren't very important any more. Who cares about them?"

[66]

"Aloysius cares."

"If he cares about my looks he'd better not keep after me about having more children. He thinks a woman isn't safe unless she's pregnant."

"Kitty, I hate to hear you talk like that!"

"All right, Mother, I won't. I'm sorry. Talking about the facts of life is out. You're too young, anyway. And too good."

"Is Aloysius calling for you?"

"I suppose he is. He has the car. He even makes a fuss about my driving now."

"He worries about you. He adores you. Don't take any more to drink, Kitty."

"But Mother, you forget I'm a married woman. He's got to keep me. I've got to keep him. And the deal was that everything was going to be all right and I could do anything I liked when I married Aloysius. You all told me how happy I would be. And so I try to do my best." She lifted her glass and stared moodily through it at the fire.

"You have everything to make a woman happy, Kitty."

"Of course I have. And I'm all right. Please don't worry about me all the time. I get enough of that." —She came out of a moment's heavy silence to say, "I can't get over Kenneth Craig and that girl. I just wonder what went on between those two beforehand. And what she said to him afterward. But still, she backed him up, you say. She came across in spite of what you or anyone else thought. People do. All the time. If they have what it takes."

"Kitty, you must know—"

"I know. She'll go to hell. Well, you just have to choose when and where to do that."

She spoke softly, a little thickly. She did not turn her head when the pallid, anxious man who was her husband came into the room seeking her.

Kenneth Craig's sister-in-law, who lived just outside of Philadelphia in an elaborately simple way, read the letter which her husband brought home on a November evening. Her neat eyebrows lifted in surprise and her lips made a little sigh like disappointment. But before she finished reading the pages, scrawled blackly and awkwardly as if every word was a signature, Mrs. Malcolm Craig had decided that it need not make much difference to their plans and to the general setup of the family. She wouldn't have to go to the wedding. Malcolm could fly out, if he thought he had to, and since Ken was his only brother, he probably should.

She thought too, it means another wedding present right before Christmas, as she said, "Well, there's nothing we can do about it. Ken's just telling us."

"It's all right," said Malcolm. "It's a good thing. I wish in a way it wasn't a widow. Mrs. Field, you notice, he writes. To me there's always something about marrying a widow—"

"Do you know anything about her?"

"No. But I had an idea last time I saw Ken that he might be interested in some quarter."

"Did he tell you so? You should have let me know."

"Not a word. It was more because of the way he looked. Just as he used to. There was a time, after that divorce of his, when I was a little disturbed about Ken."

"How old is he now? I forget."

"Let's see—Ken is five years younger that I am—I was born in 1902—Ken's close to thirty-nine."

"Of course it's time he married again, if he's going to. He's doing well, you always say."

"From what I hear, Ken is coming right along. It was tough sledding at the start—that's always true of the transportation business—but now I understand that he's pretty close to being executive vice-president of that line."

"I hope this woman has some money. It always helps."

She herself had a personal fortune and it had helped very much, for furs, and private schools, and extra servants' wages and charities. She went on thoughtfully, almost resentfully, "That was why when he was here in March for those few days, I featured

Mary Crandall. She would be such a marvelous wife—and all that money! In her own name. I couldn't make out whether Ken was even interested. I thought he might still be in love with his first wife."

"Oh, no, she gave him a bad deal. I'm sure of that though he never would talk about it. Just said they were splitting up."

"She did very well for herself afterward. I saw a picture of her in *Town and Country* not long ago. Look, Malcolm, Ken won't expect us to be there for this wedding, will he?"

"I've been wondering what we should do. After all, he and I are the only two left in the family. He doesn't put it up to us but he gives us the date."

Helen Craig read that again. "*December seventh. A civil ceremony because Barbara is a Roman Catholic*—that's funny. I thought they always wanted priests."

"Maybe Ken wouldn't stand for that."

"I thought they had to. I wish she weren't a Catholic."

"You ought to be more broad-minded. What difference does it make?"

"I don't know. But they always seem to me to be a little secretive. You know, not quite American, with all those schools for their own people. There's something funny about it. It sets them apart."

"That's what the Pope wants."

"I suppose," she said in vague agreement. "Well, anyway, the seventh of December is impossible. The children will be coming home for their holidays by the sixteenth and there is so much to do before they get here. I'm chairman of the committee for the holiday dance at Foxhole and I've a fitting in New York—you could go without me, if you have to, couldn't you?"

"Well, I could—"

"You can fly out. And you can explain why I couldn't get away—because of the children coming home for Christmas so soon. That will be better too because after you've seen what she's like, we'll know whether we want to get tangled up with her at all. Though

I've always liked Ken. Mary Crandall would have been just about perfect for him. Aren't men terrible?"

"Well, you did your best."

"I certainly did. I wanted your brother to be happy. It does seem too bad of him to have him spring this old Catholic widow on us."

"Now you don't know that she's old," he chuckled.

"Old enough. We'll have to send them a wedding present. One more thing."

"Yes, we should pick out something pretty nice for Ken."

"It's so difficult when you don't know what she's like. Or what she has already. Catholics are apt to be so elaborate! I suppose a silver platter is always safe enough. But you'll have to pay for it," finished Mrs. Craig, revenging herself on him for her disappointment. "He's your brother."

Barbara herself had only one relative to whom she felt obliged to tell her decision to be married again. The rest would hear about it sooner or later. When it was over, she planned, she would write a few notes to distant members of the family. But Aunt Agatha must know beforehand. That was only right. Though their lives touched lightly and infrequently now, Barbara felt close to Aunt Agatha.

Virgin and martyr, they used to call Aunt Agatha in the family. "Where's your Aunt-Agatha-virgin-and-martyr?" Barbara's father would ask teasingly, and she herself used to chant the words because they were such fun. When she grew old enough for a better perspective, Barbara realized that the affectionate mockery was probably rooted in truth. Virginity had to be taken for granted in Agatha Braniff's life. There must have been almost no opportunity for anything else. She had come home from a convent school to be the daughter who stayed at home, while the others went out to marry. The homely daughter. The pious one. The daughter who might have been a nun, except that she was so much needed at home with her parents.

The three other Braniff girls of that generation had married and gone away. One had died long since, and Marie and Grace had become so imbedded in other communities that they came back only at the call of a death in the family to the city where they had been born. John, Stephen and Agatha stayed on. But Stephen went to the first great war. He came back unwounded, to kill himself in his own room in the old house, on a quiet winter day after all the other guns he had faced had ceased firing.

John, who was Barbara's father, was supposed to be the money-maker. He looked like old Julian and he intended to do better than his father had done in real estate and local speculation. Once in a while over the years it seemed as if he had done it, but most of his ventures had something faulty in conception or development. His money always went out as fast as it came in.

Agatha, of course, took care of the old folks. When they died and the house had to be sold at last, she went, just as much as a matter of course, to live with Barbara's parents. They were glad to have her come. Other help was hard to get and often harder to pay for, and Agatha's competent hands filled many a gap. Barbara's mother had never been used to doing her household work. Also the virgin and martyr was not a dependent. She had a small, in-vulnerable income, doled out carefully by an insurance company. Her father had arranged that before he died, after Stephen's suicide had lost Agatha one protector and it had become obvious that John could not hang on to money.

But John himself had managed to leave the virgin and martyr the house she lived in now, without any encumbrances. He took a final pride in that. John's wife was dead by that time and very handsomely buried. Barbara had recently married, not to her father's satisfaction, for he distrusted Leslie Field and his charm, but at least she had her own man. Probably John Braniff wondered what would happen to Agatha if she were severed from the possessions she had cared for so diligently. Perhaps he thought that some worldly reward was only fair, in addition to her certain eternal one.

The house was too big for Aunt Agatha's needs, but she did not mind that at all. The one in which she had been brought up had been three times the size of this one, which always seemed small

[71]

to her. Nor did she mind its increasing shabbiness or the makeshifts by which she could avoid paying for repairs, the stick to hold up a window where the old-fashioned cord was broken, the yellowed notice that the front doorbell did not ring—none of the bells in the house had rung for years—the picture half hiding the place in the front hall where the wallpaper was rain stained.

The imperfections did not matter. She was where she belonged and she knew it. The tables and chairs and desks in the house had been living together so long that there was peace between them. Dozens of framed pictures on the walls and piano top kept Agatha company and made her still the center and homekeeper of a big family, and the votive light in front of the little shrine on the stair landing had flickered and glowed there continually for twenty years. The big, bad oil paintings, the rug that always had been called the Turkey Carpet, the graceless mahogany dining room table with its lion-claw feet all had an easy suitability, drawn from slowly blending with the life of the virgin and martyr.

She was the oldest of Julian Braniff's children and now she was far into her sixties and short of breath. She ate too much. She always had eaten too much, but endless trips up and down the front and back stairs, the daily pushing of carpetsweepers, shaking rugs, lifting objects that were too heavy for her, had hardened every muscle in her body. Her gray hair was done in a twisted knot, which forty years before had been a fashion, named from a statue of Psyche. Her face powder was pale-pink and faintly sweet, like an old flower. Now that there was no reason for Agatha Braniff to be handsome, she had become more so, like the old furniture. Like it, she was there for use, looking comfortable, peaceful, quite good enough for the purpose.

When Barbara came in, Miss Braniff was greatly pleased as always. She went almost at once to get something to eat and drink.

"Yes, I will. Some hot tea will do you good."

Barbara thought perhaps it would and she knew that her aunt always welcomed an extra occasion for food. It might help the shock. She hoped that her announcement would not be too troubling. She

[72]

was very fond of her aunt, although she had refused Agatha's single invitation to come to live here. That had been made after her divorce. Agatha never wanted anything to do with Leslie Field. Barbara had said no with gratitude, that she wanted to be independent. She had an idea that her aunt was rather relieved at her decision. The invitation was not repeated. But they had established certain customs, having dinner together on Easter Sunday in the old house, and on Agatha's birthday, and supper on Christmas Eve, perhaps before Barbara went on to a party. Aunt Agatha, like most plain women who had never had many pretty clothes, loved to see Barbara dressed up.

So today Barbara had worn her mauve jersey dress and the little knitted hat with sparkles on it. Her aunt admired it immediately.

"Don't spill anything on that pretty dress. You'll never have anything that's more becoming. It makes you look like a young girl."

"Which is exactly the way I feel these days."

But she did not tell her news at once. She talked about other things as they drank the strong, green tea and ate the overbuttered slices of toast and thick sugar-sprinkled cookies. Nothing was very savory or well-cooked and yet it all tasted delicious to Barbara, for it brought back childish hungers for the same cookies and lumps of half-melted butter.

"It's always so nice here!" she exclaimed.

"Well, it's an old house," answered Agatha Braniff, as if that were full explanation. "You should come more often."

"I've been busy. A lot of things have been happening."

"You don't want to wear yourself out at your age, dear. Remember that the poor you have always with you. You won't have to work over Christmas, will you?"

This was the opportunity to tell. "I'd only have the day off if I were going to be here. But I'm not. I'm afraid that I won't be here to have our oyster stew on Christmas Eve this year. Will you be all right? Will you ask someone else for supper?"

"Don't worry about me. But where will you be? Out of town?"

"I'll be in New York. Aunt Agatha, I'm giving up my job. I'm

[73]

going to be married. On the seventh of December. We're going away for a few weeks afterward and then we'll be back here. To live."

The tick of the big bronze clock on the mantel made a number of little exclamation points against silence before Aunt Agatha said something. When she spoke she did not ask the name of the man whom Barbara was going to marry. She asked, "What has happened to Leslie Field?"

"I don't know. He's completely out of my life. He has been for years."

"Is he dead?"

"I don't know. I don't suppose so or I probably would have been notified by somebody."

"Will the Church permit it?"

"We aren't going to be married in the Church."

"Oh dear God help us," ejaculated Agatha Braniff. "Did you talk to the Bishop?"

Barbara nodded. "And so did Ken," she added.

"Is it that Mr. Craig you've been going about with so much?"

"Why, of course. He's the only man in the world I would marry. You'll like him so much, Aunt Agatha. He's just the kind of man you would like. Big, handsome, grand sense of humor. And good. He has lots of character. Everybody respects him who knows him at all."

"I suppose he's a Protestant."

"Yes."

"You were always like that," said Agatha Braniff. "Never one to stay with your own kind."

The words had a Celtic cadence. Agatha Braniff had never been in Ireland and yet, as she grew older, the heritage of her Irish ancestors became more apparent. It appeared in the turn of her phrases, the way she would crack the top off a boiled egg, fold a scarf like a shawl, or croon the slurred responses in a litany.

"My own kind," repeated Barbara. "It's a queer phrase. Our kind. I never have liked the sound of it. Who are my own kind, anyway?"

"You know well enough. Those who share your faith and practice it."

"A religious belief shouldn't fence you in. Make you one of a herd."

"I don't know about that. It may be safer so."

Barbara said, as calmly as she could, "I don't think so at all. It seems to me the worst attitude anyone, especially a Catholic, can take. It just leads to bigotry."

"It's easy to argue. When your conscience is troubling you."

"My conscience isn't troubling me at all."

"Lord help us," said Agatha Braniff rhythmically and with no accent.

"I mean what I say. Perhaps when Catholics were persecuted or there were only a few of them in some places, they did have to huddle together for self-protection. It may still be true in some places abroad. But in this county even if Catholics are a minority group they have every right and every privilege and protection. They ought to mix and not do what you call staying with their own kind."

"It's easy to argue," answered her aunt. "Look at yourself. The bad time you had, poor girl, and all that trouble. Wasn't one Protestant enough for you?"

"You don't understand. This isn't at all the same thing. Aunt Agatha, this is the best thing that ever has happened to me. I'm in love for the first time. The other was a kind of crazy, horrible dream. I can't remember myself as I was when I was married to Leslie. I've grown up since then. Now I know what to look for in a man, what there has to be in a marriage. Ken is very strong and yet he's kind. He—" She stopped because she couldn't say some things to a virgin, and finished, "And one of the main things is that he needs me. He hasn't had a happy life any more than I've had."

"Then let him find happiness elsewhere and not ask a good girl to give up her religion for him."

"I'm not giving up my religion."

"You'll give up its comforts and graces if you do this thing. I've known what was in your mind this past year and I've prayed for you,

[75]

child. Tell him no, while there is still time, and not live to regret it, poor girl," begged Agatha urgently but her voice was warm with sympathy.

"I've already told him yes," said Barbara. "I couldn't go back on it now. And I don't want to. If I didn't marry Ken, my life would be one long mess of being sorry I hadn't, and of resenting what made me give him up. I couldn't be a good Catholic if I didn't marry him. I'd feel like a slave, like a prisoner, like somebody serving a cruel sentence all my life."

Agatha Braniff's memory was a great album of family scenes. This one would have its own place, the young women in her mauve dress, with the determination on her face softened by love. It was a beautiful, hopeful, daring face. Facing that terrible risk, thought Agatha. Her thought turned a page of the album to the dreadful scenes after Stephen's death, scenes of anger and rebellion because a suicide could not be buried in consecrated ground. No day had passed since in all the intervening years without her offering a Rosary for Stephen's tortured soul, shut away from the sight of God. Or was it still, after all these years? Sometimes she had hoped against her faith.

I can no more stop her than I could the wind, she thought as she looked at Barbara. If she would not listen to the Bishop, she won't listen to her old aunt. Poor child, what a life any way you look at it. She's had more than her share. She saw another picture, the wild despair of a girl whose child was dead and taken for burial. "Let me hold him a little while longer!" Barbara had cried. And the man who should have been her comfort and given her more children—Agatha Braniff saw him too. Insolent, mocking, not meaning that laugh of his, and saying things in a two-edged way. The worse for liquor most of the time.

"Let it wait for a while then and God may be good to you," she argued.

"It's not fair, Aunt Agatha. Even if I were willing to wait. And I'm not getting any younger. Don't you think that the Lord wants me to have a family?"

"It's a poor way to bring luck to yourself, turning against your Church. Don't ask me to uphold you!"

"I won't. But don't be troubled, will you? Don't worry about my soul. I know this is the right thing to do."

Agatha Braniff thought, she's young and strong. God has his own ways. He might take that first man any day, and no loss, considering the life he's led.

"You should wait God's time," she said.

Barbara laughed. "I know exactly what you're thinking and that's a sin."

It was. When she examined her conscience that night, Agatha Braniff admitted it was and included it in her act of contrition. But she did not quite destroy a lingering hope that Leslie Field might die before December seventh.

Chapter Six

Bishop Tarrant was told by Father Paul Gilroy, who was in charge of the cathedral parish since Father Moore had been made a Monsignor and assigned to other duites. Until that day the Bishop had not believed, in spite of Kenneth Craig's defiant statement that he would marry Barbara, that she would agree to do it. He relied on his own injunctions and the fact that the Braniffs were a good Catholic family.

He had prayed for her during his Mass, as he had told Craig he would, prayed that she might resist temptation and accept God's will and the laws of His Church. It had been a special prayer for Barbara, because her case had touched him. He was not unaware that she had suffered human injustice but that often brought special graces in the end.

All sorts of people came to Bishop Tarrant to discuss marriage laws, asking for extraordinary consideration and special dispensation, trying to get out of one marriage or into another one which was forbidden. There were sulky, sex-ridden girls who would declare that they could not live without some man, angry parents, who were good supporters of their parishes, demanding that exceptions be made for their children. There were wretched women who wanted release from brutality and drunkenness, and others, hard but scrupulous, who wanted him to devise a shrewd arrangement so that they could live within the respectable immortality-insured shelter of the Church and still indulge their passions.

The Bishop was patient because they were so faulty and did not know what they needed. They sought for indulgence when they needed discipline. He could imagine the women as they would be without the shelter and bracing of the Church, helplessly preyed upon by their transient desires and passions, unfitting themselves for the destiny for which their bodies as well as their souls had been created. He was scrupulous too in examining the law in regard to each individual case, for he was almost invariably the final judge of what could be done. He was sorry for Barbara's plight, especially since she had been a Braniff and it had been a strong name in the diocese for two generations. But all the more on that account she was in a position to serve the Church well. Resistance to divorce was one of the greatest present battles of the Church and she could set a vigorous and important example.

Father Gilroy's statement that he understood that Mrs. Field was going to have a civil marriage disturbed the Bishop to the point of anger. Bishop Tarrant was in his study when the young priest was sent up to see him. He had been considering some of the vast problems which confronted the Church and how to perfect his own piece of the mosaic.

Now that the war was over, pitiful moans were coming from the wreckage. Catholics must do their share, help take care of the ones of their own faith and not let them drift away into false doctrines. The attack would be terrific morally. There would be persecutions, priests and nuns driven into exile. Never in all her history had the Church confronted such dislike and defiance. There were bound to be new martyrs.

Against the background of that thought came Father Paul Gilroy announcing another apostate, another scandal.

"It will be no credit to your parish, Father," said the Bishop shortly. "There could be no worse example. There are too many mixed marriages in that parish anyway and too many separations condoned."

"There will be fewer in the future, Bishop."

The Bishop was not quite sure of how much he liked Father Gilroy. It had been necessary to put him in Father Moore's place because the other was getting too frail to carry the heavy responsibility of the city parish. Also leniency had grown in Father Moore along with the increasing age and long-time friendliness with his parishioners, which was perhaps one reason for all the mixed marriages. This young priest, still not forty, recently back from Rome, was one of the group who wanted to be militant leaders of the faith, instead of the shepherds.

Father Gilroy sat unrelaxed, severely intent on his purposes. He had a thin, ascetic face and yet his appearance was of unlimited strength. He seemed to be controlling his energies, throttling them down into talk although he wanted to be moving, as if the effort to make his religion a dynamic force was never turned off or quite idling.

"I hope so," said the Bishop. "How do you propose to do it?"

"It is a matter of organization, I believe, Your Excellency. The young people in the parish need to be dealt with as a coherent group. Many of them hardly understand what marriage is from a Catholic standpoint. What we say on Sunday goes in one ear and out the other."

"That is always disconcerting."

"With your permission I should like to organize a course of twelve lectures on marriage to be given to the young men and young women who are in—" the word "love" seemed to bother him and his sentence shied away from it.

"Going steady," supplied the Bishop with a half-smile.

"We must do more than state the laws. We must teach young Catholic men to take charge of the morality of their households, rule their families and teach the girls what their place is in the home and their duties to their children."

"Very well. But such efforts have often been made."

The gleam in Father Gilroy's eyes seemed to imply that when he tried them, the results would be different than ever before. The Bishop thought, he loves to talk but his sermons may burn him up more than the people who hear him. He took Father Gilroy down a peg. He said, "Talk won't get very far as long as bad example persists. The example of a member of good Catholic family, like Mrs. Field, falling away from the Church is what does genuine harm in a parish."

"That has not happened yet. I am going to talk to her."

"It may not be rewarding," answered Bishop Tarrant dryly. "I discussed the matter with her myself. Mr. Craig, the man involved, also came to call on me. He's rather determined. I was counting on her, but from what you tell me I may have been wrong."

"Have you any objection to my talking to her again?"

"No, no. Not at all. Actually, it is your duty as her parish priest to try to prevent the scandal."

"I felt that way. But as I had heard that she had come to you for advice, I felt that I should consult with you before doing anything further."

"Do what seems best to you. It is most unfortunate if it should happen," answered the Bishop and the priest knew that his time was up.

Father Gilroy's assurance annoyed the Bishop. He thought, that young man is too sure of himself for his own good. He's got no grace of humility in spite of his manners. He thinks I'm old-fashioned too, and that I failed with Barbara Braniff because I wasn't vigorous enough. I doubt if that would have made any difference in this case. Well, we'll see. Perhaps Father Gilroy is right, thought the Bishop, who did have the grace of humility. I may not have put it strong enough to her.

Barbara said, "Oh—won't you come in, Father?"

He came in, very tall, dark of complexion and cloth and mood, and he seemed to be carrying a weapon. He was not, of course. It was only his breviary, but there was something about the thrust of his arm that was almost threatening.

"You are Mrs. Field?"

"Yes—"

"I am Father Gilroy."

"Oh, I know you, Father. I often hear your sermons."

"That's hardly enough for a parishioner. Religion does not grow by mere listening. I have not seen you in any of our women's groups, have I?"

"I work, Father. I'm with the Social Agencies. It keeps me pretty busy."

"And your evenings?"

She tried not to stiffen, not to resent the question.

"There is always a great deal to do," she said evasively.

He had seated himself on the hardest chair and she felt borne down upon as he stared at her in the corner of the sofa, as if inspecting her for signs of sin.

"We need you in this parish," he said, as if he demanded her, "and what you need, Mrs. Field, is closer parish affiliations. Without those one can not really be a good Catholic. I intend to build up a strong woman's organization at every age level, which will absorb the normal interests of all the parish women."

Barbara waited for what was coming.

"Every woman, according to her vocation in life, will have a niche in this over-all organization. The mothers, the young girls, the older women. Mrs. Field, I think you could lead a group of young working women like yourself. I want you to get them together for me, arrange a preliminary meeting. How about Thursday night of next week?"

[81]

"Oh, Father, I'm sorry, but I couldn't do that."

"Don't tell me that. I'm sure you could. It may take a little time but I am sure you can spare it for God's work and He needs you. As you—I am sure—need Him."

"I can't, Father. I have other obligations."

"None more important than the one to your Church."

This is double-talk, she thought. He knows about me and Kenneth.

"You have no children?"

"No living children." She always had to say it that way.

"And you live alone?"

"I do at the moment," said Barbara, "but I am going to be married again."

"Again? Then you are a widow?"

"I don't think so. I've been divorced."

"My dear lady, I seem to have come just in time. Don't you know what you contemplate is impossible?"

She said nothing.

"Why haven't you come to see me on this matter?"

"I went to see the Bishop, Father Gilroy."

"I am sure he gave you no such permission."

"No."

"And you intend to defy your Bishop?"

Barbara answered that with silence.

"Where are you bound for? Hell?" he asked, allowing himself a sudden eruption of anger.

"I don't think so. I hope not."

"Then let us hear no more of such an idea. Give up this man, whoever he is. Forget him—separate yourself from all occasions of sin—and talk no more of a second marriage while you have a living husband."

She moved her head, refusing.

"But surely you know that you would put yourself outside the grace of the sacraments. You cannot make a good confession nor be absolved. You cannot receive the Holy Eucharist if you live determinedly with a man who is not your husband."

"He will be my husband."

"Never in the sight of God or of any good Catholic. Are you unmindful of the fact that God might claim your life in the midst of sin? Would you dare to meet His judgment without preparation? Do you realize that you would be denied Catholic burial and that your time may be nearer than you think? Can any pleasure, any human satisfaction be worth taking such terrible risks?"

He was thundering at her. Her voice sounded small in the echo of his.

"I don't think it matters very much where one is buried. And I believe that God understands what I am doing and knows that it isn't just pleasure and satisfaction I want."

"Quite obviously, from the way you talk, you are losing your faith. Or have lost it."

"No, Father—sometimes it seems to feel stronger than it ever has."

"That's a peculiar way of temptation. You are deceiving yourself, creating your own heresy. You claim a strong faith, do you, and yet take it upon yourself to refuse to obey God's laws?"

"I do believe in my religion," she repeated. "But I can't accept this prohibition against my coming marriage. I haven't lived with my first husband for years. I couldn't ever live with him again. I'll obey all rules of the Church except in not marrying again."

"You mean you will accept what you choose, what suits your pleasure. That is not faith. That's too easy," he said contemptuously.

"It hasn't been easy, Father Gilroy. There have been times when I have been utterly confused and wretched. Whatever I did, I seemed to be doing harm. Hurting someone else, if not myself."

"That is the confusion always caused by a guilty conscience. What you need is to make a good confession and resolve to put these evil lusts away from you."

Barbara stood up, her eyes dark with anger.

[83]

"Get busy serving your Church and its work and try to become an honest woman," he said with deliberate cruelty.

"I am an honest woman."

"In refusing to save your soul?"

"I do not refuse to save it. I shall be a more honest woman if I do marry. And I do not believe God wants women to be frustrated and lonely and childless because of a technicality."

"You made a contract before God," he declared, angrily despising her. The tall, gaunt priest had conquered many passions, in himself and in hundreds of penitents, but it had left him with a hatred for the resistant temptation in women. He felt it surging in him now against this cause of sin which she represented, this source of division and apostasy which she dared to defend.

"My husband broke that contract," she said, "a long time ago. It no longer exists."

"Can you tell that to God?"

"I have. Again and again."

"You blaspheme when you do. You have closed your heart to grace. You already have lost your faith."

"No, I have not."

He ignored that. He stared at her and finally said slowly, "Have done—I want you to come to me tomorrow, Mrs. Field, and tell me that you will give up this man, that you repent—"

"And stand by the church door in a white sheet? Shall I wear a scarlet letter too?" She gave an involuntary gasp of laughter at this fantastic scene.

Father Gilroy said slowly, "Unfortunate woman! God is not mocked!"

Barbara heard his last distant step before she moved from where she was standing. Then she turned on another lamp because the room seemed too dark. The winter twilight had gone black during the priest's visit. She turned the lamp off again because the brightness was too much for her, until she had regained control of herself. She realized that she trembled uncontrollably. For

[84]

refuge she went to the telephone. But she did not lift it from its cradle.

"No, I won't," she said aloud as if she wanted to hear her own decision. "I mustn't tell Ken about this. It would make him so prejudiced. I'll never say a word to him about it. It would give scandal. He would believe this is usual. This never happens."

But it had happened. In bewilderment she thought, I talked back to a priest. The things I said! What came over me? No matter what a priest says to you, he has the right. No matter how you may feel about it, you never talk back.

You may have wanted to. Yes, many times, in all these years. Remember how you felt when you were a child and were told that you wouldn't have a sore throat if your throat was blessed. But you did, right afterward. You didn't dare say anything. And in the convent, when you were told to count your sins of impure thoughts, you didn't want to because it started you thinking them all over again, but you didn't say so. And so many times, on Sundays, when it was so hard to get to Mass because Leslie was raising hell, you got there and were scolded when you did and told to have more children. Scolded so often when you were trying so hard.

Father Gilroy forced himself in here. He wasn't in the pulpit or on the altar. He was deliberately insulting. I'm not sorry that I said what I did.

It's not true. I'm not losing my faith.

Chapter Seven

It was almost a beautiful wedding. Barbara had not expected that. She thought of it beforehand as something to go through, as a bridge that must be crossed. But Kenneth had done his part of it very well. Old Judge Kirk was about to retire from the bench, and usually refused to perform marriages, but he made an exception in this case, after Mr. Miller spoke to him confidentially about the situation and asked him to do it as a personal favor.

Judge Kirk married Kenneth and Barbara on the December afternoon which they had chosen. The ceremony was in his chambers, in an inner room paneled with dark wood and leather-bound lawbooks. The feeling of the place was profound and wise. There was a large silken flag on a staff beside the Judge's bench, and its colors were singularly vivid in the sober room. Portraits of other Justices on the walls, all serious and thoughtful, seemed to act as witnesses to the contract.

The human witnesses had created more of a problem. Mr. Miller was at the wedding of course, and Malcolm Craig, who, after meeting Barbara, apologized again because his wife had been prevented from coming. Without much enthusiasm, Barbara had agreed with Kenneth that Carol and Dudley Harrison should be asked, because they were Kenneth's friends and would inevitably be part of their future social group. Blair Wyatt heard about it from Carol and telephoned Barbara to ask if he might come. But it was a small company.

Agatha Braniff had not come.

"In the courthouse!" she had exclaimed in dismay when Barbara asked her to be there. "Oh, my dear child, I couldn't. I have never done anything like that. Oh, Barbara, what would your mother say! The courthouse! God help us all!"

But she had come to Barbara's apartment early in the morning, obviously avoiding the hours when she might meet Kenneth there, carrying a package. It was not too well wrapped, for Agatha's fingers were no longer very deft, but the contents made Barbara exclaim with astonishment and love.

"You mean for us? Why, it's the very old silver. The cream pot and sugarbowl that were made in Dublin by Walsh in seventeen hundred and something."

"And forty," said her aunt accurately.

"They're priceless. You should keep them."

"I never use them. I always intended you to have the set. I

never knew whether Marie or Grace's children would care for them or not, but you always had the taste to admire them. They were made for a Braniff in Ireland, and brought over with them, and the workmanship shows the style of people they must have been!"

Her eyes were proud with giving and then they saddened.

"Take care of yourself," she urged. "With God's help, it might come out all right in the end. Carry this with you. It has had great blessing."

Barbara put down the ancient silver and took a small cheap medal of the Virgin with even more gratitude.

It was in her purse when she and Kenneth came into the courtroom. She could feel the quiet stretching to tensity as they entered. They came together and unattended and went directly to the front of the room where the Judge was standing. It was a brief ceremony, but it had full weight. Their words to the Judge and to each other were the gravest of pledges.

The Judge did not release them as he completed the official part of his task. He delivered a little homily, speaking as if he were charging a jury.

"Though this is a civil and not a religious ceremony, I feel that it is not out of place to address a few words to you who are the parties to this contract of marriage. You are, I know, fully aware of its great importance. I am assured, by those who know you well, that you have considered deeply before taking this step which so deeply obligates you both. You have weighed many considerations which might have deterred you and balanced them against your love and need for each other.

"The love of man and woman is more than poetry and romance, though it inspires those branches of life and literature. It is more deeply based than attraction, or even affection. True love—" Barbara never forgot how the Judge infused those street-ballad words with an extraordinary dignity—"is rooted in duty, often in the sacrifice or abnegation of self.

"In all civilized countries—indeed in all orderly countries whose

[87]

history has been recorded, marriage has never been taken lightly. On its stability the moral character and the life of any state depends. No state can grow or progress if the family group deteriorates within it. No family is safe if the state is careless or corrupt in its protection of marriage by wise laws, ably enforced. The law in this Christian country seeks in every way to insure the continuity and stability of the married state and to uphold its proper functions.

"In accordance with the laws of this state, I have pronounced you man and wife this afternoon. I wish you well in this great undertaking which you engage upon together. May you meet the inevitable vicissitudes of living with joined wisdom, tolerance and mutual love." His voice changed and simplified as he held out his hand to Barbara and finished, "I wish you great happiness, Mrs. Craig."

Barbara said all she could say. "Thank you for marrying us, Judge Kirk."

His words had been healing and exalting to her. He offered them the sanction which she had sought from the Bishop and failed to receive. To have this grave and worthy old man of law give them approval seemed to close the open wounds in her mind and conscience.

She felt the fabric of the occasion was honorable and truthful. She was proud of Kenneth's distinction and control, which were like fine and formal clothes worn by his feelings today. The light came evenly into the room, seeking the bright bars of the flag. It was still sunlight. Everyone was glad that they had been married, everyone present. She heard Kenneth's brother declare loudly, "This is certainly fine, old boy, and you've got it coming to you!"

Yes, Kenneth had it coming to him. Everything he wanted must come.

There was no great merrymaking after the ceremony. In a private room at Kenneth's club there were a few toasts in champagne, and Carol Harrison had ordered a handsome wedding cake, which they plundered only slightly. Barbara was dressed for travel and did not go back to her apartment. Kenneth had asked her not to do that until they came back from New York. Then he knew, and so did she, that it would not be like her home. For professional movers were going in tomorrow to transfer the furniture she wanted to keep to the house which Kenneth already had bought from Mr. Miller.

As she thought of that after the door of the airplane was closed and its engines were warming up, she felt as if she were almost ruthless to walk out on the past without another backward look. This morning she had tried to meet the change with full awareness. But it was difficult. She had told herself that one life was over, and another about to begin. But she had broken her thought to water a violet plant so it would be sure not to die.

"All right, darling?" asked Kenneth.

"Better than that! The wedding was quite lovely, I thought. Didn't you?"

"I thought it went off very well. The old Judge did a good job. I was pretty sure he would, if he took it on. He's a noble old Roman, but doesn't he love to hear the echoes of his voice as he rolls it out?"

"I liked what he said. It wasn't just rote. It was for us."

"Think so? I don't remember much of it. I couldn't keep my mind on that last bit. All I could think of was that we were married. Married."

"It was much more impressive—"

"Than you thought it was going to be?" He filled her pause.

"Yes."

That was true. But her thought as she spoke had been that this second marriage ceremony of hers had been far more impressive than the first one. It was no time to speak of that, and she checked herself. But memory and contrast had risen irrepressibly in her mind. Father Moore had been quick almost to hurry, formal and cold when he had married her to Leslie twelve years ago in the bleak vestry where mixed marriages were performed. But not blessed. Not encouraged. Father Moore disapproved all mixed marriages and especially he had disliked the one between Leslie and herself. He had seemed to mistrust Leslie's reception of the necessary instructions, always given by a priest to Protestants who married Catholics. Leslie had been agreeable, with never a question or a disagreement, but a trace of amusement showed through his compliance. Barbara remembered that her father had put up with the marriage only because he could not stop it, that her mother had been disappointed and ashamed because the wedding was so unlovely and not in church. No one was glad at that first wedding. Except of course Leslie—and herself. She must have felt that way. Leslie had closed the door of the drawing room on the train and said—

"Kenneth!" She called him as if from a distance, though he was close beside her.

"What is it, darling? Forgotten something?"

"Thank you for our wedding."

"You're the one to be thanked. You're not worried or bothered about anything any more, are you?"

She knew what he meant. "Not a thing," she answered.

"That's the way it's going to be," he promised, adding one more vow to the others of that day.

Nearly all the time while they were in New York, it was that way. No doubts seemed to pursue them. Barbara remembered them as things past, distanced. Everywhere there was approval and welcome and admiration. Living together was better than they had hoped or dreamed. They were more than happy with love. Loneliness and strain had been drained off their lives, and it was like being rid of poisons.

It was happiness to feel so sure, as an hour of love waned, that the tide would soon come in again, to know that she could be lavish with time because they had so much of it ahead, to discover the variety of Kenneth's moods. To have him take care of her openly and devotedly was almost surprising. He had talked of that, but she had not guessed how warm it would make her.

She had known luxury before. In the days when she was very young and her father often had plenty of money, he had been a spender. Barbara had been sent to a convent boarding school near New York for a few years and at Thanksgiving and in the spring her parents used to come to the city and establish themselves at the Ritz, to make her and themselves a holiday. Barbara would take off the school uniform, the black wool jumper and long cotton stockings, and put on a dress for the city under her red coat with the fur lining. She loved that coat, but she had hours of renouncing the world at that age and sometimes felt she should give it up. But she did not. In the red, fur-lined coat, she had first known New York, lit a candle at St. Patrick's Cathedral, skated with an attendant at Rockefeller Center, and gone to the theater if the play had nothing bad in it, or if her mother was sure that whatever was bad would be over Barbara's head.

Later she had come to New York with Leslie when he had his foothold in a big investment firm. Those were expensive trips, and never very solvent. Leslie never paid bills if he could establish credit. He was usually short of cash. "Have you any money, Barbara?" He expected her to have some. She had soon found that out. Leslie spent money in defense and defiance, always trying to make that false confidence of his ring true. In the beginning of their life together, Barbara had not realized that, nor how much money went for liquor, nor that many of the presents he gave her might as well have been shoplifted, for Leslie could not pay for them. She used to send back those presents without telling him.

It was completely different now, securely and deliciously not at all like that. Barbara liked to see Kenneth carefully scan an account before he paid it. They could go back to restaurants a second time. Kenneth gave her presents too, but not to show that he could. They were given to gild her happiness. She unwrapped his imagination from every surprise.

"Tonight you're the star," said Kenneth, giving her a long, gay box. "It's for your show!"

The negligee inside was almost exactly like the one she had

admired on an actress in a play a few nights before. It was her show.

Each day Kenneth told her again that he loved her more. Each day it seemed lucidly true. Now that they were married, she understood with deeper sympathy how much he had wanted it, how he had needed her and how she had wanted his love unveiled and proud. She felt now that life together had been inevitable. I was parochial about the whole thing, she thought, when she was reminded of her disobedience to the Bishop and of the scene with Father Gilroy. Of course they had to say what they did at the time.

She kept proofs of her religion about her, the ivory and pearl rosary which she had always carried since she left the convent, an illuminated prayer of St. Francis on a card in her purse. She had begun to say that prayer daily in wartime. "God, make me an instrument of Thy Peace . . ." She had said it in strange places and over fears, and vowed to say it every day until peace was visible.

She was faithful to the practices of the Church, as far as she could be.

"I'll have the whitefish, Ken."

"Fish? Oh, no. Let's have a good thick steak."

"I can't tonight. It's Friday."

"Oh, so it is. Well, I'll have fish with you."

"You needn't do that. There's no reason to spoil your dinner."

"I don't mind fish. Good for me once in a while. But here— why don't you have fish tomorrow instead? Won't some other day do as well?"

"No, you can't fix it to suit yourself. All over the world Catholics don't eat meat on Friday."

"Why did they pick on Friday?"

"It's the day that Christ was crucified. The abstinence is to remind you of Christ's sacrifice for us. It isn't real fasting. That isn't required except in Lent and on certain other days, and since the war and rationing there are any number of dispensations. But you have to keep Friday—without meat. You can have anything else."

"Must be good for the fish trade. As a matter of fact, at most clubs and hotels, they feature fish on Friday. Waiter—Madam will have the whitefish, and make sure that she gets a good piece. Now first—how about the soup? That cream of chicken seems to be a specialty here."

"No, I'll have tomato juice, thanks."

"On top of that drink? You should have soup. Nothing wrong with chicken, is there?"

"Yes, it's just the same as meat. You can't eat soup with a meat base on Friday."

"That's drawing it pretty fine. You might get fooled. But chicken? You can eat eggs, can't you?"

"Yes, eggs are all right. Listen, Ken, they argued that one out in the Middle Ages. There isn't a thing you can do about it. For a Catholic a chicken is meat. An egg isn't."

"Just as you say, darling."

And later Kenneth said, "You know, you can give me fish on Friday any time. I like fish."

He was trying to go as far as he could with her, and she loved him for it. But though he offered to go to church with her on their first married Sunday, Barbara did not let him come.

"No, you sit here and finish the newspapers. I'll be back in an hour and a half."

"Sure you don't want me to come? I'll be glad to."

"No, I'd really rather you didn't this morning."

"I want to do what you want."

"I know, dear. This is it."

"Well, be careful crossing streets."

"I will. I'll get a policeman or a Boy Scout to go across with me whenever the light's green."

"Just the same, you be careful. Have you got money for the box?"

"Plenty. I won't be too long."

He followed her to the door of their suite.

[93]

"Barbara—"

She turned willingly to him again. It was sweet to be so loved.

"Only don't knock my hat off."

"You won't let anything bother you now? You won't be disturbed?"

"You mustn't worry about that."

"You are happy, aren't you, my darling?"

"You know I am."

It was a late, High Mass. Barbara had hardly entered before the choir began the repentance of the Kyrie in a magnificent arrangement that seemed to blend notes of despair and confidence. Barbara knelt and joined the voices silently. It was good to be here. Nothing was strange, not even the strangers. The familiar service belonged to her and she to it. There was no rejection of her, no isolation. It was as it had been before she married Kenneth. She had that too now to thank God for. She did, as the preparation for the sacrifice went on.

The choir was silent. A priest came into the pulpit, for it was time for the announcements and the sermon. She thought, all over the world it is the same way. She did not listen closely until suddenly his words attacked her. He was speaking of the Christmas services.

"Every Catholic who in the true sense is a Catholic will make his first present to God, by approaching and receiving the Sacrament of Penance at some time during this week. He will receive from God, in return, that greatest gift ever made to man, the Holy Eucharist. That is Christmas, my dear people. The truth of Christmas is not found by a Catholic in the shops which line and brighten the avenues and streets of New York or any other city. It cannot be bought in the jewelry shops, the toy shops, or in the food markets. The only Christmas gift that a Catholic really wants, the only Christmas gift that it is obligatory upon him to give, is available at this church and at this altar—"

Barbara had heard that all her life. It was always said in words like these at Christmastime from almost every altar. This sermon, usually overstated, was an old one. But this morning every word seemed hurled at her. I can't go near, she thought. It's always been the first thing—the most important, except that you don't go around saying so—and I can't go to Communion on Christmas.

You knew that. Are you going to be terrorized because you can't? You knew that was part of it when you married Ken. You can't have it both ways. Get hold of yourself now and don't let yourself be superstitious. The sacraments were devised to increase spirituality. You'll have to manage without them—at least for a while. There won't be any thunderbolts—or any bad luck. That's mixed up with your fear of not going to Communion on Christmas. Maybe it will be good for you not to go in one way. You won't be following a habit. It may give you clearer perspective.

The sermon was over. The ushers took up the collection. Barbara put in a ten-dollar bill. It was a large contribution for a church she had no responsibility to support. But they were spending so much on themselves.

Was that why you did it? Or are you trying to make up for something? Stop thinking—pray.

"It was a beautiful service," she reported. "It always is over there. Have you ever been in the cathedral, Ken?"

"No, I never have. I wish you'd take me."

"I will. It's something to see. They say that only St. Peter's is more beautiful."

They went into St. Patrick's on a snowy afternoon and walked around, looking at all the chapels. Beside one of the small altars, Barbara lit a votive candle and knelt for a moment in prayer. As she rose she found Kenneth watching her tenderly.

"What's that for?" he asked in a whisper.

"For you."

"For me?"

"I'll tell you when we go out."

He reminded her as they walked up the Avenue.

"Why did you say the candle was for me?"

"Because I said a prayer for you. For your happiness. The candles

[95]

are lit for special hopes and intentions. There's one burning in there now for what I want for you. At the altar of the Holy Family."

"I like that idea. The family altar. I should have lit one for your happiness. Let's go back and do it now."

"Oh, no," she laughed at him. "It's the prayer, you know, not the candle."

"I'll pray for you. In any church. I'll never forget you as you stood there lighting that candle. You were beautiful."

She said, "Some people don't approve of votive candles. There are priests who won't have them in their churches."

"Why not? You pay for your own, don't you?"

"It's not the cost! But some people light the candles, ask for all sorts of things that are impossible, and somehow identify it with faith. It can be bad for people. Like superstition."

"You don't have to light candles unless you want to?"

"Good heavens, no. It's just a piety."

"Always light one for me when you can."

"That's beginning at exactly the wrong end of Catholicism," she answered.

"It's an amazing institution," said Kenneth thoughtfully. "Think of what that property is worth. And all over the country—the world for that matter, except where they've been run out—the Catholic Church does hold property. It must have an enormous income too. The Catholic Church is the best example of actual world organization that exists."

"It's the religion that fits any soul," she replied.

"I like the way you stick up for it."

"Darling, I'm part of it. I always have been. I always will be. In spite of everything."

"That's the way to talk. You know I wish that Bishop Tarrant could see you right now."

"Why? What do you mean?"

"I'd just like to show him how it's working out."

"Our living in sin?" She sounded almost amused by the idea now.

"That's what he says. He knows better."

"It's what he believes."

"Well, a life of sin, if that's what it is, doesn't seem to hurt you much. You've never looked lovelier."

"I don't believe that the Bishop would think that very important."

"Aren't you glad that you didn't let him dictate to us?"

"Let's not talk about it."

"Right. There's no use in gloating over it."

"We couldn't do that," she protested. "We didn't win, you know, as they look at it. I lost. You see, Ken, I haven't changed the Bishop's attitude or the rules of the Church. I broke the rules so I'm an outlaw now. I've fallen away. That's what they call it."

"You don't mind as much as you feared, do you?"

"Yes, I mind—never let me say I don't—but I would do it over again."

"Don't be troubled now. I never should have mentioned the Bishop. But he certainly tried to throw a scare into me that day when I saw him. He said I couldn't make you happy. Tell me, darling, was he right?"

"What do you think?"

"I know he wasn't."

They stopped to look in Tiffany's windows for Barbara to choose jewels that Kenneth said he might buy for her ten years from now.

"It's the ten years that excite me," she told him.

"Don't you want those things in cases?"

"They're all right," Barbara said of the diamonds and rubies. "But jewelry never made a man love a woman any more, did it?"

He thought of Nina, of certain grim presents.

"Sometimes it can make a man hate a woman, I suppose," he answered.

"I never could understand why some women want it so much, unless it proves their hold on a man. But it isn't proof enough. Don't worry about buying me diamonds. I'd rather have lots of other things."

"What?"

"What I have right now," she said radiantly.

The falling snow was like a transparency through which they saw acts in a pantomime. A man came out of a toy store carrying an unwrapped rocking horse to a waiting taxi, and there was a grin of anticipation on his face. Something clutched Barbara's heart as she saw him. The window of a fashionable store had been decorated as a country kitchen, with a coal stove and a turkey in the oven, and stuffed stockings hung on the backs of chairs. Angels floated over a stylized manger in another window.

They crossed the Avenue and went into the Oak Room of the Plaza for a drink. They had been here several times in the last week, and with the quick affectionate attachment of New York, it seemed now like their own place.

"How about a Manhattan for a change?"

She said quickly, "No. I hate them."

That had been Leslie's favorite drink. One after another. Pitchers of them. A swift, interrupting thought wondered where he was, where he was drinking now. It would be in some very sordid place. Or it might be that he was in an institution again. It would have to be a public one. You can't help it—that's all over—Manhattans—"you should learn to let yourself go, Barby, try another Manhattan." She had, more than once.

"A Daiquiri. Rum's for Christmas," she told Kenneth.

Kenneth ordered, and settling back in his chair to observe, saw a man he knew.

"There's Ben Whitney. Old Ben. I've known Ben for years! I'd like him to meet you. Excuse me a minute, darling."

Barbara watched her husband cross the room, reminding herself that was who he was, for the memory of Leslie had scratched her mind unpleasantly. It was horrid speculation. Did Leslie have anyone to turn to now, to help him—to exploit and borrow from? He always had people. There was always someone to believe something could be done with him. Nothing could. He couldn't be counted upon, not ever. But to think of what Christmas for him must be now when—that was why the man carrying the rocking horse had seemed so painfully familiar. There was the time Leslie brought one

[98]

home for Davy—oh, poor Davy—those few Christmases. Don't think of it. You'll get sad and spoil Kenneth's day. For Kenneth is very sensitive to every mood you have. He loves you, and it is the most wonderful thing that ever happened to you, to have him love you. Look—how handsome he is, how glad that man is to see him. Kenneth looks just right in this room. It's a good background for him, worldly, distinguished, everything under control—he's much more than he looks, not so cut and dried as most of these men. He's very emotional. That candle! He'd have gone back and lit one, if I'd let him. To him it's just a picturesque notion, of course. He really believes that we put something over. He has no idea that anything was lost.

Kenneth was bringing his friend to meet her. She became very completely young Mrs. Craig, attractive in the firm, soft black wool that men always admired, wearing a pale pink camellia, the trademark of Ken's love, at the top hook of the jacket. How beautiful she is, thought Kenneth. She's a beauty when you see her close up, Ben Whitney's thought agreed.

"Well, to be honest, only two weeks," she admitted, laughing.

"The best two weeks of my life—so far—" said Kenneth.

"I don't wonder at that at all."

"Ben's just back from South America, he tells me. Sit down and have a drink with us."

"I wish I could. But I have to get out to the country in time for dinner." His eyes stayed on the provocative camellia, the beauty of the throat above it. "We'll have to get together while you're in New York."

"Where were you in South America?"

"Buenos Aires mostly. We have some clients down there."

"Ben's a lawyer," explained Kenneth. "On the upper levels now. But I knew him when."

Ben Whitney laughed. "From what I hear, nobody's keeping you down. But speaking of upper levels, you should see the way they live down there. Estates big as whole counties up here. Almost feudal. You get out in the country and there's a medieval feel

[99]

about the way the people live. Uneducated, priest-ridden—of course, the priests don't want the people to be educated. That's too dangerous."

"Why?"

"The priests don't want to lose their soft jobs." Whitney laughed again, and Ken smiled. But Barbara said, "I've always found that priests do more for uneducated people than anyone else does. I'm a Catholic myself."

Whitney sobered instantly, almost to stiffness. "I hope I didn't say anything that seemed offensive. Of course down there it's a different situation from anything in this country. Well, Ken, I must run along. This certainly has been fine. I'm awfully glad to have met you, Mrs. Craig."

After he had left she said, "That was a little disastrous. I'm sorry."

"Of course he had no idea you were a Catholic."

"You think I should have let it pass?"

"I don't know. I don't think it mattered too much. He was just giving his impression."

"But it was a wrong impression."

"Sure of that, darling? You've not been there."

"I know that. But I've seen plenty of ignorant people. I often heard just the same thing, that they're priest-ridden. I suppose maybe it's true. But without their religion those people would have nothing at all. It's the Church that gives them the only beauty and hope they get. It takes them through birth and marriage and death. What have they got but the Church and their priests?"

"Ben didn't mean anything. Don't get excited about it."

"I could have let it pass. But that's so cowardly. We were taught to defend the Church."

"Never mind now. You did, at the drop of the hat. Ben didn't know what hit him."

"I suppose, as things are, I'm a pretty queer person to defend it. Not too good an advocate."

"Let's drop the whole thing," he said. "Let's enjoy ourselves."

"I spoiled the afternoon for you, didn't I? And embarrassed you in front of your friend. I'm sorry it had to happen. But I don't like the idea of anyone being called priest-ridden, Ken. My father always used to say that the Braniffs weren't."

"Then what are you making such a fuss about?"

"Your friend saying that priests didn't want people to be educated."

Kenneth Craig was silent.

"You believe that too, don't you?" she asked. "But, after all, it was the Catholic Church that kept learning alive for centuries. Monks kept the records and made the books and illuminated them and taught the princes."

"Sure—the princes."

"They had to begin somewhere. Now the same orders of monks are teaching in high schools and colleges, and the nuns teach parochial schools. It isn't true that they don't want people to be educated."

"Not if it's done their way," said Craig.

"You mean—"

"I think we need another drink," he said.

"No, that wouldn't make me any clearer. Or more consistent. Let's go! Let's walk all the way back, shall we? I love the streets at this time of night."

They often argued and disagreed on many subjects. This should not matter. The incident left no mark on her spirit that he could see. She was more gay and swift of sight than ever as they walked back. A tired-looking woman dropped a bundle. Kenneth picked it up for her and retied the string around it in a doorway.

The woman wished them a Merry Christmas. Bareheaded boys, young girls, wearing bright head scarfs like peasants, mingled with ladies in mink and men who must be of importance.

"I feel like a Christmas card," she cried, laughing. "Let's find the gayest place in town tonight."

It was too bad about the Midnight Mass. Very carefully they did not comment on it afterward but merely let it be over. If they had gone earlier, and had better places in the cathedral, it might have been different, she thought afterward. Or it might have been wiser to have waited and gone to a Low Mass on Christmas day by herself. But Ken had not wanted to part with her on Christmas Eve.

As it was, they were packed wetly into a crowd at the back of the open vestibule. There were throngs of people and soft snow melted from coats everywhere. They sat on emergency folding chairs and the service seemed far away and unreal even to Barbara, who could only think that to Kenneth it must seem mummery indeed. In front of them was a woman who had come to see the service as if it were a show. She would not kneel nor bend her head. The service was long, the sermon a distant monologue on conditions in the world at the time of the Birth in Bethlehem.

Barbara heard the bells ring as the Canon of the Mass began and the time of Sacrifice approached. She tried to think of that alone, to recapture the feeling which she always used to have on Christmas, something like mental identification with the watchers and the shepherds. But it was impossible tonight. She was conscious of Kenneth beside her, uncomfortable, and seeing and hearing so little that he must not be aware of either beauty or mystery.

The congregation began to move. Most of them were going down the aisles. Kenneth stood up. "Do we go now? Is it over?"

She shook her head and whispered, "Not yet. They're going to Communion. We wait."

It seemed endless. She bowed her head a little, not too far lest he think she was suffering. The floor on which she was kneeling was damp and cold. Kenneth shifted, leaned on his other knee, and she thought, with a sudden flash of wild mirth, that he would only think this was badly organized.

Lifting her eyes, she saw the peace on the face of a woman returning from the altar. An old man. A girl. A boy with his mother and father. A cripple. A soldier. A woman waxen as death. A young husband and wife, their virtue a little smug on their faces. A woman in a cheap fox coat and bright blonde hair, whose recently shed sins were still obvious. A fat college boy. A Frenchwoman.

All kinds of people, yet she could not join them. Were her sins so much worse than those of some of these communicants? Surely, even humbly, they could not be. All the wickedness of the city must have washed through those confessionals this afternoon. But she could not enter one with any hope of absolution. How unfair! How cruel!

Why did it matter so much? She could pray even if she could not share the mystery. Why do you suffer, she asked herself? Is it because you are breaking a habit? Or because you are afraid, afraid because you defied the authority of the men who run this organization, as Kenneth calls it?

No, not that. She knew it was not the pain of a habit torn loose or fear. It was the lack of what all those people had, what all of them had felt, in some degree, if only for an instant, if only between their sins. There had been at least an instant when something better than living descended into their souls, a bright instant of grace for each in that motley procession. And the instant had passed by her forever.

She felt outcast. It was feeling rather than thought. Her prayers were heavy. They would not lift.

"What a crowd it draws!" was all Kenneth said about the service afterward. Barbara said nothing. As if he guessed it had been depressing for her, Kenneth set himself to make her think of other things, of themselves.

"It's our first Christmas, darling, and it's the happiest one I've ever had in my life."

"Truly, Ken?"

"Absolutely. I couldn't ask for anything better than Christmas with you. With you as my wife. Are you as happy as I am?"

"Merry Christmas, Ken!"

Now, at a distance from the church, it could be merry. She must see to that, turn her thoughts to the man who loved and needed her. She must not be emotional about what she had given up, renounced. She must be adult, rational. It was over now. An hour from now, before then perhaps, this nightmare of losing and feeling lost would be gone.

She brushed her hair, decorated herself with the ice-blue satin of the new negligee and came out to Kenneth in the sitting room.

"I think it's time for a few Christmas presents," he said. He was piling packages on the table beside a little stylized tree which she had bought yesterday.

He was trying to distract her. So he must have guessed that she was troubled. He was trying to take her mind off the service, which must have seemed utterly flat and unspiritual. Be a help to him, she told herself. Don't begin this first Christmas drearily. After all, you've been to church. You've done what you could. Of course lots of people go to Communion but lots of others don't. Her spirit mounted, springing from one defense to another, building them up as she went along.

"Open this first," he told her.

"And here's one for you."

"For me, darling? When you've given me everything already?"

She could feel the tears in her eyes but the comfort in her heart. It was all right now, when he said that.

Chapter Eight

This is where I belong now, Barbara reminded herself as her eyes opened, for sometimes, even after two months, the pleasant, almost elegant bedroom seemed strange and surprised her. This is home, she assured herself. I have a completely new daily life and it begins here every morning. This room will be my friend for years. A close, intimate friend, storing away dear, secret memories and being the scene of many of them. The master's bedroom—the mistress's bedroom too. Already it has forgotten that anyone else ever lived in this room except us. It has forgotten that its walls were once foolishly pink and it loves its new silver-gray color and its new furniture and the two people who call to each other, and laugh and make love here. I want every room in the house to enjoy its life but this must be the happiest one of all. He must never dread coming into it, she thought, and I shall never hate to have him come.

That thought touched a memory she did not want to keep and she quickly covered it up with another, thinking of the day before her. I'll take the first shower and have plenty of time to get breakfast. Ken can't get over the fact that I like to make breakfast for him and expect to do it. He figured on at least one servant. But I don't need any, not at least until we have children. When he was married before, he used to have to buy his breakfast at a lunchroom on the way down to his office. Nina was a sloven, a slut too, I guess. Pretty desolate for him. He's not desolate now. And yet she must have had some kind of attraction. Or was it loyalty? For he didn't leave her. She was the one who walked out on him. Who was it—it was Carol Harrison who hinted to me that Nina may still be in love with Ken. It won't do her much good now.

Barbara slid out of bed, and automatically her lips shaped a prayer as she did. The always rather distracted but habitual one on rising—"offer Thee the prayers, works, and sufferings of this day." She considered the works. She thought, I'm going to see the doctor this morning and find out. He can tell by this time surely. And tonight there is the Shrove Tuesday dinner dance. Evenings by ourselves are more fun. I like them better and so does Ken. But we'll probably have a good time when we get there.

The little stir woke Craig. He lay comfortably listening, thinking that it was Barbara in the shower. His glance repossessed with satisfaction the appointments of the room, the things which he had bought for her and their home. They were all handsome pieces, the tiers of modern chests, the beds and desk that had cost more than they meant to spend, the soft chaise lounge where he so liked to have her lie sometimes, deliciously within reach. There were books still unread or half-read, and a pot of pink violets blooming in the midst of them. She's done a grand job, he thought gratefully. It's a real home. It ran into money but I'll catch up with it

[105]

all right and it's a good investment. We had to take our place here in town. That's what the boss had in mind, of course, when he urged the place on me.

It was the kind of setting Barbara should have. Craig thought of the apartment where he used to call on her. It seemed even less attractive as he looked back on it, and contrast rose again very pleasantly. She had someone to take care of her now and was through with that rather fly-by-night phase. Everybody likes her, he thought. They're all glad we're married. I haven't heard a word of criticism. Of course there might be some talk I wouldn't hear. But apparently now that the thing is done, all the fuss quieted right down. As I was sure it would. Barbara herself doesn't worry the way she did about that religious business. She had herself worked up to a point of hysteria, before we were married, and even in New York the thing worried her. But now she has too much else to keep her busy.

She's very sensitive. Spiritual. She keeps right after it. Every Sunday, rain or shine, off she goes to church. I couldn't make her stay home. And prayers. I never saw a woman pray like that every night. I didn't know that anyone except children still did it.

His thoughts ran on cheerfully. One of these days, if he happened to meet Bishop Tarrant, he would try to iron out any memory of unpleasantness or difference of point of view. If he had a chance to talk frankly with the Bishop, or the thing came up naturally, he might explain that he had no personal resentment. He understood the organization problem that had been involved and hoped he hadn't been too importunate. He might say that he understood the Catholic Church better from seeing what a strong hold it had on Barbara and observing her devotion to it. No, that might be piling it on a little. Better not say too much but merely be friendly. Sooner or later some of those priests or the Bishop himself would want some subscription or favor from the railroad. Let it rest. Everything was working out all right. Barbara was no longer so disturbed. She was in better shape than she had been for months before they were married, more adjusted, happier. That was the main thing.

Nothing he could ever do for her would be too much. His mind filled with so much gratitude for what she had done to his own life that it flooded with yearning to tell her again how much he loved her. Sometimes in the middle of the day, in his office, that same mood would come over him. This was marriage as it should be, as he hadn't been sure it could be, orderly, honest, gay and yet with unlimited secret sweetness when they were most intimately together. He knew what he could expect. Yet he never quite knew. She plays so fair, he thought. She doesn't pretend it's a concession to love her husband.

Barbara came out of the shower, half wrapped in one of the biggest towels, looking very clean and young and natural.

"You know, this is the best part of the day," he said.

"I've heard you say that at other hours."

He laughed. "I guess so. Well, I always mean it, don't I? What is the best part of the day for you?"

She remembered that she had been taught in the convent school that the best hour should always be the one of final evening prayer when a sinless day might be given back to God. Easy to be sinless then. You were always scraping the bottom of your conscience to be sure it was perfectly clean.

"I don't play favorites like that. It depends on how the hours behave themselves. Or how I do."

At eleven she was in the office of Dr. Roush. That was a wonderful hour.

"There doesn't seem to be any doubt about it, Mrs. Craig."

"You're quite sure?"

He smiled at her eagerness. "Some women have a different expression when they say that. Yes, I'm sure. The womb is closed."

She sat treasuring the fact. "I was a little afraid. Because it's been so long. And I'm not very young."

"You're plenty young enough. Especially since it isn't a first child. Let me see." He looked at her record. "Not yet thirty-one That's young by most standards. And you had your first child—"

"When I was twenty-two. He was nine pounds."

"We don't believe in their being quite so large now. We'll keep an eye on that."

"Is there anything I shouldn't do?"

"Not just yet. Lead a normal life. We'll suggest a diet later. You'll find it all in the little book the nurse will give you. Go ahead in your usual way. Get plenty of sleep and don't worry about anything for there is nothing to worry about."

She would tell Ken tonight when he came home. Not on the telephone, though it would be hard to wait. She might go to his office and tell him now. It would be fun to see his face if she walked in and quite casually mentioned that his child was on the way. But no—when he came home, she would tell him. That was the proper place. Under his own roof, his paid-for roof, which he had provided for them.

She walked along the street feeling very important and rather amused at her own secret pride. She was conscious of every child she passed, each one clutching its mother's hand. There had been a long time when she could hardly bear to look at very little boys in snowsuits. After David died. But now it was different. David would always be locked in her mind and heart but she would not begrudge women their children any more.

Quite properly she felt hungry. Kenneth told her to go to the Town Club for lunch whenever she was shopping in the city or doing errands there. But today she would not, for the big dance was to be held there tonight. Barbara did not feel like meeting any of the people whom she would be sure to meet and talk to tonight. Twice a day was too often for most of those conversations. What she might do, she decided, was to stop at the office of the Social Agencies, find out how they were getting on without her and perhaps take Sally out to lunch.

The office was dreary as usual. The Board never spent anything on office equipment that it did not have to spend, for fear it might

[108]

seem that money was being diverted from the purposes for which it had been charitably subscribed. Her desk had been moved from its former place and Barbara felt that, with the rearrangement of furniture, she had completely disappeared from the office. But Sally Frick welcomed her with vehemence.

"Have I missed you in this charnel house!" she exclaimed. "And how smooth and lovely you look! I hear you have a beautiful home."

"It's a good house. I want you to come and see it and meet Ken. I hoped you'd come to the wedding."

"I intended to come. I did appreciate being asked, Barbara. But I didn't have anything very snappy to wear, and I thought I'd stick out like a sore thumb and bring down the social average —but believe me, it wasn't because I wasn't thinking of you, and pulling for you!"

"I know you were and thanks."

"Some people around here made me pretty sick about that time. That ghoul Anna Kelly really got on my nerves. I was glad that you went ahead and showed everybody that you weren't letting anybody run your life for you. When Kelly tried to say something to me afterward, I shut her up pretty quick. For my money, most of her gripe was just plain sour grapes. Not a thing in the world but jealousy."

"Well, she thought it was."

"Some of those old girls can't bear to think of a woman having a man and heaven too!"

Barbara laughed and asked how things had been going.

"We've been up to our ears. I've been spending the morning trying to make sense of this Rigg's situation. You remember those two—James and his unhappy Pearl?"

"We set them up in a flat with a budget and two jobs just before I left. Didn't it work out?"

"No—he's drinking again. Lost that job. And she's not well. One of the children is getting to be a queer character, I think.

[109]

They ought to break up that family before somebody gets going with an axe."

"I didn't think it would stay together."

"Waste of money and effort," summarized Sally. "And we're shorthanded around here. Jane Foster went abroad, you know, to do a job for UNRRA."

"Did she really? That's what I was fishing for a year ago."

"It happened just after you left. They needed somebody and an SOS for a case worker came through to Mrs. Cunningham. She mentioned you at the time and wished you were available. If I weren't married I'd have tried to go myself. It wasn't a job that paid much but I would have seen a piece of Europe anyway. But of course I couldn't leave Jack. Not for that long."

"I've got a fellow that I can't leave either. Come out and let me buy you a lunch, Sally. We'll go to the Maisonette at the hotel for a change."

"A change indeed. From the drugstore counter to splendor. That's what it is to marry money," said Sally.

At six o'clock Kenneth came up the newly carpeted stairs to their bedroom carrying, as Barbara could tell when she heard his careful tread, a tray with two cocktail glasses and the small shaker that held just enough for the two of them. The matched set was made of handsomely engraved and signed glassware and had been a wedding present from the David Ryes.

Barbara was in the dressing room, among her cupboards and mirrors. She was almost ready for the party. He sat down comfortably where he could watch her through the open door, and stirred the drink to tempt her.

"This is the best hour of the day," he said.

She came to laugh at him. "You said that this morning."

"I've changed my mind. This is it."

"What have you got there?"

"Just one apiece to start us off and get us in the mood."

"Just one," she agreed, "because this is a momentous evening."

"It ought to be a good party. You look very beautiful."

"This is my best dress. I hardly ever have a chance to wear it. Do you think it's a little too ingénue?"

"No—lovely." He was looking at her bare shoulders rising out of the bodice of the white lace dress.

"You've seen it before. A year ago on New Year's Eve."

"That was the night I fell in love with you. But I didn't dream then that one day I'd be seeing you put on that dress."

"Take a good look. It will be a long time before you see me put it on again. I won't be able to get into it."

He said, "You're not a pound heavier. I should know."

She lifted her arms to him, "I'm going to be! What a vulgar way to tell you! I should be knitting something small. I'm going to have a baby. We are. That's what I meant by its being a momentous night. Are you glad, Ken? Very glad? Could you possibly be as glad as I am! It makes everything so right!"

Pride, tenderness, devotion, a little awe. She saw and heard and felt his answer. He had never known a woman to feel like that about pregnancy. He had seen nothing but dread of it, heard refusal, calmed panic.

They considered not going to the dance and staying at home to rejoice. But she was already wearing the white lace dress and their excitement seemed too big for the house. So Craig dressed in a blur of exhilaration and pride, and they drove into the city to the handsome club where the Shrove Tuesday party was always held. Cars were already ranked along every surrounding street and a long line of them was still driving up to the opening in the long awning that guarded the ladies' entrance from too much public view. It was one of the more important social occasions of the year, a subscription dance arranged for a restricted list of patrons. Inside that general exclusiveness were the usual concentric circles of varying social importance.

The Town Club was famous throughout the region. Its name stood for wealth, conservation on the highest and most rigid levels, private gambling, social drinking where business subordinates could not see it being done, lodgings for men who were too important for the hotels, and fashionable entertaining. It was a men's club, with card and dining rooms where women were not allowed to enter. But at the other end of the building were the lounges, and amusing cocktail rooms, and the old gilded elevator that was out of date but too traditional to give up, and still creaked up to the ballroom with guests who for one reason or another could not use the red-carpeted stairs.

It had been organized by the grandfathers of many of the present members. Julian Braniff, in spite of his money, had not been asked to join it, for the early social leaders of the city had come from Eastern cities, where well-born Protestants did not mix with Catholics. His son John had joined the club in the heyday of his own fortunes but for him it was purely a business recognition. Barbara's mother was never one of the women who used the rooms for parties. She was always shy of the place.

Barbara had known it better, and unhappily, after she married Leslie Field. He was not native to the city and when he came there associated with a branch of an investment company, he had looked like an asset to local business and social life. No one could know that the perfect tailoring he came with was not paid for. Young as he was, he was put up for membership in the Town Club and voted in, on the argument that new blood would be a good thing for the organization. It turned out to be bad blood as well.

Barbara had trained herself to forget much of what had happened in connection with the Town Club and Leslie. She had to forget, if she was to go through that ladies' entrance again, and after he had been gone for several years she found she could do it, as if she were a different person from that girl whom Leslie Field kept in an agony of embarrassment so often. There were the times when Leslie had refused to go home, when they were not welcome, when they became a nuisance. She had to forget the scenes he had made, the fight with a steward, the bills that had piled up so insolently. But the worst thing, and the hardest to forget was the time he had insisted that they dine there together, and she had not known at the time that he had been asked to resign, practically been expelled from membership. In one of his secret rages, his brain on fire with crazy defiance, he had taken her as his protection, knowing that the steward would not want to insult his wife by refusing to serve them dinner.

He told her about it later. He said that they couldn't put him out of the club, that he was going to sue them if they tried it. He was obsessed with angers at his creditors and dreamed fantastic lawsuits. Barbara had tried to pay for the dinner. She sent ten dollars to the steward with a stiff little note, ten dollars that she got from selling a pin of her mother's. That was the first time she sold any jewelry. A year later she had none left.

She had vowed then that she would never enter the club again and even to pass it gave her, for a while, a slight feeling of nausea. But she got over that. She got over Leslie himself in time. He couldn't humiliate her any more, nor frighten her. Nor make her sick at heart with pity for him.

Tonight as she entered the Town Club she hardly thought back at all. She was Mrs. Kenneth Craig. She felt no one else. Her old selves had disappeared, the pretty Braniff girl who used to come here long ago to big parties and always felt a little out of them, the bewildered, ingenuous bride who had been the wife of a rascal and come here with him. Those selves were like empty houses which her mind might pass and remember without accuracy, thinking, yes, that was I, but what was it like when I lived in that self?

She knew the structure of parties like this as well as she knew the interior of the Town Club. Tables for dinner were reserved for various groups. Some of the groups were made up of old friends, some were glued together by mutual snobbery, others were composed of people trying to keep one another socially warm. The Kenneth Craigs were to sit at a table which had been organized by Carol Harrison. But it had surprised Barbara slightly to have had no invitation to a cocktail party beforehand. The crowd must have been drinking somewhere. People always gave themselves a start before coming to an affair at the club. Not that the omission mattered to Barbara. She preferred the drink at home with Kenneth. But she had vaguely wondered once or twice if there was one of the pre-parties being given by someone who did not know her and who had asked the rest of their group.

Now she saw Dudley Harrison, just being present as usual, without effort or effect. There were the two Ryes, and Blair Wyatt talking to a woman who was unfamiliar. Barbara did not know who she was. Yes, she did know. It took only an instant before she was sure. It had been a long time since she had seen the woman who had been Kenneth's wife. Barbara had believed that she would not know Nina Longman if she saw her. That was a mistake. She knew her almost at once and just as immediately realized why they had not been included in a cocktail party. Someone had not wanted to chance the combination of herself and Nina Longman.

Barbara was not sure what she was feeling as she recognized the other woman. She had to cover up any embarrassment. That was the first thing to do. To plaster it over with something. It was like feeling a curious personal exposure, and that must be hidden and not admitted.

Kenneth, beside her, muttered, "What the hell?"

There was Nina, once Mrs. Craig, now Mrs. Longman, who did not matter to him at all any more. Of course this happens all the time, Barbara told herself. It is a kind of joke now. Meeting your "ex." She would try to be casual about it, indifferent, coarse if she had to be. People were getting divorced by thousands and this situation was inevitable. Then why be unsophisticated? She had him once. You have him now. Why should it seem so shocking to see her, to be in the same room with a woman who had been Kenneth's wife?

She hadn't made him happy. She had been a rotten wife. She wasn't really beautiful. No, but she had something that must have attracted him once. He didn't like that kind of artificial, stylized woman. But he must have liked her, craved her. It is completely over. Is it ever over? Seeing her now, what does he remember? How she felt, how she looks under that dress?

[114]

"Hello, Dudley. Hello, Jennifer—Have we been keeping you waiting?—No, we had a drink or two—Of course, she'll have another, won't you, Barbara?—Looks like a good party—Your bride looks very beautiful, Kenneth—It's an old dress; I drag it out on Shrove Tuesday and New Year's Eve every year."

Some of it she said, and some of it the others were saying. It was all prelude. Were they watching, even in this noisy, moving crowd to see how Kenneth's wives would meet? She's not his wife and never was in the real sense of the word. Carol Harrison says that Nina is still in love with him. Kenneth loathes her. He's never been really happy before. He has told me that again and again. Here it comes, she comes. She's being quite deliberate. I wish I hadn't worn this dress. It's an ignorant dress, as if I wanted to be pretty.

"Why, Ken, how are you?"

Nina Longman gave him her hand, cased in the long black glove that reached to her shoulder, the one bare shoulder, the clever accent on flesh, like the one where her breasts could be seen parting. It was a black dress. It did not sparkle or float but it was exciting.

"I couldn't be better. And you?"

She said she was fine but her eyes made a little mockery of the words. Barbara wanted to hit their hands apart.

Nina let him go.

"Do you know my wife?"

My wife. That was what he should say to this woman. Thank you, Ken.

"Oh, yes," said Nina. "I think I must have." She made it a little vague as she turned to Barbara. "How are you? It's such fun to see you again."

She took the ordinary conventional words and made a memory and a situation out of them. She must have known Barbara, who had lived all of her life in St. Anthony. In a large city there are degrees of acquaintance, by friendship, social rank, by name or face. In Nina Longman's smooth words there was an overtone of condescension. It brought back part of childhood and girlhood to Barbara. She felt it again.

Since she was a child she had known that her place was not the highest in the little orbit where she lived. Not the highest though it was a better place. The other class in dancing school, the convent school instead of Foxcroft or Miss Hall's—those were the things that made the difference in one way, just as the knowledge of greater spiritual grace made the difference in another. She had been taught in school and she had heard from the altar, since she was a child, that worldliness did not matter. For the poorest tramp, with grace in his heart, would be closer to God than the rich man who was indifferent to Him. The scrubwoman might be better than the society woman and the characteristics of both were often vigorously described in sermons.

When she was a little girl that had seemed almost romantic to Barbara. She had once conceived a pious admiration for their own laundress. Later the same sort of sermons seemed not quite realistic, more true to theory than practice. Now she understood the defensiveness bound up in many such homilies, and the comfort they gave to the bruises inflicted by a life set up on the worldly plan.

To have Nina Longman even make her remember that early awareness of being diminished angered Barbara. She wouldn't smile. She couldn't. She managed a question.

"Are you living here now, Mrs. Longman?"

"No. I have to live in my mining village."

"For how much of the year?" asked Kenneth cynically.

"Quite enough."

"Where's Bill tonight?"

"He's driving down. He'll be here later. As usual, there's strike trouble. But I didn't want to miss the Shrove Tuesday party. So I came by myself and rounded up a few people beforehand. I was going to ask you for a drink but I thought it might be confusing. This place is still very farmer. Would you have come?"

She asked Kenneth but Barbara answered, "No. I'm very farmer that way."

Her voice was not smooth like those of the other two and Kenneth put a hand on her arm, asking for control. Barbara tightened but did not quite pull it away. She felt crude. And good.

Nina Longman said, and she made it sound like wistfulness, whatever it was. "Perhaps you're right. Wise." With a finishing look, her eyes silently described Barbara's gown, wrote off her beauty just as the girls in the top circles used to write off goodness as something very middle-class. It felt the same to Barbara for a second. It was the same baffling appearance of defeat, in spite of being right and so certainly winning.

"I hope you'll be very happy," said Nina. "Ken has great talent as a husband."

"Oh skip it, Nina!"

Nina had turned away before he said that. She was the one who broke up the conversation, not Barbara, who was left trembling because she hadn't.

Kenneth felt the quiver, and tried to steady it.

"Don't pay any attention to her. She always talks like that."

"She must have been very amusing to have around. Let me go. Don't hold on to me."

"I'm sorry, darling. Especially tonight. I wanted this to be a grand time."

"I won't eat at the same table with her."

"Let's duck out—shall we? Let's go."

"No, I'm not going to be driven away by her. That's what she'd enjoy. Hello, Blair. Yes, I'd love a drink. I'm a little bored. I've just been listening to Nina and Kenneth reminisce about their private life."

Kenneth hated that. His face showed that he did. But he deserved it. He shouldn't have let her in for that. How could he have helped it? Her thoughts attacked him, fought back for him.

At the bar she heard Nina's voice, poised and penetrating.

"I shall give it up entirely for Lent. Why, of course. I follow all the seasons of the Church."

"The pieties have become sophisticated," remarked Blair. "Nina must have run into Evelyn Waugh somewhere. Or perhaps she's grooming poor old Bill to be a prince of the Church. I suppose the Longmans can well afford it and a papal title is at least something. In France they look down their noses at it but it's good publicity over here."

He might laugh. Barbara couldn't. For this was the very deepest injustice, to have Nina Longman preen herself, claiming to be a Catholic. It was more than a claim. They had let her become a Catholic. When she wanted to be. When Bill Longman had put up a fight over it. They had allowed it, in spite of the personal record of Nina herself and the history of fallen away Catholics in her family.

Barbara knew certain facts about Nina's family, although there had been no personal friendship between the Braniffs and the Howes. There were some intimate things that were apt to be public property like the fact that Mrs. Howe "should have been a Catholic." Catholics always made a point of identifying prominent apostates, and passing information about them from one to another. Nina's mother had come of a Catholic family but she had sloughed off her religion when she married a Protestant. The Protestants had not paid much attention to that but the Catholics marked it down. Mrs. Howe never went to Church. Nina was not sent to parochial school, nor even to any instruction class of the kind arranged for children of mixed marriages in order to give them at least the crumbs that fell from the table of religion.

But she had been baptized. That had been done by a priest in the hospital where she was born, and probably allowed by her mother because it had been a hard birth and in her weakened condition Mrs. Howe had not been able to shake off all fears of hell for herself and limbo for her baby. There had been no follow-up of the baptism after Mrs. Howe was well enough to resume her social position, but twenty-seven years later the fact had given Nina a very strategical advantage. For by that time she wanted to marry Bill Longman and the prerequisite was not only a divorce from Kenneth Craig but a complete annulment of her first marriage. It

[118]

had been worked out. Since she was a Roman Catholic by baptism, even though through her mother's fault she had not been brought up as one, she was held to belong in the faith, and her marriage to Craig was not valid in the sight of the Catholic Church. It was not an impediment to marrying Bill Longman, and for the sake of that outcome Nina submitted, with the extraordinary effect of wistfulness that she could conjure up, to the religious instruction and admonition which had been skipped in her childhood.

Barbara had been glad when Kenneth first told her about that. He was puzzled and critical. He said, "They doped it out somehow," with scarcely concealed contempt for all the parties to the bargain. But it let him out completely. And Barbara, trying to explain Catholic marriage laws—that was the first time she made the effort—had been pleased to have his marriage to Nina erased until only the stain of a passionate and mistaken love affair was left. It happened in the first days of their own love, when it was a marvel to be together, even if Barbara could not remarry. Later, as the desire for marriage grew in both Craig and Barbara, the solution of Nina's problem seemed to make an exception in their own case all the more probable.

But there had been no solution allowed for them. Now that did not seem to matter to Kenneth, thought Barbara. It does to me. The feeling that she was suffering alone came over her and the loneliness curdled to resentment all at once, and for the first time. It was the sight of Nina, the fact of her. Bill Longman had managed to put things straight when he wanted to marry Nina. Kenneth had assured her that concessions would be made after they were married. And where were they? He hadn't cared enough to follow the matter up, had not cared that much for her restoration. He never thought of it any more. She knew she was unfair and that only added to the confusion already caused by the shock to her joy tonight, and this sudden insecurity which had possessed her.

This was no time or place for such thoughts. But Nina Longman's lightly declared orthodoxy had reopened the wound. Wyatt

[119]

knew that he must have pressed on some hurt for his light words left Barbara serious. Almost tense, he thought. Some women create drama. They can't help it. They do it unconsciously. She's one of them. He was not thinking of Nina Longman's effects but of the woman beside him, in her soft, sweet dress. She was distressed but it seemed to him that it was because her happiness was so sensitive. He was aware of Craig, who, though now on the other side of the room, was hardly able to take his attention from his wife for a minute. Wyatt said to himself with shrewd insight, I suppose it's hard for them to get together in some ways. For one thing he's a very Protestant American type and she comes from a long line of obedient Catholics. Hard for her too, I suppose, to take the fact of Nina, who can't give a tinker's damn for Bill Longman and has deliberately planted herself here tonight to stir up the old fires.

He decided, Barbara had better harden up. After all, she let herself in for this. He put the first part of it in so many words, aloud.

"Harden up?" she repeated and was quickly back with him, out of her own thoughts. "Why? You think I'm upset because Nina's here?"

"Aren't you?"

"Yes. But not for the reason you think. It's not that kind of jealousy."

"What kind?"

"The light comedy kind. I'm not worried about competition, in that sense. I'm not trying to hold my husband, you know."

"It doesn't appear to be necessary."

"But," she said rather stumblingly, "it's the cheapening of a situation like this. I take marriage seriously. You never have."

"My dear girl," said Blair, "I probably take marriage more seriously than anyone here tonight. I regard it as the most important thing that civilized life has left to bank on. I entirely agree with the Church on that point—with my own and to a large extent with yours."

"But you've dodged marriage for yourself."

"Not dodged. I'm still a student of it. When I know enough, I shall probably take up the practice."

She finally laughed. "Does it take so long to learn, Blair?"

He asked, "Aren't you still learning?"

"Yes. I surely am."

"In fact you've learned the hard way. People dose themselves with marriage without knowing what they are taking. They read what's on the bottle and in the romances. It will make them sleep better, have more energy, increase the appetite, cure snake bite. They dose themselves and look at the results. I propose to know what goes into my system."

"You do take it seriously."

"To me," said Blair, launching into his subject, "marriage is too often confused with sex, which does quite well without it. I may disagree with your Church that it is primarily an institution for the propagation of the family. I would broaden the base myself. I feel that while propagation enters into it, the social orientation of the family is the important thing. The future may depend on that."

She thought, I am going to have a child. For a minute, I'd forgotten.

"I have been slow to marry," said Blair, in a flowery but serious way, "for many reasons, most of them ones that my friends don't appreciate. For one thing, I consider that if you marry, you give up the right to change the beneficiary. The history of the world shows that civilization exists only because sound family units have been able to perpetuate themselves. The family is practically the only incorruptible institution left."

"The Church."

"Oh my dear girl," protested Blair, "you know better than that. No—governments go bad in church or state, people are subject to rot and to every pest that flies or crawls. But the family, in spite of all attempts to destroy it, remains the vessel of the best social motives that man is capable of. The primitive tribes found that out pretty quickly. The Russians had to come back to it, tighten up their

[121]

laws on marriage. They will probably decide before too long that it's got to be indissoluble."

"You're talking to the perfect person about that."

"I'm not being personal. Besides, you know as well as I do, that you and Ken will never be fully satisfied as long as Leslie lives."

"You're quite wrong, Blair. We're completely happy."

"I wasn't speaking of happiness."

"What did you mean?"

He paused, looked at her, went on. "You know what I mean. You live in a temporary adjustment, entirely legal, respectable, delightful. But you, with your background, would feel it to be temporary. No doubt, before too long, it can be made permanent quite simply."

"I never feel it's temporary—not for a moment!"

He lifted his glass to her and left the argument there. "Good."

"And how about her?" asked Barbara thoughtfully, looking at Nina. "If there's anything in what you say, where does she come in?"

He said, very lightly now, for this had gone quite far enough but he could not resist a little more, "She came in tonight, didn't she? Odd, isn't it? That marriage was annulled too. But, as you said yourself, it was something different from jealousy that disturbed you. You didn't say what. A question of claim? A not quite clear title?"

"My title is quite clear enough for me," she answered defiantly.

Barbara rarely drank much, hardly ever too much. She had learned discipline in that respect during the years when she had to get Leslie home somehow, and maintained it in the later period when she had to take care of herself. Kenneth had told her it was one of her great charms. Tonight she discarded it. People blurred as the party went on, rising shrilly to a discord of voices and glasses and music. Dinner was telescoped, and seemed to have no length. She sat at the same table with Nina Longman after all, out of her sight, but Kenneth sat opposite where he could see them both. She felt that she looked like a frowsy Irish girl. They never forgot that you were of Irish descent and a Catholic, not in this crowd, but just the

[122]

same you were proud of it. I don't think this way usually. It's because she's here. Not jealous—exactly as I said to Blair—and he said—

"Yes, it's a wonderful party."

What makes a party wonderful? A crazy, rotten situation?

"No, of course not, Ken. It's too early to go home."

"Are you all right?"

"Don't I look all right?"

Bill Longman came in before they left the table. He had a big body, not well held, and a submissive face with small, self-conscious eyes. The face of a parochial school boy, Barbara's thought flashed through the fog in her mind. She saw Nina get up to welcome him—a nice gesture—Ken would be watching that kiss, thinking of how she used to—no, he wasn't looking. Why wasn't he looking? Everyone else was.

Now it was much later.

"Aren't you ready to go home, dear?"

"Why? Are you ashamed of me?"

"Oh darling, I just want to take care of you. I have to take care of you now, you know."

"Then why don't you? Bill Longman takes care of his wife."

"Let's not talk about them."

"He even gave her a religion. Did you hear her telling about what a wonderful Catholic she is?"

"Darling, not so loud. Let's talk it over when we get home."

"I'm the renegade. The apostate. Lent begins tomorrow. It's today. I used to keep Lent very strictly. Did you know that? Even last year I did, I could."

"Come on, Barbara. I've had enough of this brawl and so have you."

In the little gilded elevator they had bad luck. The Longmans and several other people were also leaving and pushed in after them, crowding it to capacity. Bill Longman looked as if liquor had made him uncertain of time or place but Nina was clear. The evening had worn her down almost to ugliness but her outline was firm.

Wrapped in the soft fur of the coat that Kenneth had given her, Barbara stood silent as the elevator creaked down, unaware of her beauty that surprised Longman, and infuriated Nina, and would have made Kenneth proud if he had not been so worried about this final encounter.

"Good night," said Nina, perhaps to Barbara. "Good night, Ken. It was good to see you."

Barbara spoke so that everyone who was in the lobby could hear. Carefully. "I want you to remember that your marriage to Kenneth was annulled. It doesn't exist. It never did."

Somebody caught back a laugh.

"She's—"

"Obviously."

"Just the same—"

Kenneth tucked a robe around Barbara and closed her side of the car. She heard him draw a long breath as he turned on the ignition. It broke her anger and she wanted to weep, but would not let the collapse come.

"Did you mind my saying that to her?" she asked in a tightened voice.

"I don't care what you said to her. It doesn't matter. The whole evening was a mess, with her turning up like that and spoiling everything for you."

"I felt like one of your harem. Not the first wife."

"For God's sake, Barbara, don't say things like that! Can't you forget it now?"

"But what I minded most of all is her being a Catholic."

"I know," he muttered. "It shows what poppycock it all is."

"No. You don't understand."

"Please—don't start that now," he begged. "I want you to rest. Think about what you told me tonight before we left the house, about that youngster we're going to have in a few months."

"Less than seven."

"You know you'll have to take care of yourself from now on."

"I will—I always do—you know, it was just tonight—did Nina ever drink too much or is she too clever?"

"I don't want to discuss her."

"But tell me that—did she?"

"Why sure she did. And worse."

"Worse. But even then you—"

"Cut it, darling, cut it."

"She felt like evil," said Barbara. "Like one of the evil spirits roaming through the world seeking whom they might devour."

"What are you talking about?"

"It's just part of a prayer," she sighed in a fumbling way.

Chapter Nine

Theodore Kilmey, in his Chicago office and with an important project before him, was not the jovial host of his private car parties nor the gentle husband that his wife could make him. His long, narrow face was alert almost to suspicion. A glance would reach out of his bright blue eyes, gather up the reactions of his companions and retreat without leaving a trace of his own. When he spoke it was with an almost exaggerated deference that thinly concealed control of this situation and only pretended to humility.

"I may be wrong," he stated. "I may be misguided," he added, coming upon that word and liking the sound of it better. He had the Irish love of a long word instead of a short one. "But in my opinion we need a committee of the railroad industry to study our major problems. It is my belief that it could function with far-reaching results and without unduly disturbing these who guard so assiduously the virtue of the Antitrust laws."

They grinned more or less. George Van Wick, who had come on from Pennsylvania for this meeting, said, "The fact is, that if privately owned railroads are going to continue to exist, we've got to stand up on our hind legs and fight for equality of regulation with the other transportation systems. The truckers and the commercial airlines are putting it all over us with subsidies of one sort and another. And we're paying for our own roadbeds. They don't."

"But we carry seventy percent of the load."

"Ninety percent in wartime. That's what the public doesn't realize."

"We carried the whole army. And they'll be right back again in case of more trouble."

Someone regained the point at issue. "This committee, Ted—as you see it, it would be a kind of steering committee for the industry?"

"I wouldn't go so far. A purely advisory group who would meet in occasional friendly conference," said Kilmey and they grinned again.

"The idea is all right," agreed Roy Hubbard, whose rails were in the far West, "but like all those setups, it's entirely a matter of who is on the committee. This may cost us money before we're through, and there's no use wasting it on men who haven't the power or influence to do the job and do it right. Understand me, I'm for it in principle."

"I'm in accord with that, Roy. The group should be handpicked. Active experienced men are what we want. Including some of the ones who are coming to the top and going to carry on for the next twenty years."

"Ted will have to head it up."

The seven important railroad men in the room all knew that was what Kilmey intended to do. This was his baby.

"I agree to that."

"Why doesn't Ted pick his own committee?"

"I assure you, gentlemen," said Kilmey, ornately, "I am not looking for any new job for myself. Certainly not for one that doesn't carry a salary. Frankly, if I go home and tell my wife, tell Mrs. Kilmey, that I've taken on another responsibility, I'm not going to be in high favor in my own house. Any one of your gentlemen here—"

"You're elected, Ted."

"Nominations are closed."

That much had been cut and dried beforehand. But now a great bulky man, who had not done more than listen so far, spoke. His voice created something like a space around him, as if the rest drew back to become an audience for the final words. Theodore Kilmey was important but Howard Burton was more so in the railroad industry, and if Burton had not come to this meeting, it would have been a flop. They all knew that too.

"It's a move that's overdue," Barton stated easily. "Every railroad man of any consequence has felt the lack of proper liaison between the lines all over the country. It's a job that needs doing and no one can initiate it better than Ted. He gets about, knows everybody. However, I think we should be willing to give him any suggestions we have as to the composition of this committee. This group will be representing us. We want it to do just that."

In overtone, Burton told them all that it was not to be turned over to Ted Kilmey completely.

"Well, if I know Ted, he didn't get us here without having an organization worked out pretty well beforehand," said Roy Hubbard, chuckling. "Let's have his ideas first."

"You're wrong about that," replied Kilmey, "except in one respect. If I head up that committee, Roy, it's with the understanding that you do the work."

They were jovial but not careless. This committee would be news, prestige, possibly power. It might also mean grief. If Howard Burton was yielding the top spot to Kilmey, that was because he was not quite sure how it would work out. Other names began to be suggested. Hubbard from the West, Savage inevitably from the South although he was not present. Van Wick agreed to serve, reluctantly. Kip Jones said he couldn't, because he had too many other obligations.

"How about John Miller of N. and E.? He's a good man and we should have someone from that neck of the woods."

"Miller's not too well, is he? I understand he's due to retire before long."

"There's a good man right under him."

"Croy?"

"No, Marcus Croy is ready to drop out too. A younger man. What's his name, Ted? I mean the fellow who used to work for you?"

"You mean Kenneth Craig?"

"That's the name. Why wouldn't he do if he's going to step into John Miller's job? We need younger men. And he's a veteran, isn't he?"

Mr. Kilmey said slowly, as if just making up his mind, "I don't think Kenneth Craig is quite our man. I had Leonard Thomson in mind."

"Who's he?"

"A very bright fellow. Actually the executive vice-president of the ore railroad up there. The one owned by the Longman interests. He's progressive. Got the whole line Diesel-operated."

"Wouldn't Craig be better? It's a larger railroad."

"The trouble with Craig," said Kilmey, "is that he's apt to be impulsive. Likely to act without considering results. I like the boy but I'm not sure he's too stable."

That settled it. Instability was a magic word to frighten off a group of businessmen. It might include anything, odd sex interests, a tendency to try to reform the world, a nervous condition. No one asked for further analysis. Burton looked a little more deeply silent but he made no comment. The name of Leonard Thomson went down with the others tentatively chosen.

It was later in the afternoon, when Mr. Burton and one of the others were en route back to New York, that Burton showed he had not forgotten the incident.

He shuffled the cards for a second round of smear at a quarter a point, and said, "I was rather sorry not to see young Craig put on

[128]

that committee. He's quite outstanding. Been a nice spot for him and it would have pleased John Miller too."

"I wondered about that at the time. Kilmey didn't want him though. That was obvious."

"You know what was back of that, don't you?"

The other man didn't.

"Religion," said Mr. Burton in a covering word. He broke it down into explanation slowly as he dealt the cards and didn't pick up his hand at once.

"Of course Ted Kilmey is a bigot. Craig married a divorced woman and that's why Kilmey soured on him."

"What business was it of Kilmey's?"

"The Catholics make a lot of things their business now. And there was more to it than that. David Rye told me the story when he was in New York. He's president of the First National up there and it was a local scandal evidently. The woman was a Catholic, and I guess the hierarchy mixed in and tried to break up the affair. Craig wouldn't stand for that. That's why Kilmey isn't doing anything to push Craig along. They tell me that Kilmey is in line for some papal decoration or honor—one of those things—and he might even be afraid that he might endanger it if he seemed to support Craig. Of course I couldn't drag that stuff out in the open today."

"I should say not."

"And it's a good committee as it stands. I didn't want Kilmey to overload it with Papists, that's why I insisted on electing that committee on the spot. That man he stuck in at the last may be a fish-eater. Could be. The Longmans are good Micks. The old man, the father, carried a shillelagh."

His companion laughed and then sobered. He said, "The Roman Catholics play it awfully close these days. You find it undercover everywhere. It's enough to scare you in a free country. What they'd like is to get control of everything, the school system, even the government if they could."

"Well, they haven't managed it yet," answered Mr. Burton with quiet confidence. "Ted Kilmey is a very good operator. And very likeable but I never would trust his judgment too far in an organization, because if the Pope gives the nod in some direction, that's the way Kilmey will go every time."

That afternoon Ted Kilmey was digesting triumph along with the excellent lunch he had given for his associates after the meeting. It was a far more complex and more profound feeling of attainment than the natural satisfaction of a self-made man presiding at last over the councils of a group of men whom he had once regarded with envy and awe. The influence which Mr. Kilmey now wielded had greater importance than money-making and that he knew. For, though it was his own success, it was also pooled with that of his fellow Catholics and built up what he thought of as his kind. It was the same consciousness of segregation and solidarity which Agatha Braniff felt and had mentioned, and which Barbara had protested.

There was a generous, impersonal element almost like patriotism in Mr. Kilmey's effort to gather power in the hands of those who were spiritually sound. There was an element of revenge—though that was not so conscious—revenge for past slights inflicted on Catholic boys and Catholic families. Also there was of course subtlety and political design in his methods, for the end was far from accomplished and it was bitterly opposed in many quarters. What Mr. Kilmey was constantly helping to do was to make a new pattern of life in America, in which the Catholic religion would be a respected, powerful, vocal force backed by strength widely distributed.

He had no illusions about many Catholics. He could despise a Catholic as well as a non-Catholic. Mr. Burton had called him a bigot and so he was, if the word was shorn of hypocrisy. Certainly Mr. Kilmey's faith was closed to argument. He believed in heaven and hell as real places and inevitable ends. He had complete credence that his beloved mother was with God, where he ultimately planned to join her, and be joined in time by all he most humanly loved. He did not claim to understand how this could be, but relied comfortably on the teaching that it was further virtue to believe without understanding. Although he accepted the often preached dogma that no person was condemned to everlasting fire unless deliberately he had rejected or apostasized the true faith, Ted Kilmey believed that the only sure way of getting to heaven was by way of the Catholic Church. In him faith was as simple, fearful and mystic as that of his grandfather who had lived on the edge of an Irish bog in a sod hut.

Until his middle life, a decade before his greatest success, Mr. Kilmey, like most Catholics, had accepted with some humility a secondary place in the social and business orbits of his country. But that mood had changed and he had seen the change come and gone along with it. There was a new militancy in the Church. From thousands of pulpits, in thousands of Catholic laymen's meetings, the word had gone out that Catholicism was not merely for Sunday use, for times of marriage and baptism and shriving of sins. It was for business use, for politics, for the arts, for infiltration into every deed, no matter how apparently secular the deed might be. Every act of a Catholic should be consciously, openly Catholic, even though many times that did not affect performance.

To this crusade Theodore Kilmey brought his own heritage and all his ability. He had both the slyness and the courage which generations of persecution had made second nature to the Catholic Irish, and the basic feeling of being one of a group whose purposes in life and final fate were irreconcilable with those of any non-Catholic. His spirit and pride rose as he saw the successes of militant American Catholics chalked up and actually advertised. They were in high places in business, in judicial and legislative posts. Parochial schools, better built, better taught, were no longer on the wrong side of the tracks.

He had been brought up to practice his religion tenaciously but quietly. The new policy was an almost complete reversal. Catholics banded together as nurses, as veterans, as Boy Scouts, as mothers, as students in the universities. If the cause or the work was worthy, let it be known publicly that Catholics were doing it, and how many of them were.

This was the change which Ted Kilmey had seen come to Catholicism in part of his lifetime. He knew that it stemmed from Rome. In his limited way, he was student enough to realize that history had set a precedent in other crusades and great attempts toward conversion. Because he was a businessman, he knew what Rome was up against in the desperate political and economic situation abroad. It was necessary to set up defense against the enemies of the Church, in America as well as in Europe. Kilmey did his part in many ways, as he had done it this morning in the elimination of Craig, whose wife was an apostate and had given grave scandal to the Church.

As he was working on a statement for the press with his public relations man, he said to himself that he was sorry that he had to do that. But Agnes felt pretty strongly about what Craig had done, the way he'd dragged them into that affair.

His secretary came in to tell him that his daughter, Mrs. Pond, was there to see him. He had not expected her but he said at once, "That's fine. Tell her to come right in," and to the public relations man, "Make a rough draft of that and show it to me in the morning. One of my girls is here to see me and I guess that takes precedence over business, doesn't it?"

She had always been his favorite and that made his present involuntary feeling of apprehension all the more dreary. He never used to feel this way about Kitty. The other girls were fine, good girls and Tim, in Texas with an oil firm, and Gene, in Cleveland with a steamship company, were doing well enough though Tim would never be a world-beater. But Kitty was his pet, had always been his favored child. Her mother used to bring her into his office—not this office nor anything like it—wearing a little blue hood edged with white fur and he called her Bluebell because of it. And she always used to come and beg money from him for her doings and clothes, when she started running around with boys, and wanted everything she saw in the shops. But she did him credit. She always went places where the rest of them didn't. She was the beauty.

It gave him a shock to see how heavy her face was. She didn't look too well in spite of the flesh on her. Her father said:

"Aren't you the good girl to drop in on your father? Though I suppose there's a motive behind it," he said cheerfully.

"I always did come to see you to beg, didn't I?"

"And the sweet little beggar you were. You could wheedle me out of anything I had to give."

"I hope I still can. Because I do want something as usual. And I thought I knew where to come."

Her face lit up as she spoke and the charm came back to it with affection and teasing. Her father thought, she'd still be a beauty if she'd take off a few pounds and get the sleep she needs. But it's the child-bearing period for her now, and that's always hard on a woman's looks.

"Be easy on an old man now—how much? I suppose you're going to tell me about the terrible cost of living?"

"No, it's not money. Though I suppose it would mean money too for a while, until I learned to take care of myself and the kids. But lots of girls do, who aren't any more educated than I am."

"What are you talking about?" he asked, his eyebrows suddenly drawing together as if making a fort behind which those blue eyes could defend their glances.

She said, "Dad, I want a separation. I just can't go on like this. I want you to talk to Al and tell him so. He'd believe you. He'd do what you told him to do. He won't for me."

"A separation from your husband! You're asking me to help you with that?"

"Yes. I know you'll hate this, but our marriage isn't working out. I'm not any kind of wife, and as things are, I'm not even a good mother. But I could be a good mother—if I had the children off by myself—oh, in some little house in the country or some flat here

[133]

in town. I'd work. I'd really like to work. And I'm not so stupid that I couldn't."

"But what's wrong with Aloysius?"

"He's such—he's such a dope! Oh, I know, that sounds mean and ugly but he is. He hasn't any imagination. He's so narrow. He's—he's so determined. I can't tell you all about it. But I just can't take it. You'll tell him so, won't you?"

"What's wrong with you, girl? He's your husband."

"I never wanted him to be."

"Are you sitting there and telling me that you, a married woman, are yearning after someone else?"

"No, I'm not yearning. What good would it do me if I did? Now? Who'd ever want me? All I'm asking," she said in a desperate crescendo, "is to get away from Al. Not to have him around, wanting, expecting things that I just can't give. Can't feel. I don't love him. He told me—you all told me—that didn't matter and that I would afterward. But I don't. I do less and less. I don't even like him any more. He seems like a haunt, a spook! Oh, don't you understand that it must be dreadful for him too? It must be, if he'd only admit it!"

"Lower your voice. Hush now. Calm yourself. He doesn't admit it, does he?"

"No. He's much too stubborn. Too vain. He wanted to be married to a Kilmey. He is, all right."

"You don't do the man justice. He loves you."

"Love." She shuddered away from the word and then drew control around her again. "Dad, I want to be fair. I don't want to hurt Al or anyone else. But I know what this is doing to me. I'm afraid of what it will do. I'm not crying for the moon any more and remember, I did do what you and mother wanted. Now all I'm asking for is a legal separation and the children, and I'll be no more trouble to any of you. There's nothing wrong with a separation. They're allowed."

"You ask me to aid you in breaking up your home?"

"Just a separation."

[134]

"And what would the poor fellow do?"

"He—Al could see the children sometimes. I wouldn't mind that so much if he didn't put ideas in their heads. And he could find somebody else."

"With a living wife?"

"Well," she said sullenly, "he wouldn't have to marry."

"I don't know what you're talking about," said her father harshly.

"It would be better than the way it is!" she cried and her head went down upon her arms. She sobbed wearily and the noise wrung his heart. He hushed her, patted her shoulder and lifted the office interphone to tell his secretary that he did not want to be disturbed by anyone. Without allowing his thoughts to become pictures, he knew this was a bad situation. There should be happiness in married life, even with worry and quarrels. There ought to be secrets of affection and little jokes that came out of a shared bed. Not this repulsion. He had thought—well, they all had believed that with two healthy young people nature would take its course and blend them. And so it still might. There was nothing wrong with the boy. A dope—Kilmey felt himself grin involuntarily over his daughter's bowed head, at that description. She was too quick for poor Aloysius. But he was a clean fellow. There were worse things.

Al should leave her alone for a while and let her miss him, thought Kilmey frankly. And, as was often said, a separation was only the first step to divorce and after that parting with the Church. A young girl like Kitty would not live alone for long.

No. There must be no separation to tarnish the record of the Kilmey family. Certainly not now with the record of his fine family life and the Catholic marriages of his children sent to Rome by the Archbishop, and Ted Kilmey knew why. How could he offer an insult to the Church when it was about to honor him, as one of its leading American laymen?

In his present position he could countenance no such irregularity even outside of his own family. That was why he had turned thumbs down on Kenneth Craig this morning though the fellow had parts and would have been useful. If he had not heard that

Bishop Tarrant had been flouted in the matter of Craig's marriage, it might have been a different story.

The sobs had become long, helpless sighs.

"Bluebell," said Theodore Kilmey gently, "how would you like to go off on a little trip to New York?"

She sat up and rubbed her stained, swollen face. "No, thanks. It's nice of you. But it wouldn't help. I'd just have to come back. The trouble with me is that I'm a coward. I always have been. I never had a mind of my own when I needed it."

"You're a good girl, Bluebell. And you did what was right. You'll go on doing it."

"I don't know. You say it's right. It's what we were taught to believe. But people break over. Like the woman who married that Kenneth Craig in spite of being a Catholic, and everything. She got what she wanted."

"Well, he won't if I can help it!" answered Kilmey. This proved it, showed the fact of bad example, the corrupting influence. Right here in his own family.

"I thought you liked him," she said in surprise.

"I don't approve conduct like that. And never shall."

"You can't do anything about it. Dad, I didn't want to come here this afternoon and unload a lot of trouble on you. But, if you could help me, it would mean everything. If you could see it my way. Mother can't. She thinks that all marriages are bound to be all right, that if you housekeep enough and have a lot of children, you can't miss. But you can miss. And when that's wrong, you stop being good. I thought that maybe, because you're a man, you'd see that."

He flushed a little. "Maybe I'll have a talk with Aloysius one of these days."

"You mean you will tell him that you agree with me about a separation?" she asked, again excitedly.

"No, I don't mean that. Not for a minute. I know where that would lead. From bad to worse. The next thing you'd be after would be a divorce and then some other man. I'll never help you to take the first step."

[136]

"Then I wouldn't bother to talk to Al," said Kitty half to herself.

He sat down to the obvious thing that always helped, drew out his big checkbook and wrote one for two hundred, because one hundred was quite enough.

"Now spend this on yourself," he said, "or for something that you want and wouldn't get otherwise."

She gave him a bleak little smile.

"I know some things may not be easy for you, Kitty. You got off to kind of a bad start in your marriage for a number of reasons, and I've always been sorry. But keep your chin up and you'll be surprised at how many of your problems will solve themselves. Life changes as you go along. Nothing's final in this world but death," he ended cheerfully.

"I suppose not."

He knew his advice was good. She looked better now that she had colored her lips. And she had two hundred dollars more than when she came in and was not going to be allowed to ruin her life or disgrace him.

Chapter Ten

The announcement of the creation of a Board of Advisors for the railroad industry throughout the country was no surprise to Kenneth Craig. He had known that Mr. Kilmey had been fathering such an idea for some time and, with his own chief, Craig had discussed the pros and cons of what such a committee's possibilities might be.

What astonished him was the total personnel of the committee. It was incredible, in one way, and after he had taken in the full facts, Craig felt that it amounted to a personal slight. It was one of very considerable importance, for it was sure to be noticed and commented upon by persons on the inside of his own profession. To have Leonard Thomson put on the committee, and himself left out, made no real sense unless it was an attempt to diminish him. A man of his own age and stature might have been chosen from any other part of the country and that would have been understandable. But this was from his own bailiwick, and in this region there was no comparison between the importance of Thomson's railroad and the C. and E. Also Thomson, though he was a well-regarded expert in railroad machinery, had never made the slightest pretensions to any policy-making ability and that was what the work of this new committee would involve. Thomson was a specialist, not an executive.

Craig combed over every possibility, before he let himself take the full force of the implications. He tried to figure out if Thomson had eastern connections, if he was somebody's nephew or cousin with a pull, if his specialized knowledge was the point of choice. But there were other and bigger machinery men on the committee. The reasons for most of the other selections were quite obvious to anyone acquainted with the railroad picture. The various regions of the country were properly represented. The men with the greatest power were included in person or by proxy. Theodore Kilmey headed it up quite naturally, because he was a driver and had fostered the idea, and also because he liked to be out in front to the point of insisting on it. But why Thomson, if not to substitute for not asking Craig, and yet represent the area in which they both functioned?

It was not as if Theodore Kilmey had not been a friend and a former employer, who had always spoken well of Craig, as the younger man knew. Craig's first guess was that someone had put this over on Kilmey. But while he was still smarting, he recalled that he had been surprised before by an omission. He and Barbara had received some very handsome wedding presents both before they were married and in the subsequent weeks. Yet there had been nothing at all from the Kilmeys. It was not a thing to bother about, for there was no real reason why anyone should send them any gifts, and he had only wondered at one time whether Mr. Kilmey and his wife had heard of his marriage.

"We sent the Kilmeys an announcement, didn't we, Barbara?" he had asked, checking up.

"Why yes, of course. They were on the list. And you told me that you wrote him a personal note before we were married."

"That's right, I did. I just wanted to be sure we hadn't left them out by mistake because it might hurt their feelings."

It was true that he had sent a brief and cordial note to Ted Kilmey, as seemed only right after that momentous dinner on the private car. There had been no reply but that seemed all right, for there wasn't much left to say that hadn't been said that night. Craig had forgotten even his own note in the crowding and exciting months of happiness and of setting up his new life.

But now it made a pattern, unless he was imagining things that didn't exist. No acknowledgment of his note, no wedding present, and here was Leonard Thomson in a spot which surely should have been offered first to himself if the plan was to put a youngish man from this district on the new committee. It looks deliberate, thought Craig. It must be because of the religious situation. But surely they don't carry bigotry so far. Besides, Ted Kilmey was the one man I consulted beforehand. He told me to go to see the Bishop and I did. Of course I didn't report back to Ted Kilmey as to what the Bishop's attitude was. That may have been my mistake. He might have taken offense at that. Maybe Bishop Tarrant is back of this. It's incredible. I wonder how far the net spreads underneath and what intercommunication those people have on matters like this.

Certainly I thought Kilmey was with me. It could be his wife. She seemed a little stiff and sour that night. Craig thought back, trying to make the memory very clear. He wasn't sure. He didn't want to imagine things that weren't true.

In any case, there was no getting away from the fact that he had not been put on that committee and that Ted Kilmey's yes or no would have turned the trick. Craig reckoned the effect on himself, the consequences. He could not get Mr. Miller's reaction, for his chief was spending a month in Palm Springs. Marcus Croy too, the vice-president of C. and E., who took his duties lightly, as an older man with a private fortune could, was as usual at this time of year, doing deep-sea fishing in Florida. Of course both men would read about the appointment of the committee for it was important business news. They were sure to wonder, why young Thomson when it could have been Craig?

It was a matter of prestige more than anything else, a lost chance to build up his usefulness to the railroad industry at this time and become favorably known to the most important leaders of it. Would Mr. Miller even be inclined to question his own judgment in bringing Kenneth Craig so quickly to the top of his own organization? Craig didn't think so, but this was one of those things which could shake confidence. It was the subtly bad result. He was safe enough in his job. But Mr. Miller might delay his own retirement. He might look into what was behind this, inquire around.

Probably he would find nothing more than sheer bigotry—and enough to disgust him—at the bottom of the matter. Mr. Miller would not hold with that. Yet evidently it was powerful. Insidious and secretive too. It was an attempt to get a clutch on business as well as everything else. Craig's face was grim. He did not like opposition that he could not fight in the open.

But one thing was sure, Craig said to himself, with a glint of satisfaction in his mind. They didn't manage to keep me from marrying Barbara.

He must say nothing about this affair of the committee to her. It would worry her and only reopen all this argument. Not a word about it to her, he decided firmly. She was very happy these days in their home life and with her pregnancy. She seemed to have worked out a pretty good technique about her Church. She was certainly faithful to it. That thought angered him all over again. How preposterous it was that a lovely and spiritual person like Barbara, a good woman if ever there was one, should be penalized in any way for doing what was natural and right for a woman to do. What did those churchmen want anyway? To keep every string in their own hands? That was it.

He went home to her that night, feeling more tender than ever because he was protecting her from any knowledge of the slight that had been put upon him, and which he was convinced, the more he mulled the thing over, was related closely to the circumstance of their marriage. His house looked more welcoming as its outlines were marked out by lighted windows, the sense of her presence even more valuable because he was paying a little more for it than he had expected.

Coming up the stairs from the garage, he met Miss Agatha Braniff in the hall, wrapping herself in an old and evidently permanent sealskin coat that was too small for her across the bosom. He knew Barbara's aunt by this time, of course, but not well because she gave him no opportunity. Her rare visits to their house always turned into something like flight when he appeared.

Tonight he was sensitive even to that. As he kissed Barbara fondly, he had an annoyed sense that Miss Braniff preferred not to observe the caress.

"What are you running away for, Miss Braniff? Barbara, won't your aunt stay for dinner?"

"I've tried to make her. No dice."

"No thank you. Such a delicious tea. All I could possibly eat. I really must go," protested Agatha Braniff.

"But why? You know, you never give me a chance to get acquainted. Take off your coat and give me a break for once, won't you?"

She was flustered, as any old maid would be when a man was personally so attentive and cordial, but her hands fumbled even more earnestly with the reluctant fastening of her coat.

"You're very kind but I mustn't stay, Mr. Craig."

"Can't I be Kenneth one of these days, now that I'm in the family?"

"Well—you know—"

"She really has to go," warned Barbara, "if she is to get her bus."

"If you must go, let me get the car out and drive you home."

That put Agatha almost into panic. "No, no, please—I couldn't allow—thank you, Mr. Craig, but I've timed the bus. It goes right by my door. Good night, Barbara."

He followed her down the walk to the road and as the bus

rounded the corner of the boulevard, Agatha lumbered across with surprising quickness, waving and ejaculating him back. Craig went back to the open doorway and Barbara's laughter.

"There's one woman you don't get very far with," she said.

"What's the matter? Does she think I have a cloven hoof?"

"She's just shy of you."

"I usually get along pretty well with old maids like that."

"Everyone has an occasional failure," she said teasingly.

"She certainly treats me as if I were bad medicine. She wouldn't even come to the wedding, as I remember."

"You know why. She's pretty rigid. She was brought up to keep away from Protestants like you. Also she regards you as my occasion of sin."

"The old simpleton."

"She's really a very sweet person. She's a virgin-and-martyr. That's what we always called her."

He laughed with his wife. Now he was very glad that her aunt had not stayed. He was home, and, over the work of the day and the unpleasant humiliation which had gone with it, happiness spread like a covering. He felt himself anticipate every hour ahead, and many of them, for it was Friday and he had the long week end to be with her. He looked forward to the mixing of a drink, as well as its taste, to the stir of the latest news on the air, dinner, the use of all these things about him which were his own possessions, and better than adequate, proving his own competence and success. Hidden too in the coming hours—he didn't know just where—was excitement, the repeating of love that repetition never staled. And it all would be shared.

"Virgins are bound to be martyrs," said Craig.

It snowed heavily on Saturday night, and, beautiful as it was to see the laden branches of the trees on Sunday morning, any driving would be difficult, for the boulevard was not plowed and only the great buses made deep irregular ruts. It was a day to stay home and be comfortable. Kenneth wondered as he looked out at the weather if Barbara was going to insist on going to church. She certainly had a good excuse for cutting that out today, especially in her condition.

He suggested it. "You're not going to try to make it this morning, are you?"

"Church? Of course. This isn't so bad. I'll go to the eleven o'clock Mass."

"Don't you get a cut in weather like this?"

"Darling, my grandmother used to walk two or three miles through drifts to get to church."

"But you're in a delicate condition."

"She practically always was."

"Well, if you insist on going, I'm going to drive you."

"No, it's not necessary."

"Don't talk like your virgin-and-martyr aunt. I've some authority over you. If you're going, I'm going with you."

"It's a long service. It's too cold for you to wait outside."

"Can't I go in with you?"

"You can, but—"

"Don't argue with me. This is one thing I'm going to have my way about. My pregnant wife isn't going to plow her way through a snowstorm alone. What time do you want to start?"

It was bitter and blustery weather and Craig was surprised to find it difficult to park near the Cathedral.

"Is there always a crowd like this?"

"This is bigger than usual at this service, but it's because of the weather. Probably a lot of people couldn't get to the earlier Masses."

The service was just beginning as they entered. An usher who was efficiently packing in the crowd signaled them, and took them up the center aisle to places in a pew close to the middle altar. Craig thanked him. He was pleased to have a good seat where he could watch what was going on, instead of being in a vestibule as they had been on last Christmas Eve in New York. With a touch of male vanity, he wondered if the usher was some boy around town who knew who he was.

"Oh, dear," he heard Barbara say softly.

[143]

"Are you all right?"

"Yes, fine," she said with silent lips, "don't talk."

She knelt and bowed her head against clasped hands. Craig tried to find a suitable place for his hat, but the seat beside him was occupied and the floor dirty. So he balanced the hat on his knees as he inclined his head and shoulders reverently for a minute.

He prayed for what he wanted most, to whatever good and mystic force there might be. "Let me always make Barbara happy."

As had been true on the infrequent other occasions when he had attended Catholic services, the procedure seemed theatrical to him. For some reason or purpose the statues all around were wrapped in purple cloth and there was even a swath of it around what must be the figure on the central gold crucifix standing in front of a closed and gilded compartment. The tabernacle, he decided. The altar was starkly undecorated except for that crucifix, a framed piece of illuminated writing, and a large book of presumably Latin prayers, for when the priest finally read from it, that was the language he used. How many people in the church understood a word of what he was saying, wondered Craig.

Before the reading there was considerable ceremony and they ran through it as if they were well used to every detail, the priest and his helper bowing to the crucifix and each other, and the small, shock-haired altar boys moving back and forth in a well-disciplined way. It was certainly all under control, reflected Craig. He thought that these acts and postures were survivals of a long past period in history, of a time which antedated printing and few men could read except the priests. Interesting to think that it had been kept up so long, and even more astonishing that these rites still held the imagination of so many people, even in America. Once again he gave the Roman Catholic organization a measure of credit for its accomplishments. But to think that a man in Ted Kilmey's position would be so narrow-minded as to believe that fellows like these priests should regulate marriage in a free country! Someday, I'm going to have that out with him, resolved Craig. One of these days, I'll tell him, and in no uncertain terms, what I think about mixing religion with business. The prospect gave him some satisfaction and he watched, critically but with no hostility, the further progress of the service, rising when the others did but not joining them when they knelt. He watched with amusement the plight of one of the altar boys who obviously wanted to blow his nose and must either have no handkerchief or perhaps have been forbidden to use one. He noted the hole that was almost worn through in the sole of the assistant priest's shoe.

The congregation was sitting down again. Craig recalled that there was usually a break in the middle of a service. Then they took up the collection. He must slip a bill to Barbara, when they passed the plate. She didn't have to make contributions out of her allowance when he was with her. She made a little sound, or was it only that she had suddenly moved? He had the impression that she had been startled or that something had made her nerves jump, and turned his head to look at her. But she was gazing straight ahead of her, not even regarding the priest, who had mounted into the pulpit not far from them and stood now behind the voice amplifier.

How beautiful she was. The straightness of her nose, the thickness of her lashes. He knew that she would not want him to stare at her now and was careful not to bother her. But he knew that line of her profile so well that he didn't have to watch it. He knew every line of her body and there was a new curve beginning. Her breasts were larger, even lovelier. She had been very sweet last night. There were a few little things to worry about, now and then an occasion that wasn't so good like that party at the club. But that blew over and it wouldn't happen again. Barbara couldn't accept the fact that he'd been married before. He said to himself that he was glad she couldn't, and wanted him so completely to herself.

Everybody was standing. The priest was reading a gospel for the day, announcing chapter and verse, which Craig liked. Craig sized up the prelate, who was not the one who was conducting the ceremony and who now sat, flanked by the two altar boys, on a side bench in the chancel. This one had come in from a door back of it, and he was dressed more simply, in ordinary black robes. He was a tall, thin fellow, handsome in a rawboned way, probably not more than forty years old. His bearing had vigor and his diction, as he began, pleased Craig, with its lack of foreign accent.

The English words too were agreeable after so much mumbled and unintelligible Latin, and the gospel was a familiar one. If they would translate the whole works into English and let the congregation have a part in the service, as non-Catholic churches do, it would be a big improvement, thought Craig. It would modernize the thing, break down a lot of barriers. But maybe that's what they want, the barriers. The priest had a fine voice. Craig glanced at him with approval and had a feeling that the priest saw him. Or Barbara. Maybe not. In an audience you often felt that the speaker had his eye on you.

But the voice was better than the logic, Craig decided after the first five minutes of the sermon. It was the old story. The world was bad and the Catholics were the only good people in it. No wonder they got a complex about themselves, with that sort of stuff poured into their ears all the time. They were right and everybody else was wrong.

Even they weren't as right as they should be. The Catholics were catching it now. The priest was really warming up. What a line he was giving the congregation! It was astonishing that he would talk about these subjects in front of a mixed congregation, with a lot of young people in it.

"I know what you women do. I know that you think you get away with it. You murder. Yes, many of you sitting here before me with your rosaries in your hands are murderesses. You have taken human life, God-given life. You have destroyed a body and a soul. There is no defense. No one gives you the right to say, 'There was no life yet.' I say to you that when you destroy the potentiality of life, the chance of life, you become murderers and murderesses! You may escape the penalty of human law but you will never escape the penalties imposed by God's law, no matter where you go nor how far you may flee Him."

Craig thought, it's very rough talk. He must scare the life out of a lot of women. If they believed that, all of them, and acted on it, the population would certainly shoot up. Of course that's what the priests want. It's always been the policy in every Catholic country to keep families as large as possible, even when they had to count on a terrible shrinkage because of the living conditions.

His mind wandered for a few minutes. He did not like the tone of this sermon, nor particularly want to listen to it now. It was the word "divorce" uttered with particular violence, that reclaimed his attention.

"There is no divorce," said the priest. His voice had become dramatically low but the congregation was so still that his quick, harsh breathing could be heard over the amplifier as well as the words. "There is no divorce. But there is adultery. Christ did not recognize divorce but he did recognize the sins of sex, the sins of adultery, the evil of the woman who goes shamelessly from one man to another, selling herself for money or for pleasure. Or for social position. Or because her husband, the one to whom she was married in God's sight, disappoints her!" His voice rose in satire, mocking a woman's complaint. "He drinks too much. He snores. He smiled at another woman. I'm tired of him. We are not in love any more, Father."

Someone snickered at the mockery and there was a general nervous stir. The priest went on.

"The priest, the representative of God on earth, says to such women that there is no divorce. There is endurance, kindness, helpfulness. There is, at the ultimate, permitted separation if a man is mad or dangerous. For him if the woman is mad or dangerous. Always with the hope that the situation may change, that God's grace may change that unhappy marriage into a happy one once more, and that man and wife may come together as God wishes, and as they promised and covenanted with Him in the Sacrament of Matrimony. Only the priest knows how often there is such an outcome, of the miracles wrought in marriages which could have been carelessly or wickedly abandoned."

Craig felt as if the skin of his face were stretched and stiffened as he

[147]

allowed himself no movement or change of expression. He thought, I ought to get Barbara out of here, away from this tirade. But we're up in front and it's a long way to the door. It would be so damned conspicuous. I'd like to stand up and walk out. I would, if I were alone.

"—and so, because the priest and the Bishop will not yield to the selfish entreaties of the woman who wants to break her marriage vows, she runs to a judge with her story. She says, 'Your Honor, I must have a divorce. My husband is no good. He drinks. He even hit me once. I can not bear it!' Bear it! Does that woman ever think of what her Saviour bore? For her? For those terrible sins which she now contemplates secretly and is determined to commit?

"For that is what is in her heart. That is what she wants and intends, to commit adultery. Perhaps she has not chosen the partner of her crime but she will find him! She will hunt for him! She will have her divorce in the secular courts and what she calls her freedom. The freedom of hell! That is what she will have in the end. For God will not recognize that divorce, no matter if it bears a dozen seals of a dozen courts. No matter what judge grants it or if the whole Supreme Court of the United States held it valid. God will say, there is no divorce. There is only marriage, and as long as a woman has a living husband or a man a living wife, there can be no other marriage.

"It is an ancient sin, this sin of adultery. But I tell you, in the language of today, that it has never paid off. When civilization was sounder, such women were stoned to death. In our own, which will rot away if we who are Catholics do not prevent it, they make the headlines. They are called glamorous! Many of them are pagans. They know no better. God has infinite mercy for the untaught, the pagan. His wrath is directed toward those who know the Law and defy it, who, given grace, have wrenched it from their hearts, mocked it, trodden publicly and privately upon it. Mercy is not for them, nor happiness. They may satisfy their animal passions but they will know only the gratification of the animal."

Craig's mouth was a tight, hard line.

"Who are the happy women in the world today? They are the Catholic wives, who cherish their husbands even in grief, even in failure or fault, even though there be a lapse of some human faculty. They are the Catholic mothers, who bring up their daughters and their sons to know that marriage is a sacrament as holy as any other, and that there is no sin in the world which is comparable to the unworthy reception of a sacrament. In their minds there is no temptation to murder the unborn, to reject the new soul which will serve and glorify God. In their hearts there is no yearning for adultery. God will bless them. Their trials and difficulties will cry out to Him for beatification.

"But there are others who defile the name of Catholic. Who smear it, in the phrase of the day. They sit among you in this congregation, corrupt, hypocritical and brazen. Claiming to be Catholics and bringing scandal upon the Church to which they have the insolence to give a measure of lip-service. Pretending to contrition and remorse and leaving the confessional only to resume their habitual sins as soon as they have made their Easter duty! Willfully limiting their families by any foul means that degeneracy can devise. Divorced and living openly with men who cannot be their husbands in the sight and knowledge of God nor of any good Catholic! These women, and the men who aid and abet their sins, are like a cancer on the body of the Church. And I tell you—I warn any of you who may be tempted to follow their example, who may be dazzled by any appearance of worldly success, that, if you do, you will set your feet on the path of corruption and deny yourself true earthly happiness as well as eternal life."

He was done. That seemed to be the end of it. His black robes disappeared through the door by which he had entered, and the choir broke into a Latin chant as the other priest, in his ceremonial clothes, reapproached the central altar. Barbara stood up, and following her lead, Craig did also. His hand slid along the rail of the pew in front to touch hers but he could tell that she did not like that from her utter lack of response, so he drew back and folded his arms enduringly. All he wanted was to have this thing over.

Now the men were coming around with the collection boxes. Craig did not want to give them a cent, after what he characterized as a terrible harangue, but even more he did not want to embarrass Barbara. He drew out a couple of bills and tried to hand her one but she shook her head and opened her own purse and took out a small envelope. That seemed to be the way most of them did it for the box was piled high with them. Grimly placing his own contribution on top of the envelopes and scattered bills, Craig said to himself that he wasn't going to be a soft touch next time one of those priests came around to the office, if this was the sort of stuff they handed out in their sermons. They couldn't insult decent people and get away with it.

He was apprehensive. He did not know what would happen when they went out of the church, whether the congregation would be staring at Barbara and himself, or whether she could take it if they did. The rest of the service seemed to drag along and his anger hardened as the words of the sermon stayed in his mind. It was the last time he'd be caught in a spot like this. But Barbara—what was she up against that he had not realized? This sort of performance explained the business about Theodore Kilmey and that committee much more clearly.

It was over at last and he stiffened himself to take on anything that might come next, with his hand at Barbara's elbow as the congregation began to file out of the church. He found himself astonished and delighted with Barbara's manner, as they reached the outside steps.

"Good morning," he heard her say in a quite usual voice to someone whom he didn't know. "Yes, isn't it a stormy day? But we're due for it. Good morning, Mrs. Ray. How are you? Hello, Dorothy."

A doctor whom Craig knew said cordially, "How are you, Mr. Craig? Getting a bit of weather, aren't we?" A mining engineer, whom he had not known was a Catholic, gave him a warm handshake.

The sermon didn't seem to have any effect on the way people were

[150]

acting. No one seemed subdued or frightened. But was it coming out into the daylight that made Barbara look so pale?

They had to walk a block to where their car was parked. Once out of earshot Craig let loose.

"That was certainly a hell of a talk."

"Hell all right. I'm sorry that you were subjected to it."

"Who is that fellow anyway?"

"That's Father Gilroy. The pastor, actually."

"Does he carry on like that very often?"

"More often than not. It's pretty standard."

"Well, I don't think they ought to let him get away with it."

"Get away with it? It's doctrine."

"Hell's bells," said Craig, "he's a complete fanatic."

She didn't answer.

"You don't let that sort of stuff worry you, do you, darling?"

"I ought to be used to it by this time."

"Of course, I know it wasn't personal. There must be a whole lot of people in that congregation who are refusing to obey orders or he wouldn't be so worked up. He talked like a guy who was losing his hold and knew it, it seemed to me. Just ranting. And you could tell what he said went in one ear and out the other. From the way the crowd shook it off when they came out."

"Don't fool yourself."

"What do you mean?"

"About it's not being personal. It was personal enough for a few of us. He knew. We knew. They knew. Father Gilroy loathes me. He thinks I'm a bad woman and that God will punish me. He hopes so."

"Oh, he was just going through his act."

"He came to see me before we were married and forbade it. He said I was a wicked woman, mocking God."

"That fellow who talked this morning? He said that! You didn't tell me."

"I didn't want to at the time. I shouldn't tell you now. But I felt this morning as I felt that day. I wanted to stand up and talk back. I wanted to tell him that he couldn't drive me out of the

[151]

Church, that I had a right there. It's not his Church because he happens to be on the altar."

"Of course it isn't. They just hire him. Don't, dear, don't take it so seriously."

"He really believes you and I live in sin."

"Well, we don't."

"God, I hope not. Oh, Ken—let's get home. As quick as we can."

"What is it, darling? Don't you feel well?"

"A little queer, that's all. I often do. I just want to get home."

She seemed herself again when they reached the house. Quite all right. She did not need to lie down, she said, and went to get their Sunday lunch. The chicken was on the table and she was tossing the salad when the pain came back furiously. She called and Kenneth found her clinging to the metal edge of the kitchen work shelf.

Dr. Roush advised the hospital immediately. She was there by three o'clock and they did all they could. But by five o'clock the embryonic new life was gone and it seemed to Craig, haggard and sorrowing and basically angry, that a person had died. They had talked of the child until he was part of their life, their family.

"It's not at all probable," said Dr. Roush to Craig, "I shouldn't think so. This was probably due to happen. Miscarriages were formerly thought to be caused by shock or falls or this or that accident. We discount those theories a good deal now. A shock or even a fall may be coincident, but a miscarriage is really nature's way of refusing to complete a birth which might not be satisfactory. There's some fault, something that isn't quite right and she's rejecting the embryo."

"But Barbara was all right this morning," insisted Craig, "and then she heard a very disturbing, violent talk in church. Enough to upset anyone. It put her under a strain, I'm sure. Right after that, within an hour, this came on."

Dr. Roush shook his head. "I doubt if the talk had anything to do with it."

"I'm certainly glad to hear you say so," answered Craig gravely. He tried to take the doctor's scientific word for it, but it was hard to believe that sermon had not been at least partial cause. Only last night Barbara had been feeling so fine, so vigorous.

"Does this mean, Dr. Roush, that Mrs. Craig and I can't have children?"

"By no means. That's what your wife started worrying about at once. And quite naturally. I've been reassuring her. No, you don't want to get that idea into your head. There's no apparent reason why you shouldn't have all the family you want. She has carried one child full time some years ago."

"Yes." Not his child. That rascal had better luck.

"But," the doctor went on, "as I told your wife, you mustn't be in too much of a hurry now. If you crowd things and don't give her time for a perfect recovery, there's always a chance that this might happen again. One miscarriage always makes the next a bit more likely to happen and we don't want to set any such pattern."

"I should say not. How much time is advisable?"

"Well, four to six months. Six months is safest if you want to take real precaution against another disappointment."

"I don't want Barbara to have any more disappointments—that's the main thing."

Craig told her, in the dim light of the hospital room, "It was bound to happen, darling. The doctor thinks nature knew what she was doing. It doesn't signify anything except that we'll try again."

She said wearily, tired with sedatives, "Why do I lose my children? I love them so."

"You won't, darling. This was just bad luck. Nobody's fault. At first I thought that business this morning might have caused it but the doctor says not.

"Father Gilroy might like to think so. It would make his sermon very effective, wouldn't it? 'The wages of sin—' " she tried to laugh.

"A lot of crazy cant, that's what it was. I still get mad when I think of it."

"You don't think this is punishment?"

"Darling—you aren't getting any notion like that!"

"No, of course not."

The silence between them hung unconvinced.

[153]

Chapter Eleven

The difference now was in not being quite so sure. Not so certain that their happiness would not be disappointed or invaded. Not so confident as a month before of being able to do everything necessary to make the other happy. Their love was not less but there had been a shock to its nerves.

Was Kenneth baffled by restraint and disappointment? Barbara did not know. Was he covering up a letdown? Though he would never tell her if it were true, was there some comparison in his mind that she could not reach? Between living with Nina and living with herself? Had that other marriage been more exciting in spite of the way Nina had treated him? Don't think of that. You should know better than to have a doubt. Forget it, have some people in for dinner—he loves to show off the house—and give everybody a gay time. When you wake in the morning think—and be quick about it—that even if it isn't perfect now, it will be later. Plan every day and don't worry. Look your best tonight. Surprise him. You are much better looking than she ever was, without being vain about it. But it isn't always looks. A woman can forget a man she hasn't lived with for a long time—I did—but does something linger in a man's mind?

Kenneth could not help it either. Was there something more than the doctor's admonition in her mind? Was she glad to obey the doctor because it let her off? Did she really credit that hokum about living in sin? Could she help herself after the way it was drummed into her? Here they were, Mr. and Mrs. Kenneth Craig, Prospect Boulevard, and everyone respected them and was delighted that they had married, except a few fanatics. Barbara knew how he felt. He had given her everything he had or ever would have. She had seen the copy of his will. "And everything else of which I die possessed to my beloved wife, Barbara." That should make her feel a wife, prove the substance and permanence. All Barbara needed to do was to shake off any of those old superstitions. She would, of course. Just give her time. Bring her home some flowers tonight.

In early April the Kilmey private car lay in the railroad yards for a day's stopover. Craig knew it was there but he didn't set foot on it. He had a formal invitation to a stag lunch given by Kilmey, but when he heard that there was a cocktail party later on the same day, which had not been mentioned to him, he canceled out on lunch. That verified his suspicions. What made him really sore was to hear later in a roundabout way that Bill and Nina Longman had been at that cocktail party as well as Leonard Thomson. They must have flown down to the city for it.

Later in the month Malcolm Craig and his wife passed through the city on their way to California. When Kenneth got word of his brother's coming, he was definitely pleased to take the news home. He wanted to show Malcolm and Helen his new house, and Barbara especially was his showpiece. Helen had tried to marry him off, and he knew it. It would be satisfying to have her see how well he had done for himself.

"We want to be sure to give them a good time," he said to Barbara. "What kind of an affair should we set up, do you think? I'd kind of like to have something here at the house if it's all right with you."

"Is it next week they're coming?"

"Yes. Malc telephoned and said they'll be here Wednesday, Thursday and part of Friday. They have reservations on the Coast plane for Friday afternoon. We could round up a crowd to meet them on Wednesday or Thursday, just as you think best, and then have them by themselves or with just another couple on the other night. But you fix it."

"It will be Holy Week, you know."

"That's right. He said they want to be in San Francisco for Easter."

"Must they? We can't do much for them in Holy Week."

"That won't matter. It's the only time they'll be here. Holy Week won't bother them. They're not churchgoers to any great extent. Malcolm likes his Sunday golf too well."

"But we couldn't give a party on Wednesday or Holy Thursday."

"Those are the only days when they'll be here," repeated Craig, as if she were the one who did not understand. "We don't have to make a big fuss about it. But we'll want them to meet a few people. Helen has really laid herself out for me when I've been staying with them."

"Of course we ought to give them a really good time. But a cocktail party in Holy Week, Ken—"

"I thought it was just Friday when things shut down."

"Oh no. The whole week—all of Lent—"

"Yes, but how many Catholics would we be likely to ask?"

"Hardly any, I suppose. But I've never gone to parties during Holy Week, and to give one—"

"You mean it's a sin?"

"More of a scandal."

"Don't be silly, dear. No one you ask is likely to be scandalized by being asked in to have a drink and meet Helen and Malcolm. People will know they're just passing through. What's the matter? You don't want to do anything for them?"

"I want to very much. And any other time—"

"This happens to be the only time it's possible. I can't very well ask them to change their reservations and make over their plans because it doesn't suit the ideas of some priest—"

"You know that's not it."

"All right, it doesn't fit the Catholic calendar," he said impatiently. "But if you feel so strongly about it, I can take them to the club. I suppose it's all right to have them sleep here in Holy Week?"

"Don't say things like that, Ken."

"I'm just trying to find out so I'll know what to do," he told her ironically.

"I'll ask people for Wednesday."

"No, not if you don't want to."

"It's all right. As things are, it doesn't really matter."

"What do you mean, as things are?"

"I just mean it's not the important thing."

"Of course it's not important. A few people in our own house—"

What annoyed Craig was the way the religious business kept popping up, interfering like this. Sometimes he felt surrounded. The Catholic Church had been part of a very large picture up until now, not very conspicuous from his point of view. But since his marriage it had a way of interfering with the normal way of doing things, with matters that a man should decide for himself and his wife. And it didn't make sense for Barbara to pull a long face about this and that taboo in Holy Week, after the way the Church had turned her down.

But on the following Wednesday afternoon he had almost forgotten those thoughts and her reluctance. The party for Malcolm and Helen was a charming and even beautiful affair. Easter lilies and spring flowers were flooding the markets and Barbara had made the house seem to rejoice with their blossoms. The sixty or seventy guests, roaming with constant exclamations of praise through the rooms, seemed very happy to be there. It was the first time that the Craigs had entertained so large a number and the competence and capacity of the house was proved. The bar and buffet table in the dining room, served today by expert hired servants, gave Craig great satisfaction. Barbara managed everything with no flurry and had time for a special welcome for each guest.

"We could have asked twice as many people," Craig told his wife, in a minute's breathing space between greetings. "I've never been so proud of you. And Helen is having the time of her life."

"That's grand."

"Are you having a good time?" he asked, suddenly wondering.

"Of course."

"No, tell me the truth."

"I am telling you the truth."

"Are you still worrying because of its being Holy Week?"

[157]

"Oh, please leave me alone," she answered and he had no choice, for more guests were coming.

Helen Craig, warmed and excited by the party, was very flattering when they talked it over afterward. They settled down, not yet relaxed, at one end of the living room, with glasses and plates for themselves. The house was still almost like a stage setting, as Helen said.

"It has real style, and it opens up so beautifully. Such a lovely party! It is so nice to see this old Kenneth living the way he should be living, instead of being stuck in a room at a club. Of course I was after him to get married. I had a nice girl picked out for him too, Barbara, but I didn't get very far. He had his eye on you. If he hadn't—did he ever tell you about Mary Crandall?"

"No—should he have?"

"Don't be ridiculous, Helen. There was nothing to that and you know it."

"I didn't say there was, Ken. I only mean that there could have been. Mary was very much taken with you, and I know that. Always remember that he gave up a couple of million for you, Barbara. It just shows how much he loves you!"

Malcolm Craig took the conversation away from his wife, as he often did when she was more frank than tactful.

"I saw the Harrisons, who were at your wedding, here today. I didn't see that other man who was there. What was his name? He knew some people in Philadelphia that we know. Wyatt?"

"He wasn't here, was he?" said Kenneth. "You didn't forget to ask Blair Wyatt, did you, darling?"

"No, I didn't ask him. He wouldn't have come."

"Blair? He goes everywhere he's asked, doesn't he?"

"Not in Holy Week. He's always very firm about that. He's a High Church Episcopalian."

"I know some people are like that," said Helen. "Catholics especially." She remembered that Barbara was one, and tried to be tactful. "You Catholics are very strict about Holy Week too, aren't you?"

[158]

Barbara answered before Kenneth could change the subject. "Good Catholics are. I don't follow the rules very well any more. I didn't give up a couple of million for Ken, Helen. Just a religion."

She said that as if it might be serious or not. Helen looked unsure. Her words trampled on.

"Why Ken, you haven't any prejudices like that, have you? I never have had. I know some of the most delightful Catholics."

"It wasn't that Ken demanded it," explained Barbara, "but you see my husband is still alive."

They were dreadful unexpected words. She saw them strike, cut into Kenneth, before she could draw them back.

"I mean my first husband, of course," she caught at the words.

"I hope you do," said Kenneth evenly.

Helen Craig said cheerfully, "You know, Barbara, when Ken first wrote us about you, I got the impression that you were a widow."

"No. I've had a divorce."

"As who hasn't. Except Malc and me."

"There are times when I too contemplate it with interest," Malcolm remarked and they all hid behind the laugh.

The Malcolm Craigs were not sensitive people. But even they had an uncomfortable sense in that moment that something was going on beneath the surface that they saw. You can always tell, thought Helen, when two people aren't speaking their minds and saving up things to say to each other later. I suppose I shouldn't have mentioned Mary. Barbara may be the jealous type. The Irish are apt to be. I wonder where the first husband is now? Malcolm told me that the man was no good, and Barbara was certainly more than lucky to land on her feet with a man like Ken, and a house like this. She had some sort of job before she was married so she can't have had anything of her own. Probably I shouldn't have said that Mary Crandall has millions in her own name.

They had a late supper and were in their rooms for the night by eleven o'clock, after a short rubber of bridge. Everyone was tired after the party, so they said to each other. Also the conversation kept breaking off, as if it had no roots.

[159]

In their bedroom Helen Craig said to her husband, "I think she is nice, don't you?"

"I sure do. And she can be a great help to Ken. She's very charming and good-looking."

"Yes, she is quite pretty and they seem to know everyone. It's a very attractive house. I don't feel that I could ever get very close to Barbara, though. I don't know why, I always feel that way about Catholics. They keep so much to themselves, to tell their priests, I expect. I didn't feel that Ken was perfectly happy about that, for some reason. Maybe she's trying to make him go over to her religion. But he wouldn't, would he?"

"No, I don't think he would. Ken's too much of an intellectual. But they say that the combination in a marriage is apt to make more or less trouble. Sooner or later. Especially when it comes to the children. I hope that one of our boys doesn't get himself mixed up with a Roman Catholic, when the kids get old enough to be thinking of getting married."

"We'll have to look out for that," agreed Helen. "Of course Barbara said that she gave it up when she married Ken. In some ways I should think that would be sensible. I mean, considering his position."

In the other wing of the upstairs, Barbara waited. She had folded the daytime coverlets, put out Kenneth's things for the night, dusted off some powder that a guest had spilled on the dressing table, put on a dressing gown. Not the one he liked most of all, though she had fingered it on its hook. But they had a sweet joke about that one. She would not wear it now, as if she were trying to be provocative.

It was taking him a very long time to turn off a few lights, and that was all that had been left for him to do. Was he reading? Was he thinking? Was he waiting until she was in bed and asleep? Did he dread coming up? Her mind grew sick at the thought that he might not want to come into his room, their room, because she was there.

Surely he knew she had not meant to say that, not that way. He must realize that everyone's tongue slipped now and then. Barbara sat in front of her dressing table, its mirror giving back a lovely,

[160]

troubled face that she did not consciously see, for even the vision of her eyes was concentrated on that moment when she had said that her husband was alive and had meant Leslie. I didn't mean it. I never think of it like that. They didn't notice, Malcolm and his wife weren't disturbed. Ken shouldn't be. Perhaps he isn't and I'm just imagining that he hasn't been at all like himself this evening, but just putting up a front.

Now he was coming. But you want him to come! Don't feel like that. It's his house, his room. You have fun here, joy. This is your husband.

"Not in bed yet?"

"No, I've been fooling around."

He took off his coat, began the usual routine. It's so silent, she thought. As if the music had stopped. Yes, there was always something like music when they were here together.

"Did you think it went off all right?" she asked, because one of them must say something or the silence would exaggerate itself.

"The party? Yes, I thought it was very successful. I'm only sorry that I put you up against something you didn't want to do, that's all."

"I didn't mind."

"I think you did."

"It couldn't be helped under the circumstances. But you see I was brought up to think of Holy Week as tremendously set apart. We went—sort of softly through it—very solemnly—and each day had its special meaning and special prayers—"

Don't go on, or it will all come back too intensely what you miss, what shames you, what makes you feel so guilty and unhappy and lonely. Each day of this week mounting in devotion and absorption in preparation for Easter. The Mass of the Pre-sanctified and the beautiful temporary altar with the Blessed Sacrament exposed in its tabernacle, and you knelt, not carelessly on one knee, but on both, and bowed your head low. The grief of Friday —sometimes during those three hours of meditation on the Way of the Cross, your own suffering was intense, and yet you felt you could bear anything and always because the purpose of His

[161]

suffering had been so magnificent. The wonder of feeling your own prayer and meditation turn to strength—it was always that way and sometimes in those bad years—

"But I think it would be better," said Kenneth, "if you would try not to throw the whole business in my face in front of other people."

"What did I throw in your face?"

"It's not the best taste in the world, is it, to talk about what a tremendous sacrifice you made to marry me?"

"I didn't say that. I said that I gave up my religion. I was trying to be honest about it and not let Helen believe that I was a good Catholic. She knew—she said so—that Catholics are strict in observing Holy Week."

"You could have let the whole thing pass."

"I let so much pass. Sometimes I feel such a hypocrite."

"That's being silly. We've been perfectly open about this thing. I went to see your Bishop and had it out with him and then we agreed that we were going to make our own decisions and do what we thought was right. Apparently you can't stand up to it. You can't take it."

"I can take it. I do. But I don't want to lose it all. There are things I still can do. Out of respect."

"You go to church. You contribute. And you knew that they were determined to hold out on you in this other business, this confession and communion. I realize that's a great wrench for you. You were brought up to those rites and it worries you to go without them. I know that and I'm sorry. But there's no use in being morbid about it. Why try to embarrass people the way you did tonight?"

"Your sister started the discussion."

"Helen was just trying to be funny. You put the knife in."

"I didn't. I wasn't trying to do anything of the sort."

"Then, by all that's holy, I don't know what you were trying to do or why you dragged in the subject. You can't leave it alone.

I begin to think that the trouble is that you've found out that you can't eat your cake and have it too."

"You said—before—that when we were married it would all straighten out. You were so sure of it. I believed it."

"Well, maybe it would if you would let it. Give it time. I admit that I didn't know the depth of bigotry that exists."

"Bigotry? You mean me?"

"No, not you. I've come up against it in other quarters. Your Church is a very close organization, Barbara. But it can't run the world, and it can't run what is after all a Protestant country. Or set the calendar for everyone."

"It's this season of the year that's hard."

"Any season seems to make trouble for us. I think you know that I'm pretty broad-minded in my way, Barbara. I don't interfere with your practicing your religion. I want you to have as much of it as will make you happy—and more than you have now, if your priests and bishops will be reasonable. But I will say I don't like the interferences of your Church. I don't want it to tell me when I can have a party for my relatives or peek into my bedroom and set the schedule for my life with my own wife for private things. I don't like to think of myself or my children being surrounded like that. I'm getting fed up with a lot of it. And I've been pretty patient."

"Yes, you have."

"But until tonight, I thought at least that you considered me your husband."

"Ken—you know that was just a break. The stupidest thing I ever said! It meant nothing. It was a slip of the tongue. You surely must know that."

"It came out instinctively," he said with quiet bitterness.

"But—"

"There's no use arguing about what's said, Barbara. Let it ride. We can't help a lot of things. All I ask is that you will be good enough after this not to drag in the religious issue in front of people who aren't interested or involved, whether they're my relatives or anyone else."

He closed the door of the dressing room with that last word. Again she waited. After a long while she got up mechanically and finished getting ready for bed, turning off all the lights, even the tiny night one, which he liked left on so he could always see her. It would be easier in darkness. He must not see a trace of doubt or pain. What was right did not matter nor what was fair. But she must make Kenneth believe that she loved him, that he was her husband, before they slept.

Book II

Across the margent of the world I fled . . .

—"The Hound of Heaven" by
Francis Thompson

Chapter Twelve

Now there was fear as well as doubt. For if such things had been said once, they might be said again. Or thought. There was always the chance now that some incident might twist words or ideas until they screamed with pain or shouted in anger. Care had to be taken, but not mentioned. The incident of Holy Week had blown over. But did he still believe, in the back of his mind, that she couldn't stand up to her marriage, that she was sorry or inconsistent or ungrateful? Had he begun to hate the Church?

I didn't worry about such things two months ago, Barbara reminded herself. Once you begin, it's like a growth. Quick. She sat back on her heels, looking at the sudden shoots of the tulips in the garden she was weeding. They must have put the comparison into her mind. They had begun to show only two weeks ago and now they were high and pushing. It is all there in the bulb, she thought, and when it starts to grow, there's no stopping it. Unless you pull up the growth altogether and then you never get a flower. I'll do no pulling up.

She stood up, almost sorry this job was done. It was only noon. There was not enough to do on most days. The cleaning woman whom she employed was a fast and capable worker, and took a great deal of work off Barbara's hands. But neither Ken nor the doctor wanted Barbara to scrub. Meals were not difficult, for Ken was never home for lunch, and they had many invitations to dine out these days. One brought on another. Ken seemed to enjoy accepting them, and when they entertained in return he liked a measure of formality, so they hired a cateress and a waitress for those occasions.

What did other women do when their houses were clean, their flower beds weeded and their husbands at business? They had

[167]

children. It will be all right when I have children, thought Barbara. Unless that horror happens again and I can't have one. Why should it? The doctor said there was no reason in the world—but things don't go by reason.

The women who didn't have children, or who could delegate the care of them to someone else, gossiped about rumors or plans on the telephone, or arranged lunches at clubs and tearooms for the same purpose. They went to beauty parlors for long sessions. They shopped, playing one shop against another in a skillful game. They gambled, not too seriously, at bridge or canasta. Barbara had none of those habits. For too long she had not had time to build them up and, now that she had time, she found herself resisting and disliking any idle uses of it. There were of course good works to be done. Even women like Carol Harrison and Jennifer Rye occasionally might be found sponsoring benefits or working in drives to raise funds for some worthy purpose.

Barbara had formed no new connection with any such cause since she had left her professional work with the Social Agencies. It was going to be hard, as she knew, to accustom herself to the amateur side of social effort. She was cut off too from some activities which might have quite naturally claimed some of her attention, the kind that used to preoccupy her own mother, and still kept Agatha Braniff scurrying around during the period when there was an annual bazaar to raise money for the Cathedral. I must find more to do with my time, Barbara told herself this morning. But she turned her thoughts away from the recollection of the few minutes every Sunday, when she listened to the priests berating women of their parishes for not responding to the need for volunteer workers. The priest who was in charge of announcements for the day would always read out the names of the women who were heading the Altar Society, or supervising the Catholic Girls Clubs, or managing events to raise funds.

Barbara had not been asked to serve on any such tasks after she had married Kenneth and she knew why. She had a sense of being not ignored, but overnoticed, blackballed. Since the disastrous day when she and Kenneth had gone to church together, she was careful to sit inconspicuously in one of the rear pews of the cathedral, if she went there to Mass. But more often now she went to the services at St. Peter's, the church in the Italian parish, where she knew only a few of the people who were in attendance.

Kenneth had asked simply, when the first Sunday came around after she had recovered from the miscarriage, "Why do you go, darling?"

"I must. I really want to. In spite of anything, I couldn't miss Mass. It's not the sermon that matters, you know."

He had not argued that, nor referred to it again, nor suggested going with her. But she would have refused to let him come.

She was restless on this May morning. It occurred to her again that she might go to the offices of the Social Agencies and see if they did not have some part-time work that she could take over for a few hours occasionally. Several times before that idea had crossed her mind, and now it seemed to want to press past vague speculation into action. In the afternoon she took a bus into the city, for she always urged Kenneth to take the car unless there was a very important errand for her to do. They had decided that the time when they could afford two cars was a year or more in the future.

Sally Frick was, as always, glad to see her. Sally was looking hollow-eyed and yet bulkier. But she was in a state of delighted excitement and welcomed Barbara as a new audience. She announced a pregnancy.

"Think of me being caught!" she exclaimed. "As I say to people, I've got just about as much sense as one of the girls at the Rescue Home. But I won't have to prove paternity! I can't even deny it. Jack is so tickled that he goes around as if he were going to make the headlines, though how we're going to take care of a baby, and his mother, and everything else when I stop working, I don't know."

"But you are going to stop, Sally, aren't you?"

Sally said that she was. "Next month at the latest. I have to. I can't toss this event off as easily as some of our young feeble-minded friends at the Home. Probably because I'm pure intellect.

But I play out easily these days, and Jack would never forgive me if anything happened to our prospective heir-to-nothing. I'm quitting June first. I'd have stopped before if Mrs. Cunningham could have found anyone to take my place. But there isn't any mad rush after these underpaid jobs. Jane Foster will probably take over my work but I'll bet they'll have to pay her more."

"I thought Jane was in Europe on a job."

"She is. Or was, I guess, by this time. She must be on her way home. Her father died suddenly, you know."

"No, I didn't know."

"Well, you probably wouldn't have heard it in that charmed circle of yours. He's been an invalid for years and it's not so much a grief for Jane as a matter of responsibility. She has to come back and be with her mother, who's a little doddery. There's a house to sell and some bits and pieces of estate, apparently. Cunningham is pretty sunk about the whole thing. I think she wanted to make a big play in her annual report about the contribution this part of the country has made in sending workers to Europe. Now this knocks it for a loop and she'll probably be criticized for sending Jane over." Sally changed her expression abruptly as Mrs. Cunningham, the director, came into the office. She was a compact woman with a brisk gait and very short, electric-looking white hair. Barbara had liked working for her because underneath the competence there was a sense of what it was for. She greeted Barbara cordially.

Sally said, "I've just been telling Barbara about Jane's coming home."

"Yes, it's a shame. I did hope that she could stay even three more months. Then there would have been a good piece of work to our credit. As it is, it's so much waste."

"Where was she?" asked Barbara.

"In Vienna. She was making a study of the disposition of the children in the DP camps, and what we hoped was that it would be so factual that it could be a basis for some of the work we'll have to do later when we start to resettle a number of displaced persons. We'll need facts and while we always can dig them up from records here, it's always so much better to produce a first-hand report by a local person. I suppose somebody else will take it up where Jane leaves off but I wish it could be one of our own workers."

"Can't you send someone else? Dozens of people wanted to go over there, it seemed to me."

"That's not so true now, since it's definite that UNRRA is folding at the end of the year and nobody knows what will come next, if anything. Trained people don't want to give up good jobs here and go over there to get stuck without one in a few months. And you can't send just anybody who has an urge. A scatterbrain who wants to see Europe is no good. She would spend her time drinking brandy. It has to be someone who is accustomed to working with case records. Either of you girls could do it, if you were free to go. But you aren't. And Sally's got herself with husband and child."

"It would only be a three months' job?" asked Barbara.

"You don't mean that you'd consider it?"

"Why, I honestly don't know," said Barbara, "I might."

She spoke slowly, feeling her way. For an impulsive second it had seemed to her as if this were a chance to grasp distance and time and make them help her. And this was what she had always wanted to do, falling into her lap. She couldn't leave Ken for that long. Or could she? Was this a good time to be away from him, since they could not begin to have children yet and restraint was the only control authorized by her conscience. Would he mind under the circumstances? Would it be easier for him, for them both?

Sally was looking at her in complete surprise as if she could not believe what she heard. I must explain, thought Barbara. Or Sally will think it's a breakup.

"The only reason I might possibly consider it is that my husband is very busy, and may have to be away a good deal this summer."

That was not too untrue. Ken had said he might have to take some trips.

"Of course I would have to talk it over with him and I don't know what he'd say or if he'd be willing."

"Well, let's talk it over a little anyway," urged the director. "Come into my office."

Sally Frick looked after the other two. She still didn't believe it.

When Barbara telephoned him and said she was in town, Craig had a lift of spirit. He liked the suggestion of meeting at the club for dinner.

"I want to talk something over and it's pleasanter there than at your office," she explained.

"Talk over what?"

"Oh, something that came up unexpectedly. I want to get your reaction."

"Are you bothered about something?"

"No, it's exciting, not bothering. But I don't know what you'll think."

"You usually do know before I do. Feeling all right, aren't you?"

"Oh, perfect. You may think I'm crazy when I tell you this."

"I'm getting very curious. What have you done, bought a monkey?"

"No, you'd never guess."

He couldn't imagine what it might be that was on her mind. But she didn't sound worried or depressed. She'd spent too much money on something. He thought fondly, well, I won't kick. He liked the procedure of meeting her at the club, arriving there at five-thirty, asking the steward if Mrs. Craig had come in yet, hearing that she was there and finding her in the lounge. She wore a gold wool dress and there was a daffodil pinned on it. One of their own daffodils, she told him, when he admired it.

He ordered them a drink and asked, "What's up? What goes on that brought you into town?"

They sat together on a deep, square lounge that faced away from the rest of the room. He took her hand and felt its tenseness.

"What's on your mind, darling?"

"Well—what would you think about my going to Europe this summer?"

"Europe? I suppose you've been talking to travel agents. I'm afraid I couldn't swing it this summer. I couldn't afford either the time or money."

"I mean if I went alone? On a job. Let me tell you—this afternoon I stopped in at the Social Agencies—"

He let her tell him. He finished his drink and almost absently beckoned to the boy to repeat the order. He went from surprise and disbelief that it was possible to a slow realization that she was in earnest.

"You really mean it? You'd really like to go?"

"It seems such an extraordinary chance. And I was trying to think it out while I was waiting for you. You'd be well taken care of. I'm quite sure. Mrs. Dacey would give us a few hours every day, probably could come in and get your breakfast."

"That's the least of it."

"It wouldn't cost too much. I would only have to pay my fare over. Then I'd get my living over there, Mrs. Cunningham says, and they would pay my way back because they are responsible for sending people back. I think that it would actually cost less than if I spent the summer right here."

"We can skip that part of it too for the moment. I'm trying to get adjusted to the idea that you'd be away from me."

She didn't answer. There was none.

"We've only been married seven months."

"I know."

"And you want to walk out on me."

"No. No, Ken, don't say that."

"But you say you want to make this trip?"

"I've a feeling it might be the best thing for us."

"I don't think so at all. I'm definitely opposed to the whole notion. I think it would be ridiculous for you to go chasing off to Europe by yourself."

She sighed. "All right, Ken."

[173]

"You know it is ridiculous."

Her silence contradicted him. And the glow had gone out of her face.

"What you want, and aren't admitting," he insisted, "is to get away from me."

"Not from you. But—"

"Go on, be frank about it."

"I'm trying to be frank. It isn't that I want to leave you. But if I could get away from some other things—I believe I could think better at a distance, get some perspective. Here I'm in the middle of old habits—I can't shake them off or get away from them. I suppose I'm parochial, as you've told me once or twice. But I can't seem to help it. And when I heard about this chance it seemed to me that it was what I need, what we both need if we are going to be happy. I want to find out what I believe and what I'm afraid not to believe."

"You've got something there—"

"It's not you I want to run away from at all! It's an atmosphere I can't shake off unless I get away from it. It's something that claims me even more than you do—oh well, I won't talk of it any more."

"Maybe I'm the one who's wrong. Maybe you have a hunch, Barbara, about this thing that I missed. I begin to catch on to something."

"These next months," she said, "aren't going to be easy if we're together. You know instinctively how I feel. I'll be afraid that if we use birth control, we'll be punished, maybe never have a child. If we don't—you might as well not have a wife."

"I can take it."

"I know. But you don't agree. You aren't afraid the way I am. What I want to think out is whether I agree. I can't seem to do it here. The authority is too hard to shake off."

"But what you forget is that you'd have to come back to it."

"I think I might be different when I did come back. Stronger. A whole lot clearer in my own mind. Perhaps this is what I should

[174]

have done before we were married. But we wanted each other so much. And anyway, until we were married, I couldn't have realized how it would feel afterward to be so cut off, to be the person who's shouted at from the pulpit. It's impossible to realize beforehand how you are going to feel when everyone else goes to Communion. Or at least can go." She looked at him with a desperate honesty and said, "I don't even know how much of it is real yearning for God. I've come to the point where I don't know what's resentment and what is faith. Or what I do believe."

"Poor Barbara, what I did let you in for. I didn't know how bad it would be."

"It's not been bad. It's been wonderful mostly. Think how happy we've been."

"We were, weren't we? And are."

"We were. And we shall be. But there's something not quite right now. It's because of me, not you. You've done everything you can."

"Do you really believe this trip might straighten things out for you?"

She tried to laugh. "The director wouldn't offer it to me on that account! Of course the first thing is to do the job and the whole idea fascinates me. What I like most about it is that it's impersonal. I wouldn't be thinking of myself all the time. I'd get—"

"Well, look at the lovebirds!" cried Carol Harrison. "Isn't this honeymoon ever going to be over? I was wondering who was hiding in this corner and then I thought I recognized the top of Ken's head. Your hair has a definite curve to the left, Ken. Do you two want to be left alone?"

"No, of course not," said Barbara quickly, before Kenneth could make any gesture of holding back from companions. He'd had enough of this. There was nothing more to say.

"Well, the clans are gathering in the ladies' bar," said Carol. "I was just scouting for Jennifer, who should be someplace." She balanced herself on the arm of the sofa and asked, "I suppose you've heard the big news?"

[175]

"Which?"

"About Blair. He's going to marry the little Longman girl."

"Longman girl? I don't know her," answered Craig. "I know the boys but I didn't know there was a girl."

"Yes. There's a big gap between her and the boys. She's at least fifteen years younger than any of the others, must have come along when Papa and Mamma Longman thought all was settled and safe. I don't think she's even twenty, just fresh out of school and a convent at that."

"But Blair's over forty."

"I know. But he always did like the formative stage in girls. He met this utter child when he was being the old beau at one of the debutante parties here—she had come down to play with the other little girls!—and love and wisdom did the rest. Everybody's most excited. Women all over the country must be tearing up his old letters and giving up hopes."

"It's very interesting, because the Longman family—" began Barbara but Carol finished that too.

"I know what you're going to say; she's a Roman Catholic. But Blair makes a point of telling everyone he's going over to that Church. He says that it's the only thing to do."

There it was again, thought Craig. The Catholic business was pushing its way in everywhere. You never knew where it would turn up next, nor in what connection. "The only thing to do." Craig said to himself very cynically that Blair Wyatt was the sort of fellow who could swallow any religion and never gag, if enough money washed it down.

"Lovely feathers in so many caps!" declared Carol. "Everyone is claiming the credit for having put it over. Especially you-know-who in Palm Beach. She had them both there for a week end this spring. She wrote me that she had always wanted Blair related to her in some nonmarital way. That his capacity—well, you know Nina. She never cares what she says."

"When is all this coming off?"

"Not until autumn, they say. But it will make a very gay summer. And right now I want you to write down the second

[176]

week end in July on your calendars for we're going to have a house party out at Winnebago. We're moving out next week and that week end will be a very special one. I think it's the twelfth—"

"Too bad. Barbara won't be here to enjoy it," said Ken. "She's going to Europe for three months on a job."

Chapter Thirteen

From the plane window Barbara could see her husband, but she knew that he would not be able to identify her face between the little triangles of curtain which festooned the pane of glass. The sun was glaring too brightly against it. He could not hear her now, no matter how loudly she might call. It seemed to Barbara that he already was far more real to her than she to him. He stood, back where he must, behind the low barrier, waiting, though she had told him that she would prefer that he did not wait until the take-off.

It was so easy to single him out from the rest of the people who were watching the plane with its whirling propellers. Not that he was aloof. He wasn't. But he looked firmer than the other men, more of a piece, complete and sure. He was not stiffened, sagged or blemished and most of the others were, in one way or another. A tall man, proportioned as a man ought to be, lean, strong, well-behaved. There weren't so many. He looked as if he had a good place in life, one that he could count on. It isn't so good as it should be, she thought. He was beginning to tan—he'd be very brown after all those country week ends that people were already dating him for. He was lighting a cigarette now and making some remark to the man beside him. Or was he answering one? Was he saying, "My wife's just off for Europe"? Barbara suddenly wanted to know what he had said. The knowledge that she would never know came over her like sadness and she thrust the absurd thought away, a little ashamed of herself. For he said thousands, millions of things that she didn't hear. She knew only part of his life.

But the best part. He had said so. And now she was leaving that best part, breaking it up, taking that risk if only for a few months.

Why do you go, if you love him so much? She repeated unbelievingly in her mind, it's the thing to do, the best thing, we both came to that conclusion. He thought so too. Or had he merely given in to her? Ken hadn't wanted to argue about it at all, after that first evening. He wouldn't let her reopen the discussion. He was the reason she hadn't backed out. No, she thought—I probably would have come but I might have tried to back out.

He was smiling now, not with gaiety, but with civility. She knew that smile too. Beyond him, separated by a few spectators, was Miss Agatha Braniff, her plump body mashed against the railing. She had turned up surprisingly, to say good-by to Barbara, taking the bus out to the airport. She would probably refuse to let Ken drive her home, the silly, old dear thing, thought Barbara. She looks so hot and so heavy and the flowers on that print dress bloom in such queer places on her body. It was good of her to come. She's really fond of me in spite of disapproving. Aunt Agatha seemed glad when I told her I was going to Europe. From her point of view I suppose I'm leaving my sins behind. I wonder if she believes I am going away for good? If she only knew about last night, she wouldn't have any such idea. But she would never understand about last night. Virgins and martyrs don't. Wives do. Some wives. Ken, how can I go? Why did I ever let myself in for this crazy venture?

The plane trembled into motion, taxiing off from its anchorage, and the watchers at the port began to wave and cry out things that could not be heard by the passengers. Miss Braniff's handkerchief went excitedly up and down but Barbara was watching her husband. He turned away at once but her eyes went along with him and she saw him stop, turn again to look. She felt her heart crack.

Craig went on because he wanted to get this over. Then he remembered Agatha Braniff was there and he had a duty. This time he hoped that she would turn him down. He wanted to be alone

[178]

until he had full command of himself. It was only a few months' separation. It would probably be the best thing in the world for her. She'd been not quite herself ever since she'd had that miscarriage. God, it was a long way and things were still in bad and dangerous shape over there in Europe. Why hadn't he put his foot down, said he wouldn't stand for it?

"Miss Braniff, can't I drive you back to town?"

She said, bunching up the handkerchief, "I just can't get over it. The way that airplane goes off. But it is safe, isn't it?"

"Oh yes. This is beautiful flying weather. And they don't let them take off unless it's very safe."

He remembered with an ugly twinge what Barbara had said, and it was the last thing he wanted to remember right now. She had been joking, not quite being funny, when she said, "There's one thing. If the plane should go down anywhere along the way, it would solve the problem of where an apostate like me could be buried."

"Absolutely safe," he repeated with emphasis. "Can't I take you? My car's right over here."

Miss Braniff said surprisingly, "Why, thank you. If it isn't out of your way, it would be very nice."

So he was saddled with her and had to do his best. He stopped the car on the way out, so that Agatha could see the plane lift from the end of the runway and get its even flight started. He wanted her to see it. He wanted to see it himself. After a plane was airborne on a day like this, there would be no trouble. The accidents were usually in taking off and landing. But all those other planes she would take—

"I think the trip will be very good for Barbara," said Miss Braniff, "and so very interesting."

He agreed, turning the car back to the highway and stepping on the gas.

"I am sure you will miss her, Mr. Craig."

"Oh, of course. But I'll get along all right."

"You were very good to let her go," stated Miss Braniff.

"It was what Barbara wanted to do," he answered grimly, hoping that she wasn't going to chatter politely all the way back to the city.

The virgin and martyr knew grimness when she heard it in a man's voice. She knew, in fact, a great deal about men's moods. There had been times in her life when she had opened up bad moods in men as if they had been abscesses. She had done it with her brother Julian when he was disgracing the family with a young girl and everyone knew it except his wife. She had done it with her father, when he used to brood over revenges after social slights. She did it with the instrument of frank talk, probing talk, and only when she felt she had to. Once she had not done it in time. She had not opened up Stephen's mood when it was poisoning his whole system. And he had killed himself.

She was thinking as they drove along, in her untidy and comprehensive way, of that lovely house this nice man had bought for Barbara; of his going back to it alone tonight; of how happy the two of them seemed to be, and so romantic with each other; of how they couldn't possibly be happy as things were, not in the right way at least; of how young they both were, Mr. Craig and Barbara; of what a pity it was that Leslie Field was not dead, poor fellow; that the trip would do Barbara good, but some men wouldn't have allowed her to go; that perhaps a little advice would do Mr. Craig good, and he might even welcome it; that he might not have considered the possibility nor even know about it.

"I think your home is beautiful," she said for a start.

"Thanks so much. It's comfortable."

"You've given dear Barbara so much in a material way."

"That's about all I'm good for, I'm afraid."

"Oh, I don't think so, Mr. Craig. Of course I am aware of the problem. It has troubled me very much indeed."

"I'm afraid that I don't believe that talking about it does much good. It's very kind of you to be interested."

"Would you mind my saying something?"

"Not at all," he said with great reserve. Here it came again, and now from this old girl. "All I meant to imply was that Barbara and I have explored the situation quite fully, and have to meet it as seems best. For ourselves. I know that sometimes she has worried about the fixed attitude of your Church but apparently nothing can be done to alter that."

"There are arrangements sometimes," said Agatha.

"So I always had heard and believed. I got no co-operation, myself."

She said, "I'm sure it would be all right if you lived as brother and sister."

He almost drove the car off the road as he heard what she said, and wondered if she knew that she had said it. But she had, all right. Those were the words.

"I'm afraid I don't get the point, Miss Braniff."

She said, without any faltering or blushing, "You see, I know of several cases where that was done. Naturally I didn't ask too much, but, in this one case, I was told very definitely that, while this couple shared a house and went about among their friends—and no one ever said anything because people can be so understanding—that it was a brother and sister relationship."

He slowed down and looked around at her as if to be sure that she was the one who was talking and saying that. He would have expected her to be flustered as he had seen her before in his own house. But she wasn't.

"You mean that some people put it over like that?"

"Put it over?"

"You mean that the Church says it's all right for a man and woman to live under the same roof as—as brother and sister—and yet be a married couple?"

"I'm sure it is done. In these two cases that I know about—"

"But how would anybody know?"

That did flush her cheeks.

"Well, of course, that would be a very private matter."

"I should certainly hope so. Miss Braniff, does Barbara—did you ever suggest this idea to Barbara?"

"Well, no, I didn't. I thought of it once or twice because I knew what this terrible excommunication must mean to her, but I never brought the matter up with her. Barbara is so—well, emotional. It's always easier to talk to a man about some things."

"You're amazing," he said succinctly. "It's amazing."

"Please understand that I'm no authority on Church Law, Mr. Craig. I don't know under what circumstances a dispensation like that is given. But I'm quite sure that in some cases it has been given. And I was thinking, when I was out at your lovely home, what a pity it is that Barbara shouldn't have the companionship and the protection she needs and yet not feel—well, as she must feel. If you could deny yourselves—I know I speak very frankly and I hope you'll pardon me but I have had brothers, Mr. Craig—if you could make that arrangement, it would result in great graces for you both."

"Graces?"

"I mean God will bless you. After all, Mr. Field is a very dissipated man. He can't be in good health."

Craig laughed aloud. "You're wonderful, Miss Braniff! Miss Agatha, you are beyond a doubt the most sophisticated woman I have ever met. I never knew anyone like you for going right to the point."

Now that he had begun to laugh he found it hard to stop.

"I'm really quite serious," she insisted, after it had gone far enough.

"I know you are. I don't doubt it for a minute. You've given me a completely new slant on things. So that's one way—well, it's certainly an eye-opener."

"I'm afraid you think I'm presuming."

"I think you're a great woman," he told her. "If there were more straight-shooters like you, everything would be better."

But he grinned again, irrepressibly. She did not resent it. Men were like that. They always acted as if sex were a laughing matter. Unless their wives were having babies and then it didn't seem so funny. But he was nice about it too. He had not taken offense. When he came to think it over, he would realize what she meant and meditate on it more seriously perhaps. They could have every-

[182]

thing else in a worldly way, and a very pleasant life for the time being. If they made the sacrifice.

Craig took her to her own front door against the suggestion she began to make now that he could drop her anywhere. He handed her out as if she were a queen. The amusement was still lighting the back of his eyes.

"I do hope you won't consider anything I said was criticism of you personally, Mr. Craig."

"Any time you want to criticize me, I'll be flattered. Thank you, Miss Agatha."

After he left her and had driven around the corner, he let the laugh really come. To think the old girl had it in her! She was a great old sport to come right out with the idea in so many words. No beating about the bush. He certainly would like to tell Barbara that when he and her aunt did get cozy, they stopped at nothing.

Tell Barbara. That sobered him. Was it true that her aunt had not said anything to Barbara about this? Was it all hokum anyway? Or did they really fix things like that sometimes? Of course the woman would have to run and confess to the priest if they didn't keep it up, if they slipped, if they took a night off from being— brother and sister.

Not for him and Barbara! If old Agatha only had any idea of what their love was like, what it meant, if she could only imagine how they had felt last night. What was it Barbara had said that her aunt was always called? Virgin? Virgin-and-martyr. That was about right. The old girl thought that to live without sex was just as easy as skipping a meal.

The conversation had dulled the cutting edge of separation. He went back to work, not too depressed. The laugh had done him good. Much later in the afternoon he chuckled again as he thought of Miss Agatha's approach. If he could only tell Barbara. Craig looked at his wrist watch. It was nearly five o'clock. She would be in Washington by this time.

Chapter Fourteen

Barbara had hardly arrived in Washington before the reasons for the journey she was undertaking began to lose their strength and to fall out of logical sequence. It looked like the errand of a fool on the first day, as she went from one office to another, reporting her errand to people who certainly had not been waiting for her to come, but had to dig her name and credentials out of their files and sheaves of correspondence.

"Oh, yes, here it is. Barbara Craig? For the Austrian mission. Is it Miss or Mrs. Craig?"

They always asked that. It was like the first question of the quiz-master, "Are you married?" necessary to satisfy the basic curiosity about any man or woman. All the facts were there, in the question-naires which she had carefully filled out, but apparently no one read them.

Her usefulness seemed vague and inconsequential to herself as well as to everyone else, after a few interviews and conversations. She was a small replacement part being supplied to the huge wrecker that had been sent to the scenes of the world's catastrophes, but most of the people whom Barbara met that day seemed too unskilled to know just where the part was missing or how she should be fitted into place. Or they were indifferent. The indifference was sticky and wearying, like the heat. She had to hunt down the people with whom some contact was necessary. She felt unattached and yet there was a steady ache from severed habit and emotions. And there was no word from Kenneth. That was her fault, for she had made him promise not to telephone her until she reached New York.

"By that time I'll be all fixed up," she said, "and can tell you my adresses abroad and all about my job. I'll be so busy in Washington that it would be hard to reach me."

The first night was a ragged one. Worse than the day had been. She kept waking up and not believing her surroundings. She felt for a bedside lamp which was not there. She saw a window in the wrong place, open to a dim glow that was cast up from the canopy over the hotel entrance. It was a disagreeable, livid light but she did not draw down the shade, hoping that before dawn a breeze might float through the hot, stuffy room. Once in a while she heard the cries and whoops of roaming boys or a drunken shout like a taunt. Otherwise nothing broke the silence that lay stiff and heavy over her, like a too thick blanket. No breathing sound of a companion in the room. No lover. No husband. No murmured repetition of love during a moment's waking. In those half-conscious hours, Barbara's mind could make no reason vigorous enough to stand up against the absence of what she had left.

So she got up at two o'clock and tried to read a German book which she had brought with her to help her brush up on the language. In the convent school where she had been educated, German and French nuns had taught their native tongues with diligence and discipline, and that was proving lucky now. But her attention fled from the book. She began a mystery story and even the brutal characters and incidents could not shock her into interest. She stacked the books on the bureau after an hour, took her rosary out of her purse and went to bed, hoping that the beads with their prayers might bring her peace.

The rosary used to be her constant companion at night before she had married Kenneth. It was something familiar to hold on to, one thing to feel sure was continually there, even if her mind wandered or she fell asleep in the middle of a decade. When she was a child the beads had always been a link between herself and hope—I'll say a Rosary for that intention, that I may not be tempted again, that I may be pure all week, that I may pass in French. The little strings of prayers were always attached to some aspiration or desire—or that I may always take willingly whatever comes from Thy hand—sweet or bitter.

She had given up the habit of taking her rosary to bed for final or wakeful prayers. For she was reluctant now to have Kenneth

[185]

find it in her hand, or pressed against her cheek, or under her pillow, as he had done once or twice.

"What do you do with those beads anyhow?" he had asked, a little interested yet almost teasingly. "Some of the boys in the Navy used to carry them and they certainly hung on to them like lucky pieces. Have they got something to do with death or protection from it? I know that once when a friend of mine died —he was a Roman—and I went to his house to pay my respects to the family, a whole lot of people were kneeling around the casket and going full tilt with those beads. They seemed to be saying the same thing over and over."

"It sounds like that unless you understand," said Barbara, "but it really isn't repetition. The Rosary has nothing to do with death except that it's a pious custom to say it around a coffin like that. But you can say it any time and if you just pronounce the words, you're not saying it well. You see, when you repeat those prayers, you are supposed to meditate on the Mysteries."

"Mysteries? Don't make it harder."

"I'm trying not to. The Mysteries are the important things that happened in the life of the Blessed Virgin and Jesus and they're divided into Joyful and Sorrowful and Glorious ones. The Joyful Mysteries concern Mary mostly, like the Annunciation, the Visitation and the Birth. The Sorrowful ones are the mysteries of the Passion, and the Glorious ones, of course, are the Resurrection, the Ascension—" she paused because he was looking at her with admiring tenderness and she was sure he was not taking in what she said.

"I hadn't any idea there was so much to it," said Kenneth. "I thought it was just a religious chant of some sort."

"Ah no—you're supposed to think as you recite the prayers. To be joyful, and then sorrowful and to give thanks. Not that everyone does! Or that I do it the way I should, myself. It can get mechanical. You get to rattling them off. But it ought to be a beautiful devotion and it can be. You can say a Rosary for some special purpose too, for help in trouble, or for something you need very much, or for someone that you love."

"I like that. I hope you say it for me. Use the beads for me, will you, darling?"

So she knew that she had not explained, nor made him understand. It was impossible to begin with that one thing and it could throw others out of proportion. He must not think the saying of the beads was a love charm. Barbara stopped taking them to bed with her. It was often Kenneth's bed as well.

Tonight she went back to the Rosary, hoping she could rest her mind against the great meditations, and too because she was lonely and she had so often turned to those prayers in loneliness before. She began the familiar routine of prayer and, as she lay exhausted after the cleavages and efforts of the past few days, supplications long out of use drifted through her mind.

"Make him a better man—give him strength," she found her lips saying as she began the fourth decade. She had fallen back into an old habit and it woke her with a shudder because that prayer, said a thousand times for Leslie Field, was so out of place in her life now. For a second she felt that she was disloyal to Kenneth. It was like that time, she said to herself, that I spoke of Leslie as my husband before Ken and his relatives. Ken was more angry than I've ever seen him and he had every right to be.

But it was not disloyalty, not that night and not now, when Leslie crept back into my prayers. God knows someone should pray for him. But I was asleep and incoherent. He means nothing to me, hasn't for years. Leslie comes to your mind now, Barbara told herself, only because it is so near to David's birthday and you've been thinking about that. You always do and always will in early June. If David had lived until next Thursday he would be nine years old. And you probably wouldn't be going to Europe the next day.

She had not mentioned the birthday to Kenneth for he might have worried about her becoming sad or morbid on the date, when away from his own care. And Kenneth had never known David. To him the child was a remote little ghost. Barbara knew that. They never could share David. It was remembering him as vividly as

[187]

she herself did that reminded her of David's father, even to revive the old unproved, bitter feeling that it might have been Leslie's fault that David died. Leslie had a bad cold but with David it was pneumonia. Perhaps it had made no difference and Leslie had suffered terribly. In spite of everything, he had loved David as much as he was capable of loving.

All that was distant and faded. Erased now. Almost erased. There sometimes did seem to be an indelible mark, a kind of imprint that she could not rub away. In this anonymous room, where it could hurt or trouble no one but herself, Barbara let another thought out of deep hiding. Could those who said it was impossible to destroy a marriage know something cruel but true? Love could go completely, and all desire, companionship could become a horror and betrayal and shame—but even after all that was good was drained out of marriage was there a residue, something indestructible? A terrible unity that wouldn't dissolve?

So the Church said. It didn't identify marriage with happiness or contentment or even decent living. Those things were good and it was better if they went along with marriage. But if they did not, there remained the marriage. Some women accepted that as inevitable. Poor ones especially. They couldn't break away from a man, no matter what complete misery life with him meant. Like that Riggs woman, who always went back to drunken beatings. That was fear of change, ignorance, lack of imagination, the "my man" psychology—those things explained it better than any mystic indissolubility.

Kenneth seemed to have erased completely his first marriage. But of course that had been annulled. It never was a sacrament. Do you actually believe that makes the difference, Barbara asked herself? They were just as close, physically united, promised—he and Nina had it all and must have believed it all to begin with, as Leslie and I did. It is strange that since Ken and I have been married, I am much more conscious of his first marriage.

But the marriage that really is a sacrament is the one between us now. It can't be, under the circumstances, you know better. Don't think of it—don't get tangled up—think of Ken and how we love each other and that he's lying in our room now, perhaps awake, missing me, missing us. Barbara slept with the thought, the crucifix of her rosary pressed against one cheek.

She buttoned the khaki coat and turned to look at herself in the mirror on the wall of the army outfitting store. It was an unlikely image of herself but handsome and exciting in a new way. She must have a picture taken in this outfit for Ken—perhaps she could get one in the airport on Friday, if they had any of those self-photographing machines there. Would he like her in uniform? Perhaps not. They said men didn't. They wanted women to look feminine and not so impersonal as this. Perhaps she wouldn't send him a picture but try the uniform on for him when she came home again. When she came home again as she would, lovely thought!

She was started now and she had only to finish. The reasons for going were on their toes this morning and standing up very well.

"Is it okay?" asked the fat woman who did not care whether she sold anything or not. She got no commission for fitting strangers out in army regulation clothes.

"Yes, it feels fine. I really like it."

"A lot of girls feel like that at the start. But you get tired of it, they tell me. Personally I wouldn't want to wear one of those rigs for very long. Not in this weather."

"It depends on what you're going to do. I wouldn't want to wear it around home."

"Some women like to get away from home, I guess. Not me. Well, I sure wish you luck."

Then the doctor at the examining office inspected the medical certificates of inoculation that she showed him and jabbed her once more with multiple vaccine.

"That takes care of everything, as far as I can see. You're safe from practically everything, except a pregnancy. That's what you girls have to look out for over there."

"I'll wait until I get back," she said.

"It would be the best idea. Have you got some vitamins? You'll

[189]

need them with the kind of diet you're going to run up against in Europe. They're still short of a lot of things. You're underweight, aren't you?"

"Not too much."

He eyed her with shrewd carelessness. She was not his personal patient. She hadn't asked his advice about going to Austria. He could tell at a glance that she was healthy and well-kept as well as beautiful but she seemed highly charged. He wondered in which direction the man was, noting on her card that she was married.

"Husband over there?"

"No, he's on this side."

"He must be a pretty generous fellow."

"He is."

"Well, you want to take it easy. Take it as easy as you can. You can't make Europe over. And you don't want to come back sick or with shot nerves and pay for this junket for the next ten years."

"It's a job, not a junket, doctor."

"Oh sure. I know that. Well, good luck, Mrs. Craig."

They were all like that, cynical, not praising, wondering why she was doing this, especially since she had a husband.

The man she saw in the personnel office seemed to know better than the others where she was headed, and why. He found her application, looked over the data that was pinned to it, and said that he didn't really know who would be her boss in Vienna. There were a great many changes being made. A lot of people, he remarked, were getting out from under.

"You'll find out what the setup is when you get there. They can brief you on the immediate situation better than I can. The office is on the Stalinplatz. Do you know Vienna?"

"No, not at all."

He said, "Then you won't have so much of a shock. Know German, do you?"

"Yes, but my French is better."

"Two languages? Good. That will give you a tremendous advantage. Where did you pick those up?"

"I was educated in a convent." Where Mother Rahn was jealous of her German class and Mother deBuys of her French one. Barbara cast a grateful thought back at their strictures.

The personnel man had looked down again at her application.

"I see here that you're a Roman Catholic."

"Yes."

"Well, for my money, it's time that they sent more Catholics over. However, you realize, of course, that we have to maintain an attitude of detachment."

"I should think so. But I'm not too sure that I know exactly what you mean."

"I mean that you'll be attached to a government agency, not a Catholic one."

"Of course."

"And being a Catholic yourself, you want to watch your step. The situation is very tricky. You can't let yourself be used."

"I'll only be working on records."

"Records are very important. They're often all we have to go on in matters of repatriation. And that's life or death, or one kind of life against another. The liaison officers of the various countries fight for these unaccompanied children, these orphaned kids that the war left adrift. Our people have quite a time between the London Poles and the Warsaw Poles. Of course it's just a skirmish on the edge of the big battles. But our organization is a declared neutral—has got to be if it isn't to be destroyed even before its time runs out."

"What battles do you mean?"

"The ones between your Church and Communism. You must know what the situation is. Both sides want all the people they can get. They both want kids. To educate their way, to train up. Of course the conservative governments and exiled groups all over Europe are lined up with the Catholic Church, using it. Or maybe it's the other way around. I don't pretend to know which comes first, the chicken or the egg."

He paused, scanning her through a puff of smoke from his cigarette to see what her reaction might be. She waited for him to go on. She handles herself beautifully, he thought.

[191]

"Anyway, our people have developed a policy in repatriating both adults and children who come under their charge and they work of course closely with the allied military authorities. Theoretically, the Russians are our allies and working with us. In the field, it's not so clear nor so simple. You'll be briefed in all this and expected not to let any personal views affect your professional attitude. Some people tell me that Catholics can't do that, that they aren't allowed to, that they are supposed to slant everything their way. But I've seen Catholics on various jobs, playing good ball."

"I am glad you say that," she answered with cool pride, "because I know it's true. Good Catholics are convinced that what they believe is right but they are not subversive. You can trust me to follow the policy of the organization while I'm working for it. If I couldn't, I'd get out."

"You look as if you would. Between you and me there's been some criticism that we've kept Catholics out. That's not true. We've not had enough qualified Catholics to send. They have their private groups working over there that absorb their best workers. That's why I'm glad to see a person like you going over for us."

Barbara's face changed. She lifted her hand and smoothed a frown from her forehead but it stayed in her eyes and her voice.

"Since this has come up, Mr. Meader, I probably should tell you that I'm not too well qualified in that way. I'm not in good standing in my Church."

He looked again at the record. "It says here you're a Catholic."

"I am. I always have been. But recently a personal matter came up—there is no use in bothering you with it, I'm sure—but it meant that I went against the decision of the Bishop in my diocese so—there it is. The Bishop would tell you I'm not a good Catholic. It's not that I don't believe in the Church but I'm under discipline for my own conduct."

The words had come hard and truly, as the man across the desk realized. He liked her even better. They'd tried to run her life and she had bucked, he thought.

"Well," he said slowly, "we just go by the record here. We can't delve into parochial matters."

"Thank you. I just wanted to make that clear. But I'm sure that religion won't enter into this work I'm going over to do."

He gave a disbelieving snort of laughter. "My dear young woman, tell me that when you come back!"

Chapter Fifteen

It was a relief to get away from the knowledgeable obscurity which seemed to surround everyone in Washington. She tried to describe it in a quick letter to Kenneth, but the impression came out flat, and sounded rather depressed as she reread it, so she tore it up. She would write him fully from New York. Barbara disposed of her errands and secured her passport, although she waited for three anxious hours in one office, where she had been sent to pick it up, before she was told that it was quite ready for her in another. On Wednesday afternoon she took a plane for New York and found that suddenly she became an expected Mrs. Kenneth Craig, not the Barbara Braniff Craig of all her applications, who was one more social worker.

Kenneth had insisted on telephoning and making hotel reservations for her in New York. There, he said, he knew his way around. He didn't know that crowd she would be mixing with in Washington, so he kept out of that. The clerks at the desk of the New York hotel where they had stayed when they were on their wedding trip remembered her, and said they were glad to see her again, and that they were sorry that Mr. Craig was not with her. It was like a faint copy of staying here with Kenneth, and she had hardly settled her bags in her room before a bellboy arrived with a huge box of flowers from him. She ached for Kenneth and yet his arm seemed to be around her, relinquishing nothing, and that was good.

The city was their city. She must write him that there were azaleas in Rockefeller Plaza. She would tell him on the telephone tonight. She began to make a list of the things she must not forget to tell him, and also she would write that long, full letter. She would send him a present. In his favorite haberdashery next morning she bought an expensive tie for Kenneth and attached a card, saying that he probably wouldn't like it but she did.

Her spirits had risen though she still felt as if she had better not eat very much, and she had slept badly during the second night as well as the first. But three months was not long, and this was—she could credit it again now—the right thing to do. From every standpoint. Her interest had been reawakened by Mr. Meader's disillusioned tying up of her work with destinies.

There were two telephone messages attached to her door when she came back to the hotel that afternoon. It was the same call, repeated twice. Please call—the message read. The number written down meant nothing to her but she sat down to get in touch with it. The call might be from someone who was connected with her assignment.

"Hello," answered a man's voice, harshly.

"Is this Stuyvesant 2-8643?"

"That's right, lady."

"Does someone there want to speak to Mrs. Craig?"

"Mrs. Who? No, lady, you got the wrong—oh, wait a moment. Craig? Say, here's your call, fellow." He had evidently been interrupted or reminded by someone else. It seemed as if it might be some public place at the other end of the line, a drug store, more likely a bar—

"Hello. Is this Barby?"

She knew instantly who was talking. She never could, though she would try, forget that voice and the way he said that nickname. She tried to make it not come true.

"This is Mrs. Craig."

"I know that too. This is Leslie."

"Oh." Why didn't she hang up? But it seemed as if she must not. It would be so viciously hard.

"When I found out you were in town I thought I'd give you a ring."

"How did you find that out?"

"Is it supposed to be a secret?"

"No. I wondered. That was all."

"There are plenty of newstands in New York where you can pick up a paper from your old home town, you know. I do it once in a while. I like to keep up with my friends. And—family. As was. I saw an item about your going to Europe and figured you might put in a day or two here. I had to call a few hotels to track you down but I could pretty well guess you wouldn't be staying over on Sixth Avenue. How are you?"

"I'm fine. How are you?"

"I couldn't be better. As a matter of fact, things are just beginning to break right for me."

He always said that. Always. But remember, it doesn't mean a thing.

"And how is Craig?" he asked cheerfully.

"He's very well."

"Is he with you?"

"No, not on this trip. I'm on a job."

Perhaps she should have pretended that Kenneth was with her. But what difference did it make?

"Haven't ditched him already, have you?"

"No," she said coldly. "We're extremely happy. But he has a very important meeting in St. Anthony on Friday." She stopped, annoyed at making any explanation.

"Of course it isn't any of my business. I only asked because I thought I might come around and say hello to you both. I met Kenneth Craig once but he may not recall it. Since he's not here, can't I take you at least to dinner?"

"Oh no. Thanks."

"When do you leave for Europe?"

"Pretty soon. I don't quite know. Tomorrow maybe." Don't be too definite, you never know how he'll try to make use of things, or hang around.

"Too busy to see me for a little while tonight?"

"I'm not too busy," she said, "but I don't think it's a good idea."

"It would mean a lot to me, Barby."

"It wouldn't do any good."

"It would to me. Please." His voice was clear but very low as if he were talking in a corner, trying to be inaudible. She could hear other voices indistinctly. "I can't tell you how much it would mean because I'm talking in a place where there are a lot of other people right now. But I would like to have a chance to tell you about my new plans, what I have in prospect, and get your slant on it—"

His plans. His bluffs. Don't believe him for a minute. He can still be plausible, apparently.

"Leslie, there's no sense in seeing each other. We're divorced, finished."

"I appreciate that. But what seems to me more important is that it's the Little Corporal's birthday."

The words twisted her heart. That was what they used to call David because the baby folded his arms in a miniature Napoleonic way. She could see the pose now.

"Poor Little Corporal, I've been thinking of him all day," said Leslie Field.

That wasn't true. She knew it. But he had remembered the date. Leslie loved David, as much as he could love anyone. And David had adored his father. His father made him wild with joy. When Leslie came home—no matter what state he was in—of course a child didn't see—

"Don't," she said to her thoughts or to Leslie. It came out aloud.

"I'm sorry, Barby. I didn't mean to upset you or remind you—"

"I hadn't forgotten."

"You couldn't spare time for a drink? Or an early dinner? It would make so much difference to me. I know I'm getting what you think I deserve. I haven't any kick coming. But it is pretty lonely sometimes. I'd like to see you. Have you put on any weight?"

"No."

"Good girl. Just as beautiful as ever."

"Which wasn't beautiful at all."

"Craig thinks so, doesn't he?"

"I don't want to talk about what he thinks."

"I don't either, as a matter of fact. Barby, I don't want to be a nuisance but I need the lift you always give me, when I see you. It won't hurt anybody, you know. Not you or anybody else." .

"I know that. But I've last-minute things to do, packing and letters. I haven't much time, Leslie. I would have to be back early and can't play around."

"That's all right. I can pick you up any time you say."

"No, I'd rather that you didn't come here."

"Oh, well, I understand. Maybe you're right. Anything you say, Barby. Where can I meet you?"

She chose a Longchamps restaurant quickly. One at a considerable distance from her hotel. She told him she would be inside at a table, near the door, at six o'clock.

You had to, she told the self that was impatient at her yielding. You couldn't do anything else. Leslie was not sincere about many things but it was true that he loved Davy and this must be a bad day for him. With nothing left. He didn't sound as if he had been drinking. A little nervous and excitable but not worse than that. Can he possibly have improved, changed? Got hold of himself? No—remember what all the doctors told you. When he was sober he could always be charming if he wanted to be, and very persuasive too.

He probably will need money, Barbara thought. I can't give him much. I have figured the travel expenses very closely and need all my traveler's checks for that. The only extra money I have is the five hundred that Ken told me to keep in dollars and spend over there. I want to buy something beautiful with it for the house. I'll pay for the dinner tonight. I won't let Leslie do it. I couldn't stand that. Twenty dollars will more than cover it, drinks and all, and I won't get that extra pair of walking shoes.

I'll give Leslie one happy evening. One that he can remember. I'll build him up—he loves that—and remind him of how Davy loved to see him. It will be the last time I'll see him—that has to be made clear—but perhaps I can make him feel that he's not utterly outcast.

She was in the appointed place at six o'clock. Excitement and repressed apprehension made her eyes dark, navy blue like the dress she wore. Her hat was soft and small and yellow, a travel hat to match the coat that was on the back of her chair. Pretty colors and a lovely girl, thought a number of men, and looked back to realize that she was not quite so young as they had thought at first.

At half-past six she ordered a long drink, because she could not sit there doing nothing any longer. She made it last, thinking of all the things that might have happened. Leslie might have gone to another Longchamps. There might have been an accident. There were accidents all the time, only few of them came very close. This might be a close one. Oh no, she thought in pity, that would be too dreadful when he was looking forward to this dinner. But perhaps he never intended to meet her and this was his idea of a revengeful joke. No, not likely. It might be that he'd had a heart attack. The doctors had warned him. How would she ever find out? How long should she wait for him? Why had she ever agreed to this meeting? He was probably drinking somewhere and had forgotten all about it.

He had been drinking but not quite to the point of forgetting. It was nearly seven when he arrived at the restaurant and the shock of his appearance was so great that she did not immediately notice his condition. He came into the place as if he was afraid, yet he was insolent. His tallness had a stoop as if he had slept in bad beds. His blondness had gone gray, his skin was sallow and his eyes furtive, his clothes very shabby and his tie too bold. Seeing him, she remembered quite clearly that he had been conspicuously handsome, with a clean Nordic coloring and an athlete's body. What had he done to that young man who was a tennis champion?

The pity went as she realized he was very unsteady. The consequences might be bad. She had planned in the first few minutes while she waited, a delicious dinner with a couple of cool Martinis as prelude. Now she didn't want to risk a drink with him.

"Here," she said, as his look fumbled around. "Here I am, Leslie."

"Oh, hello, Barby." His voice was a little loud, a little defiant. "You got here first. I'm sorry but I had very important business. I met a man who wanted to talk to me about his affairs. Very important affairs too."

"Never mind," she told him. "Sit down. Relax."

"Same old Barby, giving out the orders. So you had to wait for me. You should have let me call for you. Like a gentleman. You never want to be ashamed, Barby, of anyone, not even an ex-husband."

"I'm not ashamed of anybody. I'm just hungry. Shall we have dinner here or would you rather go somewhere else?"

The head waiter did not have a welcoming look for Leslie, and, suddenly and completely, Barbara felt as she used to feel. She knew what she had to do, and began with the methods she had almost forgotten.

"We don't want to eat yet," declared Leslie. "This fellow can't hurry us. We want a few drinks. Waiter—boy!"

The waiter approached hesitantly. Let him have one drink, thought Barbara, and then I must get him out of here before they throw us out.

"Tell me about your plans, Leslie. What's this new project?"

He didn't seem to remember that. He was possessed by a conversation he had just had with a very important man. Barbara could guess at it.

"Don't you want a drink yourself?" he asked, as the waiter brought only one glass.

"No, I've had one."

"Don't trust me, do you? You think I'm drunk. Well, tell me this. I wasn't drunk when you talked to me on the phone, was I? Was I?"

"Not a bit. You aren't too bad now."

"Bad enough. You got rid of me. You led the procession. They all got rid of me. All the rats followed, so the ship sank."

"You're drinking enough to sink it."

"I said to this man—this very important man who wants me to handle all his affairs—and there's money in it. I said, 'The trouble with me is that I married a girl and she didn't stay by me,' I told him. 'I married a little Irish Catholic girl. I signed all the papers— then she put me in a nut house—got the priest to let her divorce me'—what did that cost?"

"Let's go, Leslie. I'm going."

[199]

The waiter put the bill for the drinks on the table. She laid money on it. Leslie protested.

"That's not the way a lady acts. That's humiliating to a man—"

She went to the door, ignoring stares and grins, and he finally followed. In the cab they took, he quarreled with her, abused first her and then himself. It was the same terrible routine. She coaxed him at last to another restaurant, a noisier and more careless one, but he would not eat the steak he ordered.

"Where do you live, Leslie?"

"You don't have to worry about me. Not from now on. I've got a very important connection—"

"Yes, I know. But tonight. Where are you going to sleep?"

"What do you want to know for?" His eyes grew sly, horrible. "I thought you were pretty well fixed."

"You're drunk, Leslie. Be careful. Listen to me. I'm leaving you now. I have to go back to my hotel."

"I'll take you there. Like a gentleman."

"I'll take myself there. You stay here, finish your drink, and pay the bill."

The thought of the bill frightened him. There must have been experiences. "I was going to explain to you," he began, "I'm just a little short."

"You don't have to explain. Leslie, will you do what I tell you to do? The way you used to, once in a while, when you really promised? Will you please?"

"Always do what you say. Hard girl. Cold girl. But always do what you say."

"Then take this money. It's quite a lot. Two hundred dollars."

His eyes glistened. How long it must be since he has had so much, she thought.

"I'll give it to you if you go now to a hotel and get some sleep. Only on that condition. And tomorrow you get yourself some clothes."

"It's a good idea." He fingered the bills. "Your money."

She said, "It's a birthday present from Davy. What you might have given him, if things had been different."

His soft battered face worked and tears gathered in his bleared eyes. She laid a hand for a second on his and left him. Forever, she thought.

Her spirit had been torn to shreds in the last few hours. She had made a mistake. She should not have seen Leslie. But at least now he had a little money. It was actually Ken's money, his gift to her. But he had told her to spend it for something she wanted, that she couldn't afford otherwise. She had. How strange it was. She had squandered it on a hopeless, helpless, irresponsible wreck of a man and it would clatter into the tills of bars. But for an instant it had seemed so right, so definite a duty.

It was not quite black dark. Not yet ten o'clock, she noticed as she passed a clock in a jewelry store. She saw the great bulk of St. Patrick's on the other side of the Avenue and wondered if it was still unlocked. It would be peaceful inside, and she could get control of herself before going back to the hotel.

The doors were open and people were still coming in and out. Was there the special service? Then Barbara saw the lines still in front of the confessionals, and remembered that tomorrow was the First Friday of the month, always a day for special Communions. She knelt in the still, quiet light, thinking almost hungrily of how she used always to observe the First Friday, of the hundreds of times she had found peace after confession, of the relief, the sense of cleanness and then the peace and exaltation of Communion, of having come close to God, receiving Him and being received. If only tonight, before she began this difficult journey, and after this hideous evening, she could have the comfort of the sacrament. She could start then with the curious, beautiful safety that was far more than physical.

She felt herself yearning for it. Was it possible? She was a stranger here. Was it not possible that, if she went into a confessional now and told a wise and unknown priest that she was on the verge of a dangerous journey, and that she repented every irregularity and sin of her life, and would straighten out her marriage relations or go without them when she came back, that he would give her absolution? She would have to promise never to live again with Ken as his wife as long as Leslie was alive. In spite of his dissipation, that might be a long, long time.

But I would have the peace, the assurance, the feeling of having straightened all this out. At least I would have three months of peace. I can receive Communion wherever I am and this trip would be blessed. Early tomorrow morning I could come here to Mass and Communion and then take the plane. I'll go to confession now. No one can look too far ahead these days. I may not live three months. I'll make a good act of contrition.

A good act? Are you sorry for loving Ken, for your marriage? Are you really repenting that happiness? Don't lie to yourself. And when you come back from Europe—or if he were here tonight—how would it be? What would you do? Do you admit that the corrupt creature you left in that restaurant tonight is your husband? Do you believe you are an adulteress?

She looked again at the dwindling line of penitents waiting at the doors of the confessionals. She stood up, not to join them, but to leave the church.

There were notices of two telephone calls for her on her door and again she saw that they were duplicates. She went to the telephone in a rush, tossing down her hat and purse.

"Long distance, Operator 8, please. This is Mrs. Craig in 1211. You have a call for me. From St. Anthony. Yes—Mrs. Kenneth Craig."

"Hold on, please." Barbara could hear the click and scraps of signals bringing them together. In a minute or two she would hear his voice, be claimed by it. "Call Meadowbrook, five thousand." That meant that Ken wasn't home. They were calling him at the Town Club.

"Go ahead, St. Anthony."

"Hello—hello—Barbara?"

"Oh, darling—how grand to hear your voice—how are you?"

"I'm all right. But how are you?"

"Fine. I just came in this minute and found your call."

"I've been trying to get you for half an hour."

"I was out for dinner."

"I knew you weren't in the hotel because I had you paged a couple of times. Where did you go?"

"Uptown. To a restaurant."

"All by yourself?"

"No." He has a right to ask but I must tell him only so much. He must not know it was Leslie. He might think that I had planned all along to meet Leslie here, that I wanted to—he hates to have me even remember that Leslie exists—"I was with a person I used to know years ago."

"Anybody I know?"

"No, you don't know him."

"A man, was it? Good for you—have fun?"

"No, not especially!" Make it sound like nothing of any consequence. "I got fed up and came back here."

"How's New York?"

"Better than Washington. I had to find my way through a fog there. But I managed to get all set—passport, shots, uniform. Would you like to see how I look in my uniform?"

"I'd like to see you, period."

"I know—so would I. More than anything in the world right now. But you're really all right? Calling from the club, aren't you?"

"Yes, I stopped here for dinner. And there's a great to-do around here tonight."

"What goes on?"

"Blair Wyatt's in the private dining room with a party. The announcement of his marriage broke in the paper tonight and everyone has been going in to congratulate them."

"Did you?"

"Yes, I saw him. Gave him the works. He sent his love to you."

"What's the girl like?"

[203]

"Very young. Very pretty. Looks as if she were just unwrapped."

"Tell Blair I think it's wonderful. When is the wedding?"

"Not till autumn."

"Then I will be back for it. I feel so far away!"

She could imagine the club tonight, Blair in the center of its activities, being worldly and witty and yet how clever of him to choose a clean, young girl. Was Nina Longman there? Probably.

"It's too damned far," said Craig. He too was imagining and he didn't like it. When Barbara answered the telephone she had sounded excited, all geared up. Who was that man she had gone out with? No point in asking but he had never forgotten what Barbara had told him once of her life after she had broken with Field and before they had met each other. She used to play around—like excitement. Barbara was his wife—and good. He could trust her. But give any woman a few too many drinks, let her go off by herself like this—I shouldn't have stood for it, Craig thought as he said, "Barbara, listen, why don't you give up this crazy trip and come home?"

"Come home? Now?"

"Yes, it's going to be too long and too far. It just doesn't make sense."

"But how could I?"

"Of course you can. You're a free agent. Tell them you've thought it over and that it is going to be too much for you. Or tell them that I won't stand for it. Ditch the whole business and come back where you belong."

I could, she thought. I could say I'm sick. I'd never have to see anyone connected with the project again. They'd write me off but what need I care?

"It's nothing but a wild goose chase anyhow," he urged. "They can find somebody else for that job."

"I know that." But in Washington Mr. Meader would say that there was a girl briefed for the job but she had fallen down on it, that she was a Catholic, that you couldn't count on Catholics. She would never find out what she had felt, as she talked to him, could

[204]

be found out. Something important, deep in explanation, that she could measure her own life and problem against.

"It's too late, Ken. I'm committed to do this, even if they could find someone else. And we thought it out—we agreed—"

You could have stopped me in the beginning, but you didn't, her thoughts were saying. We both knew that it was better for us to be really separated for a while than to be separate living together.

"Yes, I know. But you shouldn't be down there alone. Going off by yourself. Of course, now that you've gone this far—"

"It's in the right direction, Ken. Not just because of this job but because of ourselves. Oh darling, let's not tear each other to pieces like this. I love you so much."

Chapter Sixteen

In Vienna, many of the wide, old streets now had strange names, too new to be in any guidebook, and a chromo portrait of Stalin swung over the Platz which had been chosen as the thoroughfare important enough to be his namesake. In large, formally constructed mansions, which had once been the city residences of rich and important Viennese, girls in American sport shoes slid among the parquet floorings and went down the marble staircases two steps at a time, on errands from one temporary office to another. Their short khaki uniforms and bare legs made an unlikely human foreground for the painted panels and gilded wallpapers which, not so long ago, had been suitable and elegant settings for women dressed in lace, velvet, or satin, which might conceal the most delicate of pointed slippers.

Almost daily two Russian officers sat in the open window of a hotel in the Ring, playing an interminable game of chess. There were always plenty of the top-ranking ones driving fast cars, as fiercely as if they were rushing to an attack instead of back to their billets. Soldiers outside the headquarters of the occupying armies might lounge against the walls, but they were armed and sometimes at night the crack of guns would be heard telling of another incident.

The surviving buildings, on streets which had once been walled by magnificent masonry and carved façades, looked desolate and hardly more safe than nearby ruins. Odd and dangerous gaps were everywhere, for more than four thousand buildings, many of five and six *stöcke*, had been destroyed. Walls no longer fully supported swayed in the winds and dropped brick and stones menacingly. But the city was used to danger and paid little attention to accidents. Vienna was tired out by danger and calamity. Even its fears were exhausted.

In the parks people went along talking to themselves but no one thought that was very crazy. Austrian officers, once so vain of their uniforms and polished boots, now wore the same uniforms though they were dirty and shapeless and, even more humiliating, meant nothing. But they had no other clothes nor any chance of getting any. There was no longer any fashion in the city of great and historic style. For most Viennese, and for the refugees who drifted among them, there was only covering. The men who were not wearing remnants of military outfits wore unmatched parts of suits, tattered hunting jackets, shorts that exposed pale, emaciated legs, old raincoats buttoned or pinned close for decency. The women wore what they had managed to save, sometimes pieces of draperies for skirts, bundles of raffia for shoes. There was nothing useful for open sale. If any article had value it was traded in the black market. But in little sly or bold shop windows, among the boarded up and abandoned fronts of others, there might be tiny pink and white carnations for sale, or shiny brass necklaces, such as soldiers would buy for girls as a preliminary offering or as a souvenir.

By the time August had come, and it came very quickly for Barbara, none of that surprised her. She was used to the sights of tragedy, and a broken wall had become as natural to her vision as a well-plastered or brick one would have been at home. She was accustomed to the flat taste of powdered egg stuffed into a tomato, and the sweet meatball that inevitably was horsemeat. She knew that if a single potato rolled from a cart into the street it would be there only for a second, for starvation kept a constant and sharp watch. She had learned the incredible value of soap and cigarettes. If she threw away even the smallest stub of a cigarette on a path, it would be retrieved, competed for. The lucky finder would put it in a cheap holder and have a little puff or two, a minute's stimulus, a faint taste and odor of a happier past.

But she still could be astonished by other things. In the midst of all the wreckage and the creeping diseases of partial starvation, while the allied victors went about with submachine guns as a matter of course, there was no carelessness in dealing with the destinies of refugees who had become the charges of the armies of occupation. It was almost absurd, on the face of it, with evidences of wholesale destruction and waste of life everywhere, that destitute individuals should have diplomatic attention and be considered important enough to quarrel about. But they were. For each government wanted its own nationals, though it was common knowledge that a good many of the refugees would be executed if they were sent back to what once had been their homeland.

Barbara's work was with the records of the "unaccompanied children," as the understated phrase went. The various nations were demanding all the children to whom they could lay any claim. They needed them to build up depleted populations, to be educated from the start to uphold new political regimes. Children were very valuable property in devastated Europe. Most of the governments whose armies lately had been involved in Germany or Austria sent officials to find any children who had drifted or fled out of their native countries and might be repatriated. Sometimes there was no question of where a child should go. But the envoys of the Communist controlled countries, seeking their young, as they claimed, met resistance which might be open and was again subtle and devious. Exiled governments, set up in London or Paris for the time being as they hoped, had their men on the ground too. And these made every effort to keep children from going back to the countries which had been taken over by the Communists, where they would be made wards of the state. They asserted another authority, which worked with the exiles, and claimed the children as its spiritual wards. The Catholic Church. Barbara's Church.

She had found out before long that the fact that she was on the records as a Catholic was a matter for comment, and that some of her associates distrusted her because of it. But she was held in an almost embarrassingly high regard by some of the liaison officers of the exiled governments. Her religion placed her on their side automatically, so they assumed. She could not deny it, nor explain to almost strangers for the sake of honesty and clarity, "Yes, I consider myself a Catholic. But I am under Church discipline, and unable to receive the sacraments. I am a divorced woman and I remarried while my first husband was alive. He is still alive."

And, even if she had been so scrupulous, she realized that the fact that she was not in good standing in her diocese would not have mattered to these people, so long as she was willing to count herself a Catholic. In this tattered country, Church laws were often relaxed or ignored. Being a Catholic here was not dependent on going to Mass, though Barbara did go with regularity which surprised and impressed the concierge at her hotel, who told her that he too was a Catholic and then burst into a torrent of abuse of priests. No rule of fast or abstinence held, of course. People had to eat meat when they could get it, Friday or not, and dispensation was taken for granted. Nor did lack of personal morals seem to discredit an avowed Catholic. One of the exiles who was grinding political axes in Vienna was a Polish count who had been dispossessed of vast estates in the recent struggles. He had sent his wife to London and now was living with a married Austrian woman quite openly. But he was described to Barbara more than once as being "very Roman Catholic."

In the Old City where Barbara's lodging was, inside the half-circle formed by the Canal and the Ring, where the walls of old Vienna could be raised again in imagination, she saw evidence everywhere of how completely the Church had once dominated the city and threaded it with monasteries and parish churches. History was a heavy odor in Vienna that could not be dispelled even now, and part of that odor was the incense of the altar. That great Catholic family, the Hapsburgs, had built up the institutions of their faith everywhere. And perhaps quarreled with the priests as the Braniffs did every once in a while, thought Barbara. It was different here and yet quite the same. On the grand scale yet with the same pattern. Understandable and familiar.

Argument and suspicion swarmed everywhere. Cold and critical young Americans and British, in various occupation posts, did not trust the Church and said so. Their accusations against it carried plenty of evidence that Barbara could not beat down. People who had been Fascists and openly backed the Hitler conquest were now creeping to the Church for cover and assistance. The fact that the Catholic bishops had urged the people to support Hitler in the first plebiscite had not been forgotten—and there were those who were not going to let it be forgotten—even though the Church had later found itself in violent opposition to the Führer.

"Of course," they said cynically, "that was when Hitler began to confiscate Church properties."

The tangle was beyond Barbara's power to unravel, beyond her knowledge of politics or history. She could only approach it with as much honesty as she could, sometimes to be carried away by veneration in the old cathedral, and sometimes wondering if the odor in the Old City was not incense but corruption.

Mr. Meader in Washington had warned Barbara that her spot might be difficult and she found him a hundred times right in the first couple of months. She was expected not only to be an expert in the handling of records but, because she was experienced and intelligent, she was soon used as a consultant in case work as well. There might have been plenty of chance for the use of influence, the sidetracking of data, for mixing in the intrigues which were going on, if she had been willing to do anything of that sort.

In any case, even to be recorded as a Catholic meant an alignment of political significance in Vienna. The admission of her faith was taken in many quarters as acknowledgment of a tie with groups which were more militant in worldly plans and projects than in religious faith. Barbara had never felt her religion to be regarded as such a complete commitment, not only of her spiritual life but of all her ideas and loyalties. It sometimes troubled her because she felt she was cheating in not accepting the full bond. And sometimes it irritated her. She did not like the occasional suggestion which might come from someone with whom she was working, intimating that of course, being a Catholic, she was not able to make an un-weighted judgment. She did not like some of the people she met who wore the Catholic label. She was not sure that theirs was the same religion as her own, and often it did not seem to be religion at all but straight politics. Yet to criticize the Church here was more impossible than it had been at home. For that might line her up on the other side.

She sat in Aileen Bradley's office one day, talking about some Yugoslav boys, on whose incomplete histories she was working. Aileen and Barbara had a working friendship by this time and sometimes a playing one when they were not on their jobs. Aileen, who was British, liked the American girl. Barbara sometimes felt that Aileen Bradley liked her as much as she could. There was a very thin barrier between them but it was a tough one.

Aileen was in charge of relief as well as the welfare of children under the military officials of her own country, and she had ex-empted herself from wearing any uniform. Her violet linen dress today gave her a lovely look of the uses of peace and tidy feminine beauty. The top brass of two armies liked Aileen and for their sakes she managed to keep her nails even and lacquered. Every now and then some nail enamel came through for her in a diplomatic pouch. A once-famous Viennese *coiffeur*, whose shop was now operating under a Russian sign, laid Aileen's hair in a circle of smooth curls once a week. She did not look like a woman of more than forty who often worked twelve hours a day and drank too much brandy. Some-times she did look those facts but not this morning.

"There are forty-nine boys in that place in the mountains," said Aileen. "You can't call it a hotel any more, and it's certainly not a

[210]

proper orphanage. It's a kind of roost. We've got to get them out of there before winter. They would freeze to death by November. Unless they starved first. Sister Eltha keeps them alive with the vegetables that she and a couple of other nuns and the boys raise. But they eat the garden stuff as fast as they grow it. They've no reserve supply of food, and if they should be cut off by an early snowfall, God help them. We have to settle this business about those boys. Get some action and stop the bickering."

"Nikkol won't give them up?"

"But certainly not. You know how he feels. Give up fifty children? That's not what he's here for. He intends to get them back into their own country. And after all, whether one likes Nikkol personally or not, they are Yugoslavs and he's the liaison officer."

"Colonel Brush doesn't want to let him have them," said Barbara, "and the Colonel has the last word on repatriation. He has to sign the order before anyone can be moved out."

"Brush is stalling. He hates all Yugoslavs."

"He thinks they hate us. He says they're building up against us, being built up by Russia."

"Maybe they are. But that doesn't make any difference. From what I hear, there's a lot of quiet pressure being put on the Colonel to send the children to Italy. The story is that there's been an offer from Rome. The Pope will accept the boys as his personal wards and see that they're housed and fed and educated."

She paused a second to see what effect that had on Barbara, who did not seem surprised.

"So you've heard that too?"

"Those stories get around."

"But Brush isn't a Catholic," Aileen went on. "I can't see why he's holding things up this way."

"He prefers the Pope to Tito. He thinks that if the boys go to Yugoslavia they might as well be sent to Russia and that they'll be brought up to fight American soldiers ten or fifteen years from now. He says that it burns him up to reinforce the inevitable enemy."

"Maybe by that time Tito will be on our side."

[211]

"Not if the Colonel has anything to do with it. He doesn't want any part of any Communist."

"You seem to know his ideas extremely well."

"I see him now and then at the Officers' Club. You know how it is. You get to talking."

Yes, I know, thought Aileen. With looks like yours, and being young, you have them all in line. And you manage to keep them guessing.

She said, "Couldn't you talk to him again about these children?"

"And say what?"

"There's only one thing to be said, isn't there? The army has a definite policy of repatriating wherever it's possible. So have we in our organization. The Colonel is simply ignoring all that in this case, as well as the recommendations we've sent in. If you're in his confidence—"

"I'm not. The matter came up somehow the other night and he made the remark I just repeated. But he wasn't asking me for any advice. It's not my job to talk to colonels about policies."

"I suppose not. But it's my job to keep those boys from starving or freezing to death because of a stalemate at the policy level. Do you want to get up there with me and see how it is? I'm going on a quick field trip tomorrow, stopping at a couple of the camps and ending up at Sister Eltha's rookery. You can come along if you like. There's room in the car."

"If I can get away, I'd like nothing better."

"We can fix that. They can spare you for a day or two on your side of the hall. I'll ask for you, borrow you if I can. You really might be of considerable use. There must be more records of these boys than what we have. I want to see if I can pry some facts loose from Sister Eltha and your being a Catholic might help. She doesn't quite trust me."

It was made possible. They left Vienna on a fair, cool day in an old army station wagon, with a rough-looking Austrian at the wheel. Barbara had saved her morning bread ration to give him and he would take the thick slice out of his pocket, bite it with reverence

[212]

and thrust the rest safely back. The car rattled and shook as if it might fall to pieces but the engine still had plenty of power and it was exhilarating to get away from the sight of bombed areas, and the tangled, dusty rubble. Little, ancient villages began to appear along the way. Their old marketplaces and cobbled streets had outlasted many wars. Perhaps because of some special grace of humility or serenity, thought Barbara. Then her mind went off to find Kenneth, wishing that he were sharing this morning with her.

An old woman was picking up twigs in a wood so clean that the sunlight through the trees seemed to fall on a brown floor. She bent double, her petticoat flashed red, and the aged posture had a kind of stiffened charm. A girl with a poised bucket of water stopped to stare at the car and its passengers. A man on a bicycle was wearing whole leather shorts and even had a glossy feather in his hat.

"This is lovely!" exclaimed Barbara. "This is the way it ought to be. I wish that my husband could see this. I must tell him that there are parts of the country that aren't ruined."

"You always think of your husband when things are pleasant, don't you? When you feel happy. I've noticed that."

"Do I? Yes, I suppose I do. It's all tied up. Happiness, I mean, with Ken."

"The thing that puzzles me is why you're here at all."

"You must know. We're on the same kind of job, more or less, though yours is much more important."

"But you have a man over there in America. One you like, and one who must be in love with you or you wouldn't feel the way you do. And you've a home. I understand about myself and most of the rest of us who are working over here. We didn't have anything better to do. They say over three-quarters of the people in this organization are escaping from their lives, or families, or jobs they didn't fit into somewhere else."

"Are you?"

"Oh, quite. This war, and helping to clean up after it, has been personal peace to me. I once had a man I liked too. Your way. I can remember how it felt though I've long since stopped feeling it."

"Why did you stop? I'm sorry—tell me to mind my own business."

"I don't mind telling you why. It's academic with me now. And you'll never see him. He had a previous attachment when he married me. I worked—I had to—I couldn't be around all the time. And when I was out of sight or use for a while, he went back to her. Like a horse to the old stall. Like a drug addict actually. She was in his blood, even though he knew she was poison to him and he thought he wanted to break it off. But some women are like drugs. The craving for them comes back to a man and he can't resist. He'll do anything, cheat, lie, steal—to get what he wants. I took it for a while. Long enough."

Barbara was thinking of Nina Longman as the crisp, factual voice paused. She told herself sharply, secretly, that there was no parallel. She said, "I couldn't take that at all. What horrible luck."

"That's why it's so cheering to be among people who have so much worse luck," remarked Aileen and spoke in German to the driver. "To the left and at the next turn to the right. Here we shall stop but an hour."

The first stop was at a large children's camp. Newly farmed land stretched around a large group of old barracks.

"There are mines near here that the Germans worked. The workers lived in these quarters during the last two years of the war. The slaves of the Germans," explained Aileen briefly.

It was understaffed and messy, with dirty stairs. It was magnificent, for nothing that was absolutely necessary for nearly two hundred children was lacking. There were cribs and nursing bottles and small chamber pots. There was milk in great metal cans and soup cooking in aluminum kettles, the good kettles which had been abandoned by the Germans. The barren kitchen smelled yeasty and sweet from the bread which was being baked in tremendous loaves by a refugee baker. Everything was scanty and yet desperately managed to be sufficient. Routines had been established. There was a makeshift playground and even a little schooling going on for the older ones who were reciting a lesson in one room when Barbara looked in. She had been given permission to inspect the place by

[214]

herself, for the people who were managing the camp were all busy.

Soldiers and diplomats were considering the destinies of these children, she thought. Investigators were still combing villages and cities and farms to find out with as much certainty as possible who had bred each of the waifs and when. To Barbara, as her records came alive, it seemed more than ever important to be sure who had first claim on these helpless children.

She found her way finallly into a dormitory where twenty or more of the youngest ones were having midday naps. The room was half-dark, the paper windowshades flapped, and occasional sighing breaths or little cries broke the stillness of the barracks that tried to be a nursery. Barbara looked down into a crib where a child was sleeping, loosely spread out just as David used to lie in his sleep, stretched out as if unconsciously growing. She thought of all the protection that had been given to David. Yet she had not been able to keep his life for him when it was in her care. She had not been allowed to keep it. All these other children had survived abandonment, horror, danger at its very worst. Was it chance? How could it possibly be reasonable, a deliberation of God's will? What would be reasonable in keeping these children alive for their twisted fates and wasting David? What was reasonable in tearing Kenneth's child away from her and letting these live against such odds?

It wasn't because I disobeyed any law of marriage, she thought. It was chance, the physical luck of cells. I've always known that, of course. Yes, she had told herself so but she had not really believed it until this unlikely moment, when she could feel her mind slough off the idea of punishment, rid itself of a burden of guilt that had been attached to it like a parasite since her miscarriage.

If there was punishment of that sort, why were these shabby cribs full? Most of these children must have been conceived in shame or excess or despair or against the will of the women who bore them. As for marriage laws, who had paid any attention to them? Legitimacy counted only as it affected guardianship. The children were important, not when or how they were bred or under what rules.

[215]

"Where do the children in this camp come from?" she asked Aileen as the other woman came in to say that she was ready to go. "I haven't seen the records of this place."

"From Poland or Czechoslovakia for the most part. You know how it was. The Nazis would clean out a village of its children or abduct a whole school, kill the Jews and the cripples or sick ones, and send the rest to Germany for indoctrination and adoption. These kids fortunately didn't get that far before the war ended."

"The ones in this room are too small to have been in school. They must have been born in the last few years. In slave camps?"

"Some of them. And to soldiers on the march. They belong to the mothers, of course, if we can find them. Nice jobs too, some of them. If that lad belonged to me, I'd want him back, wouldn't you?"

"God, yes," said Barbara.

"That's what you ought to explain to your friend, the Colonel," Aileen suggested. "Sometimes the mothers are alive when the kids are repatriated."

They stopped next at a Polish camp, before they went up into the mountains. It was a transient camp, filled to overflowing with infiltrees who had come over the border since the war's end to add another problem to those of the occupying armies. There were bent old women with worn-out, tiny eyes, men whose personalities seemed to have faded and lost shape like the clothes they wore, until they all looked more or less alike. They were blurred in age, unless they were very old or very young. In every face were apprehension and doubt, overcast with the disciplined patience of men who have lost their own places in the world and their right to make decisions for themselves. There were women near the end of pregnancy, children who were quick-actioned and sharp-eyed, like young animals who knew the way of the woods. Broken luggage and bundles were piled carefully in the corners of the roughly partitioned rooms of a building which might have been an old abandoned school, or perhaps a cheap resort in its heyday. In each cubicle a family or more lived in terrible intimacy. The blankets on the cots looked as if all the warmth had been used out of them. Only the grayness was left.

It was not a good camp, even as emergency standards rated these cases for refugees, and Barbara knew why Aileen Bradley was here. Aileen made a quick inspection of the buildings with the director, who was a tired-looking man with a bald head and a Harvard accent. Barbara walked around with them and heard the discussion.

"We must encourage them to go back to Poland," said Aileen. "They can't stay here under these conditions and there's no other place to send them. They're not proper refugees who were here at the end of the war, and if they swarm in and manage to stay, it will be an endless job. There's no one to handle it. The military can't do it. They haven't got the money or the staff. Our organization is folding at the end of the war. This bunch has to be repatriated."

"They're terrorized," the director told her. "There have been a lot of pretty grim rumors circulated about what is happening across the border. To Catholics as well as the Jews. They're afraid to go back."

"Some of those rumors aren't true."

"But some of them must be. They give dates and places and names for the purges."

"Our people who have gone into Poland and Russia with repatriation groups come back and tell us that the children get good care."

"The children are valuable. They separate families."

"Yes. I know."

Barbara was looking at one end of the building through which they were walking. The west wall had partly fallen away or perhaps had been blasted off by a stray shell or bomb. But a family was living in what was left of the enclosure. There were a few belongings on nails and four cots in the half-exposed cubicle had blankets spread over them. She thought of storm at night, of days when the rain swept from the west, of the way rats must creep out from under the building at night. She could smell mildew. Suddenly she was not a relief worker on an inspection tour, looking at a bad condition.

[217]

She shared the suffering. These people had fled, been driven to this grudged, wretched shelter because they believed what they had been taught to believe, because it was deep in them, part of them. She realized that her feeling had sprung from the sight of a cheap crucifix hanging from a nail above one cot. That was the reason, the symbol of fate.

Aileen Bradley was looking her full age and her voice was hard. She said, "They can't stay here. The place is falling in. I shall recommend that they be repatriated with three months' rations. That will give them something to go on and also some bargaining power when they get back to Poland."

"It could be another reason to massacre them," the director said in his dispirited way.

"We don't have to anticipate that. We can talk to the liaison officers and tell them that the food musn't be diverted from the people to whom it's given."

"They'll promise anything. There's never proof."

"There's no proof either way. Some of this panic has been deliberately built up, from what we're told. It's sometimes the fanatical Catholics who start trouble and then spread a lot of this talk about Communist purges and massacres. Of course there undoubtedly is some of that—the country's in a fluid state right now—but I believe that if these people would go back to their own cities and towns and try to co-operate with the new regimes a little—"

"They can't do that," Barbara interrupted flatly.

"They could try at least."

"They can't even try. A Catholic is an enemy of Communism. He has to be."

"Well, if they take that attitude I don't see what can be done except—"

"Except send our kind back to be killed?"

It was almost a cry. It came from a feeling Barbara had never known before, a curious identification. She heard herself say "our kind" and thought, quick on the words, that she had never used them except in mockery until now. Aileen was staring at her in

[218]

surprise and the director lit a cigarette in embarrassment. Aileen became calm and brisk.

"It's quite futile to argue about it, I expect," she said with British coolness. "It's very difficult and sad. But after all the policy of repatriating where possible is established. Of course I can understand how you must feel from your personal standpoint."

But she does not understand, thought Barbara, as they overlaid her outbreak with talk of prevention of disease and very immediate needs. Soon they were gone, distancing the camp like a bad dream. Their car chugged breathlessly up the winding hills toward a mountain and the two women hung on to their seats to keep from falling forward.

The rookery, as Aileen had called it, was an old hotel built of stone and stucco on a site with a magnificent view. It must have been impractical for tourists, and failed in its hopes long ago, for the last roads leading to it had not been mended for years. They came upon it in the sunset, a strange-looking place, jumbled with unnecessary towers and bare verandas on three sides, surrounded by vegetable gardens which sloped down the steep hill in every direction. Thin boys with shaved heads who had been working in the patches had stopped at the sound of the car to watch for its appearance. They looked like brown statues in the rows of potatoes and beans. Barbara and Aileen waved at them and Aileen said, "There she is. That's Sister Eltha coming out on the terrace."

She was a big woman. Her black habit exaggerated and yet lost her silhouette but she was tall and her face had the look of very clean old driftwood. The cheekbones were almost fleshless. Above them were deep brown eyes and the brows had gone gray. She smiled as she came down the stone steps to meet her guests. The smile was not amused or jolly. It is completely a smile of reassurance and hope, thought Barbara. It makes you understand that heroic story.

Barbara knew the story from talk as well as the records. During the civil struggles in Yugoslavia many children were separated from their parents. Sometimes the partisans and sometimes the Germans murdered almost at random up and down the streets of a village and children would be orphaned or abandoned. Sister Eltha, who was a teaching nun, had gathered in as many waifs as she could into a school home, and the Germans let her do it. She was useful in taking care of boys that they might want later. When occupation times were good, they even helped her with food. But when the Russians came and defeat was certain, the Germans ordered all women and children into air raid shelters, and themselves rushed toward safety, exhorting Sister Eltha to take care of the children, for they must live and continue the work of Adolf Hitler.

Sister Eltha had salvaged the boys and followed in the wake of the retreat until she reached Austria. The legend or the miracle was that she had not lost one of the children whose care she had assumed.

"This is my friend, Mrs. Craig, from America," Aileen told the nun. "She is working with our organization and has had a great deal of experience. Mrs. Craig is a Catholic so she was especially eager to meet you, Sister."

Barbara felt the pressure of the firm, coarsened hand tighten on her own and saw interest light the brown eyes.

"You speak German?" she asked Barbara.

"Only schoolgirl German," answered Barbara, smiling. "What I learned in convent school years ago."

"A convent in America was that?"

"Yes. But the order was French. The Madames and Mothers of the Sacred Heart."

"Ah, I know of it. That was an order instituted to teach the daughters of the French nobility."

"They don't get any nobility to teach in America now, I'm afraid."

"But Americans are very good. And religious. And very generous."

"I knew you two would have a great deal in common," said Aileen Bradley. "I must tell you, Sister, that Mrs. Craig is trying to perfect our case histories. She has brought along the cards from the files about your boys and perhaps you can help her to fill in some of the gaps. The boys may have remembered more details or facts that we haven't heard about. Will you go over the cards with Mrs. Craig?"

"Yes, I will," said the Sister simply, her eyes still searching Barbara. "You will stay with us tonight?"

"Have you room for us?"

"Always there is room."

She rang a small brass bell which stood on a table and it summoned a battered-looking nun who had lost an eye. At Sister Eltha's direction she brought the guests small glasses of bitter, homemade wine and disappeared again to make a room ready. Then, quite deliberately, as Barbara realized, Aileen went to see the gardens and the boys.

Sister Eltha asked Barbara, "Would you care to visit our little chapel?"

It might have been a game room once. At one end of it, a stained glass window, coarsely patterned, showed the figure of a leaping deer and gave a colored glow to the improvised altar, a table covered with a spotless cloth that was deep-edged with lace. In the middle was a sanctuary and a light flickered before it.

"You see that by God's grace we have the Sacrament," whispered Sister Eltha. "The priest comes every week to confess us all and say the Mass."

There were a few straight chairs in a row and behind them a halfdozen crude kneeling benches which had been made by unskilled hands. Barbara genuflected and knelt before the altar on the floor, making the sign of the cross. She could feel the observation of the nun. This visit to the chapel was a courtesy and an opportunity but it was also a test, to see if she was in fact a Catholic, if the bond really existed. I'm cheating this nun, thought Barabara. She thinks I'm a good Catholic because I'm acting like one. It doesn't make any difference. No use in giving scandal.

She tried to pray, to feel the stir of devotion and reverence that should come in the presence of the Blessed Sacrament. No aspiration came and after a minute she realized that with shock. She was not praying, only pretending to pray as she knelt there. She

[221]

was not sharing what she knew Sister Eltha felt and believed. Her mind was filled with pity, her heart sore from the sight of the refugees this afternoon and yet her murmured Hail Mary was only so many words with no content of faith or hope.

I never have felt like this in a chapel before, she thought. I'm stale inside. I'm hard. I'm putting on an act, going through the motions of being a Catholic and I don't feel like one at all. Why did I say "our kind" this afternoon to Aileen? Now I don't feel as if I belong to any of this. What burned me up was her assumption that if the Catholics would be reasonable and co-operate, everything would be all right. She doesn't understand that if you're a Catholic you can't be a non-Catholic. I ought to know by this time.

Pray for the people in that dreadful camp. It won't do any good. It would only be a little wishful thinking to comfort myself. I really used to believe that when you went into a church or chapel for the first time, you could pray for three things and they would be granted. Of course that's superstition. The old fairy tale of the three wishes is practically the same thing. No, I won't pray for three things.

Have I knelt here long enough now to convince Sister Eltha of my piety, I wonder? So that I can pry into her confidence? I don't like this job. But I'll never forget this day, that camp, all those babies managing to live, and the villages this morning that seemed so pretty and so happy. Aileen said that I thought of Ken when I was happy. I do. I think of you when I'm happy and when I'm not, Ken. I think of you now and hope and pray that we may have each other again and more closely. That's the prayer I have no right to say, I suppose, and it's the only one that comes. The only one that I can feel.

She blessed herself with the sign and went out behind Sister Eltha.

The nun said, "We do not often have Catholic visitors and it makes me very happy. This will bring us graces. Your husband, is he too in Austria?"

"No, he is in America."

"Have you children too?"

[222]

"None living," answered Barbara. "I had a son but he died. Some years ago."

"And now you give your time to such work as this? That is very good."

"I'm not at all important to the work," said Barbara. "Could we go over the histories now, Sister? I'd like to ask you some questions about some of these cases."

"I shall tell you all I can."

Aileen Bradley had been right. Sister Eltha knew more than she had told previous investigators. Bits and pieces of information came out as they sat where the light was best, going through the cards. The dreadful stories of the boys filled out with names and even places that would be very valuable as records.

"I know you will be their friend," said Sister Eltha.

"They have many friends who are thinking of their futures. And some of them must have relatives alive in their own country."

"Perhaps. But they must not go back there."

"It's safe enough now, Sister."

"It is a bad country now. They have burned the churches, killed the priests. There is no religion. The poor boys must not go there."

"They may have to, Sister Eltha. I don't see how they could stay here when winter comes."

"No. But you do not know then that the Holy Father will provide for them?"

"I have heard that. But it would be difficult to get permission to send them to Italy."

"Why so?"

"Because they are Yugoslavs. They belong to their own country, as each of us does."

"They belong to the Virgin," said Sister Eltha. "Long ago I have given them to our Blessed Mother."

She spoke with quiet finality. She went on, "The boys know that is so. They pray to her as their mother, their only parent. They know she has saved their lives, that she will care for them. Sometimes on the journey they were hungry, cold, a little sick, very frightened. But the Virgin was always with us. In the woods she

[223]

would hide with us. She found food and water and shelter for these orphans, she blinded the eyes of the wicked, made tender the hearts of those who gave us help."

It was complete belief, mysticism so real that Barbara was silent in wonder.

"And now she sends you to us."

"Oh, not me, Sister."

"I believe she sends you. These other kind men and women, with their talk of papers and laws and government, do not understand. But you will not permit these souls to be stolen from their mother, Our Lady." She made a kindly deprecating gesture in the direction Aileen had taken. "You will not think only of the body."

"But there's nothing I can do. I have no authority."

"Our Blessed Mother will help you. I shall pray to her. So shall all the boys pray that the Virgin will help you to accomplish this."

It's almost funny, thought Barbara miserably. Me!

They had cabbage and potatoes and a salad for their supper and dark crusty bread. They said the Rosary with a chanting rhythm and afterward Barbara talked to the boys. Their shy, curious eyes watched every movement she made and they hung on every word she said. She told them about farms and cities in America, fumbling with her vocabulary but managing to make them understand a little at least. Sister Eltha sat straight and tall, smiling.

"Truly you were extraordinary," said Aileen when they were finally alone in a bedroom with rain-streaked plaster walls and two rather sunken cots. "Sister Eltha is eating out of your hand. Did you get much out of her?"

"Quite a lot."

"It all adds up, doesn't it? Proves they are all Yugoslavs?"

"No doubt of it. They're Serbs for the most part. A few Croats."

"You were good to come. You've been a great help to me."

"But not to Sister Eltha," answered Barbara. Nor to the Virgin, she thought without prayer.

On the way back to Vienna they argued about it.

"For one thing it's cruel to send them back to the places that they fled from. It will revive dreadful memories in those boys. Some of them saw their parents killed and have hideous nightmares. Sister Eltha told me that," Barbara said.

Aileen sighed, not casually. "Nothing about this business is easy. You just have to follow basic principles. It may be bad psychologically for some of the boys. But most of them probably have some living relative, and if they don't go back they grow up without a country, without a citizenship, and as things are going, one day they might be in the position of fighting their own people."

"They will anyway, if you turn them over to the Communists."

"But is that any more unfair than turning them over to the Catholics?"

"They are Catholics. That's the whole point."

"Barbara, do you really believe that should be the deciding factor? Do you think Catholics should set themselves apart as Catholics? Always put that first?"

"Good Catholics must put it first. It doesn't interfere with patriotism."

"It seems to in this case," said Aileen rather coolly, "and isn't it the whole history of Austria? A church-dominated state that only allowed a qualified patriotism? Same thing in Spain. On the face of it Catholicism does interfere with patriotism."

"The religion doesn't."

Aileen looked skeptical.

"I just object to sacrificing children to Communism," Barbara went on. "Those boys should be brought up to have faith in something. To believe something."

"Exactly what Nikkol says. He wants to give them faith in Communism."

"That's not faith. That's worshipping a false god."

"Maybe all gods are false."

"You know better than that."

"I don't know either. I don't believe those fixations of Nikkol and his gang, of course, but I don't believe your creed either. Brush said to me once at a conference that, if he could have his way, he'd divide all these children into two groups and give half to the Catholics and half to the Quakers."

"That's the most cynical plan since Solomon nearly cut the baby in two."

"Brush is in Solomon's spot. The Communists won't give an inch. They want every child to whom they have any legal claim. And the Catholics counter with an over-all spiritual claim. Well— if we're going to back a Catholic underground, no matter how noble it may be, and build up a spiritual guerrilla warfare, we disqualify our own purposes as an international body."

"But the poor kids would have a good bringing-up."

"Under the control of monks and nuns?"

Barbara said, "Yes. Of course there are bad spots but most of the teaching orders are excellent now. I know what I'm talking about. I was brought up in a convent school."

"Did it fit you for the world you have to live in?"

"I manage."

"I should think it would be hard. You talk about the system of the Communists, but doesn't your Church try to control your whole life? Doesn't it set up fixed rules about what you can eat and what you can read and how you have to vote and what man you marry?"

"That's very exaggerated."

"Is your husband a Catholic?"

"No. He isn't."

"Oh well, then you have a different situation," said Aileen, with an odd note of relief. "That's why you don't seem so bigoted as most Roman Catholics. So many of them have such a high wall around everything they think that you can't talk to them."

Barbara tried to be frank without telling all of it. She said, "I'm not too good a Catholic. I haven't lived up to all the laws of the Church. But I believe in my religion, and what got me down in that dreadful Polish camp yesterday was the actual closeness to people who were probably going to be massacred because they believe as I do. It's incredible! The world's gone medieval."

"Some people say that's because your own Church won't let it become modern. I don't mean to be rude. There aren't many Catholics that I could say that to."

"Am I to be proud of that?" Barbara asked, mocking herself.

"I would be, if I were you. Well, here we are, nearly back in battered old Vienna. Barbara, will you break down the records of those Yugoslav boys from your notes, so that I can have a clear statement of their ages, places of birth and any other facts that identify them and their nationality. I want to show the facts to Colonel Brush."

"Yes, I'll do that at once."

"Are you dining with Brush soon?"

"Tomorrow, maybe."

"Won't you whisper in his ear that those boys have to be repatriated to Yugoslavia?"

"I can't. That's not my job."

"Isn't it your job to support the policy of the organization?"

"Not after hours."

Barbara went back to her own office, a great high-ceilinged room with an oaken frieze around it. She worked for hours and when all the records were arranged and classified, she herself was still in confusion. She called a page and sent the papers to Aileen Bradley and then walked back to the hotel where she had been billeted. It was a shabby, old one but she preferred it to the grandeur in which some of the occupying forces, and even the relief workers, had managed for their temporary settings.

The first gloom of evening, unrelieved on every ragged, unlighted side street made the ruins look ghastly and threatening. Walls fitted with empty windows and shapeless heaps of rubble made hide-outs for any crime. On a bench under a tree a man sat with his head in his hands, not as a loafer might sit, but in an attitude of final despair. Where would he be in the morning, Barbara wondered. She felt small and cheap before his suffering, in the midst of so much total and permanent loss for so many people.

She thought of Aileen Bradley's comment that it was strange that Barbara was here, if she had a good life at home. Why am I here,

Barbara asked herself. It was because of a chain of happenings, because an urge fitted an opportunity, not because I wanted to escape from my life, as Aileen says so many of the others do. All the good things are waiting for me. But why did I leave them, how could I leave them, the love and safety and marriage and happiness? Why did I never feel that my happiness belonged to me? Why don't I feel it now as mine and sure?

She had never let herself think that before. The question was like a light searching her mind.

Her hotel was narrow, wooden, and high, a lodging that must have been third-class in the days when the city had form and style. Barbara had not described it too fully in letters to her husband because she was afraid he would realize that it might be a firetrap. She herself did not worry about that. It was unsafe, but in the strange, suffering city Barbara too had grown numb to personal danger. She had become accustomed to her room, almost fond of it. It had held the first cruel loneliness that was like constant nausea during her first days in Vienna and kept the secret of that misery to itself. It was a place where she had measured her worth and her luck and destiny against the size and sufferings of the world.

The concierge, who was old and dropsical, took her big key from its hook and handed her a letter. From Kenneth. She studied the envelope with joy to see when it had been mailed, and then, because the lift was not working, as was habitual, she hurried up the four flights to unlock her door and be alone with what he had written.

The wallpaper was green and spotted, the bed lumpy, with patched linen sheets turned back, and a dingy flowered puff. A hard couch upholstered in green velvet tried to make the furnishing impressive, but only crowded the room into a narrow lane between bed and sofa. A picture of Kenneth and one of David stood on the small bureau. Barbara sat on the couch before the photographs and opened her letter. This was good. It felt a little like hearing Ken come home at the end of the day. What would he say first?

He had written the news, chronologically, as if trying to dutifully remember, on the day when he had sat down to write, what he had done on the Tuesday before. The events seemed distant to Barbara, as if she were regarding them through a field glass that did not bring them quite into focus. He had dined with the Ryes. The Harrisons had given a large party. Blair Wyatt and the girl he was going to marry were making it a gay summer, wrote Ken. *Everyone is entertaining for them. I don't go to half the things. She's a very nice girl. Blair seems to have fallen on his feet all right.*

Were you thinking when you wrote that sentence that you have not been so lucky? It's not fair to Ken for me to be here and yet all that seems so trivial. He sounds cheerful, amused. He doesn't mention Nina's being at any of those parties. But he wouldn't mention her, and of course she must be. Am I a fool, completely, to put this distance between us? What a disgusting remark that was of Aileen's, about a man going back to the old stall. It won't be long before I'm back. And things will be better for us than they ever were. I'll be able to have a baby. We can live like normal human beings. I'm a broader person for having been here, not so simple and parochial. I won't take some things so hard. I had a queer attitude from the beginning of our marriage. I suppose there was an ingenuous guilt sense—but it's gone—really gone—

And on the third page he had written, *The weather keeps good and the house is in nice shape but it has been a long summer. You will be home before long now and it may have been a good idea for you to take the trip.* Then he has been happy without me. Perhaps I'm not necessary.

I've done a lot of thinking in these months and I want to tell you now, before you get back, that any arrangement that's best for you and your peace of mind is what I want too. I have some ideas to suggest. We can talk all that over.

What does he mean by arrangement? We'll go on living like any married people, like people in love. What is in his mind? He can't mean to suggest a separation. It sounds so cold. She searched the rest of the page for explanation but all she found was—*take care of yourself. I'm glad that you get good army food and have a comfortable place to live. It's been a great experience for you, I know. With all my love, Ken.*

All his love. He had written that. But it would have been so much better if he had said more, repeated it, written that it was misery without her, signed himself "your husband." It was not enough. She felt hungry for more.

What's the matter with you, she scolded impatiently. It's a fine letter, a wonderful letter. He doesn't mean anything by that word "arrangement" except—what does he mean by "my peace of mind"? He's thinking about religion, making plans for my going to church and keeping fast days, and perhaps he's still worrying because I didn't like that party in Holy Week. It must be that. What else could it be? Not that he's come to think our life together won't work—

She folded the letter and put it by her pillow for reading again later. She brushed her hair, washed her hands, using the thin wisp of soap sparingly, for she was saving the few whole ones she had to give to the hotel servants when she went back to America. She looked at the clock and saw that if she wanted any dinner she would have to hurry. But she was not sure she could eat tonight. She would go into the bar instead and have a brandy.

It was a dreary little bar with a few shabby tables set around the room which enclosed it. She sat at one of them with the glass of brandy, trying not to let that word "arrangement" ride her mind, speaking to an acquaintance, wondering who was the person with the Czech doctor. She saw Nikkol, the Yugoslav liaison officer, come in and ask for a drink. That was unusual, for Nikkol did not live in this hotel. But the bartender had some secret source of good brandy, and that was probably what drew Nikkol. She did not want to speak or talk with him, but he kept his eyes upon her until she nodded a cool greeting.

It brought him over to her. Perhaps he would have come anyway.

"Good evening, Mrs. Craig," he said with his stiff little bow. His English was excellent. Only the accent and an occasional arrangement of words showed that it was not his native language.

She said good evening, and that the weather was good, and that the brandy was indeed excellent, and that she did not want another now.

[230]

"May I sit with you here?"

"Certainly. But I shall not be here long."

"A moment at least. I understand you have made a visit to our young wards in the mountains."

"You are very quickly informed, Mr. Nikkol."

He smiled or something like it, intent upon what he had to say. She guessed now that he had come here, seeking her.

"It is a very unfortunate situation," he said. "The boys are not well fed and they are neglected. We have made great efforts to send them to their homes and families."

"From the records I saw, few of them have families, Mr. Nikkol."

"They still have their country. The government will care well for them when they are repatriated."

She said nothing.

"I hope that your organization will use its great influence to move them immediately, Mrs. Craig."

"I do not handle such matters. I am a clerk."

"Not a clerk at the Officers' Club, Mrs. Craig."

"No—not on my evenings off."

"When great ladies come from America to be clerks—"

"I am not a great lady, Mr. Nikkol. For once your information is incorrect."

"A most beautiful one, at least, if you will pardon me. And I am sure that your knowledge of the true facts could carry much weight. That is why I wish to ask you to use it in order to—as you say in America—get action quick for these starving boys."

"It's not as bad as that. They're hungry, but Sister Eltha does her best."

"Ah, the old woman. The nun. She is—" he tapped his fore-head—"not right from war. She must let them go."

"She would let them go if she thought they would be safe, Mr. Nikkol. In a minute."

"The Yugoslav government will provide for them. They are Yugoslavs."

"They are also Catholic children," said Barbara slowly.

"That does not concern me."

[231]

"It concerns me very much personally."

"So you are an agent of Rome. So I have heard. Now from your own mouth."

Barbara laughed aloud. "I've never been called that before. Not by those in a position to know. Would you please—go away, Mr. Nikkol?"

Chapter Seventeen

There was one piece of local news which Kenneth Craig had left out of that letter to Barbara. It had been one of the reasons why the urgency to write to his wife had been especially great that day. He had come upon an item in the morning paper which seemed to him to be extremely tragic. Obviously, all details had been cut to the bone out of consideration for the feelings of so important a family, or more likely because the Kilmeys had brought pressure to bear on the press. But the main fact could not be suppressed. Craig did not know what was back of the tragedy but for the next twenty-four hours so many people talked about it in his hearing that he soon filled in the sparse outline that had been printed.

He heard men speaking of it at noon, between the cold hands which they played to see which of them would pay for the lunch.

"That was a bad business about poor Kilmey's daughter, wasn't it?"

"Very sad. He's a fine fellow in many ways. What was the matter with the girl?"

"I don't really know. But my wife tells me that she heard it was a case of alcoholism. Something ought to be done about those kids. The girls especially. There's too much of it going on, too much drinking."

"Was she an only child?"

"Oh no, Ted Kilmey had quite a family. As I understand it, this was the youngest girl. Married a few years ago and had children of her own."

"It's a terrible thing. What was it? An overdose? Those sedatives— anyone can get hold of them."

"No, it was worse than that. She hanged herself in her bathroom and the husband found her there. That's what I was told, anyway."

"That's bad. A man would have a hard time getting over an experience like that."

"It's particularly bad in one way." The man who was talking looked around and sized up the group, to be sure that there was no one in it before whom he couldn't speak freely. Satisfied of that, he went on. "Catholics—the Kilmeys are Romans, you know—are very squeamish about suicide."

"There isn't very much they can do about it if a person knocks himself off, is there?"

"It's a matter of burial, the rites, and all those things they make such a point of."

"That's quite true. I remember years ago," said one of the older men, "that there was a big commotion in the city about burying a veteran who went haywire and shot himself. That was thirty years ago, after World War I. I was just back myself and I never forgot it. This fellow came back from the war and I suppose he had a case of shellshock but they didn't know as much about those things then as they do now. Anyway, he turned a gun on himself one day and they wouldn't let him be buried in the Catholic cemetery. The family had a plot—it was one of the Braniff family, Stephen Braniff—and there was one hell of a row about it. The veterans were all stirred up about it too but they couldn't budge the old Bishop or make him open up the holy ground for the poor fellow."

Craig's expression had not changed, but someone evidently managed to remind the speaker that there was a man present who had a close connection with a Braniff, and the story was not elaborated further.

"Ted Kilmey will take it very hard," said another commentator.

"He's a great family man. Always travels with his wife on that private car of his."

The last time that he had been on that car came back to Craig's mind. Barbara—his attempt to get advice from Mr. Kilmey—if he had known what he did now, he wouldn't have brought the matter up. Or made the announcement at that dinner.

Not that it would have made any difference in the final event. But he had not realized how deep such bigotry went. It had spoiled his own relationship with Kilmey. But at this minute Craig resented nothing that had been done to him. What he was remembering was the joking bits of affection and scolding and tenderness he had seen between Ted Kilmey and his wife. He could remember farther back, to the time when, as a younger man working for Ted Kilmey's organization, he had called at the roomy, hospitable Chicago house and dated one of the girls. Was it Louise? Not Kitty. She was the very pretty one, a few years younger. He had never wanted to marry one of those girls, never been serious about Louise. For a second he wondered if that was because they were Catholics. No. It wasn't their religion. It was the almost racial way they kept inside it. It was a cult with the Kilmeys. He remembered something he had quite forgotten, that there was a red light burning under a picture of a saint in that house, halfway up the front stairs. And one of the girls had told him that they never let it go out.

I never thought much about it at the time, he said to himself. It seemed curious, sort of primitive. But until I married Barbara I never knew how deep it goes, how hard they come down on people with all those rules and practices.

Restlessly and with worry, he wished Barbara were home. He found that story about her uncle sticking in his mind. And she had said, that if there was an accident to the plane it would solve his burial problem. God, what a thought! What they had drummed into her mind. How she had been tortured by the lot of them and by himself too. When she came back, there must be no more of that. No more at any cost. No more if he never laid his hands on her again.

[234]

He heard a detailed discussion of the suicide that evening. He was too lonely to go to his home, so he had accepted an invitation from the Lymans. The party, one more given in honor of the girl whom Blair Wyatt was going to marry, centered around the beautiful and elaborate swimming pool which the Lymans had added to the resources of a big house on Prospect Boulevard, which they had recently acquired and which still made them nervous. It was the best pool in the city and gave Joe Lyman satisfaction because he could show off its modern construction. His wife liked it because if she gave a buffet supper on her terrace and let the guests swim beforehand, there was no need for her to preside over a formal table and to seat people cleverly. She encouraged the people at her parties to do exactly as they pleased and though sometimes they carried that permission to a remarkable extent, she did not protest.

Tonight, when Kenneth arrived, he found the company excited by what had happened to Kitty Kilmey. They always needed a story to circle around and when it was both scandalous and fashionable in content, so that, listening, they felt a vague identification with it, it was the very best kind of gossip.

"She was the very pretty one. She came up here for several cotillion parties a few years ago."

"She'd gotten quite fat. Lost her looks."

"Who did she marry?"

"Awful for her husband, wasn't that? Imagine, just swinging at him when he opened the door!"

"Don't be so gruesome."

"She must have hated him. Or been in love with somebody else. I didn't know the Kilmeys."

"She drank, that was it. Simply alcoholic!"

"Who was it she married?" someone asked again.

Nina Longman, out of the water now, was wrapped in a long, white fleecy coat with great red initials that were also pockets. She stuck her cap in one of them and shook out her hair. Completely covered, she gave the idea of starkness just underneath. She said, "She certainly didn't marry the man she wanted. That was the trouble. She was wild about Sidney Chase. And at one point he really would have gone to town for her, divorced Elise and what not. I know. I got the whole story in Florida. He and Elise were just patching it up and she adored talking about it."

"Why didn't he marry the Kilmey girl if he was so keen and she was all set to hang herself for him?"

Nina answered in her informed way, her voice unaccented and striking each word with neat percision. "Her family wouldn't let her. They marched her off to Europe because they wouldn't let her marry a divorced man. They're very pious. And Sidney certainly wasn't prepared to chase after her and fight the whole Irish nation and the College of Cardinals for her. There was a limit to love as far as he was concerned. I suppose that her mother produced this other guy and she had to marry someone to get it out of her system. But I don't believe that she ever got over Sidney. I wonder if he's heard?"

"They say it was because she was drinking too much."

Nina shrugged that off. "It's a symptom of not being well-adjusted, isn't it? She probably would have been all right if she'd managed to get the man she wanted."

Blair Wyatt said that he didn't agree. He spoke with the rather conscious air of authority which he had taken on lately, aware that the girl he was going to marry was listening, setting a pattern. Catherine Longman was a lean girl who looked as if she might still be growing. Her face was very natural. No concealments of thought or make-up altered it except that her lips were perfectly colored and it seemed as if they had just been taught to kiss. She held them that way, listening to Blair Wyatt and admiring him.

"I don't agree with you at all, Nina, and I knew little Kitty very well. I'm extremely fond of the Kilmeys. She was an utterly beautiful child but not at all the type to think for herself and of course nobody ever expected her to do anything of the sort. She believed Sidney when he told her he loved her—if he did, and even Sidney seemed to think that it was possible. Then she believed her mother and father—and no doubt much higher authorities—when she was told that if she did marry him she would go straight to hell. The poor girl never had any more chance than a tennis ball between two rackets. She would have been just as unhappy married to Sidney as she was when she didn't have him. And he wouldn't have been at all patient with her doubts and fears. She was born to tragedy, marked for it. I'm extremely sorry for all of them. Such cordial, cozy people. And I understand that Ted Kilmey was about to be made a Prince of the Church. This will put a crimp in that."

Listening silently, Craig made his own comparisons, understanding why the Kilmeys had been so hostile and unrelenting after he married Barbara. Those two apparently cheerful, fond family people could deny their own daughter the man she wanted, drive her to drunkenness and suicide. Wyatt's didactic summary struck home with Craig. No happiness for the girl either way, he said. That would have seemed so much nonsense if Craig had heard it a year ago. But he knew now that the pull was strong, much more powerful than an outsider realized.

"How is Barbara, Ken?"

"Very fine. Having a wonderful experience."

"Will she be home soon?"

"Not much more than a month from now, I hope."

"It seemed such a shame that she had to go to Europe right now just when you'd got your lovely new house finished."

"You can't time such opportunities," said Craig. "You have to take them when they come."

"Speaking of opportunity," murmured Carol Harrison to David Rye, "how about Nina? Can you imagine any sane girl playing into another woman's hands like that? I mean Barbara Craig. But I never have believed that her going to Europe was just because of a noble impulse to help refugees. There's more packing in that box."

Nina Longman went into the house on the pool level, where there was a row of amusingly decorated dressing rooms. She came out wearing a white dress and a dark blue turtle neck sweater and a closely wound turban which held her eyebrows very straight and made her eyes look Asiatic. She made almost all the other women feel at once that they were trying too hard to be pretty. Though she did not seek him out, most of her friends knew that before long she would be where Kenneth Craig was, on the lawn where very old statues were newly placed, or at the end of the terrace, the pool's edge, or in one of the empty rooms of the house. It had been like that lately. Bill Longman was not here tonight. Often he was not at parties with his wife. The summer was the busy season in his industry. But Nina herself was spending so much time in St. Anthony that she kept an apartment in a hotel. She explained, and let them take it or leave it, that she had hay fever and that it was always less uncomfortable in St. Anthony. "What fever does she say?" mocked Carol Harrison.

For a while tonight Craig kept away from her, lingering with a group of men who were talking politics, and then doing a little fetching and carrying for a pretty woman who was visiting in the city. He liked beauty in women and he was hungry for it tonight. Temporarily he satisfied himself with the sight of the stranger's perfectly browned and almost moist skin, and by the return of admiration in her eyes which he suspected she turned on at will and often with men.

The thought of Barbara nagged at him. He resented her absence tonight, and the resentment had begun with worry after hearing of the Kilmey girl's death. Tonight, before he came here, he had written and air-mailed a letter to Barbara, bringing her up to date on most things but saying nothing about the suicide. Also he had tried, without putting too much in a letter, to reassure her about their relations when she came home. If they had to, if it was what she wanted, they would live according to the plan suggested by that funny, blunt old girl, Agatha Braniff.

He had written it in good faith but just the same it galled him. What a damned situation it was when a man couldn't have his own wife to himself. These Catholic priests were going to ride to a fall one of these days. There was no end to their demands. Now they wanted public support for their schools and, once let them in, they'd try to control all the schools in the country. But they weren't going to have it their way. There were some candidates who weren't going to be elected this fall and they were never going to know what hit them either.

[238]

They had driven Barbara to the edge of a nervous breakdown before she went to Europe. She'd never been quite herself since that miscarriage, on the day that foul-mouthed priest had let loose and she'd taken it seriously. With his eyes on the lovely skin of the woman to whom he was paying compliments, Craig thought, in some ways it was better before we were married. Of course the priests didn't care about that. That was minor. Marriage, when the property interest came in, was what they wanted to control.

His hostess was calling something about games of canasta being set up. Craig felt too restless to play but the beautiful stranger went away to gamble. He walked down to see the pool again, playing with the idea that perhaps someday, when he could afford it, he and Barbara might have one at their place. While he stood there—waiting or hoping she wouldn't turn up, even he wasn't sure which it was—Nina came, and the noise and laughter of the party seemed to retreat into the house, as if to leave them alone, as if to get away from them.

"Mooning?" she asked.

"I was just wondering what the specifications of this tank are. I must ask Joe."

She said, "When longer and better pools are made—the Lymans will have one."

"They're fine people," he said curtly, not to be caught in any collusion of mockery with her. "Cigarette?"

"Please."

He wished that he had not offered her one or lit it, because her face was so uncomfortably familiar, the cigarette held loosely in that perfectly painted mouth so that a man wanted to pull it out and toss it away and have the mouth for himself, the eyelashes brushed until each hair seemed to cast a separate tiny shadow against the thin, pallid, waiting face.

"Where's Bill tonight?"

"He has a meeting. I suppose he has a meeting. He doesn't like this kind of party. Too long and too buffet for him."

"Does he mind your coming without him?"

"I don't know. I never asked him. I must find out about that. It's

[239]

probably a relief. I'm not easy to live with, as you know. A man needs respite. Anyway, I'm here tonight as duenna for his little virgin sister. I brought her." She laughed on one contemptuous note and added, "Actually. The whole Longman family puts that up to me at these prenuptial affairs. They want the unmarried girl to be accompanied by the keen-eyed married matron. Me! Isn't that a wonderful notion? As if old Blair would take a piece out of the girl beforehand. He's much too great an epicure to want his dish until it's properly prepared and served."

"You're certainly hardly in character as chaperon."

"I have my points. I'm fairly well informed on the facts of life."

"Some few of the facts."

"Well, you can't be expert in all lines, can you?"

He didn't answer. They smoked in silence until she tossed the stub away. It was still lit and the grass was dry so he moved to stamp out the ember. As he turned back, he could feel her glance move over him like a physical touch.

She said, "I miss you, Ken. Terribly at times. I have ever since. I've never had anything so good."

"I don't believe it. And I don't want to hear any of that kind of talk."

"But you have heard it now, Ken. May it ring in your ears."

"I didn't listen."

"Then I'll say it again. I used to want you more than anything on earth. And the odd, unexpected thing—now."

"You didn't want me!" he told her roughly, pacing away from her. "Don't give me any of that, Nina. You wanted money—what money could buy!"

"Of course I did. And you never understood how much I wanted it."

"I understood when you walked out on me."

She spoke in a contemplative way. "You see I had to have something to work with. I'm not beautiful. But I'm decorative at a price. I need what money can buy."

"Well, now you've got it so you're all fixed."

"You still are bitter, aren't you?"

"I'm not bitter at all. I'm all over that long ago. Of course when a man comes back from a war, thinking what he can do for a woman, making plans so that things will go better for them and he finds she's walked out—"

"It had to be done that way."

"I realize that now. It took me a little time. Now I can yield to your excellent judgment." It was his turn to laugh. She didn't.

"But if I had it to do over again," she began.

"You won't ever have it to do over again, at least not with me, fortunately."

"No—it's history that repeats. Not people."

"You traded me off in cold blood. For a lot of money, a bunch of junk. Or maybe you love the fellow. I hope you do."

"No, you wouldn't hope that."

"Why wouldn't I? I do."

"The deepest male vanity prevents you. Every man wants to be the best in some ways. And I admit that you were. I'm having a bad time about you now, Ken. It's not easy to be around you."

"Cut it out, Nina. Come on—I'm going back with the crowd."

"Don't be so restless. Let me say my piece now that you've unburdened yourself. The trouble with you, Ken, is that you don't want a thing until you're sure that you can afford it. You look at the price first. I'm different. I choose and look at the price afterward. Or let someone else worry about it. Certainly I'm greedy and demanding. That's the breed I am. I like the rarest, the best, the thing no one else has, the thing that's hard to get. And I don't mind being the way I am, since I live with myself so closely. Neither did you mind my being that way as much as you pretend. If I'd been a sentimental sloven, always washing dishes and diapers, would we have had as much fun?"

"It might have been real. Something to bank on."

"But I didn't want to bank on it. I lived it, spent it, got my money's worth. So did you, darling."

He felt her voice curl around him. He knew he was being invited, tempted as she could do so well. This was the way a man felt when he began to decide that he might as well be drunk as be the way he was, when he knew he ought to stop, that if he didn't he would probably act like a damned fool and be sorry for it. Yet in this minute he wanted, almost craved the discarding of reason, the loss of self, the defiance of control and decency. She could be so completely intoxicating when she wanted to be. He knew—

"Come on," he said shortly. "Get back on your chaperoning job."

"What makes you so nervous? Remembering?"

"It took me a long time to forget how bad it was."

"Remember the rest of it," was all she answered.

She had placed herself so he must look at her unless he walked away and he stared at her almost expressionless face. It used to be like that and then when he would make her lips open—a man had a right to something of that once in a while—brother and sister, he thought, what a proposition—

"All right, I'll remember—I remember, don't I?"

They drew apart at last. Her eyes were bright with triumph and his were dark with anger.

"Nina," he said, "that's all over. That's all past and the hell with it."

"It doesn't seem to be so past."

"I'm not going to start anything. And I'm not going to let you start anything. I'm married. To someone I love. Just keep that in mind."

"Why don't you keep her around to be loved, darling? Why did you let her go? Or couldn't you keep her from going?"

"My wife," he said with accent, "is doing a job. It's important to her."

"More important than you are, Ken?"

"Why don't you mind your own business?"

"I am," she murmured, "and why must you hide your head in the sand when it's fairly obvious to everyone that a marriage isn't working out when a bride of a few months goes away and stays away?"

"Listen," he said, "get this into your head. Barbara and I are happy. You don't know what she's up against. You would never understand."

Nina laughed again and there was triumph in the laugh too. "No, I probably wouldn't understand the fine points because of my coarse nature. But I've heard a good deal about these European jaunts. She's probably up against a bar, if you ask me, with some man beside her."

Chapter Eighteen

If allowance was made for certain differences in time around the world, the guess was not far from truth. Barbara put on her pale green silk dress, because the officers hated to see uniforms on their women guests in the evening, and went from her shabby hotel to the magnificent palace where the Officers' Club made its headquarters. The great baroque residence had been an extravagance of one of the last Austrian princes who had a fortune to spend on fine living, and the bombings had missed it by some freak of providence or intention of history. So it remained, as an example of past grandeur, and a very present piece of luck for those in the occupying armies who rated a card to its luxury.

Entering the courtyard on foot, Barbara thought inevitably of the way that ladies who used to be guests here must have approached in their carriages, their waists tight laced, hair dressed high, pretty bosoms poked out of their bodices a little, ready to offer a beautiful hand for a kiss or to spread vast skirts in a curtsey. And here she was, a young American woman in a short dress, gloveless, hatless and without an escort, saying to the orderly who guarded the entrance, "Colonel Brush expects me. Yes, I'll sign of course."

But the purpose may not have been so different, she said to herself. I suppose a lot of the girls in white wigs were wondering how the evening was going to work out, and how some man was going to act, and wishing it were another man.

The staircases were still carpeted in deep-piled rose velvet and brass rods held down the heavy fabric on each tread. They were delicious to walk on, after the broken pavements of the sidewalks. Over Barbara's head, cherubs and beautiful women rolled on colorful clouds along the painted sky of the famous ceiling. The many reception and drawing and withdrawing rooms were still full of polished tables, *bergères* embroidered in priceless petit point, great armchairs covered with brocaded satin and little fragile gilt ones. They had somehow survived the invasion and the use of the army, perhaps because orders had been strict or perhaps because men were often surprisingly tender with fragility and beauty after battle.

In one upper room the officers had set up a bar on an enormously long console table against a mirrored wall which gave the proper American effect of night club or saloon. Barbara said to herself that the evening noises sounded like the Town Club and people were acting as if they were in St. Anthony. But where were the people who used to belong here? They were dead, drifting in the streets. The man on the park bench could have frequented this place once. They were lost, unable to be saved or brought back. Like Leslie. Why think of him? Colonel Brush was coming to meet her.

He was a sandy-haired man, very neat just now, with a face that had grown mature without losing a look of boyishness. He was very deliberately sure of himself and normally kept his chin at an aggressive angle. But seeing Barbara he sacrificed something of the manner of the man in power in order to be gallant.

"Lovely—lovely!" he told her. "Where do you get all these beautiful clothes?"

"You've seen the three of them now," she said. "I've no more surprises. Before I go back I shall give them away."

"Don't talk about going back. What would I do?"

She was the prettiest woman in the Officers' Club tonight. She usually had been lately. Her coming to Vienna had been regarded

[244]

as a piece of good luck by a number of people who were stationed there in army and civilian jobs. Her predecessor, Jane Foster, had not had the same kind of attention. But Barbara had been quickly noticed, placed, invited. One officer stationed here used to live in St. Anthony and they had mutual acquaintances. Another remembered Kenneth Craig, who had been in the same company with him during the war. What they could not understand, any more than the people in Washington had understood, or Aileen Bradley, was why she was here if she had a home of her own, or why the man to whom she was married had let her come. Unless there was trouble between them. Barbara had given no hint of anything like that. But she talked very little about herself and it made her rather mysterious.

She herself felt sometimes, meeting Colonel Brush this way tonight, as she had in the years when she had lived alone, after her separation from Leslie. On personal guard. Ready to take what was offered of admiration and fun, of drinks and dinner. Dinner especially was important here. There might be a piece of chicken. Or veal. Maybe even cheese afterward. It was exciting to think of the food but tonight it was not. Usually, when she had been here before, food was the most important thing. Barbara reminded herself that she must not forget she had a project in mind. Careful on the drinks, she thought.

"Where were you off to yesterday, Barbara? I called your hotel and couldn't raise you."

"I went with Aileen Bradley on a field trip. We saw several pretty tough spots. One rooks' nest in the mountains where there are a lot of boys."

The wise thing was not to sound like a do-gooder.

"I know about those kids," said the Colonel. "That's a problem. That's a real headache."

"That Nikkol seems to think that they're his oyster. That they all belong to him."

"The hell they do—excuse me."

"He came around last night to my hotel trying to snoop around."

"Around you? He ought to have his face pushed in."

"I wasn't his interest. He wanted to find out what goes on here. At the Officers' Club."

"He can keep right on guessing. They wouldn't let him past the courtyard. I don't like that bird."

She acted as if she had not known that and admired the Colonel for his keen judgment.

"I'm glad to hear that," she said. "I didn't know whether I was right or wrong about him. But there is something sinister about our Mr. Nikkol. The way he's so determined to get control of those children. Of course there's the nationality thing. I suppose nothing can be done except hand them over to him."

"We haven't handed them over, you may notice," said Colonel Brush. "But we don't have to talk about that mess now. Have another cocktail? You can't do better at the Stork Club."

Colonel Jerome Brush sat beside Barbara on a velvet sofa and made a little love to her after his hard day's work. She liked him in the way she often used to like men, not too much, but with gratitude for the admiration, and especially for the company.

"You're giving me something to live for," he said. "You know that? I was getting to be a tired old man."

"Tired old man of thirty-five?" she flattered him.

"Forty-four. There it is, on the line."

"There aren't so many men of that age who have so much authority. Or who can take a girl to dinner in a palace at any age. From my point of view you're a very remarkable person, Colonel Brush."

"Known as Jerry to his friends."

"Known as Jerry to me," she smiled. "Even as dear Jerry."

"But I suppose there's someone you like better."

"There's my husband."

"What did you leave him for?"

"I haven't left him. I'm over here and he's there but that's not leaving Kenneth. I'm going back when this job is finished."

"But isn't he afraid to let you wander around in a world full of men all by yourself, or doesn't he know how lovely you are?"

"He doesn't have to worry about that."

"If he doesn't, he's a fool. Don't you worry about him and what he may be up to?"

"No. Yes, I do. A little. But I knew what I was chancing when I came. It was the thing to do. We both agreed on that."

"When a man and a woman begin to 'agree on things,' " grinned the Colonel, "the end is in sight. I know all about that. Why don't you get yourself a divorce and marry me? I think we'd get along. You're not always pushing a man around or telling him what to do."

"But you have a wife, haven't you?"

His face grew sullen. All of a sudden the scars of old angers showed on it.

He said, "I won't have one too long. That's why I know so much about this 'agreeing on things.' She went home for good six months ago. To get the thing started. I'll be free pretty soon and waiting for you."

It was only a kind of trial flight, as she knew. Not quite a joke and not really said in earnest. But she thought she had better make one thing clear. As she used to make it clear to men, after she and Leslie had separated.

"You'd get very tired waiting for me, Jerry. I'll never be free."

"No divorce?"

She shook her head.

"Some people think that was why you came over here."

"They're wrong."

"You're a Catholic girl, aren't you?"

She said yes, feeling a hypocrite, feeling even more strongly that she could not expose the truth, the privacy and pain of her life, and tell this man who wanted to play and flirt with her that she had been divorced already. She lifted the brandy glass and set it down almost empty.

"My wife hasn't got that problem anyway," said Brush, "though I do know Catholic girls who have had divorces. I guess it can be done, no matter what they say."

She broke that up by telling him how hungry she was. They went to dinner in a gilded dining room and there was chicken, wizened and thin-legged but unmistakably a fowl. Barbara was grateful for the food and said so, but she wanted still more from the Colonel. Over their coffee she managed to bring the talk around to the urgency in her mind.

"It is wonderful here tonight," she said. "Good to be back. It was grim up on that mountaintop. Beautiful, for the fall flowers are out, all the purple and gold ones. But it was cold and of course in another month it will be a lot worse. I suppose those wretched boys will have to go back to Yugoslavia soon. They certainly can't stay there."

"That's not the only possibility for these kids."

"But what else could you do?" she asked ingenuously.

"I haven't worked it out. But I might end by sending the lot of them to Italy. I would, if I could see my way clear."

"Our friend Nikkol would never agree to that."

"Nikkol wouldn't have any say in the matter. I'm going to see that he's shipped out of here. So you say he's even been trying to infiltrate the Officers' Club?"

"You know how they are. Pretty subtle. I don't think he's particularly trustworthy," said Barbara, seeing that idea had already taken hold. She was doing something tonight that was reminiscent. She had often done this with Leslie, implanted an idea in his head until he thought it was his and then he would begin to announce it as his own, and finally do what she wanted him to do.

"I'm going to fix that guy," brooded Brush. "I'm going to get him recalled to his native land that he loves so much. I know just where to say the right word that will do it too. And for two cents do you know what I'd do then? I'd have those kids flown to Italy overnight."

"Would you really?" she asked with enough admiration.

"Yes. Why send them—how many are there?—why turn fifty boys over to be brought up Communists? They'll be pointing their guns at us in the next war. And pointing guns we give them, if we don't pull up our socks. That's what concerns me. It's not that I want these boys to be brought up as wards of the Pope."

"You object to that?"

"Well, I'm not a Catholic."

"But you were one, weren't you?"

"Now who's been talking to you about that?" He sounded surprised and not pleased. "How did you get on to that?"

"I was just guessing. Nobody said a word about it. But there's something that a Catholic never quite loses."

She had been guessing and she might have been wrong. But that boyish face could so easily be imagined standing in line in front of a confessional or even serving at Mass, being respectful and a little wary of a priest. Was it something in the eyes or an infinitesimal curve of the shoulders which came from bending when the bell rang during the services? Was it nothing at all visible but only a deduction because he had been so quick to think and speak of the doctrine of no divorce in the Church, because he had held out on Nikkol, because he considered the Italian proposition where another officer might have gone ahead and decided the matter on a technical basis? She didn't know why she had guessed right.

"And then you're called Jerome. It's a Saint's name," she added plausibly.

"You're a pretty smart girl. I was a Catholic boy but that was a long time ago. I broke away before I was grown up. There was too much interference for my stomach, too much I couldn't take." He chuckled. "Too much I was afraid to tell the priest maybe. But just the same, it's all right for kids. A Catholic school is a good place to give a boy a start, and I'll never say it isn't. As you say, something sticks to you."

"Sister Eltha has given them a wonderful start in spite of what they've had to face."

"That old nun must have something."

"She has everything," answered Barbara, "competence, courage, and determination. I watched her with the boys and she loves them. She understands them from the inside out. Bodies and

[249]

souls. She could never have done what she did without tremendous faith. And how she counts on you and your judgment!"

"I wish I knew what to do," he muttered.

"Nobody knows better."

"There's no doubt about the nationality. That's the rub. Bradley sent me a lot of data. She's run it down and got the facts and she's riding me hard. I don't like a woman who does that."

"But there's no doubt about their religion either, is there? You have to decide which is more important, religion or nationality, religion or Communism. I suppose someone might say that their souls are the only personal possessions those children have."

"I guess that's about right."

"Little bundles of faith and hope and belief," she said, "that's absolutely all they have, and if they're sent back to Yugoslavia the Communists will take those away from them. Of course that government may not last. Perhaps later it would be all right for them to go back, if there are a few less Nikkols and their kind in the picture. But it seems too bad to send them now, as things are."

"That's what I've been saying to some of these people. But the hell of it is that this policy has been set up."

"I know. And basically it's right that they should be repatriated. But couldn't they have a holiday in Italy first? I tell you, Jerry, those boys didn't look too strong. They've been underfed for a long while. If it could be considered a temporary arrangement, perhaps no one would object to it."

"You may have something there," said Brush. "To tell you the truth it's more or less what I've had in mind. I'm going to get rid of Nikkol first and then use my own judgment. I've been worrying over this wretched business long enough."

"Oh, you shouldn't let it worry you," she said in the tone of the woman who reassures and comforts. "You know what I believe? This will be one of the great human stories that will come out of the war. Eventually the world will hear the full story and realize the responsibility you took for the destiny of a group of utterly helpless boys. And what credit you'll be given for what you can do!"

"I don't want any credit," he answered. But the hint of future fame tickled him and he became very affable again. "You're a great help to me, sweetheart. I wish I had you around all the time. Holiday—health reasons—that's exactly what I had in mind. Well —shall we go and have a brandy?"

"Can we?" she asked happily.

In the room that had been Americanized into a lounge-bar, Aileen Bradley was sitting with a writer of considerable transatlantic fame, who had come to study the military and political situation at first hand. His source of information tonight was Aileen, wearing a dress with little, clean prints of flowers on it and looking dainty and delicate. The Colonel and Barbara paused for a word with the other couple and then sat down for conversation and a drink to go with it.

Dilworth, the literary man, had just returned from a trip he had made as observer with the convoy of a group of families who had been repatriated to Poland. He was full of what he had seen. The Colonel listened with a look of knowledge in reserve. He had more respect for Dilworth than he had for the run of correspondents, for he had seen Dilworth's name made large and important on the covers of many American periodicals. But he doubted that any writer would be allowed to see or hear much of importance in these politically sensitive countries and his own expression almost said so, as did his own short comments.

"You might as well gas the lot of them as send them back. Maybe it would be more merciful, if you could do it."

"I don't think so," said Dilworth. "From what I heard, many of these people find families and friends and re-establish themselves in a comparatively short time."

"And then what?" asked the Colonel. "A life of slave labor?"

"Not necessarily, it seemed. Not if they accepted a completely revised way of life."

"Fine words to describe Communism," grumbled the Colonel.

Aileen intercepted. "Did you have time to look over that new data I sent you, Colonel Brush?"

"I glanced at it. There's nothing very new in it."

"No, but it nails down the facts. It fills out the histories completely in some cases. Barbara went up there with me. She was the one who worked on the records."

The Colonel smiled at his own girl. "She worries too much about these things. Takes them too hard. Anyway the question remains as to whether we can afford to hand those boys over to the Communists, either for their sake or our own."

Aileen outlined the case in a few sentences for Dilworth's benefit. She ended, "Is it better, you think, to turn them over to the Fascists, Colonel?"

"What do you mean by that?"

"That might easily happen if they were wards of the Catholic Church."

The Colonel stiffened, with another glance at Barbara.

"That's not a reasonable assumption. We had better leave religion out of this."

"But we can't leave religion out. I know Barbara is a Catholic, Colonel. We've talked this over. Barbara is broad-minded enough to recognize that the political situation is conditioned by the religious one."

"It's certainly that way over here," said Barbara. "You only have to live here to feel it. They say that the real cement in Vienna was religion and when it was knocked out the place began to fall apart."

"There's a good deal to that," Dilworth said. "When she was fighting the Turks, Austria was a great Catholic nation. She was defending the Christianity of Europe then and she did a job."

Barbara said, "Now Christianity needs to be defended all over again."

"But many Christians don't want to be defended by the Catholic Church," Aileen reminded her.

"Who else is going to do it? Or can do it?" asked Barbara.

Dilworth smiled. "The cement, as you say, has fallen out. Even between the Christian groups."

[252]

"That's not the fault of the Church," Barbara heard herself answer.

"Yes, it is. Because it became political," Aileen said.

"But it was always political," said Dilworth, "and it had to be. The Catholic Church has undoubtedly been able to project spiritual and mystical values to great masses of people for the last nineteen hundred years but it's also had continual political roles and some that even its good communicants couldn't possibly approve of all the way. There's not much question now that the Church is the screen for a new Fascist alliance. It is true enough that we may eventually have to make allies of some Fascist countries if the time comes when we oppose Communism militarily—"

"It'll come all right," stated the Colonel. "You work with those Russians and you know they're spoiling for it already."

"But nobody knows what the line-up of nations may be," said Aileen. "Whatever's done with those boys now, they may grow up to shoot at us, Colonel, as you say. Or maybe with us. And isn't nationality a more basic birthright than a superimposed one of religion? Isn't it?"

The Colonel sounded off, donning his full authority. Barbara said nothing more. He would take the brunt of this and the better if he thought he was protecting her. Besides, fallen away or not, he would resist an attack on the Church. She knew at the moment that he felt as she did.

"I don't like to have religion dragged into this, Aileen. The matter will have to be decided on its merits, according to what seems best to the authorities."

He put Aileen Bradley on the side of bigotry and perhaps she knew she had lost, for her face was inscrutable.

The Colonel had had enough of conversation and broke it up. He drove Barbara back to her hotel in his car but on the way he stopped it beneath the high and broken rows of buildings along the Canal. The shadows were so black that she could not see him, only feel his arms and mouth. She did not resist his kisses. He had given her a great deal tonight and she owed his nervous

[253]

weariness some solace and pleasure in return. She would be gone very soon now, she thought in the darkness. After tonight she had no right to stay on her job.

Two days later she went to Aileen's office with a package wrapped in a piece of newspaper. Aileen looked at her, eyebrows asking.

"I'm leaving tomorrow. The Travel Department is getting me off on the Orient Express for Paris."

"You're really going? For good? Someone said so but I didn't believe it."

"Yes, I resigned yesterday. The work is pretty well organized, and they can get along without me. If you want anything from that office, ask for Lena Schwarzburger, who's been my best worker and can carry on. They might send someone else over in my place but I doubt it if the whole organization is folding up in midwinter."

"Don't you want to see it through? Anyway?"

"I was only to stay three months and it is nearly that. And I can't stay in an organization when I'm not supporting its policy. Mr. Meader in Washington told me that something like this might happen. I didn't think so at the time. But I told him then that if it ever did, I'd get out. I haven't mentioned this to any of the others by the way. There's really nothing to mention. I have to go home for personal reasons."

"I heard this noon that Nikkol has been recalled to Belgrade. They must have swung the whip at Headquarters."

"You won't miss that character too much, will you?"

"Not emotionally. But with him out of the way I suppose Brush will send the Yugoslav boys to Italy before anyone replaces Nikkol."

"Will he, do you think? It should be nice there when spring comes. The boys would probably have a good holiday at least."

"I thought you were the one who didn't influence policies after hours."

"What makes you think I have?"

"Your resignation. And what you just said."

"Oh, leave it that I'm needed at home. My husband wants me to come back."

"I don't doubt that. Anyway, I shan't raise any stink. I can't with Brush in his position or I'd never get any co-operation for anything else. But," said Aileen, "I didn't think you were like that. That kind of Catholic, I mean. Devout. Jesuitical. I know that all Catholics are trained to put the interests of their Church first. But you've always seemed so fair. So open to reason. Like anyone else. I suppose I should have guessed, when you blew up that day at the Polish camp. But I wrote that off as emotional shock. Those things are hard to see for the first time."

Barbara ignored the comments. She did not try to explain or excuse or plead for anything. All she said was, putting down the package, "I'm leaving you these dresses, if you don't mind. I'll be wearing uniforms all the way home. I gave one to Lena but here are the other two well-worn glamour outfits. They should fit you more or less. Jerry Brush particularly likes that green one so give him a treat some night. He's a simple guy but really kind."

"It won't be a treat for him unless you're in it," answered Aileen, lifting the dress, "but it's very generous of you. I'm getting so shabby. And Barbara, I do want you to know one thing. I can't agree with you but I admire anyone who has strong convictions and stays by them as you do."

"Don't fool yourself," said Barbara bitterly. "I stay by nothing!"

She looked very tired, thought Aileen, as if she had not been sleeping but was going along on her nerve. Her eyes were bright and too intent. She laid her hand for a moment in Aileen's and hurried out of the office.

The praise was worse than condemnation or mockery. It did not belong to her and she had no right to it. What she had helped to accomplish had not been done with conviction nor with a sureness of faith behind it. She did not have as much as Colonel Brush, after all his years of apostasy, so she told herself. There was no peace in her mind now, no sense of belonging to anything, to a religion, or to the opposition of religion.

[255]

Aileen is the one with convictions, thought Barbara. I only put something over. I helped to force out Nikkol because I didn't like him. I detested him most when he called me an agent of Rome and then I acted like one, according to Aileen. I persuaded Jerry Brush to see things in a certain way because I made him like me and I know how to handle that kind of man. So does any hussy. Conviction? I had none.

Sister Eltha will be happy at least. Her great eyes will shine and she will believe that it is an answer to her prayers, and that I, because I am a good devout Catholic from America, helped to manage it. And so I did, but the Virgin wasn't walking with me, though Sister Eltha will think so. It proves how false all that kind of mysticism is. I know that now. I'm clear and realistic about a great many things. Ken will be glad of that. I'm not frightened any more, not of what they call sin.

I gave up my religion for Ken. I gave it up for my own self, because I wanted to marry him. But I ran away from him because I wanted to have my religion back, because I felt as if there was a curse on me, on us. It was a kind of mad penance, I suppose, a way of avoiding the occasion of sin. For in my heart I was really afraid to live with him all the time. I was afraid to be really happy for fear of punishment, earthly punishment, and eternal.

At least I know now that distance isn't the answer. It didn't give me back my religion. I'm less a Catholic than when I came. I've stopped being so afraid of the hierarchy. It's a political body, an organization, as Ken said once. I shall be closer to him now that we see things together. I must have annoyed him almost beyond endurance with my fears and scruples and pieties. I'm getting beyond all that. I'm not in the Church—and that's not my fault. I wouldn't be out of it if they would let me live a good life with a good man. Their rules are medieval and people here know it. They should be defied, until they're changed.

Her heart ached and her mind was shamed. But she was going home and she clung to that thought.

It's where I belong. With my husband. Not in this work, as

Aileen does, who can give her whole thought to it. Somehow they all seemed to feel that I shouldn't be here. They wondered, even when I was being useful, why I wasn't home with my husband. And so did I, all the time. If you let anything, any fear, drive you from your home, you're a kind of refugee. Only I can go back and there are all those helpless crowds who can't. I go back to welcome and safety. It isn't fair but thank God for it. I'll try to deserve it. Ah, Ken, if you haven't by this time lost all patience and desire, wait just a little longer.

In the corridor of the Orient Express, late the next night, Barbara stood, lighting cigarettes and waiting for the train to move through its wartime delays and restrictions. The sentimental, uneasy leave-taking with Jerome Brush was over. He had believed the fable she told about being needed at home, and, what was worse, honored her for respecting that marital duty. For comfort to his vanity and attractions, she had let him think that it was very hard for her to leave him. He could not wait for the train to leave because he had a conference, and she knew that in his fatalistic, military way he had already written her off as a lovely girl and a happy incident. But he had said, "And by the way, Barbara, don't you worry about those kids in the mountains. I've got that started."

"I want to know the whole story some day when you come back," she had insisted. "Someday that should be told to the public."

The thought of his published good works will keep him going, you hypocrite, she said to herself. She threw the cigarette out among the strollers who moved like shadows along the station platform, waiting for such wasteful actions on the part of travelers, lit another and threw it out without a puff. Colonel Brush had given her the cigarettes in parting and she would leave them here. It was humiliating to be able to do so little. It was dreadful to leave so much misery prisoned here.

Across the tracks several boxcars were being filled with men and women. They were of all ages but even at this distance Barbara could not define the old and younger. They were dressed in a terrible effort to be ready for cold though the night was fairly warm, with coats stuffed on coats, and strips of mangy fur, and blankets. They clung to their packages and boxes. She knew who they were. They were people who were being sent back to places from which they had fled in terror. Someone was trying to bring a cow but there was no room for the valuable cow if the people were all to be packed in with their less precious belongings. She stood watching, suffering at the thought of their long incoherent trip, the lack of decent facilities, the lice that would creep in, the disease that would flare up, the fate of the ones who would steal away when the car stopped at some unknown destination and try to live in strange, already plucked woods.

Dark people going to their dark fates, she thought, and tried helplessly to believe that prayer would do them any good. For a second she remembered the children who would fly to warmth and sunlight in Italy, and saw again the face of a boy who had listened with fascination to a story she had told when she was visiting the orphans. It was a face full of natural hope. Was it going in the right direction?

The train began to move and separated her—as much as it ever could—from the bulky ghosts in the boxcar, from the children whose destiny she had figured. She flung out the last cigarettes unlit and turned to see her face in the glass door of the compartment, darkly mirrored. She was going home, going back. So were those others. She felt herself shiver. Could even she know what return would be like?

Book III

Thou dravest love from thee, who dravest Me.

—"The Hound of Heaven" by
Francis Thompson

Chapter Nineteen

When Craig telephoned to Barbara in Paris, she asked him so earnestly not to meet her in New York that he gave up a half-made plan. He had been excited but slightly concerned when she cabled that she was coming back some weeks earlier than she had intended, but, after talking to her, there seemed nothing to worry about.

"Not a bit ill," came her voice. "I was afraid you might think that. I'm fine. It was just that there was nothing more I could do on that job. I'd exhausted my usefulness—exhausted my usefulness, I said—never mind, I wanted to come home. Yes—really. They think they can get me on a plane tomorrow."

"Cable me the time and I'll meet you at La Guardia. This railroad man will ride the sky for once to get there in time."

"No, please don't come on. Meetings in New York are no good. Besides I have to report to Washington immediately. I'll get that over in one day and come straight home."

"Is that what you really want?"

"I'd like it much better."

"All right, but get here as quickly as possible. I can't wait now that I know you're on the way. Barbara, can you hear me all right?"

"Perfectly."

"You're not worried about anything, are you?"

"No. Are you?"

"Not a thing. I've had a chance to think over a lot of things. I understand much better. I'm going to take care of you."

"Oh, darling—"

"What was that?"

"I said you're wonderful, darling. Take care of your own self until I get there."

So he had contained his eagerness until he saw her on Thursday at the airport. They did not meet even then, but only saw and touched each other in that first embrace. There were too many people around them, and a few were watching them personally, with curiosity. David Rye had come back from Chicago on the same plane and Jennifer was there to meet him. She exclaimed over the sight of Barbara in uniform.

"It's very becoming. You should live in it!"

"I'll be very glad to take it off permanently."

"Then you're back for good?"

Barbara could feel the fine edge of gossip scratch her.

"Of course.".

"I'm so glad. So glad for this husband of yours! We've been trying to take care of him for you."

"I hope you gave him a good time."

"Come on, darling," said Ken. "The car's over here."

In those first hours the shyness in each of them had to be driven away, and the fear that the other would be disappointed or let down by actuality. He seemed taller than she remembered. She liked the blue shirt he wore and had never seen the necktie. The uniform made her look formal, as if she didn't quite belong to him. But she was beautiful, more so than he had realized. There was no pretense about him, no bombast. She was so glad.

He did not go back to his office, and as the plane came in before three in the afternoon, they had unusual extra daytime hours together that were strangely hard to fill. Everything in the house was ready for her. It was too dustless and polished. It blossomed with expensive flowers, was conscious of celebration, almost self-conscious. Barbara had nothing to do except set a picture straight on the wall. No function yet. Mrs. Dacey was staying to get dinner for them tonight, Craig explained, for he knew that Barbara would be too tired to do anything.

She tried to tell Kenneth about Vienna but the description came out to her own ears as the ordinary story of blitz, with the flatness of pictures which he must have seen hundreds of times in magazines and papers. The agony, the broken beauty, the stir of life in death eluded her. She talked a little about the work of the organization but that too he had heard before and to her own ears, it sounded like a tale of slumming. She asked what he had been doing.

He repeated his last letter, that there had been a lot going on for Blair Wyatt's fiancée. Craig too felt half tongue-tied. How could he begin to describe, sitting here and watching her take things out of her suitcase, the way a man could yearn for his wife—in his office, in a moment of success or pride, when he was doing something he was ashamed of, at five o'clock in the morning, suddenly in the afternoon, at night.

The house—her house—seemed charming to Barbara in a rather unimportant way for her eye had become accustomed to higher rooms and the shape of old grandeur. I am competely happy to be back, she thought to herself and said it out loud, but as yet she felt little except the shyness and the need not to disappoint Kenneth.

She was gayer than he had expected she would be, and more sophisticated.

"Did you fall in love with anyone over there?"

"Not very hard. I suppose you kept in practice."

"It's certainly time my wife came back to me."

He was very conscious of her in this house which had been so empty and useless to him. She streamed through every room whether she was in it or not. Everything is all right now, he kept telling himself and told her so even more buoyantly. And it would be all right when they had a chance to talk and settle a few things. They would, when dinner was over and the old cook went home and they had the house to themselves.

"Does Aunt Agatha know I'm back?"

"Yes. I gave her a ring after I talked to you in Paris. I thought you'd want me to do that."

"It was good of you. Have you seen her at all?"

"Only on that day you left."

Barbara laughed. "I was really sorry for you, Ken, left with the virgin and martyr on your hands. I suppose she ran away from you as usual."

"On the contrary. I drove her home and we had quite a talk. Got very cozy. I like the old girl. She has a lot of sense. I think she'd like me if she didn't think I was corrupting you."

"I must call her up and tell her you aren't."

Craig heard one end of the conversation and wondered what Agatha Braniff was thinking. It would be realistic, whatever it was.

Then, finally, they were alone. They could not pretend that there was anything left to do but be together. Barbara had put on, laughing at her own delight in the feel of it, a negligee which she had not taken to Austria with her because it was too luxurious. It was the ice-blue satin one that Kenneth had bought for her on their wedding trip. Its lavishness trailed on the carpet and she brushed her hair, trying to make it shine as deeply as the fabric. She began to feel sure of her beauty. The house too had taken on more dignity with night and was full of colors and gentle lights. Closing the dressing-room door for a very few minutes she said her prayers hurriedly. She did not want them in Kenneth's way tonight.

When she opened the door he was walking in their room. He looked at her, said, "God Almighty" as if he prayed too, and gathered her into his arms, one held high, one low, feeling and remembering her.

It was not natural. He surprised her. For he had let her go as if she could choose her own direction or next move. He was sitting in the big chair by the table, picking up a book.

"They say this is good."

"Is it?" she asked dumbly.

"I haven't read it but I think I will." He put it down and asked, "Really glad to be back?"

"Of course. It's wonderful."

"Find everything all right?"

[264]

"It's perfection. I feel guilty but I'll take over my housekeeping and homelife now. I'll do better."

"I'm the one who's got to do better. That's what I want to talk to you about, Barbara."

"You do well enough, darling."

"No." He made a few more passes at things on the table and stood up. "It's funny. I've said this to myself often enough so it should come easy now. But I don't seem able to get it out, now that I'm looking at you. Now that you're really here."

She said, feeling a chill inside of what must be her heart, "What is it? What's on your mind, Ken?"

"You know that last letter I wrote you?"

"Yes. Part of it wasn't very clear. You wrote something about an arrangement?"

"That's it. As I wrote you, I've done a lot of thinking since we've been separated. I knew things weren't going too well with us before you left, and I knew the reason why. But I wouldn't face it, I guess. I turned my back on it. I suppose I was sour, in a way. I confess I didn't realize before we were married that your religion meant so much to you. And another thing that an outsider rarely does understand, I suppose, is the hold your Church has on the people who belong to it."   •

"I broke away from the hold. You know that."

"I know you tried to. For my sake. But you didn't get very far, poor girl. I was blind to it for a while. I thought you were just as happy as I was."

"I was just as happy!"

"Sometimes—for a while—and then it would catch up with you. Maybe I overpersuaded you at the start. I'm damned glad I did too for now I can take care of you anyway. But I underestimated the power of the whole thing, the controls it has. When Ted Kilmey began to take it out on me in a business way because I had married you when your Church said no—well, for a while I just didn't believe it."

"What are you talking about? What did Mr. Kilmey do?"

"It doesn't matter. I never told you about it. I was afraid it would bother you at the time. And I was sore as a boil myself. But I got over that."

"You must tell me what it was," she demanded. "Tell me."

He explained about the committee, playing down the humiliation. "It's not important. A lot of those men are good friends of mine. They'll continue to be. Poor old Kilmey can't cut me off that way."

"So I did that to you and didn't even know it."

"You didn't do anything to me, darling. As for Kilmey—by the way, did you hear that his daughter killed herself?"

"Killed herself? Suicide in that family? Oh, that's awful—they're so religious."

"Religious is right. So he's got his own troubles. I heard something of the story. What they say around town is that Kilmey wouldn't let his daughter marry a man she wanted and that was at the bottom of it."

"Oh, poor thing! I heard that story long ago. The man she wanted was divorced."

"Well, we don't want to hash it over. But it shows how deep the thing goes with them, I suppose. When I heard about it, it gave me a kind of shock. I got to thinking about you—worrying about what I'd let you in for—"

"I won't kill myself. Don't worry."

"It's your happiness I worry about," he said, "your peace of mind. I know how you felt last spring. When that priest lambasted us that Sunday. When you lost the baby you believed it was a punishment, no matter what the doctor said. You can't look at it the way I do. And conceivably that could happen again. As things are, you're pulled every which way. We've got to make some arrangement so that, even at the bottom of your mind, even subconsciously, you don't have this idea of living in sin."

"You think I have felt that way?"

"I know you've tried not to. But didn't you, underneath—often—pretty much all the time?"

"Maybe I did," she answered slowly, "but I'm over all that. I won't feel that way any more. If there ever was a sense of guilt, it's gone."

"That's what you think. But I know you well enough now to realize that you can't help yourself. That's why I think—hard as it is to say this on this particular night—that we ought to get off to a fresh start."

"Are you telling me that you want a divorce?"

"Good God no! I only want to make you happy, to keep you at peace. I'm going to try to make things easy for you so you won't be worried or unstable. The basic fact is that, as long as that other fellow is alive, your Church won't recognize our marriage and so you don't feel completely married to me."

"But I do."

"I know you say you do."

She said, above the pounding in her throat, "But if we live together, we can't do anything about it."

"I understand there's one thing we can do. We can live together —but as brother and sister—and it will be all right."

After a minute she repeated the words. Incredulously. "Brother and sister?"

"That would make it all right, wouldn't it?"

"Who told you so?"

He didn't want to give Aunt Agatha away. And suddenly she seemed a little absurd. "A person in a position to know. Who knew of cases where it was done."

"But" she said slowly, "I wouldn't ask that of you. It's not fair. There's no reason why you—"

"Don't bother about me. It's my job to keep you happy. I know that you can't be happy if you're doing anything that you've been brought up to believe is sin. I knew that before we were married. I've found it out even more completely since. Your religion is too deep in you. It means too much to you."

Now is the time to tell him that it's not true. To say that it means very little, if anything; to explain that for weeks you have just been going through the motions of Catholicism, without grace, without faith. She felt the urge to tell him and pride

[267]

resisted it. Or was it shame? She could not tell which it was. But she could not make her loss of belief a reason to have him take her in his arms. He wouldn't credit it.

"And I love you for it," he said tenderly. "I love you because you are good, Barbara."

She thought, he doesn't want me. He says he doesn't need me. Until he does, unless he does, you can't say anything. Perhaps he would have been glad if you hadn't come home. He's been having a good time. Has he been sleeping around? Her heart had never been cold in Vienna even in the first days of nauseous loneliness, but now it felt frozen to stiffness. Nothing moved in her except with difficulty but finally she made her lips speak.

"But would you be all right, Ken? Wouldn't it be terribly hard on you?"

Craig thought, she likes the idea all right. She thinks it's an out. It sickened him suddenly with disappointment. For though he had bound himself to say this, promised himself he would, he knew now that until this minute he hadn't credited her acceptance. He had really thought that, if he made such an offer, she would say, "Don't be preposterous. We're too human, too alive. We love each other too much." But no. She wasn't throwing out the idea at all.

"No. I was in the army a long while you know. And it wouldn't be forever, I suppose."

"Perhaps not."

I did this to him, she thought. To our love. I dragged him through all that argument and bullying, and I put him up against those sermons, and he's fed up with the whole situation.

At last she said it. "If you really mean this, Ken, it's very generous."

He couldn't go back on it now. He asked, "Do we have to talk to a priest about it, or anything like that?"

She didn't know whether people in such a situation saw a priest or not. In any case, it was fantastic. She thought, if I had a sense of guilt before, it was nothing to the one I have now.

"I don't know. I don't think it's necessary. I'd rather not."

"Good. We'll keep it to ourselves. And you will feel better about everything, won't you?"

"There's one thing."

"What is it?"

"If you don't have a wife, there's no reason you should be faithful to a wife you don't have."

"That's all right," he said abruptly.

"But I want that to be understood."

He moved to take her into his arms again, lonely and in a wave of realizing deprivation, trying to find some comfort.

"I just want to do what's best for you, darling. Don't draw away like that. We can have a little of each other."

But she did draw away and she laughed, as she said, "We'd better be careful, brother."

Chapter Twenty

The wedding of Blair Wyatt and young Catherine Longman in late September was a social function of the first water. The caterers who were brought from Chicago to handle all the technicalities of the wedding reception in the immense Longman house gave the most expensive service they could render. The musicians who played softly in the conservatory were some of the best members of the symphony orchestra in St. Anthony. The champagne was vintage wine to the last bottle and the lobsters had been flown from Maine for the salad. It was one of the weddings photographed for *Town and Country* that month, and the Chicago and New York papers gave it much more lineage than was customary for a wedding in the Middle West. The lace cap the bride wore had belonged to a Belgian princess, which was mentioned in all the printed accounts.

It was also a religious ceremony, carried out with great solemnity and impressiveness. Blair Wyatt had gone all the way to claim his bride, straight into the communion of her Church. He had become a convert and as was always true of anything Blair did, he became a convert in the most excellent form. There were few Catholic weddings that would receive such wide attention. It was an outstanding example of a proper marriage in the Church, which was where Longman marriages always took place. The Longman family did not have mixed marriages, though occasionally a conversion was necessary, because of some unbreakable attachment or, as had happened once, an annulment of a previous contract had to be obtained. Longman money had built the church in which Blair and Catherine were married and Bishop Tarrant himself did the family and the couple the honor of being present. Although he did not marry the pair, his presence added color and dignity to the ceremony.

Kenneth Craig had said he did not care about attending, but rather stubbornly Barbara had insisted that Blair was an old friend and that she wanted to see it. So they sat, well-placed in the church, on the groom's side of the congregation. Neither of them glanced at the array of lilies and smilax that had been the marvel of many members of the parish who had not been asked to the ceremony, but had drifted in nonetheless to say a prayer today.

The Mass was long and seemed exceptionally complicated to Kenneth. He folded his arms and wished that they would get through with all the preliminaries and actually marry those two who were kneeling on the satin pillows. Wyatt was too old for the girl. He'd find that out and so would she. But the Catholic Church didn't make any fuss about that. They didn't take nature into account. They didn't object to a lot of things that might stand criticism. He wondered if Nina had confessed to her priest yet that she had tried to seduce her first husband and had probably often made her second one wear horns. No, she probably didn't confess anything. She couldn't. She didn't know how to tell the truth. But perhaps they didn't insist on truth or ask for too much of it, if you just went through the motions.

What was Barbara thinking? What was going on inside her mind? She had been hell-bent on coming today. Craig had not felt lately that he knew what Barbara thought. Not really since she had come back from Europe. Had she ever been in love with Blair Wyatt? Was she sitting there imagining marriage with him, thinking of how nice it would be to marry someone kneeling on a satin pillow with priests swinging incense all around? She couldn't have married Wyatt in a church any more than she could have married him. Or had he missed a bet? Could it have been managed?

She's different from the way she used to be, he thought of his wife. There's something I can't get at. Once or twice I thought it was because she really wanted to be normal. But she put up with me and then sort of turned me out. She wouldn't talk about it afterward the way we used to talk. She likes the way we're living. If you can call it living for a man and a woman. Feeling that you ought to climb out the window in your own house.

He saw Bishop Tarrant's profile, serene and firm under his curiously shaped hat. Well Bishop, you win, thought Kenneth, secretly, I don't seem able to make her happy. But you stacked the cards. He watched the Bishop. Beside him he felt the soft figure of his wife whom the churchmen prevented somehow from being his wife. He let the bitterness rise until it almost shocked him and he felt his teeth on his lip. He wondered again what Barbara was thinking and what effect this show today would have on her nerves.

She was wishing that they had not come. Why had she insisted? Because she had thought she was ready to look at anything coldly and impersonally now. But it still hurt. She had seen Nina Longman go down the aisle in a black suit collared in sable that everyone would talk more about tomorrow than about what the bride was wearing. But I do not mind her clothes, thought Barbara. I mind the hold she has on Ken, who has never quite got away from her. Was it she who suggested that we live this way? Ken saw her often this summer. People keep telling me that, saying that it was time I came home and pretending it's a joke. Does he see her secretly now?

Rising for the Credo, she caught a full glimpse of Blair in the chancel. His formal clothes made him look old. And wise. He was

[271]

getting what he wanted, doing what he wanted. She remembered fragments of what he had said to her on that rather blurred Shrove Tuesday night. "Marriage is too often confused with sex," and "you give up the right to change the beneficiary." They were sharp sayings but not as true as they might sound. For what was marriage when it was denied intimacy, or when the deepest relations were made almost furtive and became broken promises?

Did Ken hate her by this time? He must. Of course he had suggested this way of living in the first place. Did he have a girl in a room somewhere, sometimes? Was it not a girl but Nina Longman? Who was it who said that a man went back to the old stall? Aileen Bradley had said that, in Vienna. Perhaps she knew. There certainly was no profit in being ingenuous. If a man had a memory of satisfied desire it wouldn't matter what the woman was like in other ways. But if a man was continually unsatisfied, humiliated, punished by rules and dogmas that he had never accepted for himself, how could he help resenting more and more the woman who had involved him in such a situation?

She too could see the Bishop and anger rose in her as it had in Kenneth. The Bishop comes to honor this wedding, she thought, and yet he must know that Blair would never have become a convert to marry a shopgirl. To Blair religion is a formal, proper thing, not a deep faith that can tear you to pieces. I suppose that doesn't matter. The important thing is to keep the letter of the law. Look at the holy Nina, on her knees.

How can Ken possibly believe that he has straightened things out and that I am pleased because we are not living together? Or making an escapade of it if we do? Does he think I feel virtuous? I have never felt so shabby, so furtive, so unmoral. When I was in Vienna I thought I couldn't stand it any longer if I didn't get back to him. And now I think it would have been better for both of us if I'd stayed on there indefinitely and played with the Colonel.

Stand up again. It is the last Gospel and Blair will be married very soon. It's always a short ceremony after the Mass. It can't be too short. I can't stand much more.

"Barbara, dear," exclaimed Blair in the reception line, "how sweet of you to come all this way for our wedding."

"I had to see it to believe it, Blair. And I do hope you'll be very happy."

"I am already happy," said Blair. "I feel enlarged and permanent and in balance. I remember telling you one night at the club, Barbara, that marriage is the greatest institution in the world. And so it is."

He smiled at his bride who looked so sweet and resolute that Barbara felt a lump in her own throat. For this girl would be happy. She would always identify her love, her experiences with it, her childbearing with spiritual sanction. She would never be without the Virgin or a guardian angel in her house, and like Sister Eltha, she would be sure of those presences. She would love Blair because she was permitted and obliged to love him, because God was in it with her and it was a holy as well as a joyful union. As for Blair, he would love her the rest of his life with all the devotion he had never yet given anyone. They would have as many children as Catherine could have, beautiful, safe children with two parents.

She had been holding Catherine's hand but she turned again to Blair and this time said it truly, "It is a beautiful marriage, Blair. I'm very glad for you."

He leaned to her, whispered in her ear, and he might have been paying her a compliment in his fulsome way. But what he said was, "In time you'll have it too, dear."

Barbara lost Kenneth for a few minutes in the crowd of guests and saw from a distance that Nina had found him. She went in the other direction and began to drink champagne.

Nina said, "Blair does things so well. He marries like an Old Master."

"He has a lovely bride."

"A trifle unlicked," said Nina.

"You won't have to do any chaperoning now," Craig told her with a grin.

"No. I'll have more time for my old friends."

He ignored that.

"Or for old husbands," she said with her still, bold look.

"They won't take up any of your time."

"The more fool, he," said Nina. "You look a little sharp at the cheekbones. You're getting too thin."

"I was too heavy."

"I never thought so," she said politely.

"Nina, how do you get away with it?"

"With what?"

"What do you tell your priest?"

"In confession? Why, that I've sinned."

"But not that you mean to stop."

She smiled, "The best way is to tell a sin when you're quite through with it. When you're ready to stop."

"Tricky as ever."

"Not tricky, dear. Just wise in my way. Tell me, if I happen to be in town what is the best time to call you?"

"There isn't any best time."

"Well, I'll try the wrong one someday. Come, there'll be fresh caviar for a while and I know you love it. Do you remember when you afforded it one night and brought some home?"

"No, I don't. I must find Barbara."

"She's right over there being very gay."

She was too gay after a half hour of celebration. Kenneth asked her if she wanted to stay any longer.

"No, but I thought you might," said Barbara, a little wildly. "You and Nina looked so absorbed. So family."

"I didn't want to come in the first place."

It was worse now. The long drive home was empty of companionship. They had endured fifty miles of it before she said, "I really think you should get a divorce, Ken."

"You've had too much champagne."

"No, I'm clear as a bell now. I said that in earnest."

"Why? Is that what you want?"

"This isn't much of a marriage that we have."

"That's not my fault, is it?"

[274]

"No, nothing's your fault."

"I'm not complaining. But if you weren't so afraid of a lot of black robes maybe we could live like human beings."

"What makes you think I'm afraid?"

"I've seen the effect they have on you."

"Not any more."

"What do you mean?"

"Just that I'm not afraid. You've been wrong about that for some time."

He did not know what to say. It should have been a welcome statement. It was what he had hoped for. But there was something dead about the way she spoke. He couldn't summon any emotion to meet it. Besides, he didn't believe it was true.

It was early evening when they arrived home. He never forgot that arrival nor did Barbara. The house was dark and he switched on a light over the door. The edge of an envelope showed under the sill. He unlocked the door and picked it up before he let Barbara pass him.

"It's a telegram. I suppose the boy didn't know what else to do with it. For you. Wait a minute." He had seen the stars that indicated that it was a message of bereavement. "Let me open it."

Kenneth was the first to read that Leslie Field was dead.

He gave it to her. "I can't say I'm sorry, dear," he said quietly.

"No one could say it," she answered, after she realized the fact. "I saw Leslie in New York. But it's so terribly sad."

"Of course it is. The fellow didn't handle himself right and he made life hard for you but maybe it wasn't altogether his fault. Some people have queer kinks in them from the start. But try not to get worked up over this, will you, dear? You were far better to him than he deserved and you've nothing to regret."

"Yes," she said in a meaningless way, "I think I'll go out for a while." She walked through the house to the dark terrace that stretched along the back of it and Craig knew that she wanted to be alone and did not follow.

At first there was no thought, no pattern in her mind. Something had happened that was important but there was no crash or shock. Or I can't feel it, she thought. I don't feel things at all any more. Leslie's dead. I don't have to keep myself from wishing that any more because it's happened. Without my wishing it. I never did.

He's gone. Safe. He's not roaming around those streets half crazy, not any more. There was nothing I could do but always in my mind, deep, there's been the worry, the burden, that awful sense of failure. I did all I could. Did I? If someone else had married him in the days when he was all right—only seemed all right, the doctors said, remember that.

But I was the one who did marry him. When he was a beautiful young man. Too good-looking. He traded on it. He traded on everything. I musn't remember that now. No, I musn't forget it. But we were married. He taught me what it was to be married. I really didn't know a thing. And David was his child. Without him there would have been no David and I wouldn't have wanted that no matter if Leslie had been worse, if I had to go on with him forever—

It was the loss of David that brought the tears, the silent shaking sobs. It had been so long since she had wept that it was like a new experience. Coming to find her, Kenneth thought, I've never seen her cry like that. I've seen tears in her eyes but this is different. It will do her good.

But he had to try to comfort her. "Don't suffer over it, darling. This had to come some day. It's the best thing."

She lifted her head from her arms on the wall.

"I know it is for him."

"And for us. That's what you want to remember now. Tomorrow we'll get in touch with the people who sent this wire and see if there's anything civilized we can do. But that chapter of your life was closed long ago."

She did not answer.

"You know that's true."

"It's closed now, anyway."

"And now everything is clear ahead for us."

"Is it?"

"Isn't it? You and I can get fixed up."

"Fixed up," she repeated as if those were curious words.

"That's no way to say it, I know, but they won't have anything to object to now in your Church. No more of those impediments. You won't have any strings on you now, even according to the Bishop."

"No. I'm a widow now, in the eyes of the Church."

"You're my wife," he said. "I was just wondering what the procedure is? Do we have to be married again or does our marriage just automatically become sanctified?"

"We'd have to be married by a priest."

"Well, that's all right," he said tolerantly. "We don't have to make a big fuss about it. It can be done quietly."

"It could be very quiet, I suppose."

"You can fix it up anyway you like. I'll go along."

"Ken, do you realize that you would have to promise to bring up any children we might have as Catholics?"

"Yes, I know that. I won't say that it's the easiest thing in the world for me to agree to. It commits a child in advance to something that might bear down pretty hard on him in later life. And it's pretty hard and fast dogma. But kids need something to tie to. If that's what is required, and what you want, it's all right with me."

"And then I'd have to want you to become a Catholic too."

"Me!" he exclaimed in protest. "Oh, leave me out of it, dear. They haven't got to the point where they demand that, have they? I'm sure not. That would be out of the question. I don't mean that I haven't got a great respect for the Catholic Church but there are some things I couldn't go along with personally. I'm not the type."

"They don't demand it. But if I marry a non-Catholic in the Church, I must hope for his conversion, pray for it."

"Oh, that's different," he said with amused relief. "You go ahead and pray all you like for me." He bent and kissed her hair, and went on.

"The main thing is that from here in no one can find any fault with our marriage or say you aren't my wife in every sense. It's all in the clear now. We'll be married your way as soon as you like and

[277]

I'll give them all the assurances they want except any promise about my going over to Rome. Do you think we can set it up immediately? Don't you want me to go with you to the Bishop or priest or whoever is the right person?"

"I don't want to do it at all," said Barbara, quietly.

"Don't want—why, what's the matter, dear? Surely you knew I didn't have it in me to be a Catholic. It's not in my blood. I never pretended—"

"It's not you, Ken. It's myself. I can't marry you in the Church. I couldn't promise to bring our children up Catholics. I couldn't pray that you'd become one. I haven't been a Catholic myself in my mind or heart for quite a long while, since before I came back from Europe. So why should we be married in the Church?"

"But that was what you wanted. That was what made all the trouble. It was what we went to see the Bishop about."

"I know."

"And now there's no obstacle."

"It should be the happy ending," she said in a tired way. "It comes just when it should, when nobody would believe it in real life. But it is real life—and not the happy ending. It's a sad, bitter one."

"Look, dear, you've had a shock. And a long day before that. Forget what's happened as much as you can for tonight. We'll talk about this some time soon."

"I'd rather talk now, if you don't mind. I want to tell you. I'm not a Catholic any more."

"Of course you are," he said. "What are you talking about?"

"No. I found that out one day in a makeshift chapel in Austria. There I was, on my knees, feeling exactly as a non-Catholic feels when he has no sense of the supernatural, when a gilded box is only a gilded box and not a tabernacle."

He stared at her, helpless for the moment.

"I have no sense of sin," she said. "I can't feel any contrition and that's what you must feel to go to confession. If they were right—and perhaps they may have been, I don't know—in saying that I was married to Leslie as long as he lived, then the sin really was there, in our life, yours and mine. And I'm not sorry for it. I told you tonight that I saw Leslie in New York."

"Why did you do a thing like that?"

"I had to. He called me and asked. There was a pull. Not anything remotely like desire, but a pull. It was a horrible evening. He was drunk when we met. He was half-crazy, hating me, panhandling. And yet I felt a kind of unbreakable tie between us, more than duty, more than pity. Because he was Davy's father. Because we had been married. It had nothing to do with the way I felt about you. I loved you. Every minute I was loving you." She closed her eyes and shivered. "But there it is. Maybe the Church has something in its indissolubility."

"Nonsense. You've been letting this prey on you. You're too sensitive, that's all. Never mind any of that now. You're free at last, thank God."

"One thing I didn't do," she went on after a minute, "and this I must tell you. I didn't deny us. I went into a church when I got away from Leslie that night. Everyone was going to confession. The place was full of comfort and forgiveness for everyone else and I wanted some for myself. Desperately. I might have gone into a confessional and said I was sorry that I had broken the rules of the Church in marrying you, and that I wouldn't live with you again as your wife while he was alive. I thought of doing that. I knew I could hypnotize myself into believing it was true for long enough to get absolution. I'm not sure that something of that sort wasn't in the back of my mind when I left here. But I didn't do it. I didn't commit sacrilege and I didn't deny us."

"Bless you for not saying you were sorry you married me."

She did not seem to hear what he said. He felt as if his words only brushed the hard surface of her thoughts.

"When I went to Europe I suppose I thought it would be an easy way to avoid the occasion of sin—"

"I'm sure you thought that."

She heard that, looked up at him. "Yes, you told me that when

[279]

I came back. You saw it more clearly and before I did. What I felt myself was a sense of escaping. Not from you. But I was trying to get away from the hold the Church had on me, to leave it behind me. I expected that when I got out of the diocese, it wouldn't be so strong."

"I never should have let you go," he said.

"I found out," she told him, "that the Church went with me, branding me as its own, claiming me, telling me which side I was on and what to think. The pieties don't matter so much over there. But the control is stronger and more complete. It's political and mental as well as spiritual. You're in an army and you aren't even told who your allies are. It isn't just for an hour on Sunday or as a monthly communicant that the Church wants you over there. It expects you to line up and die for it if necessary, or to be a refugee living in a room with three sides and the rats around your feet and a crucifix on the wall—or to go back where you ran from and be shot. It wants you all the time, all the way. It may be that way here someday."

"I wouldn't be surprised. That's what a whole lot of Protestants are afraid of. But I thought that basically was what you wanted, Barbara."

"It can't have been," she said obscurely.

"But you've been a devout Catholic."

"Oh no. It looked that way to you. But if I had been, Ken, I wouldn't have married you. Not if I believed what I said I believed. I used the Church for comfort, for keeping myself safe, as a refuge, long after I'd begun to be critical of it and even after I openly defied it and married you. Then I defied it again—I said it couldn't take my faith away from me. But it did. One day I found the faith withdrawn. It is their faith, not mine any longer. Maybe I'm better off without it and will be a stronger person. But anyway, I've stopped lying to myself or to you. And you do see now why we can't be married in the Church, don't you?"

"I think this is a touch of hysteria. All that's happened has been too much for you. And I know you too well to believe you could ever let your religion go."

[280]

"It let me go. Before I came back from Vienna."

"Then—" he paused but couldn't help finishing it, "why on earth couldn't we live together as man and wife?"

"That was your suggestion."

"But I was trying to make you happier. You agreed—"

"You were the one who gave in to the Church," she said harshly. "I never did."

Chapter Twenty-One

It was not what Barbara said that night that made Craig believe her. Nor even their conversation three days later when, sure that Leslie Field was safely buried, he brought the other matter up again. It was after dinner and the evening had been pleasant but not intimate, an evening of scanning newspapers, listening to a broadcast, remembering to check over a few bills, and wondering what she was thinking.

"You do know, Barbara, that I stand ready to do anything that's necessary. About this religion business, I mean."

"There's nothing to do, Ken. Don't worry about it."

"I don't at all. But you'll want to get back into good standing. You're going to feel better when you do, when they can't hold out on you." He said awkwardly, "The sacraments and all that. If it's in any way embarrassing for you to open up the matter, let me go and talk to the Bishop. It wouldn't faze me a bit."

She said quickly, getting up from her chair and seeming to tighten all over, "Oh, you mustn't do that! You wouldn't, without telling me?"

"Of course not. But I do believe you'll be a whole lot happier when this is settled."

"It is settled. I told you how I felt the other night."

"I know, but you aren't going to go on feeling that way. I don't wonder at it at all. You must have had some pretty disillusioning experiences. But it's obvious that the Church in Europe is fighting for its life."

"It's fighting for Christianity."

"With no holds barred. But if it's what you believe in, you have to overlook some of the methods, I suppose."

"Yes, if you believe."

"Naturally, you feel resentful and sort of pushed around after the way you and I were treated."

"There was no other possible way to treat us."

"I still doubt that. But anyway it's time now to bury the hatchet. Your family has always been identified with the Catholic Church here, you were brought up in it and they are going to be delighted to have you back in good standing. The rest of it will blow over in no time. We did the right thing and it's working out pretty much as I thought it would. But I think you'll feel better—"

"Don't say it again. I wouldn't."

"Well, I won't urge it on you. It's your business. But I want you to be sure that, as far as I'm concerned, you just have to make the move."

It wasn't what she said that convinced him. It was the queer shocks that her lapses, her changes of habit gave him. It wasn't like Barbara to toss her negligee against a chair and get into bed like that. For a minute he didn't realize what was wrong with the timing and then knew that he had expected to see her kneel down, make that swift sign and lock her head in her hands to pray. Craig had often joined her mentally, he thought, with a meditation on how lucky he was, a fervent hope that they would be happy and well for years, and gratitude to that lovely kneeling figure offering up their life together to whatever she found good, to the mysticism she trusted.

"Feeling all right, dear?"

"Yes, of course. Why?"

"I wondered if you were very tired."

"Not specially. Open the west windows a little more, will you please?"

[282]

There was the Sunday morning—it was the first one after the news of Leslie Field's death when he looked at his watch and said, "You're going to be late if you don't get a move on."

"Late for what?"

"It's nearly eleven. Isn't that the last Mass?"

"I'm not going."

"Feeling all right?"

"Absolutely. I'm going to dig up those tulip bulbs and separate them this morning."

He didn't know what to do about it. There was no reason why he should do anything, he told himself. People stopped going to church. Hardly anybody went every Sunday. Except Catholics, who had to.

What had they done to her over there in Europe? Or was the reason she'd turned against the Church because of that proposition he had put up to her when she came home? Brother and sister. He could do something about that anyway, destroy that idea, make her forget it.

He was not sure that he had succeeded. And it was so unlike Barbara not to want a child.

"Everything's so uncertain—"

"I ought to see the doctor first. I will someday."

The final reluctance, "I'm not sure enough—"

"Not sure of what?"

She whispered, "Of us. Of our marriage. Just love me."

She had never been more desirable or more unreserved and yet, waking, he knew first of all that he was not happy about them. She was gone already, shy or withdrawn into one of the locked moods she had so often now. He found her downstairs, the breakfast almost ready. On mornings like these, they used to be gay with emotional secrets, amused at themselves, very tender.

"Feeling all right?"

"Oh, absolutely."

"What are you going to do today?"

"I don't know exactly. There are some places I have to go."

"Well, you have your own car."

"Yes, it's wonderful to have that."

They had two cars now. He had bought the little coupé while she was away and explained that her absence made their expenses so low for a couple of months that he could afford it. He was not quite sure now that he was glad he had done it. There was no reason to plan their days so they would fit together and often he had no way of knowing where she was. During those first months of their marriage her life at home had been the background for his work. He could always see it clearly then. But now it was different. His not knowing where she was was part of the pattern of not knowing what she thought, a pattern that was being set and glazed.

When he had left her alone with the day, Barbara thought again that it was the First Friday of the month, the first one of October. She had remembered that as she came downstairs this morning, wondering how much he loved her, wondering if she gave him all that Nina ever had or could. It was a sordid thought, one of those she could not keep out of her mind lately. Horrid thoughts that smeared horrid words on her mind and came back even after she thought she had chased them away. But she had to think about something.

The First Friday in the month. It used to be a well-marked day because a member of the League of the Sacred Heart always went to Communion on that day. Ever since she was a little girl in the convent and a Child of Mary she had gone to Communion on the First Friday unless she was ill. For years—she thought back over them, the Friday mornings in the white marble chapel, with a white veil over her head and very chapped fingers for the convent soap was harsh, and the ones later on, after she was married—no matter what, whether they'd been out until dawn but she never ate or drank anything after midnight, she was careful about that—afterward when she was living alone and sometimes it was so hard with no car and the Cathedral was usually cold in the early morning. But so often if she didn't get to Mass early she couldn't have gone at all.

She could see that crowd at weekday Mass as it was this morning, girls on their way to work, old men piling up benefits for heaven, people who were always there in queer, ancient hats, men you never saw anywhere else and men you saw every day running an elevator or on a policemen's corner. It was easy to go on fine days in the summer, on beautiful exalted spring mornings when she got a head start on the day by going to early church and earned special graces because it was the First Friday, and breakfast always tasted so good and rewarding after fasting.

That church will be full this morning, thought Barbara. All Catholic churches will. No, I don't want to be there. It's a kind of self-hypnotism. In the beginning you believe something—when you are small and credulous and have to believe what you are told—and later on the repetition gets hold of you. You love the succession, doing it over, not breaking the chain. At some point you stop believing but that's not important unless you find it out.

Many people never stop believing. But they become afraid. I've been afraid for a long while. I shan't be any more.

She washed her pretty dishes and the steel and porcelain of her kitchen was soon shining. Where had she left her diamond and sapphire ring? Could it have gone down the garbage disposal unit? Oh, St. Anthony, help me to find it. St. Anthony—don't be so ridiculous. You'll find the ring. Look on the shelf with the glasses. There it is, right where you left it.

What should she plan for dinner? The order must be telephoned in before ten o'clock if it is to be delivered. Friday—fish day—not for me any more. I ate bacon with Ken this morning without a qualm and a veal steak would be good tonight, sautéed with butter— Ken likes that—and chicken soup. Chicken is forbidden too, of course. I tried to explain that to Ken when we were in New York on our wedding trip. She remembered the incident and how amused he had been. The chicken and the eggs.

And now he is actually urging me to be married in the Church. He talks as if it were a matter of joining a club where you've been posted until you were dropped. Pay your dues up and get back in good standing. He doesn't understand that I'm helpless. I don't believe and I can't believe. What is the use of saying five Hail Marys when you are just repeating a woman's name? Yet I think he was shocked when I didn't say my prayers on that first night.

I wonder if he calls Nina up in the daytime. Everyone has been making broad hints that she is after him again. They looked so terribly intimate at Blair's wedding. I told him on the way home he could have a divorce if he wants one and that was before Leslie died. It's one more reason for not getting married in the Church even if I would. If, later on, he wanted a divorce, there would be another religious mess and I'd be right back where I was before. And I couldn't bear to be married to Ken in the eyes of the Church if he was off with someone else. That I could not take.

She heard the mailman's ring and brought in the letters and papers. There was the parish paper. It kept on coming. She was on some list. She dropped it in the wastebasket but a picture of Father Gilroy stared up at her and she picked it out again curious to see what he was doing. He was organizing a course of lectures on marriage. Barbara laughed aloud as if she hoped he could hear her. "And if any one knows less about marriage than the dear Father," she mocked with the old Irishwoman's joke.

No mail of consequence. An expected bill or two, a few begging letters. One from a friar in India. I must be on the Catholic sucker list, she said to herself. One from a group of missionary sisters who offered to trade nine prayers a day for a dollar a year. Quite a bargain, Barbara thought, dropping the appeals in the basket, but they would be useless prayers for me.

Ten o'clock, after she had ordered the meat, and not much to do today. I must get myself an interest, she thought, something to keep me busy. Go on some board. But of course the Catholic institutions wouldn't want me and the others won't consider me because they all know I'm a fallen away Catholic.

The telephone. It might be Ken. No. It was some woman, representing some woman's club.

"And I'll be frank with you, Mrs. Craig. Our speaker for the week has disappointed us and someone told me that you have recently come back from Austria, and had first-hand knowledge of conditions there. We wondered if we might presume upon your time—"

"I'm so sorry," said Barbara. "I couldn't find time to do that."

Time. She had nothing but time. But how could she tell that group of women, with their ears set to hear another speaker and not caring much what they heard anyway, about the life that was led in refugee camps? Why expose the refugees? It wasn't as if those women could or would help them.

But there was so much time before Ken would come home again. Tomorrow there would be more time before the Rye's dinner at the club and on Sunday Ken would be home and they would idle through the day. No church any more. What I miss about church, she thought suddenly, is seeing all the people. No, it's not that. I don't mean that. But I have so few friends. I never realized it before.

She looked at the calendar of the month on her desk. The First Friday—yes, and her mother's birthday. She would take some flowers out to the cemetery. Perhaps it was only a sentimental custom but her mother had always loved flowers, and the Braniffs respected birthdays even when they could not celebrate them. Several times a year Barbara made these pilgrimages.

It was a pleasant drive through the outskirts of the city where thin woods were bright with the primary autumn colors. She had a basket of small chrysanthemums on the seat beside her, and the old cemetery never depressed her but only brought back childhood memories, of having admired and thought beautiful a long-limbed marble angel clinging awkwardly to a cross. It was still there.

Here she did not feel lonely. These people, even if dead, were her congregation. She knew the names on hundreds of the stones. And the Braniff lot was large and dominated by a great Celtic cross which she had come to realize as beautiful, though the angel was her childhood choice.

John Braniff. Anne Kathleen. Cecilia, who had died young. For a moment Barbara resisted and then knelt to say a prayer at each

[287]

grave. This was different. This was keeping them close. If their souls hovered, eager for prayers, they must not be denied, and perhaps in some mysterious way that was true.

David Field. "Darling David are you safe and happy?" It was never as dreadful here as anywhere else, for some reason. She chose the brightest pink chrysanthemum for the little vase beside his marker and put the rest on her mother's grave. It was very peaceful. She used to say as if David could hear her, "Someday I'll be here too, David." She almost said it now and then realized that she would not. They would not bury her here, not an apostate, in consecrated ground.

The thought struck her hard and she struck back. What did it matter? What could it matter? But now the peace was gone and she quickly finished tending the graves. She must stop and tell the sexton to keep that basket until spring, when he took it off the grave, in case she did not come again this winter.

It was becoming a very big cemetery. Slopes she could remember as only fields were studded with graves. She saw the sexton mowing a section and drove her car to him along the narrow little road that wound around the graveyard. He was a new man. She didn't know him.

"Yes ma'am, I'll take care of it."

"It's getting to be a very big cemetery, isn't it? This is the Angel's Row, isn't it?"

"That's what it is and filling up fast."

Angel's Row, where the bodies of children who died almost at birth and whose parents had no cemetery lots could be buried. She used to bring flowers for it sometimes, when she came so often after David died. She used to pray that they would keep David company.

"And what's that new part over there? Across the road, I mean?"

It was a large ragged oval of ground, with some rather pretentious tombstones and yet it seemed oddly placed.

"I haven't seen that before. But I usually go out the other gate."

"That's the unconsecrated ground, ma'am."

"What kind?"

"It's where they bury the suicides and divorced ones and the ones who die out of the Church and want to be near their own."

She looked at him, back at the lot.

"It's unconsecrated," he repeated.

She said, "Do the worms know?" and left him staring, and slowly beginning to grin.

Chapter Twenty-Two

In answer to Craig's question, Barbara said that she didn't know what she was going to do this morning. She might stay in bed, where she was at the moment, or she might get up after a little while and write some letters.

"I've sort of a head this morning," she said. "I drank too much at the club last night."

"I thought you were overdoing it."

"So was everybody else."

"Maybe a walk would do you good. Don't you want to get out in the air?"

"Not now," she answered and her voice was almost sullen.

He looked at the array of miscellaneous reading by her bed, the empty coffee cup. Fashion and news magazines, a detective story, the latest political analysis of Europe. It was an untidy mess of printed thought and imagination.

"I'll do those dishes later. When I get up," she said, and he remembered what fun it used to be to do them together on Sunday mornings, hurrying so she could go off to church. He frowned. She was surrounded by comforts and luxuries but all he wished to God was that he could do something for her.

"Well, I think I'll get some exercise myself."

"All right. Don't forget we have the Wyatts and those other people coming here for supper."

On Sunday they lived in the deliberately informal modern way.

Craig got his own breakfast. He used to get it for both of them while Barbara made an amused queen of herself for an hour. She did not do that any more. The day used to be their own, except for the hour or two that she spent at church, and it was always too short. Now he didn't know what to do with himself.

They had gone on with the housekeeping of living together for the six weeks since Leslie Field had died, with attention to meals and food, to winter landscaping and care of the flower borders, taking care of repairs, paying bills, entertaining and dining out. Sometimes it seemed so smooth and ordinary that, running his thought over their days, Craig could not find a flaw. Yet he knew that this apparent comfort and well-being, which might look like happiness, was synthetic, and he did not trust the materials from which it was made.

It was no secret that Field was dead. He had been killed in an accident, perhaps a brawl, and mention of it had been picked up by a news service and sent along to the city which he had once claimed as his place of residence. It was unimportant news, not featured. A few people gave it a word of pity or reminiscence, or pointed a moral. Some others realized its full implications to his divorced wife and mentioned that to one another. But Craig and Barbara never spoke of it to anyone. Nor to each other now. The balance between them had become too delicate.

Craig looked at his watch. It was already eleven o'clock. But the time meant nothing for the day had no shape.

"Well, get a good rest," he advised her and hesitated on the verge of saying something more. But she gave him no chance. She seemed to be there, soft, accessible, his wife. But he felt it was mirage. If he tried to touch her, she would be farther away and he dreaded the disappointment.

It was cold and he walked briskly, trying to adjust himself to be reasonable. There was after all nothing to worry about. He had a good place in life, a lovely and beautiful wife, safe at home, guests coming in later in the day. All women were more or less nervous. The bloom came off a marriage.

He went out of the boulevard district down into the city proper and kept on walking for there was nothing else to do. With more than three miles between himself and his own house, he was in the old part of the city. He heard a church bell summoning its congregation but at that moment the name on a street reminded him again of Barbara. That was where she used to live, down two blocks —the many times he had gone there, the happy hours struck painfully on his memory. He wouldn't walk that way. He turned and bumped into a woman.

"I beg your pardon—oh, I'm especially sorry. How are you, Miss Agatha?"

"Nice to see you, Mr. Craig. Out for a walk? How is Barbara?"

"She's in bed this morning."

"Is she sick?"

"Oh, no. Just resting."

"She wasn't well enough to go to church?"

"A headache. You're just coming from the service?"

"No. I'm going to the last Mass, a thing I rarely do, but my furnace gave me trouble and I had to have a man look at it. So I'm going to twelve-thirty. You're sure Barbara isn't ill?"

"She's all right." Craig said on impulse, "I'd like to talk to you about Barbara someday, Miss Agatha."

She looked at him gravely. He thought, of course she knows that Leslie Field is dead and is wondering what we're going to do about that. Or why we haven't.

Agatha Braniff said, "Why, any time. If the house wasn't locked, I'd tell you to stop in as you pass. You wouldn't care to come along with me now," she hesitated and he realized why, "we could talk after Mass then."

"Yes, I'd be glad to go with you," he told her. Instantly he regretted the impulse, which had been to demonstrate that he had no prejudice. But Miss Braniff had no time to demur or argue. She took him at his word and hurried him along.

"We'll have a nice talk afterward and a cup of coffee," she promised.

[291]

She led him, as one well accustomed to her special place, far up a side aisle to a pew which was close to the altar. But after his first reluctance, he found he did not feel conspicuous. The service was simple, the altar lit by only two candles. This was a Low Mass. He remembered Barbara called the short services that.

Miss Braniff knelt, her beads moving slowly through her fingers. He thought of the Rosary under Barbara's pillow. He thought of Barbara and forgot the service, heard the bell, lowered his head for he felt the solemnity around him.

There was one priest on the altar and a couple of clumsy, very young boys assisting him. Nothing was understandable to Craig as they moved and bowed. But he saw a young woman rise from a side pew and go up to the altar rail. She knelt far at the side, almost in shadow. Craig could see her and one look told him a good deal about her. She'd been about. It showed in the bleached yellow of her hair, the cracked patent leather slippers. Magdalen in person, thought Craig.

Because the Mass was so late, no one else approached the altar to receive Communion. Craig sat watching the girl, thinking bitterly that they didn't rule out a person like that who must have committed every sin in the book. But Barbara—and then he realized that there was a kind of apprehension around him. Miss Agatha was looking tense, watching the priest who seemed oblivious to the girl. Craig gave a curious glance at people kneeling nearby and saw the same tension in all their faces. The priest had not seen the girl in the shadows. Perhaps when the boys looked around she had not been there. Not come up in time.

He found himself, like the rest of the watchers, hoping that the priest would turn, that the boys would notice her. He heard the quick indrawing of Miss Agatha's breath and guessed that the time for Communion had passed. They saw—they all saw—the girl's head suddenly fall on her arms and her shoulders shake with sobs. It was a dreadful sight, to Craig as well as the others. He could feel the effort, the yearning, the terrible denial. He could think only of Barbara going through this Sunday after Sunday. And now the priest

[292]

was saying final prayers. The girl rose and stumbled back into a pew.

Miss Agatha rose almost before the priest did and went to the girl. She spoke to her gently. Another woman came and Miss Agatha returned to walk out with Craig. Once outside the church she spoke.

"Father didn't see her," she said in a shocked voice, "I never saw anything like that in my life! The poor girl! Of course you don't realize how dreadful that was for her!"

"Strangely enough, I think I do," answered Craig.

"Ah—but she'll be all right, you know. That other woman is going to take her into the parish house. She'll be given Communion there."

"She'll be all right."

"But I'm sorry you saw that. I never saw it happen before in any church."

"I'm glad I saw it. It brought some things home to me."

"Barbara—" sighed Miss Agatha— "but she'll be all right now. Tell me—I don't want to pry—but has it all been fixed up for you? I was sad about the poor unfortunate fellow but he was never a good or steady man. I had a Mass said for him. Don't tell Barbara."

"I shan't."

"And it has made everything happy for you. Who will marry you? Or has it happened yet?"

"I'm afraid it's not going to happen, Miss Agatha."

"But Mr. Craig—" she stopped walking and looked at him fully— "for Barbara's sake."

"Barbara won't have it."

"Why of course she will!"

"She says not. She doesn't want a priest to marry us."

"I don't understand this."

"I don't myself. But I think they hurt her too much. That's what I think. She's turned against the Catholic Church."

"I can't believe it. Why, there's no trouble now."

He gave a grim chuckle. "Oh yes, there is."

"Then she's lost her faith."

"That's exactly what she told me. I don't know what to do about it, Miss Agatha. I suppose I'm to blame. But I'd do anything on God's earth she wanted. Except join her Church, which I couldn't do in good faith."

"It's not required. But you don't object to a priest marrying you?"

"I assure you it's she who objects to a priest. And what can I do about it? Tell me, Miss Agatha, what should I do? I can't force the thing on her."

"But she isn't happy?"

"Oh, I don't know. No—she's not very happy. Neither of us is, in some ways."

Agatha gave a little moan.

"Can't you help me?" he repeated. "You know the ropes. Maybe you can tell me what to do."

"You can do nothing. You're not the one."

"Then I don't know what will happen. On the surface it's all right yet in a way. But Barbara's not herself."

"How could she be," asked Agatha Braniff, "if she has lost her soul? Part of her must be gone—wandering—"

Those words rang in his head until he got home that afternoon. The memory of the girl at the altar rail stuck in his mind too. He felt so sure of Barbara's unhappiness that to see her surprised him and he wondered, for the uncounted time, whether he was exaggerating the whole thing and making a fuss about nothing. The apathy he had felt in his house this morning was quite gone. It was alive, being made ready for guests and Barbara, with a merry red apron over a bright wool dress, was giving instructions to the maid who had been hired for the evening. The copper dishes which they used for their buffet suppers were ranged on the hunt board, and white geraniums and bowls of tangerines carried out the special style that Barbara had invented for these affairs.

He kissed her, sniffed, and said, "I see you've had a nip already."

"Just one. I had nothing else to do."

"Well, better go a little slow tonight."

"I shall."

She had needed that drink to get started, to wind herself up.

Sundays were the worst days. Ken did not know, she thought, and she was not going to tell him about it. But when you have gone to church every Sunday of your life and stop going, it is as if the day did not belong to you. Until noon it was very bad. Then when the time came when there was no chance of going, nothing to go to, it was better. And now it was only another evening, and people were coming to destroy the loneliness and strain. There would be fast, bright talk. Blair Wyatt and his bride were just back from their wedding trip and that made it a very special occasion. She would wear the gray dress with the black velvet collar and look her best.

"You always startle me, Barbara," said Blair. "I see so many more beautiful women who can't compare with you."

"Blair, you are better than ever. Always with the perfect insult offered as a compliment. As for you, you look ten years younger."

"The outward sign of the inward happiness, my dear."

Barbara's glance went past Wyatt to her own husband. No, she thought, Ken doesn't glow like that. You can always tell when a man would rather be with his wife than with anyone else, when they have lovely secrets. Blair and his wife are like that now.

The bride had lost the look of exalted resolution which she had worn at her wedding. She was very sure of herself and a little smile kept moving around her face.

"Oh no, we won't go to Florida. Not this winter, We'll stay right here. We want to settle down," Barbara heard Catherine Wyatt say.

"She's pregnant already. She told me upstairs," Carol Harrison said to Barbara. "She'll have one after another like a rabbit. Isn't Blair beautifully smug?"

"He has every right to be."

Barbara felt jealousy smothering her. She took a drink she had meant to go without, and knew that Kenneth had observed that. He was frowning a little. Why couldn't he leave her alone? If he was ashamed of her, he knew what he could do.

Blair took her aside, into the little empty study, after the supper was over, where they could be alone.

"Barbara, dear, I was going to write you and then I didn't. There

[295]

are some things that don't fit into letters. But I'm so glad that everything has worked out for you and Ken. I know you must have suffered a great deal under the circumstances. But it's all right now and a few extra years in purgatory won't hurt a strong girl like you. I'd like to have been at this wedding too but I suppose it's all over."

"What wedding?"

"I mean the one you had in the Church."

"There hasn't been one."

"Then I can come. I'm glad. Do let me."

"I'm afraid you can't. I'm not going to be remarried in the Church."

"But of course you are, Barbara. Why shouldn't you be with poor old Leslie out of the picture?"

"Because I don't want to."

"Ken Craig certainly wouldn't object."

"Really, Blair, it's our own business."

"Of course. But I'm an old friend, Barbara, and I may say quite frankly that the situation has distressed me. A Catholic like yourself, without the sacraments, is bound to be unhappy. I don't think many of your friends blamed you for marrying Ken at all—he's the nicest fellow in the world—but I knew all along that the decision must have been very difficult for you."

"We did what we thought was right. And it was right. It was." Her voice was hard and angry.

"Have you talked to the Bishop?"

"No, and I don't intend to. Let's drop the subject."

He didn't. He said, "I have thought of this many times. Don't leave the Church, Barbara."

"You must know the Church well enough to realize that I did leave it when I married Ken. I had to. I was excommunicated. You certainly know how it is."

"But you can make all that right now. And apostasy doesn't excuse you from the law."

"I have to go and be a hostess," she said.

"Barbara, will you talk to me about this at another time?"

"No. I never want you to mention it again. To me or to anyone else, I hope."

She moved but he held her arm. "I shan't talk about it to anyone else, but there will be talk, of course. Practically, it won't do your husband any good in some circles. It will be laid at his door."

"That's not fair. It's not true."

"I'm quite sure it isn't. You're changed, Barbara."

"I've had a few drinks, that's all."

"I don't mean the drinks. I mean what you are doing to yourself, to your character and nature. Marrying outside of the Church was rebellion and it hardened you. But to refuse the grace you can have now will destroy you. A person may disobey God and still love God or long to love Him. But—"

Barbara laughed. "Blair, you're a marvelous theologian! As they say, converts are always the worst."

She slipped away from his hand and went into the room with the others.

Craig came up to her. "Are you all right? Steady?"

"I wish you wouldn't act as if I were a dipsomaniac," she said in anger, careless as to whether Carol Harrison heard or not.

Carol heard. She thought, I knew they were having trouble.

Chapter Twenty-Three

Craig carried the worry with him all the time now. The days had become uncertain. There were the hours of tenderness when she clung to him like a tired child. There were still delights of the flesh but he never knew what was coming afterward, what would hurt her or light a flare of anger.

He telephoned his wife on a November afternoon to ask if she was going to the Harrison's house for a cocktail.

"No, Carol didn't say anything about it to me," said Barbara. "Why should I?"

"She probably tried to get you and couldn't. That's why she called the office."

"It could be. I was out for a while. Why don't you go?"

"Not without you."

"My guess is that she wants you without me. And I wish you would go. We don't have to go around like a bride and groom any more."

There it was. She was pushing him off again, as if their lives were separating. She seemed to try to make him feel that all the time. There was a new unyielding quality about her now, as if she wanted to resist.

He wondered whether she would really like to be rid of him. Perhaps she wanted to go back to that kind of bachelor woman life she had led before she married him. She was the one who had spoken of divorce and though she claimed it was on his account, was it?

His life looked cloudy ahead. If Barbara really took to drinking it would be bad. Of course she should have children—that would stabilize her. But she was refusing to have children though it shouldn't be a risk now. If she would take care of herself. If it did come to the point of separation, there would be more scandal and there had been far too much already for a man who wanted a respectable business career. Mr. Miller wouldn't like it. He would be sore if his house, which he'd sold as a bargain because Craig was the purchaser, was suddenly thrown on the market again. People would think I am unstable, thought Craig, especially since this would be one more divorce, a second time for me. But if it came to that, it would have to be done. I could get a job somewhere else, on another railroad. Unless Ted Kilmey puts the Indian sign on me. And what happens to seniority, and my chance that looked so sure to be president of the railroad in a few years? That would all have to go by the board.

He felt bitterly depressed as he picked up the evening paper which

[298]

his secretary had brought in. But he tried not to let her see it, thanking her briskly and telling her that he was through for the day in a tone that tried to imply that he was glad to go home, that he was a happy and successful man.

The front page of the paper annoyed him. How could they give the space to that stuff? A statue in a Catholic church in some remote village was reported to be dripping blood. And the little, distant town was filling up with cripples hoping for miracles. That was cheap magic or the kind of hypnotism you'd see on any vaudeville stage. He read that the Bishop of the diocese gave no credence to the miracle. That was what they always said. But they kept their hold on the people with just such dodges.

Well, Barbara didn't care whether he came home or not. So he'd go to Carol Harrison's party and have a few drinks. He'd stop at the Town Club and get a start. Craig felt in himself a defiance of everything, a growing desire to kick over the whole structure that supported his life, business, social and personal.

In the men's lounge at the club he ran into Ted Kilmey before he could avoid the meeting. Kilmey was the last person he wanted to see and his greeting was stiff. But Mr. Kilmey seemed bent on being cordial.

He had aged since Craig had last seen him. His shoulders had gathered together and there was something uncanny about the sharp blue eyes today. He looks, thought Craig, as if he had been beaten and was too stiff to straighten up but he won't give in.

"Well, my boy, how are you?"

Craig said that he was fine.

"Good. You look it. Sit down with me a minute. I haven't seen you in a long time."

"No. I didn't even know you were in town."

"Well, I didn't bring the car up. It costs a lot to run a private car these days. And my wife isn't too well so we aren't doing any entertaining."

"I'm sorry to hear that," said Craig courteously.

"Yes," said Kilmey, "she's not been well but she's going to come back all right. We had a loss, you know."

"I'd like to offer my sympathy, sir. I didn't write you at the time but I thought of you."

Mr. Kilmey sat thinking. He gave Craig the curious impression that he had sat just like this for endless hours, contemplating something.

"She was my little pet," he said. "I called her Bluebell. Did you ever know Kitty?"

"I met her at your house. She was younger."

"Of course. You used to come around to the house. I remember. I thought at one time you might pick one of my girls. Kitty was my pet. She had a nervous breakdown. After her children were born. Lovely little mother she was."

It is the story he tells, Craig said to himself. He wants me to believe it, to pass it on. Poor old man.

"She was a charming girl," he said.

"Everybody loved Kitty. You couldn't get into the church the day of her funeral," said Kilmey. "You couldn't get into St. Joseph's Church. That was where the services were. It's a big church but you couldn't get into it that day."

He made such a point of it that Craig clearly understood that Mr. Kilmey was telling that his daughter had been buried with proper services. He couldn't answer. What was there to say? You managed it somehow, he thought, but you went through hell from the look of you.

"Everything going well, Ken?"

"Yes. I think so."

"I want to have a talk with you next time I come up. I want to get you on the steering committee for the industry one of these days. We need stronger representation from this area."

Craig, startled, muttered something in the way of gratitude. He got up and said he was sorry but he had an appointment.

The old man's hand went out to him. "It's good to see you, boy." Mr. Kilmey dropped his voice. "And I was glad to hear that everything worked out for you. I was hoping it would. The good Lord takes care of these things for us."

So he too had heard that Leslie Field was dead and assumed that everything had been regularized in a religious way. It was impossible for Craig to say bluntly that he and Barbara had no plans to be married in the Church. Kilmey would hear that in time no doubt and change his mind about the steering committee, Craig thought cynically as he went on to the Harrison house.

Carol had said on the telephone that it wasn't really a party, but he was surprised to see no cars parked in front of the big city house which Carol had married along with her husband. He heard no high sounds of voices as he gave his hat to a servant but he might be late. Or perhaps early. He was glad there wasn't a crowd.

"Where's the party?"

"In the library, I think sir."

"Fine. I know my way."

The library door was half closed. He pushed it open, saw a fire, a cocktail tray and one woman. Craig stopped when he saw Nina.

"Well—are you the party?" he asked.

"Carol will be here soon. She said to tell you she'd be a little late. What would you like to drink?"

"Where's Dudley?"

"Isn't he in Chicago or some place?"

"I didn't know that."

He stood looking at Nina, wondering what sort of deal this was. What sort of trade. The two women, Carol and Nina, had put this over on him for some reason.

"Can't you sit down?" she asked.

"I don't want to interrupt this solitude of yours. Carol asked me to stop by for a drink—"

"Here it is."

He mixed himself one, thoughtfully, figuring it out. Then he asked, "How did you know Barbara wouldn't come with me?"

"Carol didn't ask her, did she?"

"I don't know. I did. What's going on anyway?"

"I wanted to see you," said Nina. "It's no mystery."

"Carol ought to be ashamed of herself."

"No. Don't blame it on her. As a matter of fact I may have made her think she was doing me a favor too."

"Why you—"

"And maybe she was. Oh, Ken, be adult. Why should I have to play hide and seek with a man I used to live with? I want to talk to you—tell you some things. Can't you drop this pose of controlled heroism and be realistic?"

"Realistic about what?"

"About me. About yourself. You must have known ever since that night this summer that we aren't through."

"I told you that we were. Told you then."

"That was what you said, not what you know. You were being loyal or something Boy Scout."

"And you don't believe in being loyal."

"Not past the point of no return. Ken, listen, Carol really may be back any minute. I've always come out with things. I told you when I wanted to leave you. I was honest about it. But we really belong together. I made a mistake. Or perhaps it was just as well that we did separate and try our wings. We'll do better now. Because we both know more."

"You sound crazy, Nina. What on earth is in your mind?"

"I'm ready to get a divorce from Bill to begin with. I'm bored to death. With the stuffiness and the whole Longman tribe and all their rites."

"But," he said, "you joined up with them. You haven't forgotten that. You annulled me and swallowed the rest of it whole. You've got it for life now."

"Don't be silly. You know I'm not really a Catholic."

"No. I suppose not. Of course not."

"Any more than you are. We certainly got ourselves in fine jams, picking two of them on the rebound. But I'd chuck it any time. If Bill takes it seriously and thinks he can't marry again, that's too bad for him. And if he tries for annulment, he'll pay for it. Pay both the Pope and Nina!"

"And where do I come into this picture?"

She laughed. The firelight jingled on a gold chain on her green velvet dress, on the heavy earrings that made her face so fragile.

"I wonder what makes your resistance so attractive. I suppose it's because when you let yourself go it's with such force. You know you're as bored as I am and up against pretty much the same proposition. I don't blame you—and neither does anyone else—for not wanting to marry in the Catholic Church, now that Leslie Field is dead. It's obvious to anyone with eyes in his head that you and Barbara aren't happy together. I don't mean that you beat her but it's there to see. Of course I know her point of view. Too well. She will do everything she can to make you give in and be married by a priest, but you take my advice and hold out. It's complicating. There are all sorts of stipulations that they pile on."

"What will you do about them if you leave your husband?"

"I?" That too was funny. "Just watch me."

She leaned forward and he could smell the rich, not sweet perfume. He watched her with fascination. She made Barbara so clear. Barbara suffering, believing, capable of all that this sterile woman would never know existed. Barbara—my love.

"Ken," she said softly, caressingly, "you don't get over the person you cared for first. The person who made you know what it was all about."

Craig didn't draw back. He only put the words between them, sharp as knives. "No. You don't. That's the reason I shall never get over Barbara. I was never married to you, Nina. There was never the thought or intention of real marriage between us. We had an affair, legalized more or less. But Barbara and I were married. No matter what. And I'd marry her again and anyway if she would only let me."

Then Carol Harrison did come in, breathless, full of apologies and untruths. It took Craig a minute to break through them and get out in the air.

[303]

Chapter Twenty-Four

When he was in residence, Bishop Tarrant always asked some of the priests of the diocese for a late Sunday dinner and allowed them to air and compare their problems. Today, after the others had left, Father Gilroy lingered, which annoyed the Bishop because Father Gilroy had already done more than his share of talking.

"Well, Father—" he said, indicating dismissal.

"There was one matter I would like to speak of to you privately, Your Excellency."

"I'll have to ask you to be brief. But go on. What's it about?"

"It's about the Craig situation. There's no reason, I understand, why that marriage can not be regularized. The first husband is dead."

"Ah yes," said the Bishop, "so I understand."

"Apparently there's no doubt of the facts though I've only had them secondhand. It was accident, probably due to misconduct of some sort, and was reported in the New York papers and picked up here. It's common knowledge. I expected, of course, that with the impediment removed, Mrs. Craig would immediately take steps to be properly married."

"And she hasn't done so?"

"She hasn't come to me. I wondered if, since in the first instance she approached you—"

"No, she hasn't come to me."

"I would like to have that straightened out," said Father Gilroy. "There's no reason why not and they both could be of great help to the parish and diocese. I hear it discussed here and there. Perhaps I should make the effort to convince her. It is difficult, I admit. In a way humiliating. But to point out her duty—" his voice began to take on an oratorical cast and the Bishop interrupted.

He said, "Let the penitent seek the priest, Father." And added, very simply, "I wouldn't do it. You might do more harm than good."

It was not what the priest wanted him to say.

"If that's your advice, Your Excellency—"

"It's my very strong suggestion," said Bishop Tarrant definitely.

No, he thought afterward, Father Gilroy wasn't the one to handle that situation. Perhaps no one could. Mr. Craig, he recalled, had been very coldly angry under his restraint. He was probably unwilling to make any more effort. But she might. One day she might come. In fear or trouble they came back to the shelter of the Church. When all was well they thought, poor creatures, that they could do without it. A pity she had not been willing to wait. How long was it? She had come to him last autumn. It must have been a little more than a year ago now. The man had died some time ago as the Bishop remembered. This was late November.

It was early December when she came. He had gone upstairs, resolved to see no more callers that day, but when the housekeeper brought up her name, he changed his mind.

"Mrs. Kenneth Craig, you say?"

"Yes, Your Excellency, that was the name she gave me. And I know her by sight."

The Bishop went down almost immediately. He did not remember how Barbara looked until he saw her again and then he remembered very distinctly and realized that she had changed. It was the manner more than anything else. She had been very handsome when he saw her before, and still was beautiful, even more elegant. But this time he felt no pliancy. There was almost hostility.

"Well, it's been some time since I've seen you, young lady," he said, ready to put her at ease with cordiality if he could. She was probably ashamed of herself and that accounted for her bearing, he thought.

"I shan't keep you very long, Bishop Tarrant," said Barbara, leaning forward from the chair that was built like a witness chair, "but I came to explain something that I thought you should know."

"I shall be glad to hear about it."

"There has been some talk about my husband and myself. I've had some of it repeated to me by a friend and it's disturbed me."

"Gossip is always tiresome and pitiful."

"Yes, and it can do harm. What is being said is that my husband refuses to have us married in the Catholic Church. You may not know that the man—the man I married first—died some time ago."

"Indeed."

"Yes. And it is absolutely untrue that my husband had any objection to our being remarried in the Church. That sort of talk does him harm, Bishop Tarrant. Actually, in a business way. I know that, because of a previous thing that happened after we were married. He was actually penalized because he had married me. That sort of thing shouldn't enter into business relations but some people are bigots, so it does sometimes."

"Perhaps it is inevitable."

"Then people should know the truth and not take it out on him. I thought perhaps that you would say a word here and there. To people like Mr. Kilmey. It is not Kenneth who refuses to have a Catholic marriage."

"But you?" asked the Bishop quietly.

"Yes, I'm the one."

"And why is that?"

"Because I've lost my faith."

"That," he said, "was the terrible chance you took when you went into this relationship without sanctification."

"It wasn't my husband's fault."

"Certainly not. It was your responsibility, not his."

"Then couldn't you tell people if the matter comes up that Kenneth is not to blame? It's a strange thing to ask but I didn't know who else to come to. And you would be believed."

He smiled. "I'm not inclined to join in gossip. Have your union validated, make a good Catholic marriage of it now that God has made it possible, and you'll hear no more cruel talk. And perhaps God will forgive you, if you ask Him, for your impatience in not waiting for His time. Give yourself a penance in addition to what your confessor may require. Always repent the scandal you have given to God and His Sacraments. Make the arrangement with your parish priest as soon as possible."

"I can't, Bishop Tarrant."

She said it in a hopeless way. He checked one reply and asked instead, gently, "What troubles you so much, my child?"

"I have no faith," she repeated. "It went out of me. I can't believe in the Church, that it is always right. I don't feel it was just. I was angry at all the scolding when I was trying to live a good life. And then when I went to Europe there were the politics and pressure and trickery all hiding behind Catholicism, and so many Catholics weren't praying. They were plotting. It didn't seem like religion. Not the religion I had believed in. And people seem to be able to call themselves Catholics no matter what they do."

"We are in the middle of wars," said the Bishop. "Strategy is necessary. We are subject to every kind of overt and subversive attack. We must mobilize against our enemies. There are always times in history when the Church must be militant."

"Why?"

He spoke sternly. "Because the Church fights for you. Fights for its worthy members. And for its unworthy ones as well. It fights for your right to believe, even for your right to challenge, to disobey, to choose. Surely you know that the enemy of the Catholic Church would not permit such things."

"Yes, I know that."

"What army is a beautiful sight?" he asked her. "And are all soldiers noble or possessed only by good impulses? But the Church accepts its soldiers with their faults, their sins and their failures. You should honor the cause for which they battle and forgive imperfections, pray for forgiveness for your own sins. Had you no impulse to join that battle when you were over there?"

"I did join it, Bishop. And that was when I found I had no faith."

"You must have had faith if you did God's work."

She shook her head. "There were some refugee boys—I won't bother you with the story."

"Tell me," he said with authority.

She told most of the story, not quite all about her persuasion of the Colonel.

"Then they were sent to Italy?"

"Yes, I've had word from a friend who's still there."

"You did a magnificent thing. Those fifty lads may owe salvation in part to your efforts."

"But it was a trick, as I did it. If I had done it because I believed they must be brought up as Catholics, I would have respected myself. As it was—"

"Why did you do it?"

"Sister Eltha put it up to me. And it meant everything to her. But I fooled her as well as the rest into thinking I was a good Catholic. And finally it seemed to me that honesty was more important than anything else. I couldn't go to Church, kneel and not believe. Isn't that a worse sin than not going?"

"You're very unhappy. A very unhappy woman."

She moved her head without speaking.

"As I recall, I told Mr. Craig you would be."

"It's not his fault," she said again.

"But God, in punishing you, is punishing him as well."

"I'm spoiling his life. I know."

"And what are you going to do about it?"

"Let him go. If he will go. That's another reason for not marrying him in the Church now. I don't want to complicate things. This was only a civil marriage and he can get out of it more easily."

"And if this should happen and your civil union is dissolved, will you return to the Church? Is that your plan?"

"I can't go back."

"Sin exacts a heavy toll," he said.

"But I still don't feel it was sin to marry him, Bishop."

"You have sinned in many ways. There was the sin of presumption, in believing you could save your soul by your unaided efforts. There was the sin of living with this man against the law of God in His Church. But your great sin is your denial of grace when now it is offered you. And you tremble on the edge of still another sin, that of despair, the sin against hope. Do you pray?"

"How can I when I've lost my faith?"

"You haven't lost it, poor child. You are pursued by it. And the pursuit will never cease until you fall exhausted. Unless you pray for grace."

"The prayers won't come. I don't feel anything."

"That is your punishment. In denying and refusing the great love of God, you lost capacity for feeling love, perhaps even human love. You did violence to your greatest loyalty, destroyed your deepest affections, went against your greatest desire. You crippled yourself and went as a spiritual cripple into these other human relationships, here and in Europe."

He paused until she accepted that. His voice was very quiet and very sure.

"No one can help you but God. But you must turn to God yourself and ask Him to restore in you—love. Stop trying to run away from Him. Cease this foolish flight which only takes you farther from everything you love, human and divine."

She lifted her face and he saw that the hostility had gone. It was spread with suffering.

The Bishop said, "These excuses you make for anger and defiance are only petty excuses. The irksome things never bother a strong soul. The Church is a great spiritual body, with the aspirations of the spirit and some of the failures and sufferings of the body. Its only function is to help the soul toward God. But you must save your own soul. That is why you are on earth, as long ago you were taught. Go now and try to pray."

Agatha Braniff was thinking fondly of a cup of tea but she did not like to get it for herself alone. She was glad to hear a knock on her door and open it on the sight of Barbara.

"What a blessing! I was just wishing for company. Come in dear, it's so very cold. How nice of you to come." Then she saw Barbara's face in the light and asked, "Is anything the matter?"

"No. I was driving by. I wanted to see you—somebody."

"Sit down and rest. I'll make a nice hot cup of tea."

Barbara sat down. She looked like one dazed, thought her aunt.

[309]

"A ginger cookie and a piece of toast with a little cinnamon sugar on it? Or would you like an egg, Barbara?"

"No, thanks," said Barbara and the words were an effort. "Nothing."

"Ah, it will do you good."

"Just let me stay for a minute. I didn't know where else to go."

"And you don't come half often enough to your family house." Agatha went on making tea. "How is Mr. Craig?"

"Kenneth's pretty well."

"He is a good man and a kind one. Have you married him yet?"

"What do you mean?"

"I mean married him as you should."

"No."

"And why the delay?"

"I don't want to talk about it, please, Agatha."

"He told me he was willing."

"Yes. He was. I'm the one who wouldn't."

"Well, that's a strange thing certainly. A Catholic girl preferring to live in sin. My own niece tells me that!"

"We weren't living in sin."

"Still, that's hard on a man. It's against a man's nature."

"What is?"

"To live in the brother and sister way. A strong, vigorous man—like Mr. Craig—"

"What makes you think—did you talk to him about that? Were you the one?"

"Now don't be thinking me bold or interfering. I was only considering the unhappy situation you were in and of a way to help you. Poor girl, running across the ocean, to get away from it. You've been distracted. Sinning and ashamed."

Barbara said, pressing her hands on her temples, "Oh! Agatha, I don't know what to do. The Bishop says I am pursued, that I will be, and that's the way it feels—as if I'd be driven until I fall from exhaustion—I wish I could—"

"Have you seen the Bishop?"

"I've come from there now."

"And what did he tell you?"

Barbara only shook her head.

"You look half-sick. Are you in the family way?"

"Family way! No, not that."

"It's what you need now. There's always been an ache in you since the poor little baby went—"

"Don't—"

"Have your marriage blessed by God and let the children come to comfort you."

"I'm afraid."

"Of what?"

"Oh, I thought I could make him so happy! And look what I'm dragging him through! He ought to get rid of me. I don't want to tie him down with a marriage in the Church."

"Who are you to deny that good man the sacrament?"

Barbara stiffened at the words.

"He loves you," said Agatha, "I saw it in his face and heard it in the pity of his voice. He loves you body and soul. And why are you trying to destroy the soul he loves? And maybe the body too. What are you without your soul but a miserable thing to live with?"

"If I could only believe—"

"You do believe," said her aunt, "and it is that which is tearing you to pieces. You believe in God and in Jesus Christ, His only Son. You believe in the commandments of God and the seven deadly sins and the virtues that are their opposites. I know what you believe, deny it though you may, what was bred in you, taught to you, loosed in your blood by those now dead. If this man you love does not and cannot believe as you do, let him have at least the sight of your faith in his house. It is a wicked battle between you and a devil tempting you that has made you refuse to let him be your husband in God's sight and with His blessing. And why? Because the Church would not let you have your own way, to do as you please, to live as you fancy. But you cannot live in peace without God's grace and you know well where it is to be found!"

[311]

"Oh stop—I can't stand any more!"

Her aunt stopped her at the door.

"Where are you going, child?"

"I don't know."

"You know where He lives," said her aunt. "Go there."

She had never been frightened to enter a church before, even in these months when she sometimes had dreaded it. But now it seemed almost as if she could not, as if the great oak door of the Cathedral was closed against her and her alone. Barbara paused before it, tempted to turn away, to get back into her car and drive fast, hard, without direction.

Then she opened it and for all its size and weight it swung easily and silently. She went down the shadowed aisle and the sense of welcome that swept through her absorbed every other feeling. This was where she belonged. There was no refusal, no sense that she had no right here. Confusion stopped roaring in her mind. She knelt before the altar and the reverence she felt was like a drink of water after a long thirst. In a quiet pew she found her prayers come easily, naturally again.

They were prayers she always said in any church, that she had tried to say in Sister Eltha's chapel and failed. The familiar ones. The Act of Contrition came now in its turn—the confession—how long since she had been able to put truth in it? Before she had married Ken, long before.

"Oh, my God, I am heartily sorry that I have sinned—"

Am I sorry? How can I be sorry that I married him? Yes—not for love, but for loving him too little to know what he needed of me most, sorry that I was not wise enough to know that I could not give him the person he loved like that. Sorry for the pride, the presumption, the angers, the despair, sorry for everything, for all the sins of my past life—as she knelt she felt forgiveness flow into her and knew that she had made a perfect act of contrition.

It was the first hour in months when she had not been lonely. She could feel the desire to begin again rise in her mind, not to be defeated this time by bitterness, but willing and brave. What had all the angers been about? Against myself, she thought. I destroyed all my loyalties. I could not even love Ken as much as I should, as a wife should. I was yearning for this, jealous of everyone who had faith. Jealous of that man in the camp with his crucifix nailed to the wall, jealous of Sister Eltha walking with the Virgin.

She felt herself real again, recognizable, no longer the woman she had been living with and hating recently. Belief went through her like a transfusion and lack of doubt was happiness.

The tea grew cold in Agatha Braniff's cup because she forgot to lift it to her lips. She ate a cookie without tasting the snap of the ginger. Finally she took the telephone book and searched for a number.

"I would like to speak to Mr. Craig, if he is there."

"May I have the name, please?"

"You may. Miss Agatha Braniff."

Craig's voice came anxiously, "Why, hello, Miss Agatha. Nothing is wrong?"

"I hope not," she said. "Barbara was here a while ago."

"She was? Is she all right?"

"She would like you to meet her at the Cathedral."

"The Cathedral? Is that what she said?"

"No," said Agatha, "she did not say so. But it is what she wants, I am sure. And would hope for."

"Is she there now?"

"It would not surprise me. She often went there in the past in her trouble."

"I see. Thank you, Miss Agatha. Thank you from the bottom of my heart."

The Cathedral was dim but not somber. Craig's eyes roved over two women in black, an old man crouched in a corner of a pew, a fair-haired girl wearing a smart hat. Then at last he saw Barbara, alone and in front before a side altar, her head lowered into her hands, motionless in prayer. Craig took a seat far at the back and waited. A long absent comfort and peace began to steal through him. He felt Barbara safe, and along with that came a feeling of gratitude and kindliness toward this place which had given her refuge and drawn her back to it. She was herself again, this woman he loved, released from that prison of suffering in which she had been confined by her own will. Something had opened the door. So, strangely, he too was released.

He thought ahead, able to hope and plan without fear. They would marry again, her way, since she had come back to this. They would try to have a family. That was what she needed. And about this other, he'd go along as far as he could. Not into these mysteries and all this ceremony. That wasn't for him. It took a certain temperament. But it seemed to be good and maybe necessary for many people. They put on pressure and were stiff in their rules and they had their ways of doing things, this Catholic Church. But they'd had centuries of experience, of course. Anyway, Barbara was better off with her religion. She wasn't herself without it. He'd found that out. He thought that with no resentment or jealousy now. The bitterness in his mind melted like dark ice under a clean flow of generosity and thankfulness. He loved her. He loved beyond his love for her.